Rampart

Truscott Jones

Trenton, Georgia

Copyright © 2024 Truscott Jones

Paperback ISBN: 978-1-959621-11-9
Hardcover ISBN: 978-1-959621-12-6
Ebook ISBN: 979-8-88531-842-6

All rights reserved. No part of this publication may be reproduced, stored in a retrieval system, or transmitted in any form or by any means, electronic, mechanical, recording or otherwise, without the prior written permission of the author.

Published by BookLocker.com, Inc., Trenton, Georgia.

The characters and events in this book are fictitious. Any similarity to real persons, living or dead, is coincidental and not intended by the author.

BookLocker.com, Inc.
2024

First Edition

Library of Congress Cataloging in Publication Data
Jones, Truscott
Rampart by Truscott Jones
Library of Congress Control Number: 2024920430

Treason

noun
\ˈtrēzən\

1. the crime of betraying one's country, especially by attempting to kill the sovereign or overthrow the government
//They were convicted of treason

2. the action of betraying someone or something
//Doubt is the ultimate treason against faith

March 30

(Five Months plus Seven Days before Trial)

Entering the "Red Zone," the inner most security perimeter, was the easiest of all. Further out, on the fringes of the North Carolina State Fairgrounds, overzealous sheriff's deputies and hyperalert local cops took their jobs seriously – for most of them, a presidential visit was a once in a lifetime event. For these officers, someone with Sam Kilbrough's preternatural vigilance, whose erect posture and purposeful movements contrasted with the excited frenzy of the arriving crowd, might draw attention.

As it turns out, he needn't have worried. No one questioned him. He knew where to find the gaps, how to bypass the funneling ropes and mobile chain link barriers and avoid the first ring of metal detectors. Not once did he have to flash his old United States Secret Service identification.

But the final access point was different. The 300 or so specially selected guests granted entry to the apron of grass fronting the central stage required specific credentials. By appearances this portal posed the greatest challenge: parallel-rowed steel barricades buttressed by laser sensors in the wide no-man's land; a ring of state troopers spaced 12 feet apart; and but one way in, a tall, gray pulse induction magnetometer, manned by four very dour, very stout members of the USSS. Precisely why, for Sam Kilbrough, it was no hurdle at all.

Even without the electronics, they would sense the 9mm Glock G43 tucked inside his bright blue Gore-Tex windbreaker. They would assume any agent, even a former one, would carry something in so public a setting. Accordingly, as he approached the machine he removed his hands from the jacket's pockets and, catching the attention of one of his old colleagues, motioned his head toward his right side. With a jerk of her chin, she directed him around the scanner.

"Missing us already?" she commented, her expression flat, her aviators concealing the subtle inflection in her eyes.

"Oh, you know ... I miss the excitement."

Official word was Kilbrough had resigned. Rumor was he was fired. The reasons for the axing, as happens with gossip, varied wildly. He had pissed off his super, or the director, or the president *himself!* He had slept with the wrong person. He drank too hard, too long, in the wrong place, or at the wrong time. He'd lost a step.

The sheer volume of chatter meant anything was possible, none of which affected his popularity with the guys and gals in the field, all of whom thought, "But for the grace of God, there go I."

For the agents manning this particular checkpoint, his presence at today's rally implied something new entirely – Kilbrough was on assignment. Ask nothing, stay out of his way.

"Enjoy the speech," she said, returning to her scrutiny of the inflow.

"Thanks." He quickly moved on, finding a spot on the field six feet stage right of the podium. He *ran his fingers through a sheen of sandy blond hair that floated like ocean-churned foam atop a base of dark brown roots. There were already two fluid rows of excited invitees between himself and the elevated plywood platform, which was fine. For now, they would partially conceal him, not that it mattered, as he knew how to avoid drawing attention. Even if someone on the president's detail recognized him, their biggest challenge would be not smiling. When the time came, he'd push his muscular frame forward with ease.*

Sam used the time before the president's arrival – 40 minutes per schedule, in reality closer to an hour – to assess his surroundings: profiling each of the growing number of people within a ten-foot circle, which he judged the outer reach of potential interference with his plans; noting the layout of the dais to predict, based on his past experience, the precise sequence of POTUS' route; taking stock of the sun's position, cloud cover and any other conditions that might affect visibility or Kilbrough's movements, or those of the target and his protectees.

And, he had to be prepared to pleasantly interact with any eager enthusiast choosing to engage him, lest he appear the odd loner, which even an amateur might mark as a problem.

All of these things Sam did. As the minutes passed, he settled confidently into his mission, maintaining vigilance, growing comfortable, like a swimmer acclimating to the water's initial chill.

At 10:38, though Kilbrough didn't need to check his watch, the wail of distant sirens seeped in, steady and incrementally louder. The motorcade approached. Dignitaries began taking their seats along the back side of the platform. The buzz around him heightened.

"Guess we're getting close," an older man to his left said, failing miserably to hide his excitement. He wore a MAGNUS THORNE campaign button on the lapel of his off-the-rack sports coat. Not a big donor by the looks of him; his presence on the VIP grounds and his age – early 70s, Sam guessed – likely meant he was a Super Volunteer. "I think you're right," Kilbrough replied with the smallest smile possible, then looked away. The last thing he wanted was an extended conversation.

A helicopter swung overhead, its thump ... thump ... thump *pulsing through bodies as it hovered close, making one last check of the president's approach before banking and moving away, its rhythmic beat replaced by the rumble of the lead motorcycles rolling into place behind a high curtain running behind the stage. Although blocked from view, clouds of dust announced the arrival of what Sam knew was a train of black SUVs, and ultimately The Beast, the president's armored limousine.*

A diminutive, bald man in a rumpled suit approached a podium bearing the distinctive Great Seal of the President, its majestic eagle clutching both olive branch and arrows as if unsure whether peace or war should prevail. The speaker stepped onto a small rostrum to compensate for his short stature. He grasped the microphone and pulled it downward to the consternation, Kilbrough noticed, of the advance man off to the side, who would now have to readjust it when he removed the riser, readying the lectern for the much taller president.

"Good mornin' ev'body," the host shouted, jolting the audience in his direction. "I'm Clive Green, chairman of your North Carolina Republican Party." He droned on, welcoming everyone, giving each of the minor dignitaries seated behind him a moment of recognition, and praising the efforts of the local GOP machine.

Sam ignored him, instead scanning the movements between himself and the enormous security tent set up behind the grandstand. He knew the drill, knew which motions, which gestures would signal "Go" time.

Two agents made their way into the crowd, immediately in front of the stage, the closest a mere five feet away.

Two more took positions at either end of the platform.

Atop the short stairs at the rear, yet another suited, sunglass adorned bodyguard looked back and forth between the tent beneath him and the podium, suddenly leaping up and onto the main deck.

Simultaneously, the advance man waived at Clive, who, taking the signal to end his warmup act, stopped mid-sentence and yelled, "Ladies and Gentlemen, it is now with great pleasure, and Eee-mense pride ..."

Sam saw the familiar shock of perfectly coiffed blondish hair bobbing up the steps, a smile already pasted on the practiced politician's face.

"... that I present to you ..."

As expected, all eyes turned to the commotion. Cell phones rose, their owners hitting the big red "Record" buttons.

"... the President of the United States, Magnus Thorne!!!"

Kilbrough felt his weapon with his mind; he dared not reach for it until he was ready.

Thorne, because he was a ubiquitous presence on TV and online, on magazine covers and front pages, seemed imaginary in the flesh, almost other worldly as he strode across the stage. Those present doubled-checked their senses as if ensuring his authenticity.

The president stopped halfway, slowly waving his hand above his head, deep, short, right, left.

Sam clapped, like those around him with free hands. Directly in front of him a middle-aged woman lofted a Thorne★Styles *sign from the previous campaign, serendipitously shielding him from the stage.*

The president's feet resumed their trek to the podium. He was 30 feet away. Twenty. Twelve.

And then, as Kilbrough anticipated, as Thorne had done at every rally before, the president cut toward the stage's edge.

Sam lowered his arms to his sides, wiggling the fingers on his dominant right hand.

Thorne looked down into the crowd with his trademark sheepish grin, stretching out his arms to allow his subjects to briefly touch him. Agents appeared at Thorne's sides to unobtrusively grab his waist, preventing him from being pulled in.

Kilbrough slowly moved his hand toward the opening in his jacket, maintaining focus on the target area, his actions now on auto-pilot.

The president grazed outreached fingers, moving still closer, brushing another trembling hand, and another. Four feet.

Kilbrough, in one deft movement, slipped the 18-ounce weapon from its holster, his finger secure on its heavy trigger.

Thorne, having completed his routine, was lifting up with the help of his men, their attention divided between control of his body and any potential threats below.

Sam lunged forward, easily wedging aside the people in front of him, closing the short gap with his extended arm.

Thorne looked into his eyes, recognizing both Kilbrough and his own fate. There was anticipation in his gaze. Resignation.

In the split second before Sam squeezed, the president didn't freeze in bewildered panic as would be expected. Instead, he tensed, and twisted.

The blast was deafening. But even before its echo finished rippling, even before the acrid smell of gunfire permeated the air, before Thorne had time to feel the 9mm bullet pierce his flesh, Kilbrough had already tossed the weapon across the stage, spreading his face and arms flat onto the raised hardwood, ready to be tackled.

As they brutally wrestled him to the ground, Sam ignored the pain. Instead, his mind concentrated on the memory of his late father, a giant presence taken from him too soon. Sam wondered if he could ever justify to his dad why he had done this.

Probably, he decided.

After all, he had the blessing of the man most important to them both.

Prologue

"Mr. Vice President, let's talk about your close relationship with Rachel Maslow."

The tall, athletic African American man looming over me, from a less than respectful three feet away, shows his talent as a prosecutor. In only nine words he has introduced Maslow, unapologetic leader of the group Americans believe is democracy's greatest threat; has linked *me* to *her*; and has branded our fleeting connection as a "close relationship." All of this without asking a question, leaving me no avenue for escape.

I wasn't coached on this, and although popular opinion regards me as intelligent, a quick thinker and good talker, they are unaware of my true superpower: preparation. As far back as high school my M.O. has been to hoard data, sluice it for the best nuggets, and draw what I need depending on the circumstances. Point is, I don't "wing" it. I knew we'd talk about Maslow – extensively – but wasn't planning to start behind the Eightball like this. I need to remain calm, know I can't let the jury see me sweat. But I feel naked.

"Multiple records place the two of you at a Dallas fundraiser for her radical organization, The Aberdeen Circle, seven years ago this month."

Again, no question. Just a sinister framing of what, back then, was considered smart politics. In symphony with his statement, on a large portable screen set up across the room from the jury, there is a still in glorious high definition showing me smiling broadly, my left arm around Maslow's waist, the pair of us waving from behind a dais as if life-long BFF's.

"Had you and this terrorist leader ever met, or otherwise collaborated before *that* show of support?" he asks, pointing accusingly at the picture.

I have been warned not to be argumentative. I've been instructed a million times to answer *only* the question asked, don't *volunteer* any information. Besides, he has already implied too much for me to unwind without appearing super defensive. So, I answer simply, truthfully ... frustratedly.

"Yes."

The prosecutor feigns surprise, like I've just admitted something extraordinary, though he knows damn well Maslow and I go back years, even before that portrait of mutual affection *still* reflecting off the taught 63-inch surface.

"Really," he says, his voice halfway between query and underline. I don't bite, so he twirls his index finger in an unspooling motion, and then commands, "Tell us about that."

Where to begin, especially with all of the half-truth admissions he's already made on my behalf? I'm not confused about the history – my team and I have been over this in excruciating detail a zillion times. My concern is to convey the *innocence* of my connection to a woman whose followers are accused of scheming to assassinate my boss.

"Mr. Vice President?"

I focus on the prosecutor, unable to keep myself from a slight smile. It's my go-to gesture for disarming hostile adversaries. Looks good on air. Has worked well over the years. At the moment, however, it draws puzzled frowns around the room and suddenly seems smarmy.

"I first met her ..."

"Met who?" he interrupts sharply. "For the record, you understand," he adds, waving the back of his hand at the court reporter behind him, whose middle-aged fingers are stabbing her stenotype keyboard as she glares at me. I realize he is going to make me say her poisonous name as many times as possible.

"Ms. Maslow," I clarify in a neutral voice, attempting to convey neither pride nor shame. "I first met Rachel Maslow about 10 years ago, a week or so before I announced I was running for mayor of Dallas."

Some of the jurors are leaning forward. Most of them are taking notes. All of them are very, very serious.

"A decade," he declares, widening his eyes. "You became involved ... politically, that is," he purrs, "with The Aberdeen Circle *over a decade ago!*"

"No, I met Ms. Maslow at that point," I correct.

The prosecutor fingers his red power tie, the puzzled look on his face hiding his glee that, after an hour on the stand, I have finally slipped up. I have finally tried to parse words, to split hairs, to show my fear of his implications. For a man as skilled as this inquisitor, that's all it takes.

"Now, Mr. Vice President, let's make sure we are talking about the same set of facts." He turns his back to me, faces the jury, and uses one hand to pinch the other's index finger. "One," he says. I hear his voice as the cocking of a gun's hammer. "Rachel Maslow is the founder and supreme leader of *TAC*. You know that today, and you knew it when you first engaged her 10 years ago, correct?"

"Yes." I mentally hunker down into a defensive ball, doing what I was told to do all along: one-word answers. Don't fight on his turf.

"Two," he says, waving a "V", "You knew Maslow and The Aberdeen Circle were one in the same when they were the very first to endorse your campaign, right?"

I'm biting my tongue, because on the day I announced, I released the names of over 100 endorsements. The prosecutor is making it sound like Maslow and *TAC* were my lifeblood. "Yes."

"Three." With a Boy Scout salute he adds a patina of honor to his next point. "You also knew *TAC* was an extension of the terrorist Maslow when she became the co-chair of your presidential campaign six years ago, true?"

I don't want to concede that Rachel is a terrorist, or even a criminal, and despite all the popular innuendo, all the assumptions, no one has *proven* she or Aberdeen were behind the shooting. Six years ago, in fact, when I made Rachel an *honorary* co-chair, both Maslow and *TAC*, except for those on the hardcore fringe, still had pretty good reputations.

"Yes." I try not to choke on the word.

"In fact," he continues, no longer bothering to number his assaults, "The Aberdeen Circle contributed ten thousand dollars to your mayoral campaign, and another fifty thousand to your presidential committee, correct?"

"Something like that," I answer. The prosecutor's brow furrows in disappointment. His crown is empty, only a margin of closely shaved gray stubble encircling it, so those wrinkles extend high in an exaggerated fashion.

"Are you disputing the large amounts of cash they gave you?" he challenges, even though I didn't. I wasn't. But before I can clarify that we received numerous donations from varied sources, that I simply don't remember precise numbers, he has flashed copies of both checks onto the screen, as if to cut me off from lying about it.

"No, I was only ..."

"Are these the checks?"

"They appear to be."

The prosecutor moves his head slowly from side to side, and glances at the jury, a bemused look as he repeats my words, "They *appear* to be," suggesting with his eyes and his emphasis that I am somehow in denial. Who wouldn't want to distance himself from these miscreants, he implies.

"Maslow, too," he announces. "Separate and apart from *TAC*, she also gave you money over the years, right?"

"To my campaigns, yes." Apologies to my attorney, but I couldn't let that slide. Maslow was a political supporter. She didn't buy my family's groceries.

He ignores my clarification, pressing on with "Let's talk about the inauguration five years ago." A picture of the festooned West Front of the U.S. Capitol goes up, showing the lower section's tiered rows immediately surrounding the podium. There I am, my right hand raised, my left on the Bible held by my husband Brady as I take the oath of office. He, and standing next to him Anna, our daughter, are beaming. I am serious, as usual.

"This was an extraordinary moment for you, wasn't it Mr. Styles? The first homosexual vice president in American history being sworn in."

Inside I wince – it is only recently that society returned to the pejorative "homosexual" rather than the lighter, more accepting "gay." Outwardly, I display a small, amiable smile. "My family and I were all quite thrilled, and honored." I want to say more, but again, *Keep it Short*. My attorney will let me share my story when it's our turn.

"Now, Mr. Vice President, do you see this lower bowl area closest to the action," he asks from the screen, sweeping his hand from one side to the other. I nod. He nods back. "I checked with the office of the Architect of the Capitol, and they tell me this sector seated 598 guests." He pauses to see if I will comment. I don't.

"Other than your husband and daughter, were you specifically allowed to invite any guests?" Good lawyers never ask a question unless they know the answer. This prosecutor knows Magnus Thorne didn't want me as his running mate. In a tight race, I merely checked enough boxes to help him win. That's it. He began shutting me out the moment the rally announcing my selection ended. This is going to be embarrassing, but worse, I see where he's going.

"Yes, I was, but it is the president's ..."

"How many, Mr. Vice President?" he cuts in. "How many people did you get to choose? Or should we simply consult the Inaugural Committee's final report, which I believe has an appendix labeled, 'Guests of the Vice President'?" The prosecutor makes a move toward the stacks of documents on his table, as if saying, "I'll make you tell the truth," again implying a predilection to fabricate.

"Maybe, half a dozen," I say as nonchalantly as possible. No resentment here!

He tilts his head and pouches out his lips as if considering my answer, seeming to decide if it's good enough. "So, about six. Six people out of 598." He lets the math work its own, simple humiliation. Then, he thrusts. "Can you name them for us?"

With the indifference of narrating a grocery list, I comply. But the effort to act like there's nothing to see is pointless – everyone knows who one of the names will be. It's the other people I recite, though, which makes her inclusion even more ominous. "Let's see. My father. Brady's parents and his brother. Winnie Butler. Rachel Maslow."

The prosecutor lifts his chin, looking up, either in wonder, in contemplation, or in shock. "Your immediate family," he begins, "Ms. Butler, who happens to be your loyal lifelong friend and campaign manager, ..." He pauses, pivots to the jury, an action blatant in its purpose, but still effective to underline his next three words. "And Rachel Maslow."

I could explain that most everyone else I would have considered – important public officials, high dollar donors – had already been invited by the Inaugural Committee, or that I had dozens of other guests in the equally fantastic seats of the upper bowl. But that would be like diving into quicksand, every exculpatory word merely highlighting the prosecutor's point: Maslow and I were *tight*!

I never actually saw her that day ... or ever again. My schedule was tightly scripted by the White House, and she wasn't on any of those guest lists. Pretty quickly during our first term, The Aberdeen Circle began its rapid descent into public disrepute. Natural enemies on the far right waited patiently for the public to grow weary of *TAC's* lofty human rights origins, and when radicals in Maslow's orbit went too far, they pounced. By the midterms, even the Thorne administration, of which I was a technical if irrelevant part, piled on against "The Homo Horde," "The Pink Peril," showcasing the dangers of the "Gay Mafioso" as a feature of its very effective culture war.

The prosecutor walks me through all of those homophobic official policies, making me squirm again and again for my loyalty to the president; coating me in a hypocritical tinge for failing to stand up to the assaults against the gay community; implying the resentments surely building inside me.

It's no wonder, he leaves unsaid, I was working so hard behind the scenes to help Maslow and *TAC* undermine the president, *my* president! The prosecutor "proves" this by trotting out call logs from both my office at the White House, and the "USNO," the United States Naval Observatory, my official residence. They showed numerous calls to Maslow and other *TAC* leaders. This shouldn't be a surprise. I was tasked with trying to calm the waters, trying to explain how Thorne's onslaughts – the bans on gay adoption and same sex marriage, the criminalization of gender-affirming care, even the removal of federal funding for schools employing gay teachers – weren't as bad as they seemed (they were!). He makes it sound like I was plotting against the administration when I was actually doing its disgusting dirty work – literally trying to avoid bloodshed.

"Not only," he thunders, waving a sheaf of papers in the air, "were you using official channels to communicate with the people who would soon shoot President Thorne, you also did so surreptitiously." The prosecutor has me identify a stack of CelluServe bills, my private mobile carrier, and then projects copies onto the large screen, all of the numbers blocked out with thick black strokes as if hiding sinister secrets, except for certain yellow-highlighted lines. "Yes," I acknowledge, over and over and over, every item emphasizing a call to Rachel Maslow. He makes sure her name crosses my lips each time. He doesn't ask me what we talked about, knowing the jurors' imaginations will fill in the blanks much better than the truth.

"All of this," he points at the accumulating pile of documents on his table, "leads to your final dispatch only five months ago, March 29, the day before the assassination attempt. *The ... very ... last ... time* you contacted Rachel Maslow."

And there it is, a small four-by-six-inch scrap of paper, more authentic for its slightly worn, wrinkled appearance, illuminated to many times its size on the rectangular canvas. No matter how well I spin my tale – which is the truth, by the way – the story will wind its way to this note I never should have written.

The prosecutor makes it look worse by overlaying, one-by-one, "incriminating" graphics: first my thumbprint, which he swears he's ready to authenticate with an expert if I wish to deny the oily marking is mine; an arrow pointing from a bubble explaining the ink matches a special pen from my desk – one given me by President Thorne at the signing ceremony for an urban renewal bill I, as a former mayor, was allowed to shepherd through the Senate (how ungrateful, or sick, my choosing *this* symbol of gratitude for my betrayal); the friendly "E" at the end, "for Eli, right?" he asks, overstating our friendship. All of this proving the damning document is mine – something I never denied!

Yes, the note. The one Maslow was supposed to destroy, but kept, either through negligence, or because even then she sensed some advantage. We were stunned during "discovery," the process before trial requiring parties to exchange what they intend to show the jury, when the prosecution produced a copy.

Thirteen little words. The jurors are engrossed, squinting, or slanting their torsos toward it, or grimacing, or looking down. Regardless of the movement, it is clear they, to say the least, disapprove. But none of them look at me. Not a single one.

> *R –*
> *I can't help anymore. You need to act now, before it's too late.*
>
> *E*

Having plunged the knife, leaving me bleeding in my small, uncomfortable wooden chair, the prosecutor walks over, a strange look of sympathy emerging from his dark features. All eyes are on him, anticipating his next action.

Then he crouches down, his face a mere foot from mine, his eyes dancing. A small smile appears. "It's not that bad, Mr. Vice President," he says. He reaches out his arm and places a large hand on the point of my shoulder, squeezing it. "It's not that bad."

I struggle to return to the real world. Hell, it's hard for me to breathe after the whipping I've just endured.

I look around the room. A "juror" is whispering into a very young "judge's" ear. Others on the "jury" are comparing notes, two of them dismantling the screen where so many horrors were projected. Slowly I realize, I remember, like the adjustment one makes awakening from a nightmare, that my now kindly tormentor is Mandela Briggs, my own lawyer. As devastatingly authentic as it seemed, this was all ... pretend. A "mock session," they call it. My trial is a good month away.

The characters in *this* courthouse – actually, Briggs' conference room – all work for him, and thus, for me: associate attorneys, legal assistants, secretaries, technicians.

This drama was one big practice run, an elaborate scrimmage. "We need to put you through your paces," Mandela had explained, "show you what it's going to be like." Now I know.

Hell. That's what it's going to be like. Hell.

And the punishment for the crime, treason, with which I am charged?

The death penalty.

PreTrial

One

Carolyn Bering never shied from a fight. Her father abandoned their family when she was too little to really remember. Her mother worked so many hours at so many jobs, sheer maternal exhaustion and absence forced young Carolyn into the role of caretaker for both herself and her younger sister.

No teacher or administrator in high school, no professor in college or law school, no colleague or partner at her law firm, and no husband (she had cycled through two) proved too intimidating or too great an obstacle for the headstrong girl, then woman, whose motivation – survival – was stronger than them all.

And survive she did. At least so far, anyway. Chief Judge of the United States District Court for the District of Columbia. Yet she could not rest, could not ease her focus, not even for a moment. *The United States of America vs. Elijah Wilson Styles, Vice President of the United States* was on her docket. It could have landed with any of 15 judges comprising the D.C. federal courts, but the random, rotating assignment of cases mandated by the local rules found her. One more test in a lifetime of challenges from which Carolyn would not shirk.

She sat behind a massive desk, actually more of a table on ornately carved legs, pulling erect her five-foot-seven frame. The high-backed leather chair was elevated so that only the fronts of her feet touched the floor, allowing her a leveled look into her guests. Carolyn enhanced this gravitas by pulling her naturally blond hair into a severe, no-nonsense bun, censoring the lighter streaks and warmer honey tones peeking through here and there. She made only a modest effort to cosmeticize the effects of 58 years, somehow sensing that the absence of such vanity allowed age to advertise wisdom.

Atop Volume VII of the Styles case's massive, metastasizing files, she lay her right hand. Glinting on its ring finger was a simple silver band, not from Yale where she completed her law degree, nor from her undergraduate study of European history at Purdue, but that of St. Margaret's. The small, Midwestern boarding school for young women molded her more than the glitzy institutions that followed, turning anger into enterprise and fear into resolve, qualities the days ahead would require.

Carolyn shut her eyes, propped the back of her head against the chair, and inhaled a slow, exaggerated lungful, only slowly easing the air out. In a moment she would call in the opposing gladiators to discuss the terms of battle: Fact or truth? Swords or axes?

Her country staggered toward a precipice, beneath which swirled disintegration. This case, this trial, could either save it, or shove it over the edge. The nation awaited. And, Carolyn accepted, the judge would be judged.

†††

"Zee, I'm ready," she said into the desktop console's speaker. No other words were needed, as her long-time administrator, Zenith, knew the choreography well.

A pair of thick wood-paneled doors glided open, Zee at attention with his back to one of them, his hand on its long, gilded handle as he subtly motioned the lawyers into Carolyn's spacious chambers.

The short, fit, angular United States attorney charged in first, a confident gust of energy. As the government's top lawyer in this district, Sidney McGehee was more than familiar with both the judge and her terrain, which he immediately sought to dominate with his presence. He thrust his arm out, Carolyn watching its lance-like approach as it reached, then crossed her desk. She remained seated, expressionless, and grasped McGehee's hand firmly, granting him only a quick, small nod.

Much less obtrusively, Mandela Briggs followed, more cautious, more respectful of the ornate space. Carolyn knew him by reputation, but other than a brief couple of hearings on a quickly settled commercial lawsuit a few years ago, this was their first real introduction. His urbane nature impressed her, the comfortable pride with which he wore his dark skin, politely refusing to allow his race to define him as society so consciously demanded. How would that play, she wondered, with the several African Americans who would wind up on the jury – this was the District of Columbia, after all.

Last into the room was Carolyn's senior clerk, Debbie, who discreetly took a seat on a window bench off to the side, pen poised over a yellow legal pad. Later, they would compare her written notes with Carolyn's mental ones.

Carolyn motioned the attorneys into the tufted Britton back chairs spaced at the corners of her desk. These were not GSA issue; Carolyn had purchased the tasteful, ivory-colored pieces precisely because they not only added a touch of grace to her dark compartment, but their open design also left her visitors more exposed.

As was custom, McGehee, the prosecutor, took the one to the Judge's left. And somewhat outside of protocol, but in keeping with his self-assured nature, he spoke first.

"Judge, I am very pleased to advise that I have been able to reach agreement with Mr. Briggs," he proclaimed, implying full credit for the deed, "on most of the Motion in Limine items, saving just a few for your consideration."

Despite herself, Carolyn bristled.

The routine procedural motion, one filed by each side on the eve of trial, derived its name, like so much of the law, from Latin: in this instance, *līmen*, meaning "at the threshold." Limines seek to exclude information a party thinks will be unfairly prejudicial, rather than aiding the jury's ability to decide the case. Thus, evidence a defendant beat his spouse would not be allowed in a tax evasion case – his scumbaggery would surely inflame the jury's passions, but wouldn't fairly show if he intended to cheat the government.

Carolyn had, as always, asked the parties to work out what they could, bringing her only the most intractable items. She also reminded them of her strict skepticism against the garish, sensational stuff lawyers loved to fling about the courtroom.

She should have greeted McGehee's pronouncement with praise. What riled her was his arrogance, a self-righteousness that oozed from his pores. Even the man's easy posture suggested the prosecutor intended to own this trial.

Not a chance in hell, Carolyn thought.

"Thank you, Mr. McGehee," she said without smiling. "We'll hold that for later," she added, diminishing his achievement. This was her turf, and she would set the agenda, even though on her small white pad Carolyn's elegant penmanship had crafted the word, "Limine," next to "No. 1."

He held her gaze. His smile thickened.

"What I want to discuss first," she continued, shifting her attention to defense counsel, "is the matter of pretrial publicity." He frowned, as she knew he would, reflecting his supposition as to what was coming next.

"I am going to sequester the jury." She held up a hand to his tensing body, arguments forming behind a determined gaze. "Allow me, Mr. Briggs, to explain.

"First, I understand the downsides to separating jurors from their families, from their lives, for days on end. I read your Response, and I do not dispute any of those points. However, we cannot ignore what is happening online or on TV, and I am even more concerned about what is developing on the streets all across this country."

She paused, folding her hands on the desk as she looked back and forth from Briggs to McGehee. "There is too much on the line in this case, not just for the Vice President, but for our democracy. This is going to be a fair fight, gentlemen, and that requires us to protect our jurors in every way we can."

"May I be heard, Your Honor," Briggs asked in an even voice. He knew the matter was decided, but like a player working the Ref for the next call, he wanted her to feel his pain. She nodded.

"No one is going to want to be one of the 12 in that box," he began, pointing toward the wall behind him, and through it the courtroom beyond, "unless they have an agenda. And I'm sure we'll weed those folks out. Which means those remaining will start off angry, which is never good for the accused. Locking them up in a hotel room, with no access to the outside world, will add isolation, boredom and crazy anxiety to the mix, leaving a bunch of people driven to rush their deliberations so they can return to their normal lives."

Briggs leaned back, emphasizing his exasperation. "More times than not," he whispered, "that means a guilty verdict." He shook his head sadly. "And not because of the evidence."

Carolyn gazed at him sympathetically. "As I said, Mr. Briggs, I fully appreciate your concerns." Her tone was of the *Mother Knows Best* variety. "But in my mind, they do not outweigh the need for this jury to focus solely on the trial, without having to filter outside influences. And to be quite honest," she added, lowering her voice an octave, "I'm worried about intimidation, and even their safety."

"I concur," the prosecutor interjected, unhelpfully. He was an experienced and accomplished counselor, and well knew the maxim, *Don't fight when you've won*, or the more direct version, *If the judge is arguing your side, keep your mouth shut*. But Sidney McGehee was nothing if not a showman, no matter how small the audience. "The prospect of those Aberdeen Circle nuts threatening our jurors is terrifying."

Carolyn glared at him. "In reaching my conclusion, Mr. McGehee, I was frankly thinking more about the militias supporting President Thorne." The U.S. attorney feigned surprise. "I'm sure we have all seen their posts, showing off how well armed they are."

She almost immediately regretted having allowed McGehee to draw her out. This was going to be a long trial.

"Anyway," the judge quickly transitioned, "I am also denying the prosecution's motion to allow cameras during trial."

"But Your Honor," McGehee thundered, half rising from his seat. Again, her hand.

"This case will not be broadcast," Carolyn proclaimed, "live or otherwise, at any stage of the proceedings, for three primary reasons." She looked to Briggs. "First, my ruling follows my concerns about security. If we allow cameras, we increase the chances that one or more jurors are identified, which puts not only them, but their families, at risk."

The prosecutor readied his counterattack, his mouth opening, only for Carolyn to raise her voice as she barreled ahead. "Second, I don't want a circus. With all due respect, gentlemen, we don't need lawyers playing to cameras, or witnesses auditioning for stardom." McGehee's look soured. He knew damned well she meant *him*.

"Finally, it just slows things down. There will be pleas for time to fix technical glitches, a mess of set up issues, cables running everywhere. I plan to tightly control these proceedings, to work long days, to get a resolution as expeditiously as possible – no delays or distractions."

"Your Honor," the prosecutor uttered, somewhat bitterly.

"Yes sir?" Carolyn offered him a weak smile.

"As I know you are aware, Congress passed the 'Courthouse Sunshine Act' last month ..."

"They seemed to have us in mind, didn't they Mr. McGehee?"

"Perhaps, Your Honor. But the more important point is, they overrode the prohibition against cameras in federal criminal proceedings, and in fact, encouraged judges to allow as many Americans as possible to see their justice system in action. I think we should respect what the people's representatives have mandated. Show them ... show the world, we have nothing to hide!"

Carolyn couldn't conceal her amusement, and didn't really try. For years, a presidential appointment as U.S. attorney had been a pathway to political advancement. It was no secret McGehee had designs on the senate seat in his home state. What better way to launch his campaign than to dominate the airwaves during the trial of the century?

"I read your brief, counselor. And I certainly understand your ..." She groped for a suitable word, one that would not betray her distaste for this man's obsessive preening. "... your *preference* for maximum exposure." She furrowed her brow, concentrating the intensity of her green eyes, drilling them into the prosecutor. "But as you are surely aware, the Act is permissive, not a command, and leaves it to each judge's discretion in each individual case." She didn't bother to repeat her reasons. McGehee sat back, not troubling to hide his disapproval.

"Gentlemen, this trial begins in three weeks. We have a lot of ground to cover today, so let's get moving." She ticked down her list, dispensing with one dispute, one request, one logistic after another, usually disappointing one side if not both.

As they neared the end of the long session, Carolyn glanced at the picture on the corner of her desk, a five-by-seven wood frame angled so that only she could see it.

Dressed in a pale blue sweater, a tasteful string of faux pearls encircling her neck, an unsmiling woman regarded Carolyn with a stubborn, expectant pose. Rose Bering was not a fountain of warmth. She was a dependable mother, though, if not a particularly present one. Her doggedness, her resilience, were her legacy. Carolyn missed her, longed for her approval, hopeful but not certain the daughter's accomplishments would suffice.

What she knew for sure, however, was that she carried forth Rose's refusal to relent in the face of adversity. There had always been food on the table, as well as the sustenance of love, even if the latter was largely assumed. In Carolyn's courtroom, there would be a similar consistency.

"Okay, counselors," she said as the sunlight outside began to fade. "Last item." She considered McGehee pleasantly. "The Motions in Limine."

Two

"So, do you think he might testify? I mean Styles. Boy oh boy, he's a master. I've seen him on MSNBC, and he even has the liberal anchors eating out of his hand." Horace Hollingsworth, founder of Mayflower Capital Resources, sat to McGehee's left, three places down the long, oak dining room table. The moderately overweight leader of the eastern seaboard's largest hedge fund looked like a bowling ball with a sport coat. But he was unavoidably important, which was why he was here.

"He makes everything sound ... *reasonable*," Dolly, Horace's wife, chimed in. From the other place of prominence at the table's opposite end, McGehee's wife nodded reassuringly, making sure Dolly knew her comment was respected. Laura was the perfect partner. Sooner than not, McGehee thought, she would be a tremendous First Lady.

"He's also clever, though," August Wolfe said from McGehee's right. "Smart enough to realize that if he ever takes the stand, Sidney here will rip him to shreds." *The Washington Post*'s owner pursed his lips and raised a glass of Malbec in praise of his host.

McGehee loved these dinners. His and Laura's Georgetown brownstone was a coveted invitation. D.C. society knew the power couple were on the way up and wanted to be along for the ride. Each date, therefore, was carefully selected with the attendees purposefully curated. Always eight, four along each flank. Always the perfect mix of helpful significance.

Pretty much everything in Sidney McGehee's life had been just as prudently planned. First, by his parents: public or private education (public would seem less elitist); which sports (baseball, of course, as it was way more "American" than soccer, and much less prone to brain injury than football); what clubs to join (Chess too nerdy, Spanish too ethnic, Drama too gay – Future Farmers of America and Robotics were better fits, even though neither Mom, Dad nor young Sidney foresaw a future in either field).

"Still, does he have a choice?" asked Penny Gillespie, using her proximity to touch McGehee's hand for emphasis. "The coverage has been brutal. His relationship with that horrible Rachel Maslow!" The tough-as-nails former chair of the Colorado Republican Party lacked diplomatic nuance. Of course, her current appointment as ambassador to Barbados didn't really require any.

Seated next to the chaotic Penny, Lewis Dearborn couldn't help himself from lecturing. "Then again, the president's popularity here in the District isn't, for example, what you would find in Tennessee or Wyoming." As Chair of Howard University's Political Science department, pontificating was his lifeblood. "All due respect to the undisputed talent of our favorite prosecutor ..." he paused, bowing theatrically from his chair, "a unanimous verdict is not an easy task."

McGehee raised his eyebrows ambiguously. It was one of many lessons learned from his dad. Hold your cards close. Even after Sidney began charting his own course, the influence of his mother and father remained. She, creator of a hugely successful home accessories website, provided him exquisite marketing acumen, an ability to judge his words and actions by how they would be perceived by those who mattered. His dad, majority owner and CEO of the largest independent bank in Indiana, introduced his son to the fine arts of networking and leverage. Perhaps not Joe and Rose Kennedy when it came to managing Sid, as one uncle joked, but they sure didn't mind the comparison.

"Sort of reminds me of one of our episodes," Hugo d'Clément offered pleasantly. Easily the more recognizable "prosecutor" at this gathering, courtesy of his CBS Drama *Steel Verdict*, he chuckled at his own lighthearted contribution. "There was this corrupt police chief. I mean, a *really* bad guy. Money from drug busts. Covering up murders.

But he had a great public image, just like Styles. And I ... well, my character, Sam Steel ... had to prove the chief was all show, a total fraud." d'Clément paused for dramatic effect.

"What happened?" Laura asked raptly, ever the perfect hostess.

"Oh, I remember," Dolly jumped in. "That was one of my favorite scenes!" The debonair actor leaned back and opened his palm, happily yielding to a fawning review.

"Well, Hugo here, or should I say District Attorney Sam Steel," she gushed, "led the crook right down the path. Showed that he wasn't the common guy he pretended to be, you know, that he attended boarding schools and had private tutors and such, that his father bribed his way onto the force, that he cheated on his wife, blackmailed his way to promotion. He was a complete fake, like Styles. The jury hated him. Life sentence!"

McGehee chuckled along with everyone else, though in contrast to the hapless fictionalized chief, he was more confident in his precisely crafted image. Choosing Indiana State for his undergraduate B.B.M, and then the University of Chicago for his law degree, followed this pattern: fine schools which avoided the snobbish coastal stigma future Hoosier voters might detect in a Harvard, or a Stanford. And in a detour from the path of financial success – not a factor with the inheritance Sidney could expect – he joined the Air Force Judge Advocate General's Corp as soon as he passed the bar. Another line on a carefully compiled resume.

Tonight, only 35, Sidney looked at his gathering with equal measures of pride and satisfaction. Its very composition confirmed the success of the design he and his folks envisioned from the beginning.

"Sidney," Congressman Neal chirped sheepishly – or was it Nell; McGehee didn't know why Laura included this lowly freshman from a non-swing state, but was sure she had a good reason. "I have a question," he declared. Or was he asking permission? Sidney nodded. *Go ahead.*

"I was wondering, well, treason. Not attempted assassination, or conspiracy to murder or whatever. Why is the vice president being charged with treason? That seems ... I guess, nebulous? Harder to prove?" McGehee contemplated Representative Neal, or Nell, for a long moment, causing a rise of discomfort in the young elected official. The man's wife tried to affect a rescue.

"Honey, maybe he's not supposed to talk about that."

"Of course," the congressman grasped at the rope, "of course. No, that's true, thank you Barbara," he said, patting her arm appreciatively. "I understand completely, Sidney," he explained, turning to McGehee. "My apologies."

McGehee's high forehead served to amplify his expressions like a billboard, his bristly military crew exponentially strengthening whichever emotion he chose to render. Thus, when he burst into a grin, as he did now, there was unmistakable clarity in his intent. Sidney leaned over from his perch and slapped Nell, or Neal, on the back for emphasis. "Oh, hell," he began, waving off any concern with his free hand, "this is just a dinner among friends, right? What happens in Vegas, stays in Vegas, and all that," he chuckled, scanning everyone's consenting gestures. He knew every word he was about to say would be shared multiple times before the next sunrise. That was the whole point.

McGehee visibly composed himself, allowing them to feel the seriousness of his coming remarks. Barely two years from his appointment by President Thorne, the stakes had unexpectedly risen. The failed coup, and the vice president's role in it, accelerated Sidney's timetable, drawing a welcomed spotlight.

"The thing is, our dear Mr. Styles' actions violate multiple laws, as you so correctly point out," he said to Barbara's husband, now positively beaming. "In due time, he can be charged for them all."

"What about double jeopardy?" the *Post*'s Wolfe challenged.

"Doesn't apply," d'Clément interjected with authority. "Double jeopardy is putting someone on trial twice for the *same* crime based on the *same* event. So, if you rob a bank, you can't be tried more than once for that robbery. But you could be tried for robbery, murder, illegal weapons possession, whatever, even though it all happened in a single incident. Same event, different crimes, and you can be prosecuted for each." Everyone glanced back and forth between the impertinent actor and his host. "Season Five," d'Clément explained, sensing the tension. "We had a two-parter on that very question."

McGehee roared with delight, clapping his hands. "Sam Steel to the rescue!" he declared. "Maybe I should let you handle this case," he added with a wink.

"No, no," d'Clément flashed his hands in deference. "I think we all agree, something this serious needs a real prosecutor, not a TV star."

"Be that as it may," McGehee resumed, "you are correct, Hugo. I'm not worried about double jeopardy. The vice president's conduct, as you so elegantly explained, triggered several distinct crimes, giving us several different ways to hold him responsible."

"But why treason?" Dolly asked. "That seems like the hardest one of all to prove."

Sidney smiled patiently. The intrusions into his elucidation were tiresome, but like with members of his juries, he wanted all of tonight's attendees to feel valued. Doubt, or stupidity, was nothing more than an opportunity to score more points.

"Good question," he flattered Dolly, a quick, knowing glance to her husband – *these women, right Horace?* "The answer's actually quite simple." McGehee rounded the table, invading each pair of eyes, making sure everyone noticed the fire in his. "It is the only one of the possible charges that carries the death penalty."

The room fell into such a silence that the only sound was the *tick, tick, tick* of the grandfather clock in the hallway. Dolly looked into her lap; the Congressman and his wife exchanged uneasy expressions; Professor Dearborn stared vacantly into the distance, his napkin dabbing aimlessly about his lips; d'Clément's eyes widened, as if this were too much for even a Hollywood script. The brassy Ambassador Gillespie, rarely at a loss, was still.

Only Laura maintained her husband's gaze. "I suppose it is startling to hear the words," she whispered calmly. She lifted her pinot grigio ambiguously, its sweat glistening from the chandelier's illumination. A salute to her husband, or just the prelude to another sip? "But I am proud our country has the courage to put accountability over politics." Laura and Sidney shared resolute, grave smiles.

"Here, here!" August Wolfe exclaimed, lifting his glass more forcefully, and everyone else scrambled to join in the acclaim for the vice president's imminent demise.

McGehee feigned a bashful acknowledgment before launching into his now familiar talking points.

"The thing is, we mustn't look at this as garden variety attempted murder, or relabel it, in view of the target, as an assassination attempt. Such would be a *big* mistake, because it reduces the act to that of simple violence by one human against another. Bad, granted, but missing the larger, more vital implication: this was an act of violence against our *nation*." McGehee pounded the table with his fist, the cutlery tinkling as it jumped with the vibration. "More evil still, it was an act of violence *against our very democracy*!"

Every face was his, transfixed by his fervor.

"So, then," Wolfe offered politely, his publisher's blood unable to resist, "you *know* that Styles wanted the president dead." There was no lilt at the end indicating a question.

Sidney sloped back into his chair and lowered his gaze, pretending to absorb the statement's gravity, though his reply was already in his throat. Rubbing his chin thoughtfully with thumb and forefinger, a perfect sadness filling the sharp contours of his face, he eventually spoke. "August, I am afraid it is worse than that." McGehee finally looked up from the floor, pausing, forcing his guests to contemplate what desire could be worse than wishing a president's murder.

"Styles craved power. Absolute power. And he was willing to do anything to get it."

Sidney knew each person here understood, from his or her unique perspective, the lure of unbridled authority, the ability to exert one's will without challenge. They all strived for such within their own realm, setting themselves above the common masses who could only dream of such. This compulsion to dominate one's environment, turning whim to fate, was a feature of humankind, especially in the political world. Harming one's fellow man to achieve this goal – destroyed reputations, toppled careers, financial ruin – was tolerable, an unavoidable cost of nature.

But physical harm? *Murder?* That was the stuff of hoodlums, thugs and mobsters, so far beneath the dignity of proper society. Insufferable. Unspeakable!

And yet, McGehee had just uttered that precise charge at the vice president.

"Well," he exhaled sharply, attempting to puncture the darkening mood, "that's all my problem to deal with, isn't it."

Sidney grinned broadly, attempting to levitate the assemblage's morose spirits. The prosecution of Elijah Styles was important, and McGehee believed in the mantra that would convict him. As vital, however, were the affections of these important people. In less than two years, an open senate seat back home could be his, but not without the enthusiastic backing of leaders like those now surrounding him. A good prosecutor must summon ominous clouds; but a future senator like McGehee needed the association of strength, not darkness; confidence, not misery. More Indiana Jones, less Grim Reaper.

And so, Sidney winked, then chuckled, letting a sense of ease permeate the room until, by sheer force of his personality, the tension seeped away. Tentatively, uncertainly, first the actor d'Clément, then the publisher Wolfe, and like dominos, Horace and Dolly and the rest, began to breathe, to smile back.

Satisfied with the more pleasant vibe, the host quickly turned the page by looking lengthwise to his wife, her perfectly proportioned eyebrows raised with sunny anticipation.

"Laura, what's for dessert?"

Three

"Where did you get them?" Mandela Briggs asked, his tenor harsh. He was angry, not with the bearer of the bad news, Izzy, but with the news itself.

"A friend," his paralegal replied vaguely, a defiant stare communicating, *you don't want to know!* Her boss had a pretty good idea. She and *Washington Post* reporter Sebastian Montes had been cycling through the various stages of "relationship."

"Am I actually seeing what I think I'm seeing?" he asked.

Izzy folded her bare arms, the left one on top, its full sleeve of tattooed ink like the pages of a comic book, colorful figures and designs indecipherable to Briggs, making him feel much older than 43.

"'Fraid so."

He returned to an 8 x 10 black-and-white glossy, holding it with both hands, excuses for his client branching out in his mind. It showed two men bundled up against the cold with upturned collars and scarves, one with a fur cap and mufflers, the other a dark beanie over his ears, yet both recognizable. Blakely Kurtz, The Aberdeen Circle's communications director on the left, and mere inches from his face, the clouds of their breath intermingling, Sam Kilbrough, would be presidential assassin.

"In front of ..."

"In front of the Ritz-Carlton. Yep. The very same downtown Cleveland hotel where Kurtz met with the vice president. In fact," Izzy rubbed the heart tattoo on her left ear lobe, a tic she exhibited when revving up, "you can see the time on the pharmacy's marquee down the street."

As Briggs squinted, the LED display in the background became legible. Izzy was right. It was the same as the ominous red stamp on the photo's lower left-hand corner, which likewise stated 10:48 a.m., along with the date, February 17.

"Do you think," Briggs' senior associate, Ryan, interjected, "this could be why the vice president didn't tell us?"

"Captain Obvious!" Izzy needled her colleague. She actually loved Ryan like a little brother, but his linear mind drove her crazy. "Of course it's the reason. Not exactly a good look if you're trying to disprove a conspiracy."

Briggs didn't look up, ignoring the team's jostling, his gears turning. "There's no proof," he said finally, then let out a sigh, taking in their small conference room. It felt even tighter among stacks of sturdy Bankers Boxes, with exhibits and transcripts strewn about the round table, chairs and floor. "We can presume the vice president will say he had no idea Kurtz would leave his suite and meet with Kilbrough moments later."

Ryan and Izzy turned from Briggs to each other, their expressions confirming their agreement. Their employer was one of the most coveted defense attorneys in the nation. Elijah Styles was lucky to have him. And Briggs was correct: Styles would claim Kurtz acted on his own in meeting with the man who, six weeks later, would fire a gun at the president.

But was that even remotely believable? As they say, pictures speak a thousand words, and this monochrome doozy screamed *GUILTY*! What were the odds of Blakely Kurtz, who the vice president had dealt with for years, The Aberdeen Circle being one of Styles' most fervent supporters, and Sam Kilbrough, once lead agent on the vice president's own security detail, running into each other by coincidence outside Styles' hotel? Pretty low, and U.S. attorney Sidney McGehee would make a mockery of anyone suggesting otherwise.

Briggs knew this. The question was, who would be the first to say it out loud, to start the process of untangling an ugly mess and crafting a comeback?

Izzy. Always Izzy, as if spurred on by the green-tinted, angry Lady Liberty adorning her exposed deltoid.

"Maybe there's no proof," she began matter-of-factly, "but what Tom, Dick or Harriet will need any?"

Ryan's eyebrows rose into a steeple, not in surprise, but quizzically, a perfect imitation of Mr. Spock, Izzy decided. Fitting, she thought, for someone so entwined in logic. "Because," he said blandly, "the jury can't rely on speculation. Facts have to be established with valid evidence."

Izzy trilled her lips. "They teach you that in law school, Ryan? Glad I saved my money."

"Actually, they did," he said evenly, not rising to the bait.

"Okay, fine." She raised her hands in mock surrender. "But, I mean, look at it the other way around? The jury sees the picture of Kurtz and Kilbrough. They are reminded when this little meeting took place, and that sitting in a suite upstairs is our client, who just met with the very same Mr. Kurtz."

She stroked her chin in playful contemplation, the colorful butterfly tattoos on her knuckles seemingly flapping their tiny wings. "Now, counselor, where do their minds go?"

Ryan frowned.

"If criminal justice were all about appearances," Briggs said to Izzy, "there would be little need for trials. Defendants almost always have an odor of guilt in the public's perception, precisely because they have been accused. Our job is to make sure the jury holds its collective nose, or failing that, to apply liberal amounts of perfume."

Izzy puckered her lips, another of her non-verbal cues, this one representing defiance. The movement jiggled the slender gold bar piercing her septum, one of many features that unnerved Ryan. At the moment, however, he was more pleased that the boss had taken his side.

"Unfortunately," Briggs added, his attention now on his associate, "if Izzy was referring to the dangers of circumstantial evidence, I think she's hit the target."

"Ha!" she yelled, punching Ryan in the arm.

"The question is," Briggs continued, ignoring the competition, "what did the vice president know?"

"Nothing good, I'm guessing," Izzy said, "or else why would he lie to us about even meeting with Kurtz that morning."

"He didn't lie," Ryan leapt to the client's defense. "As soon as we asked, he admitted it."

Izzy grew animated, waving her arms. "That's exactly what I'm telling you, Ryan! Until we brought it up, Styles didn't bother to mention a meeting with Blakely Frickin' Kurtz, 40 days before the assassination, 'cause he *knew* what a big deal it would be!" She pounded her hand into her palm. "If hiding stuff from your own lawyer isn't lying, what is?"

Briggs enjoyed the fireworks. The cerebral, legalistic Ryan Townsend – his office's only, and therefore "senior" associate attorney – represented a certain rationality, that sense of caution and fairness residing in most Americans, though buried more deeply in some than others. Equally relevant, maybe more, was the rush of emotional intuition presented by Isabella "Izzy" Petritoli, Mandela's jack of all trades. She was his organizer, his investigator, and above all, the firm's barometer, the one attuned to society's pulse.

As he looked through the second story window of the firm's office, a delicately restored Queen Anne Victorian on Q Street, Briggs watched the pedestrians amble, presumably to and from Dupont Circle a few blocks away. A young man on a skateboard. An older woman carefully making her way in small steps, a black pillbox hat firmly attached to her stylized mound of gray curls. A Black man about Mandela's own age, though more worn, limping along in a frayed Commanders sweatshirt. It was a diverse array, indeed, the mélange of humanity that would be called to Judge Bering's courtroom for jury duty in less than three weeks.

A squawk from the doorway, "Mandela," broke his musings. It was the smokers' rasp of the fourth member of their little family, Joan, his forever secretary. "They're on the way," the cantankerous but supernaturally efficient 81-year-old blared. "They" was the vice president's entourage, "on the way" from Styles' residence, The United States Naval Observatory – a 12-minute drive for normal citizens, more like five with the advantage of an escorted motorcade.

"Thanks, Joan."

Given the new photograph, today's visit would be another tense one. For Styles, meetings with his lawyer were one of the few exceptions to his severely enforced house arrest, and the sessions never lacked for drama. That was to be expected, Briggs supposed, given the pressures of this case, with the very life of the vice president at stake.

Still, he reflected, *how damned lucky am I?* His father drove city buses for the Denver RTD for 35 years. His mother toiled almost as long in the public schools' cafeterias. And here he was, God rest their souls, at the center of their nation's biggest legal and political battle ever. His name had long ago become a benchmark for controversy, a celebrity status rivaling F. Lee Bailey's and Johnnie Cochran's, evoking vitriol that worried Mama and delighted Pop.

This fight would surpass all the others. It would forever brand Briggs in partisan shades from blue hero to red devil. And for that very reason, as he prepared to rally his motley band, Mandela swelled with confidence, happy it was just the four of them, that Styles chose this small, devoted crew – Mandela, Ryan, Izzy and Joan – over the glossyshoed, Armani-suited 500-lawyer firms lording over D.C. and New York.

Maybe they were hired because of longstanding friendship: the two met after Styles, then a 25-year-old rising star at the prominent brokerage Borgen Railey, retained Briggs, fresh off his first headline verdict, to represent a BR client in deep trouble. Their connection was immediate, strengthened by Mandela's huge support for each of Styles' subsequent campaigns.

Or it could be Briggs' fierce reputation. This was, after all, an African American lawyer who defended an unabashedly racist White governor on corruption charges, never once apologizing for his work. "I may loathe the man, but I love Lady Justice," he said in a fiery speech on the courthouse steps as the trial began. "As a Black man, I know well how my people often get the short end of the stick – that is, if the stick isn't being used to beat us. As Black Americans, therefore, we must demand a country where no one, no matter how reprehensible in the eyes of public opinion, is *beneath* the law. The jurors in this matter are free to vote Governor Lark out of office in the next campaign. Were I a citizen of Louisiana, I may join them. But on this jury, they must treat him as one of their peers, and vote only as the evidence requires." The defendant was acquitted unanimously by a jury of four Whites, one Hispanic woman, and seven Black citizens. He lost the next election.

Or perhaps it was simply that Mandela, and Briggs Law, would be as underestimated as Styles himself had always been: the smart little dark-skinned child, who does he think he is, the ambitious gay kid who'll never amount to anything, combining for yet another surprise.

At the moment, the reason for his hiring didn't matter. The only "Why" that did? Why was Eli Styles lying, and what else was he hiding?

Briggs considered Ryan and Izzy one last time as the rumble of police motorcycles swelled outside. He thought of the gargantuan tasks ahead of them, steeled himself, and placed the photo back into its folder as he barked, "Okay, folks, let's see what our client has to say today."

†††

Streets Erupt as Trial Approaches

SEATTLE – With the treason trial of Vice President Elijah W. Styles only 18 days away, violence continues to grow across the country. Most of the protests, which have broken out in cities from coast to coast, are fueled by supporters of Mr. Styles, many claiming he is the scapegoat for a plot by President Magnus Thorne to curb or even end democracy in the United States.

In Chicago, The Miracle Mile was closed after multiple cars were attacked with bricks, bottles and other projectiles, and several storefronts were breached. In Midtown Manhattan, a massive fire erupted in the lobby of The 725 Building, formerly Trump Tower. Surrounding retail establishments were ravaged by looters, and Fifth Avenue was rendered impassable by thousands of demonstrators. San Francisco closed its central business district after numerous assaults on businesses, vehicles, and even pedestrians. In total, 37 cities reported rioting.

None were worse than here in Seattle, where protests of varying intensity have erupted in dozens of communities. In the Capitol Hill neighborhood east of downtown, marchers, many carrying signs supporting

Mr. Styles or denigrating the president, closed down the major Broadway thoroughfare early Friday morning.

By midday, defenders of President Thorne had arrived on the scene. "I'm not going to let these homos and druggies destroy our country," said Colton Reedy, sporting a red ballcap emblazoned with the familiar white script, *Restore America's Greatest Era*.

Scores of the counter protestors wore those iconic RAGE hats, some expensively stitched, others screen printed like Mr. Reedy's. Regardless of how fancy their gear, they were united in support of the president. Predictably, brutality followed. Glass containers, rocks, smoke bombs and other homemade incendiaries flew between the opposing sides, eventually progressing to gunfire. Some blamed militant followers of The Aberdeen Circle, others claimed the pro-Thorne militia group Mighty Sword initiated the mayhem.

Nearby hospitals reported a steady stream of injured, both combatants and bystanders. There were at least 11 confirmed fatalities.

The Seattle Police Department never gained control of what is being called the "Battle of Broadway," their resources strained by chaos in disparate locations of the large metropolitan area. Before nightfall, Governor Malcolm Bergquist dispatched the national guard which succeeded, at least temporarily, in separating the dueling factions. The physical destruction of the Capitol Hill area, including widespread blazes, continues, as does the turmoil in other parts of the city.

U.S. attorney Sidney McGehee, who leads the vice president's prosecution in Washington D.C., issued a statement condemning the uprisings, blaming them squarely on Mr. Styles. "Every one of the defendant's admirers who try to destroy America by causing death, injury and destruction of property must be held accountable," he said, adding, "Make no mistake, however, this is exactly why justice for the vice president's attempt to overthrow the government cannot come soon enough."

Styles is the first sitting vice president to be charged with treason. Former vice president Aaron Burr was acquitted of the same offense in 1807, for alleged insurrectionist activities after he left office. Spiro Agnew plead no contest to tax evasion and resigned as vice president in 1973.

Continued on Page 8

Four

Lars Whitehorse Presents
Episode 443: The Funny Thing About Treason

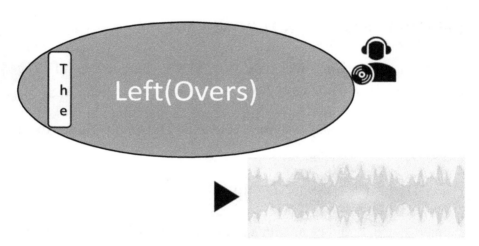

Transcript

(AMERICANA STREAMING NETWORK JINGLE)

Americana Narrator: Good afternoon all. This is the Americana Streaming Network studio in New York.

Lars Whitehorse: It's time we tell the truth ... while we still can.

(BEATING HEART SOUND)

Americana Narrator: Today is Sunday, August 21, 16 days before the treason trial of Vice President Elijah Wilson Styles.

(BEATING HEART SOUND GROWS LOUDER)

Lars Whitehorse: And here on The Left, those passionate few of us left over, we believe the best way to tell the truth is to start at the beginning.

(BEATING HEART SOUND GROWS FASTER)

Americana Narrator: Welcome to ASN's production of *The Left(Overs), Lars Whitehorse Presents*, Episode 443.

Lars Whitehorse: Today's show is called ... "The Funny Thing About Treason."

(HEARTBEAT FADES INTO SILENCE)

Female Voice: It all began with a thrashing. A massive, brutal beating in the sleepy settlement of Aberdeen in Washington State, on the eastern shore of Grays Harbor, nestled between the Pacific Ocean and Seattle. A proud community with long ago ties to timber and fishing, Aberdeen was, sadly, well past its heyday. Most of the old mills and canneries were long since closed.
Like many other towns forgotten by time, its residents struggled day-by-day, far from the lights of the big city. They worked low-paying jobs, suffered the scourge of drugs, and drew on the strength of family, friends and neighbors. They persisted. Until, that is, 13 years ago. That's when everything blew up.

Lars Whitehorse: Wow. Has it really been 13 years? Hard to believe, but it's true. This very month, 13 years ago, young Tanner Centurion pulled his car to the curb of Simpson Avenue, in front of a local bakery.

He was after a bagel, his usual before going to work. Unfortunately for the slightly built 22-year-old, two local toughs wanted the same spot. They were not pleased when Tanner claimed it.

(JINGLE FOR KING 5 [SEATTLE] NEWS)
Local Anchor: Welcome to 5 at Noon, and thank you for joining us. Disturbing news out of Aberdeen this morning, where we have video of a shocking physical assault in what is already being described as a potential hate crime. And we must warn, what we are about to play may be very upsetting for many of you.

(CRIES OF AGONY, GRUNTING AND "THUD" SOUNDS; MUFFLED LAUGHTER)
Voice of Witness on Video: Oh, my God, do something! They're just standing there watching. Why aren't they *doing* something?

Lars Whitehorse: "They" were the two Aberdeen police officers called to the scene, who everyone remembers from the ubiquitous video just stood by and watched as Tanner was pummeled. Two minutes. Five minutes. Finally, at seven minutes and 37 seconds, one of them stepped in. Too late for the victim, who after three days in a coma, mercifully passed away.

(CHANTING VOICES IN UNISON)
Justice for Tanner, the police killed him too. Justice for Tanner, you know what to do.

Lars Whitehorse: The gruesome images were the worst since George Floyd. And while in that case, the knee of an officer snuffed out a young man's life, here it was the callous eyes of law enforcement, passively permitting blow after blow from unrestrained fists and steel-toed boots. A young gay man locals knew as out and proud lolled on the asphalt like a rag doll.

I am joined today by *Washington Post* reporter Sebastian Montes who, no less than Woodward, Bernstein and Watergate, is one of our nation's primary voices for the upcoming trial of *United States vs. Styles*. Sebastian, greetings.

Sebastian Montes: Thank you for having me, Lars.

Lars Whitehorse: Perhaps you can explain what the death of Tanner Centurion has to do with the government's quest to execute our vice president, other than each having a gay person at its core.

Sebastian Montes: I'd be glad to. The Centurion murder, as I'm sure your audience knows, led to the rise of The Aberdeen Circle, started as a group of local activists focused on accountability for the two cops involved. However, under the guidance of its founder, Rachel Maslow, it grew into a million-member, multi-racial, multi-generational human rights crusader spanning all 50 states. Police abuse, job and pay equity, educational opportunity, gender and gay rights, you name it, *TAC* became America's conscience, and a powerful force in its politics.

Lars Whitehorse: Enter Elijah Styles.

Sebastian Montes: Correct. No matter what you think of the guy, no one denies he's a master at reading the public mood. Ten years ago, Styles leaned heavily on *TAC* when he launched his campaign to become mayor of Dallas. Five years later, when he became the first major gay candidate for the Republican presidential nomination, The Aberdeen Circle was right there with him again.

Lars Whitehorse: And gave Magnus Thorne a beautiful fig leaf of acceptability when he selected Styles as his running mate. Who could forget that acceptance speech in Minneapolis.

(ROARING APPLAUSE, DRUMS BEATING, NOISE MAKERS BLEATING, CROWD CHANTING "THORNE, THORNE, THORNE")

Voice of Elijah Wilson Styles: So it is only fair to ask, if Governor Thorne is the monster his detractors say he is ... what am I doing here? Is he conservative? Yes. But so am I, and it is time for the Left to realize, progressivism merely as a pose is no virtue, and conservatism in the name of progress is no sin."

Lars Whitehouse: Little did he know.

Sebastian Montes: For sure, but then again, Styles was a new breed. A gifted orator and effortless campaigner, yes, but also an out, proud, gay Republican who spoke of traditional values, a fighter for equality who used the language of personal responsibility, someone who believed he could bridge the gap between Red and Blue. Styles trusted that he and Thorne would actually be a team.

Lars Whitehouse: And then?

Sebastian Montes: A tsunami of bad luck hit the new administration right out of the gate. Before Thorne was even sworn in, the stock market crashed. Inflation soared past nine percent in his first hundred days, and the financial collapse propelled millions of desperate Latin Americans toward our southern border.

Lars Whitehorse: And as often happens in times of economic crisis, crime soared. People were frightened. A desperate search began for a savior, and a scapegoat. The president deftly became the nation's Redeemer by finding just the right whipping boy, didn't he Sebastian?

Sebastian Montes: He did indeed, with The Aberdeen Circle handed to him on a silver platter.

(XBN BREAKING NEWS THEME)
Male Voice: Good evening to our viewers. We interrupt normal programming to report on dramatic events at this hour in Butte, Montana, where a gay activist group calling itself Tanner's Vengeance have taken over the studio for local TV station KTLZ. Since their armed incursion, for approximately the last 20 minutes, the affiliate's broadcasters have been forced to read from a lengthy statement of grievances and demands ...

Sebastian Montes: When it all ended, Lars, four KTLZ employees, including beloved anchor Rhea Hickson, were dead, as well as the six members of the extremist group. Within hours, the leader of Tanner's Vengeance was identified as a former executive director of The Aberdeen Circle.

Lars Whitehouse: And that's all the rope Magnus Thorne needed, right? By then, *TAC* had morphed into a political juggernaut more than a human rights organization, and not one friendly to the president, despite his selection of Eli Styles.

Sebastian Montes: Exactly. As a fierce, unapologetic advocate for gay Americans, Black Americans, immigrants, the poor, *TAC* ran head first into the fundamentalist, nativist, far-right, anti-woke, White Lives

Matter, Restore America's Greatest Era RAGErs who, led by their new hero Magnus Thorne, convinced enough voters the root of their miseries was a gay mafia. It was time to take their country back. A raft of anti-LGBTQ legislation and executive orders followed.

Lars Whitehouse: Which prompted more violent reprisals by bad actors, some small cells but mostly lone wolves, all acting in *TAC*'s name.

Sebastian Montes: Yes. The cycle spiraled, and while Rachel Maslow and the leadership at The Aberdeen Circle tried to distance themselves from the mayhem, it was too little, too late.

Lars Whitehouse: It's pretty easy to see how The Aberdeen Circle went from champion to villain. But that still leaves us, Sebastian, with the startling downfall of Eli Styles. He was a red-hot GOP star, their poster boy for diversity and inclusion, and most experts agree, Thorne would never have squeaked his way to the White House without him. Now he's Public Enemy Number One?

Sebastian Montes: Stunning, isn't it? But here's the thing. The president was shot. And while my reporting casts doubt on whether *TAC* really had anything to do with it, that's certainly the prosecutor's position. And there is no question Vice President Styles has long standing ties to The Aberdeen Circle. In a nutshell, that's why he's under house arrest. That's why he's accused of treason. And that's why his very life is on the line when jury selection starts in a couple of weeks.

Lars Whitehouse: We'll see, my friend. We'll see. We know the government isn't interested in the truth, Mr. Montes, so please don't stop digging. It's only reporting like yours that keeps them honest.

Sebastian Montes: Thank you, Lars. And I will. There's a lot more to this story than people know.

Lars Whitehouse: Folks, I want to close with this.

(BATTLE HYMN OF THE REPUBLIC PLAYS QUIETLY IN THE BACKGROUND)

Lars Whitehouse: I'm a Leftie, I'll admit it. One of the few remaining, sadly. Those in power, especially the president and his goons, don't like us, don't want us, and they're doing everything they can to eliminate us. I honestly don't know how long my voice will reach your ears. Government regulators are after us. The so-called Domestic Terrorism Act, and Thorne's efforts to take over the communications grid. I mean, is there a First Amendment anymore?
But while I'm still alive and kicking, let's make one thing clear. Vice President Elijah Styles is a fall guy. To use the old school mafia term, he's the "patsy." I hope Judge Bering gives him the chance to prove this at trial.

(LARS WHITEHOUSE CHUCKLES)

Lars Whitehouse: Forgive me. There's nothing at all funny about the situation. It's only, well, a little tidbit that just crossed my mind which speaks volumes about where our country is, about this whole thing. The word "Rampart."

Did you know that is the vice president's Secret Service call sign? Yep. Not some Liberal virtue tagging. This was the name the tough guys with the dark sunglasses and the Uzis gave him.

And when I first heard that, I thought, "Right on!" It's the perfect nickname. A flawless symbol for the man.

See, ramparts are the defensive wall around a castle, or a city. Barriers of stone protecting what matters most, and even in their ruins around the world, they symbolize security. Guarding. Shielding.

We may not, literally, have castles and ramparts any longer, but we still have, barely, something worth defending. Our republic. The right to speak freely. The privilege of seeking from the government a redress of grievances, without fear of retribution. And anyone who has followed the career of Elijah Wilson Styles, anyone who has actually listened to the man, knows he stands for those sacred principles, for the downtrodden, the voiceless, the least among us.

(MUSIC INTENSIFIES)

He is, as his code name envisions, a last fortification surrounding what should matter to us all: the very democracy slipping between our fingers. Which is precisely why Marcus Thorne and his RAGE crowd are determined to knock down this particular "Rampart" – to kill our vice president!

Lift your voices, my friends. Do not be silent. Be heard, while you still can. *ASN*

(AMERICANA STREAMING NETWORK JINGLE)

END

June 10

(Two Months plus Twenty-Six Days before Trial)

"Here's what I'm confused about." For the publisher of one of the nation's flagship news organizations, August Wolfe had a very modest working office. The Washington Post's *majority owner had much nicer digs one floor up, a large corner office with memorabilia – framed photos with presidents, kings and movie stars, an autographed baseball from the Nationals' World Series win and signed football from the Redskins' now distant Super Bowl victory, ornately framed front pages from the paper's most explosive scoops – all designed to impress visitors.*

Wolfe preferred this small, square space with its heavily scuffed wood desk, plastic blinds hanging crooked on a single, dirt coated window, and two old, worn guest chairs stacked high with miscellaneous written materials needing his attention. Sitting in one of them now, having carefully removed its debris to the floor, was his top investigative reporter, Sebastian Montes.

"Why," Wolfe continued, "would a relatively young guy like Kilbrough, well educated, passed all the Service's personality tests and mental health screenings, why would a guy like that literally risk his life, willingly sacrifice his freedom, to do something crazy like kill the president?"

"That's the thing." Montes began excitedly, scooting to the very edge of his chair. "I'm not so sure he saw it that way."

Wolfe's brow crunched into a plateau of deep caverns. "Whattaya mean?"

"I'm not so sure Kilbrough thought he would go down for this. At least not for very long."

Wolfe attacked an unlit Padrón, absent-mindedly twirling it. He stopped, removing the cigar from his mouth. "What are you getting at, Sebastian?" He stared incredulously at his ace. "You saying he believed he would get away with it?"

"I'm saying that my sources are painting a very complicated picture." Montes' goldish brown eyes bore into his chief, high cheekbones intensifying his seriousness. "Something way more involved than the 'vengeful madman' theory everyone else is pushing."

Wolfe settled into his threadbare mesh high-back, which squeaked as he leaned it into a recline. He resumed the nervous chewing of the cigar. "Okay." Wolfe steadied his emotions, focusing on the stained ceiling but envisioning banner headlines and Pulitzers. "Go on."

Sebastian lived by words. Carefully vetted, doggedly researched words. As he considered which ones to use now, his fingers pushed through thick, jet-black hair. "To your point, sir, Kilbrough wasn't an impulsive, irrational actor. Far from it, he was a calculating, analytical machine."

"Yeah, I know. Marine. NYPD special ops sniper or whatever it was."

"Strategic Response Group, actually. But its more than that, Mr. Wolfe. Sam Kilbrough wasn't some one dimensional, made-for-TV trained killer.

The USMC drilled him in counter-intelligence, and NYC recruited him to run their ISR program ..."

"Their what?"

"Intelligence, Surveillance, and Reconnaissance. The really nightmare situations where you must be prepared to take out the bad boys if all else fails. Anyway, I interviewed the Marine major who got him that job. Old buds with the NY police chief. He said Kilbrough was the coolest cat he ever commanded, and probably the smartest too."

Montes scrolled through his tablet for an exact quote. "I asked the major, 'So how do you explain the Corporeal Kilbrough you knew doing something like this?' And he said, 'Son, first of all, Sam wasn't someone I once knew a long time ago. We maintained regular contact after he left the Corps, even after I retired.' Says Kilbrough visited him at his home a couple of months before the assassination attempt. As you can imagine, the FBI spent hours asking about that."

Wolfe grew impatient. "And? I presume he claims Kilbrough was as ordinary as Sunday, no ticking time bomb, no snapped twig. That doesn't lead us anywhere," he huffed. "Psychopaths often appear completely normal."

Sebastian knew his boss would be a tough sell. This wasn't the first of his investigations to be met with skepticism. "True enough," he conceded. "But Kilbrough doesn't fit the profile. Lots of friend and family relationships. Everyone who knows him describes a super empathetic man, very involved with an org for kids with Down Syndrome."

Wolfe's face became a puzzle. "Kilbrough has a younger brother with the condition," Montes explained. "The two are very, very close. My point is, he's not one of those detached, narcissistic types sneaking through life looking to hurt someone."

Sebastian paused, contemplative. "And even if Kilbrough had any of the traits of an attention seeking nutcase, which he doesn't, that bumper sticker leaves too many unanswered questions."

"For example?"

"For example, why March 30, a month after Kilbrough left the Service? If his goal was to take out the president, he had daily opportunities for almost a year."

"Maybe getting fired pushed him over the edge."

"That's the thing, though. I'm pretty certain Kilbrough wasn't terminated. I think he left on his own, and, in fact, I've got some solid leads suggesting they begged him to stay."

Wolfe grew quiet, steepling his hands under his nose as he fell deeper into thought.

Montes barreled ahead. "And why is the president still among us? Why isn't Elijah Styles in the Oval Office this morning, instead of under house arrest? Point blank range. One of the best marksmen ever, yet he missed? Five rounds to spare, and he didn't fire a second shot?"

The reporter watched as his publisher soaked in the full implications of his queries. And then he unleashed his lead. "Kilbrough wasn't shooting to kill."

August Wolfe's paper had run several astonishing stories over the years. This one might top them all. "In that case ..." Wolfe faltered. The boss was having trouble organizing his thoughts, a rarity. Sebastian pounced.

"Thorne needed an excuse. An accelerant. Something to juice his dominance, his power. The riots, the marches, all the backlash to his first term and his so-called re-election."

"He had to re-establish control."

"Exactly, as we've seen over the last few months. I mean, the new Domestic Terrorism Act, Thorne's executive order giving him effective control over the communications grid, which is kind of ironic, given that's the big thing he accuses TAC *and Styles of plotting to do. And of course the National Guard call-ups, the disappearances, arresting his own vice president – none of that happens without the shooting, right?" Montes knew this was the crazy part, the conclusion which he feared only the seediest of tabloids would dare blare across its front page – not a legacy like the* Post. *Perhaps it was all too much even for his adventurous captain. "We're this far," he pressed on, holding his thumb and index finger a hair's width apart, "from full-on martial law."*

Wolfe very slowly rotated his chair toward the dim sunlight filtering through the gritty panes and half-closed slats behind him. As he manipulated the expensive tobacco through slow rotations, Wolfe contemplated not only what his star journalist was telling him, but also what he implied.

"Am I wrong?" Sebastian finally asked.

"About which part?" Wolfe fired back sternly.

Montes lowered his gaze to the floor, not in defeat, but certainly in retreat, hiding the fire in his eyes. He didn't want to provoke Wolfe.

A long minute passed in silence.

"Okay," Wolfe eventually sighed. "Tell me what you've got."

Sebastian lifted his small frame as tall in his chair as he could, and took a deep breath. "What I've got," he said, "is a source. A really, really good, high placed, reliable source."

Wolfe lowered the cigar to his side. He pivoted his stout neck 90 degrees and, with a commanding voice, asked the unavoidable question. "Who says what?"

"Who says Kilbrough never intended to fire more than one shot, and knew from protocols that if he did that, then tossed his gun, they wouldn't kill him, wouldn't even shoot him, which is exactly the way it went down. Kilbrough also knew, once Thorne's plan reached its conclusion, once Thorne had complete control, that he'd get a pardon and be allowed to disappear comfortably."

Even for an ambitious publisher like August Wolfe, the story was outlandish. He glared at Montes, then turned back to his dirty window, his thoughts drifting into its haze. Wolfe wondered if his predecessor at the Post believed Woodward and Bernstein were nuts too – until they weren't. He ticked through a mental checklist: Montes had never steered him wrong, was meticulous in his investigations, and while daring, wouldn't risk his entire reputation and career on some flimsy conspiracy theory. Moreover, Thorne was an odd, *power-hungry narcissist who made Nixon and Trump look like demure boy scouts.*

On the other hand ...

Still lost in the murky distance, Wolfe almost whispered, "You think the president hired someone to shoot him? The actual fucking President of the United States?"

Sebastian eased back into a slouch, not out of disrespect, but in anticipation of a long, long meeting. "I think that's only the beginning."

Jury Selection

Five

"I voted for President Thorne, both times" a tall woman I would guess to be in her mid- to late-thirties says. The judge smiles at her benignly, then scans all sixty veniremen, as these potential jurors are called: six to a bench, two benches to a row, five rows deep.

"I appreciate your disclosure, ma'am," Judge Bering soothes, "and let me remind everyone on the panel, you are certainly free to declare for whom you cast your ballot. However," she adds, "my question is only whether your vote in either of the last two presidential elections might in *any* way affect your ability to fairly consider the evidence in this case."

She returns her friendly gaze to the woman, seated at the far-right end of the third row. "Venirewoman Number 36, does your support for the president in the last two elections impact your ability to listen to all of the facts and testimony to be presented, and to weigh that evidence in accordance with my instructions?"

"No, Your Honor."

We have been at this since shortly before ten o'clock this morning, except for a ninety-minute break at lunch. The black arrows of the old-fashioned analog clock line up to three minutes past three. So, if the court sticks to the schedule announced at the start of the day, we'll continue another couple of hours.

In the beginning, I was laser focused on each response – every nuance, expression, tic – intently searching for tells. Who's with me? Or, who wants to go down in history hanging a vice president?

As time grinds along, though, it gets harder. Tedium sets in. One answer tends to drone on into the next. Judge Bering started with the same three questions of each individual, starting with the young Black man in the first position at the left end of the first row, Venireman Number 1, then moving to his left, one person at a time.

They all held a blue 3 x 5 card, and the first of her questions was whether its information was correct. At lunch, Mandela explained the small rectangles contained the venireman's number, name, date of birth, address, employer and marital status; the court simply wanted to verify everyone's identity, and that they were seated in the correct spot.

Next, the judge asked the same man, "Do you know, socially or professionally, the defendant, his lawyer Mr. Briggs, anyone on the defense team, the prosecutor Mr. McGehee or anyone on his side, me, my bailiff, my clerk or our court reporter?" This entire cast, including me, arguably the star, had all been introduced first thing today.

She concluded her opening triad of inquiries with, "Are you *presently* caring for anyone who, either because of their age or a medical or mental health issue, would be *endangered* by your absence if you served on this jury?" Her inflections made it clear anyone answering in the affirmative better have a darn good explanation – it was not a golden ticket out.

Number 1's responses were immediate. "Yes," the card was correct; "No," he didn't know anyone involved in the show, and "No," no one would be in jeopardy if he made the final panel.

"Yes," "No," and "No." Three words, and Judge Bering moved on to the elderly Hispanic woman perched next to him, and so on down the line, row by row, until an hour and a half later everyone had responded. I thought two or three offered pretty good reasons to go home – a man who claimed to be all but legally blind, though he had found his way to the courthouse on his own; a single mother with no access to day care whose sister supposedly watched her three-year-old at night while she worked at a bar; a gentleman who worked remotely so he could keep tabs on his wife, who he said had not been officially diagnosed with Alzheimer's "but she forgets more than she remembers." None were dismissed. Mandela says the judge will eventually excuse some of them, but fears a stampede of woes if she starts releasing people now. She doesn't want a jury made up only of folks with nothing better to do.

After a mid-morning break, another triad of questions to each potential juror. Then lunch, followed by round three, and here we are at the question which somehow prompted Number 36 to overshare: "If you cast a ballot in either of the last two presidential elections, would your vote in *any* way affect your ability to fairly consider the evidence in this case." Question nine, and I have no idea how many of these sets of three the judge intends.

At lunch, Mandela asked, "So, Mr. Vice President, any impressions?" I've told him a hundred times, "It's Eli," but despite how long we've known each other, he refuses to dispense with the formality.

I answered his question this way. "Honestly, I think it's hard to tell anything about any of them. The questions are so narrow, and no one wants to sound bad by telling the truth. Mostly 'Yes' and 'No,' and I'm not even sure how much of *that* to believe."

Mandela nodded solemnly. Izzy looked dissatisfied with my reaction. Izzy often looks disappointed. Ryan studied the notes he'd furiously scribbled all morning, as if each juror provided a trove of useful hints.

Mandela and I picked at our lunch as we talked, neither possessing much of an appetite. "That's often how it seems," he continued, "and we'll get more expansive answers when the prosecutor and I have our turns. The judge is really only trying to weed out the ones who are obviously unqualified."

"That's good to hear," I said, unconvinced. I am not confident we will gain any meaningful insight into the twelve people chosen to decide my fate.

"What I'm really asking," he clarified, "is what vibe you're getting from different folks."

"Like Number 13," Izzy jumped in, unable to contain herself. "I think that woman has a major crush."

Ignoring for a second the serious consequences of this trial, I had to chuckle. Izzy made the whole thing sound like one giant bar scene. *Hey, don't look now, but I think that one over there might be into you.*

"I'd just be guessing," I told them honestly. "I tried paying attention to body language the first hour or so, but it's all basically blurring together at this point. Does a smile mean 'You're cool, don't worry?' Are arms folded across the chest boredom, or 'Let's execute this guy?' I find them all pretty much impossible to read."

This was the truth. I don't know if my lawyer is being polite, trying to include me in everything, but if he really needs my "vibe" on these people, we're in trouble.

"Mr. Vice President," Izzy again, "there's no science to it. Just go with your gut."

"Well," Ryan, the quiet, studious one chimed in, "it's more than 'vibe,' Izzy." Those two always seemed in competition, which I suppose is healthy for any team. "We consider age, employment, race, gender – a whole host of demographic factors to figure out who is most likely receptive to our defense."

Izzy rolled her eyes. "'Single, 40-year-old female Southeast Asian school teacher' might give you a clue, but if she's shooting darts through the client, you might not want her on your Twelve." She shrugged her shoulders. "Call me crazy."

Probably fearing Ryan may do exactly that, Mandela intervened. "You see, Mr. Vice President! Equal parts science and art."

I understood his point. And Ryan's, and Izzy's. The selection of a jury is a crapshoot. In fact, as Mandela explained yesterday, juries aren't actually "selected." A bunch of people are randomly summoned up by computer based on the mere fact they have a driver's license or are registered to vote. They are seated in arbitrary order, again determined by a processor somewhere, and after questioning, like we are doing this week, folks who can't be fair or have some obvious conflict are supposedly eliminated by the judge. Then the lawyers get a certain number of discretionary "strikes" to cut others they can't convince the court to remove. The first twelve left, well, that's your jury. Not necessarily your "peers" it turns out. Merely a collection of the least objectionable.

So, as I sit here shortly after 3 p.m. listening to Number 36 proudly reveal her votes for the man who wants me convicted of treason, all I know is, this system feels pretty haphazard for deciding great questions like, say, life and death!

Onward we press, though, another dozen denying that their votes in the last big elections, if they voted, will in any way affect their verdict. Some of them, I'm sure, are being less than honest. There's no way to know who, or whether, their lies are intended to help me, or screw me.

But then, out of nowhere, a burst of transparency, a jolt of truth! From my perspective, this whole proceeding's first real moment. On the very back row, a short, balding, gray-haired man, early 50s I'd say, answers the election question, "Yes." Yes, his vote would affect his service in this case. Yes, he admits, he might not be fair.

It woke me up, or maybe it was all the lawyers' heads jerking that snapped me to attention, or maybe the lifted eyebrows of the man's fellow would-be jurors. The reaction we are all keen for, however, is Judge Bering's. Everyone looks to her perch atop the bench and searches her face where we find ... nothing.

"Thank you, Venireman Number 49, for your honesty," she says calmly. "I will ask that you keep the specifics of your response private until I have an opportunity to discuss them with you." The man nods his understanding, and she smiles warmly, as if his answer is of little concern.

My first sensation is disappointment. The single drama in hours of pointless, bureaucratic nonsense, and the judge snuffs it out like a cheap candle.

Then it dawns on me. Judge Bering knows the balding, gray-haired man's story, whatever it is, could poison the impartiality of the panel's other 59 people, or worse, give them ideas. So as soon as he reveals his flawed neutrality, she quickly moves on.

I wonder, though, is this the best path to justice? An imperious judge overpowering an honest citizen's urge to unveil disqualifying bias. Maybe he says he loves Magnus Thorne, agrees with the president that I am a traitor, and thinks I should get the electric chair. Shouldn't we know that? If letting out that kind of bias encourages two, or five, or twenty of the rest to come forward, isn't that a good thing? Surely they're sharing these feelings during breaks anyway, right? How many are being convinced to convict me before the first witness even testifies?

I wish the world could see this. This *injustice* system at work. Alas, there are no cameras in the courtroom; Judge Bering made sure of that. There are only three pool reporters way in the back using only old fashioned notepads, their recording devices confiscated. And there is a sketch artist making, I'm sure, totally unflattering caricatures of me that look like a fifth grader's bad watercolor experiment.

Yet, outside, crowds are screaming at each other across barricades. I saw them when my motorcade sped by early this morning. On one side, a sea of long whiskered Caucasians in red RAGE caps, many in Confederate t-shirts, lifting Thorne placards and holding signs that mostly riff on my being gay. On the other, a much younger, multi-hued mass of people heavy on leather and hoodies, waving pride banners, upside down American flags, and posters with expletives directed at the president. The common denominator were faces contorted with hostility, spittle flying as they hurled insults over the Guardsmen and police officers separating them.

How much of that anger is sitting on this courtroom's benches, right in front of me, one step away from deciding my life? Mandela assures me we'll find out. Maybe his vast experience makes that possible. Maybe Ryan has an algorithm, or Izzy a sixth sense, that will sniff them out.

Right now, though, I'm feeling pretty damn vulnerable.

Six

"I voted for President Thorne, both times" an impeccably dressed woman in her thirties proudly announces. Judge Bering smiles at her benignly, as if at a child who has, as children sometimes do, blurted out something a little too personal.

Her Honor then scrutinizes all five rows, all sixty veniremen, looking for reactions. She knows the legal teams are doing the same. This woman will likely not survive the screening process – too eager, too headstrong. The judge and both sides scan for others maybe identifying with her.

"I appreciate your disclosure, ma'am," Judge Bering says compassionately. She doesn't want to scare anyone away from being truthful, especially later when the group phase ends and individual interrogations begin. But Carolyn Bering must maintain control. "Let me remind everyone on the panel, you are certainly free to declare for whom you cast your ballot. However," she adds, "my question is only whether your vote in either of the last two presidential elections might in *any* way affect your ability to fairly consider the evidence in this case."

She returns to Venirewoman Number 36 and asks, "Does your support for the president in the last two elections impact your ability to listen to all of the facts and testimony to be presented, and to weigh that evidence in accordance with my instructions?"

"No, Your Honor," she replies, chastened.

As Chief Judge, the administrative leadership position afforded the longest serving judge in each district, Carolyn has managed big cases before. Billion-dollar corporate battles. High profile drug cases, including that of a notorious Honduran cartel boss. The sex trafficking scandal against a prominent Middle Eastern royal.

The stakes in this one, though, were much higher, more than tabloid fodder. This trial could very well determine the survival of American democracy. She had to get it right.

Carolyn prepared 27 questions, more than usual, breaking them into nine batches of three. She started by surveying each potential juror with a single trio of queries before moving on to the next candidate, beginning with Venireman Number 1. For the second triad, she commenced on the far side of row three, Number 36, moving backward, then to rows four and five, then back to the first three rows, but in reverse order. The point was to keep everyone uncertain as to whom the next volley would come. Even for a case this important, boredom and disengagement were real risks.

Carolyn recorded each answer on a spreadsheet prepared by her senior clerk, Debbie, noting which ones would require follow-up. As she proceeded, the judge could not avoid absorbing her courtroom's personality, which changed with each case and each new collection of occupants.

Dark-stained paneling on the walls contrasted starkly with the smooth, faded white ceiling, grimy gray dust surrounding the air grills of the large space's ancient, rumbling HVAC system. A faux chandelier hung in the center, its plastic candles always illuminated – no one could figure out how to turn them off, or had the slightest idea why the fixture was there in the first place. Eighteen wood benches, divided by a wide aisle into nine rows of two, showed the abrasion of thousands of guests palming them and shifting upon their uncomfortable design.

Carolyn examined the long three-foot-tall balustrade dividing her courtroom into front and back sections, its plump-bellied spindles scratched and gouged, decades of polypropylene cup and travel mug rings marking its top rail. On this side of that battle-scarred demarcation were the more familiar features of her world: the jury box against the wall to her left; the two table islands floating on the linoleum-tiled floors, one for each of the warring sides; Noah on his ancient roller chair off to the right, fingers drumming on his old-fashioned stenotype machine. And grandest of all, "the bench," her lordly, elevated domain, polished oak concealing steel security plates, approached only with reverence, and from which she now snapped back to the present.

"Venireman Number 60," she announced, skipping back to the right edge of the fifth row, now intending to work inversely to Number 1. "Without revealing what you may have communicated, have you posted any opinions or observations about the president, the vice president, or anything whatsoever regarding this lawsuit, on Facebook, X, Snapchat, Instagram, TikTok or any other social media account, whether in your name or a pseudonym?"

The elderly gentleman appeared confused, perhaps, Carolyn wondered, trying to decipher the strange names she had hurled at him. Eighty or so, she guessed, the man's encounters with the cyberworld were probably limited to printing out e-mails from his grandchildren. But you never knew, and considering how revealing people were online, this was an important question.

"No, I'm not on any of that stuff," he finally said, eliciting a few chuckles from the crowd. Carolyn smiled at him appreciatively. Given her position, she couldn't come within a mile of such virtual communities.

"I understand, sir," she said breezily. "Now," she continued, looking at the old fellow intently, "this case has received extensive media coverage." Carolyn paused, letting that massive understatement soak in. "Regardless of what or how much of it you have seen, do you understand that none of those reports are evidence, and if selected for this jury, your verdict must ignore all that noise and consider *only* the testimony and documents you receive during the actual trial?"

As Number 60 mulled his answer, she stole a glance at the *Post*'s Sebastian Montes on the back row, flinching. *Noise?* he appeared to say, mockingly offended. But the judge had chosen this word with great care, fully intending to denigrate the opinion-makers, from *FOX*'s conspiracy-laced condemnations of Maslow and Styles, to *MSNBC*'s fawning defenses of them, to the offbeat ponderings of popular podcasters like Lars Whitehorse. She wanted to put her thumb on the scale against the influence of the monetized influencers, to wield her authority now, at its peak, in the beginning, when the newness of the courtroom and the oddity of its procedures remained a bit terrifying for the pool of potential jurors. Carolyn hoped her dismissive attitude would bend them into ignoring as much of their exposure to pundits and "experts" as possible. Fantasy, she acknowledged, but if she could just make them feel guilty about it ... well, maybe that would help.

"I really don't listen to them much, Your Honor," Number 60 began, understanding by this point Judge Bering wanted a more specific commitment. But he was proud to assert his independence.

Carolyn sensed where he was going, and nodded her encouragement.

"They're all certain they know everything," he continued, setting his face in a determined, wizened glare. "I prefer to think for myself."

Not the "Yes" or "No" the judge had so rigorously demanded all day, but *score one for us*, Carolyn thought. "That's good to hear, sir," she said firmly, as if handing out a gold star. "And now one last question."

She skimmed all sixty, visually reminding them they would each be subjected to the same crucial test. "At the end of this case, should the jury find the Defendant guilty, and *only* if it does so, you will be given the sentencing options of life imprisonment without the possibility of parole, or the death penalty. Will you follow the court's instructions, consider both alternatives carefully, and impose the sentence best justified by the evidence, regardless of any personal feelings?"

"Yes," he answered without the slightest hesitation. Too fast, in fact. She didn't dare glance at Mandela Briggs, the defense counsel, but could guess he was making a note to be wary of the old man. Anyone that unemotional about the death penalty probably had no qualms about it.

"Thank you, sir," she said, and shifted her focus to the young woman seated next to him. Korean, Carolyn guessed from the last name. Not unusual for her panels inasmuch as D.C. had the second largest Korean population in the country, after New York. "Venirewoman 59," the judge started, her voice maintaining its pleasant, even tone. "Without revealing what you may have communicated, have you posted any opinions or observations about the president, the vice president, or anything whatsoever regarding this lawsuit, on Facebook, X, Snapchat, Instagram, TikTok or any other social media account, whether in your name or a pseudonym?"

And on she went, methodically completing her list, vetting one after another. The lawyers were both given Carolyn's questions in advance. Neither dared object to a single of the judge's propositions, even those they thought could cause trouble. Each team furiously ascribed meaning to every answer. Whether yes, no, up, down or a nonsensical ramble, the two sides gauged each reply into circles as different candidates moved up or down their "Must Go" projections.

This long march had begun early the morning after Labor Day. And with only a couple of short breaks each morning, and another two in the afternoons, the slog through one thousand six hundred and twenty individual questions and answers finally ended after three on Thursday afternoon. Carolyn would love to press on, but also appreciated how tired these folks must be from the emotional tug of war exerted by stress and ennui.

So, reluctantly, she pulled herself into a commanding pose. "Ladies and Gentlemen, I am pleased to announce I have finished my questions for you, ending this stage of the process."

Smiles erupted. The judge had told them at the beginning that only twelve would make the final jury, plus two alternates, meaning three-quarters of the assemblage, most calculated, would be going home soon.

And then, as if a drain had been unplugged, their optimism faded when Carolyn added, "Tomorrow, the prosecution will begin its examination of the panel. I will see you all at nine o'clock sharp, and let me remind you of my instruction that you not discuss this case, or any of our proceedings, with anyone, not even members of your own family. Before we adjourn for the day, are there questions?"

She browsed the unhappy flock. No one spoke up, and no hands were raised, only purses and paperbacks gathered here and there amid a general shuffling on the benches.

"Okay, then," she smiled, "I wish you all a safe rest of your day."

With that, she banged her gavel.

As Carolyn collected her notes, she reflected on what had been accomplished in her three days of work. Lacking the excitement of a TV drama, she sensed the disappointment of her 60 veniremen. They had expected fireworks from the beginning in a case like this. What they got instead was tedium.

Even the lawyers were unimpressed, she was sure, and they had been through dozens of jury selections. The sad fact was, every attorney thought he or she could do a better job of interviewing a panel than the hapless judge, the way a quarterback scoffs at the talentless referee.

And in truth, she knew – every judge did – her grand inquisition had probably made little progress toward finding justice. *Voir Dire* is what jury selection is called in legal circles, Latin for "to speak the truth." Yet hundreds of answers later, how much honesty was actually shared? Very few gave responses hinting at an inability to be fair, and those who did – the four who said their presidential ballots may impact how they decided this case; the seven who claimed news reports might influence their view; the one who went so far as to say the vice president's homosexuality "is a real problem for me" – even those disclosures may be more calculated as a ticket home than sincere confession.

Regardless, Carolyn accepted, it was the system they had. It wasn't mob rule. It wasn't the Star Chamber or the Spanish Inquisition or a Stalinist show trial. It was 60 ordinary Americans, most trying their best to do their duty. Her queries were designed more to make these people look within, to reinforce their stirrings of fairness, than to actually ferret out the ones who had already decided Elijah Styles' innocence or guilt.

As the courtroom emptied, Carolyn sighed. The enormity of their endeavor hung in the air. It was going to be a long march.

Seven
Atlanta Jean Breckenridge
Jury Selection – Day 5

She just knew they were examining her hair. Judging it, like they always did with Black women, like they always had, like they never would a pasty-skinned blonde girl. No one said anything, of course, but Lanta could read it in their faces: the prosecutor, his leggy, short-skirted legal assistant whispering to that privileged young Italian-looking associate in the Armani with his slicked-back pelt. She could guess what they were saying, what they'd been furiously scribbling 'bout her full-on round-haloed *Mod Squad* afro. Militant. Skeptical of authority. Partial to underdogs. Bleeding heart.

They were probably right about some of that. Lord, how could you teach Ninth graders in D.C.'s Ward 7 – especially World History as Lanta had been doing for 11 years at Central High – and not be a little upset with *God Bless America*. All those beautiful Black faces, living in a city beholden to the federal government for all its needs and getting slop in return: no surprise, as the District's 844,315 residents didn't merit a single representative in Congress, and never would under the ruling Republicans, under Magus Thorne. She did her best with those kids, but she still understood how most of them would live out their lives.

From the fourth row of benches, Venirewoman 45 as she'd been known the past week, eyed the U.S. attorney skeptically. He was too smooth by half in her book, his smile slimy, his voice patronizing. The man had been at it almost two full days now, taking over for the Judge first thing Friday morning. Now it was late afternoon Monday, and she was about the only one left untouched by McGehee's questions. Had he decided she wasn't worth it? That started to piss Lanta off, her mind spiraling as to his reasons.

Her first guess was quite natural. The Black woman would do whatever the Black defense attorney wanted. That was offensive. She didn't know Mandela Briggs, had barely heard him speak up to now. *Nelson* Mandela was a feature unit every Spring with her 14-year-old students, an inspiring part of a curriculum that never failed to give those kids at least a tiny glimpse at the possible. Lanta wasn't sure how she felt about the man appropriating that exalted name, not like he chose it himself.

Besides, as a grown woman who for more than a decade had distilled the whole story of mankind for 160 kids, Lanta knew something about right and wrong, about justice. Race had nothing to do with whether the vice president tried to *1-8-7* his boss, and besides, Styles was as white as the prosecutor.

That wasn't it, anyhow. That wasn't why McGehee ignored her. Of the 60 on the panel, at least 27 were African American, maybe one or two more. Yes, with plenty of idle time during this excruciating process, Lanta had counted. Thirty-seven women. Three Asians, maybe one Pacific Islander. A couple of college kids, a lot of very mature folk, average age, she guessed, quite a bit over her 35.

Why, then, had she escaped his attention? The truth was, Lanta wanted to engage with McGehee. She wanted to show him who she was, to make him think twice about discounting her.

"Last Tuesday, when you were assigned to this case," he started with a Latino man seated on the bench behind her, before careening into what he thought was charm, "seems like a year ago, doesn't it?" That sickly grin as he chuckled. Most everyone politely tittered in response. "Anyway, at that time, what did you know, or what were your impressions, of The Aberdeen Circle?"

She honestly didn't hear the man's answer. Lanta was too wrapped up in her own silent reply. *The Aberdeen Circle? Let me tell you, they had their own George Floyd moment, 'cept those folks had our blueprint AND something we never had – MONEY! And that Rachel Maslow, I gotta hand it to her, she's one smart cookie. Before long, she's got BLM and LULAC and the HRC and, what's the Asian Americans' group? Whatever, she's got them all marching under the same banner, arm-in-arm. That was powerful. Then some of her disciples went too far. What is it the rich people say? "Got out over their skis."*

See, if he had called on her, all that could have been shared.

Instead, ever since the judge finished her list – that woman was *impressive*, wasn't going to put up with any *you-know-what* from either side – ever since then, Lanta was stuck listening to Mr. U.S. attorney amaze everyone with how smart he is, adjusting her butt on the hard-ass wooden bench and trying as best she could to stay focused, to be ready, to not think about how her Sub, unfortunately not her preferred choice, was screwing up her lesson plans or how her kids were checking out and sliding into disarray with Ms. Breckenridge gone. Pray to Jesus, this will be over by Friday.

†††

Aiden Tinsley
Jury Selection – Day 6

He wished he could record this. Fact was, he couldn't even take notes, though Judge Bering said those who made the actual jury could do so once evidence began, notes which would be locked up at the courthouse each night and returned to them in the morning.

Every evening, after they were dismissed, Aiden Tinsley stopped by The George Washington Law School library. He had spent all weekend there as well, getting caught up and cramming for the classes he was missing.

His professors told him not to worry, they'd work with him, while nonchalantly pumping him for an inside scoop they, better than anyone, knew he was sworn not to provide. That was okay, though. These academic elders looked at him with respect, completely unearned, and a thinly disguised jealousy. He was a prospective juror on *the* case!

Aiden's classmates were even less subtle, treating him as a legal celebrity. Oh, would they be mesmerized by the stories he could tell! He didn't dare breathe a word, of course, no matter how much it would elevate his status. Judge Bering was explicit on that point, and undoubtedly knew some of his teachers. Given how people talk, anything he let slip bore a high risk of getting him into very hot water, kicked off the panel, humiliated.

This mandated silence was really the only downside to his service, and even that wasn't so bad: once the trial was over, he'd be free to tell all. Until then, he'd enjoy his stardom with a teasing wink and a knowing nod.

Presently, Venireman Number 3 followed defense counsel's every move with equal measures of envy and amazement. *This* was what he wanted to be, what the last two years of dusty legal opinions and intricate statutes and obtuse regulations were all about. Another couple of semesters of writing papers, of preparing outlines, of enduring "lectures" that served more as target practice for his instructors hunting the unprepared. Eight months, followed by the bar examination, and then Aiden Tinsley would be transformed into Atticus Finch, or one of the stars of a John Grisham novel, or the very Mandela Briggs now performing Jedi mind tricks on his unsuspecting audience.

Freckled with a sun-bleached shaggy flaxen mop making him appear much younger than his actual 24 years, the third-year law student from Hermosa Beach looked every inch the California surfer scholar he was. Smart, informed, and eager, Aiden was excited when the summons arrived from the Clerk of the U.S. District Court. Federal cases, he knew, were a cut above the garden variety disputes found in state courts. Where drunk driving, slip and falls and custody battles filled the local dockets, in the U.S. courts the stakes were typically higher: battling corporate titans, FBI-busted drug lords, First Amendment clashes. And the lawyers a higher quality too – none of the ambulance chasers that gave the profession its bad name – with the judges all appointed by the freaking President!

The handsome young man from a wealthy family on his hometown's glistening enclave, The Strand – his parents' Pacific-facing, three thousand square foot home was worth $12 million – always dreamed of being a trial gladiator, not some pencil-pushing diviner of contracts in a quiet corner office. That's why he chose an elite school like GW.

Thus, while an invite to jury service elicited groans from most, to Aiden it meant opportunity, bearing witness to live action from the front row. Never, though, did he imagine winning a legal lottery: *The United States of America vs. The Honorable Vice President Elijah Wilson Styles*.

Therein was the challenge. As Aiden knew from his Law 6640 Trial Advocacy course, only twelve people on the panel *not* eliminated during *voir dire* would be jurors. His goal, therefore, was simple: don't give either side, or the judge, any reason to cut him. Making history meant being inoffensive.

"Now, this next one is going to be tough," Briggs started, peaking the assemblage's interest. It was mid-afternoon of defense counsel's first day with them, following Friday and Monday's grilling by the

U.S. attorney. Already the lawyer was proving himself a master at both being liked and maintaining attention, traits young Aiden knew he had to learn.

"Let me preface it by stating the obvious: we all have leanings, biases, prejudices. Nothing to be ashamed about, it's part of being human. In this courtroom, however," he dramatically swept his hands across the dignified space, "those tendencies must be set aside." His glare intensified. "They *must*."

Briggs pivoted on the faux-tiled floor, taking two steps toward the judge and her throne, his back to Aiden and the rest. He gazed up with silent reverence, as if drawing out from her majesty the very essence of justice.

"The best way to flatten those urges is to call them forth," he said, slowly pacing back to them, "to speak and confront them." Briggs placed his large, strong hands on the rail directly in front of Aiden, boring into his eyes. Tinsley felt himself sweat.

"Young man," Briggs continued in a familiar, fatherly tone, "Let me not beat around the bush. What do you think of homosexuality?"

Stunned by the directness, Aiden paused, straining to keep his poise. "I really don't," he said, and heard a smattering of nervous laughter around him. Briggs' face softened, and Aiden moved quickly to show that he took the question seriously.

"I mean, I have friends who are gay, and friends who think it's wrong. Where I come from ..."

"... Where's that again?"

"Hermosa Beach. In California. Out there, I don't know, it's pretty much just background."

"So, you don't think it bears on someone's character?"

"No."

"You do realize, however, that many consider it a mortal sin?"

"Yes sir. Like the Pope. But even he says we should love the sinner." Murmurs of approval fluttered. Briggs stood straight, placing his hands behind his back. Aiden sensed he was pleased with the exchange.

"So, in this matter, the well-known fact that Vice President Styles is married to Brady Galway, and has a daughter, Anna, will in no way affect your judgment as to his guilt or innocence of the crimes alleged?"

"Honestly, all I'm concerned with is whether he plotted to kill the president." Out of the corner of his eye, he saw the prosecutor nodding his head vigorously enough for everyone to see. Aiden turned to him. "Whether that's proven." McGehee winked.

"Venirewoman Number 7, what are your thoughts on the matter?"

Aiden relaxed, feeling he had passed a very important test.

†††

Emmanuel Arroyo
Jury Selection – Day 9

His restaurants were his life. Emmanuel paid little notice to the goings on the past two weeks, his mind instead fixated on the details of *his* business. Except now, Venireman Number 55 was in the judge's chamber. He guessed his tiny office at *Abuela Catalina* on Kenyon Street, permeated by aromas of grilling onions and peppers, bubbling pozole, and vats of spicy frijoles negros, would fit into her stale inner sanctum six times.

He sat in a large, comfortable armchair directly facing Her Honor, still formal and enrobed behind the aircraft carrier she called a desk, her court reporter off to one side with the attorneys flanking him, relaxed, friendly, their minions out of sight along the back wall ready to parse his every word.

"Venireman Number 55," she began, "the lawyers and I have a few follow-ups for you based upon your public responses out there," motioning toward the courtroom beyond the doors behind him. This he already knew. The judge told them as they were dismissed Wednesday that the group session was over, now to be followed by individual interrogations. It was finally his turn.

"I'll start," she said, reading her notes. "Last week, I stated that under our Constitution's Bill of Rights, the Fifth Amendment, no defendant in a criminal case can be made a witness against himself. I explained it is entirely the prosecution's burden to prove guilt, and advised, should the Vice President choose not to testify, that I would instruct the jury not to consider, draw implications from, or even discuss his decision."

She looked up, squarely at Emmanuel, a visage of concern as she added, "When I asked whether you would follow my instruction, you said ..." She returned to the papers on her desk, "'I'm not sure I can.'"

Perhaps it was his imagination, but Emmanuel felt she, and everyone else in her chamber, glared at him as if he had committed some terrible sin. As he reflected on it, perhaps he had, though not for the reason they might suspect. Regardless, he began to perspire.

"This is an important civil right, sir," Judge Bering almost whispered, her tone more pleading than offended, "one that sets our nation apart from many others. It eliminates the ugly forced confessions that are so common in countries with less respect for justice and due process of law."

Emmanuel felt the shock of being exposed. Shamed. He loved his homeland deeply, more than many who could trace their American heritage much further than his. For their daring escape from Tapalpa in the far western Mexican state of Jalisco, Arroyo would always be proud of his parents, and indebted to them.

Truth be told, he did think an accused should explain himself, that a defendant's silence was suspicious. But, unlike the crude judicial system of his ancestral land, he respected the careful safeguards the United States imbedded in its criminal law, the presumption of innocence, the rigors of proof required. So why had he lied?

"Now, understanding how fundamental this privilege is," she continued, "that it is up to the prosecution to establish its case, not the Defendant to prove innocence, Venireman 55, can you consider only the evidence in this case, and reach a verdict without any regard for whether or not Vice President Styles takes the witness stand?"

He cleverly believed his original answer might get him excused, thinking only of the burden jury service put upon his own business. Others had done it, shamelessly, saying things they didn't believe, cynically calculating it would disqualify them. Why not him? Why should he have to get up at 4 a.m. to shower, shave, dress, race from his old three-bedroom in Mount Pleasant to the restaurant in Columbia Heights, get as much done as he could before taking the Green Line, then the Red Line, to the E. Barrett Prettyman Courthouse by nine sharp – the judge did not continence tardiness – and after a full day of "civic duty" hustle by cab to the newer Georgetown location, check on the staff there, bus to DuPont Circle and the Metro back to Kenyon for closing, then home by midnight.

Embarrassed at his selfishness, Emmanuel grabbed for the judge's lifeline, the redemption she offered. "Yes, I can do that. I am sorry, I ... I hadn't thought it through."

Judge Bering smiled, clearly pleased. She looked to either side of him. "Gentlemen?" The prosecutor shook his head. He needn't ask a thing. He knew this man, deep down, would have a problem if Styles took the Fifth. McGehee's impression was of a rather conservative first generation American, always good for his side.

From Emmanuel's left, however, the defense lawyer spoke. "Sir, I appreciate your honesty," Briggs pandered. Although he didn't look forward to being cross-examined, Arroyo liked this man. Knowing nothing of his actual history, he assumed simply from the color of his skin that Briggs had fought and scratched his way from nothing, just as had Emmanuel. Moreover, his competence over the last couple of weeks was impressive.

"Tell us, though, what you've now 'thought through,' what it is that's changed."

Arroyo dared not divulge his ploy. So, he lied again, this time to justify his honesty. "TV. It's how, on all the TV shows, the mobsters and bad guys always take the Fifth." Emmanuel laughed nervously to highlight his own foolishness. "Obviously, now that I remember the history, and you know they taught us this in school, I understand, like the judge said, it is an important right."

Briggs sized him up, his contemplation unrelenting, his head ever so slightly bobbing up and down. Arroyo wondered if his lie – his *lies* – were obvious to this skilled litigator. He worried Briggs would lay bare his deceit, humiliate him under a withering fusillade of follow-ups. Fear moistened his torso, his forehead.

Instead, Briggs turned to Judge Bering and said, "That's all, Your Honor," and then back to Emmanuel, "Thank you, sir."

"Venireman Number 55," she announced, "you are free to go, and we will see you on Monday, when I anticipate we will announce the jury. Until then, we again very much appreciate your patience, and hope you have a wonderful weekend!"

He hesitated, disbelieving his luck, until a wave of relief coursed through him and he awkwardly stood, mumbling "Thank you!" to the judge, and "Thank you" to Mr. Briggs, and finally, as he turned for the door, "Thank you" to the prosecutor. The Bailiff opened it and Arroyo made his escape to the courtroom, where he looked guiltily at the five prospective jurors still awaiting their solo interviews. He wanted to warn them, to tell them to be honest, to not commit his horrible depravities against this beautiful nation.

Instead, he furtively read the clock over the entry doors, 3:16, considered his great fortune, and made haste toward *Abuela Catalina*. For now, he was a free man.

Eight

"Come on, people. Focus!" Sidney McGehee barked. The chief's unflappable public persona didn't exist for his team in the actual day-to-day. "They only need one to keep us from getting a unanimous verdict," he lectured. "We can't screw this up."

It was almost midnight. Those inside the U.S. attorney's office were running on fumes. That didn't excuse his brusque treatment. He wasn't the only one stressed, or the only one working his butt off. Some of the young professionals scrambling around McGehee's mammoth, stately office might even point out they typically worked longer hours than the boss. Instead, they were incredibly grateful to be a part of such a momentous, career-building case.

"We've got ..." The prosecutor looked at his shiny silver and blue Rolex, which he boldly and proudly brandished as a symbol of success, "... eight hours to get this right. She's not going to hear more than five or six from each side, so we've got to be goddamned sure who we want off!" He was yelling now.

"This" which must be right was the list of targets for "cause" challenges, one of three ways to exclude a venireman from jury service; "She" was the judge. Bering, of course, could excuse anyone she wanted, usually for extenuating circumstances like a debilitating medical condition, or being the sole provider for an infant or elderly parent. Some judges would dismiss folks with urgent work demands or long-planned vacations, though Carolyn Bering almost never did – everyone, in her view, had to perform this sacrosanct service to society unless the hardship bordered on dangerous. Important banking executives and families with Disney trips found no quarter in her courtroom.

The second off-ramp, however, the subject of McGehee's present rant, was the "Challenge for Cause" motion. A party asked the court to release someone because it was obvious he or she could not be objective and even-handed. That was a big reason the court invested nine full days in *voir dire*, to flesh out as many of the sixty candidates' biases and prejudices as possible so each side could determine who was pre-disposed to screw them.

McGehee was upset *precisely* because he knew Judge Bering frowned upon this procedure, even though it was engrained in the law and essential to a fair trial. He was well aware she would tune him out if he complained about too many veniremen. Yet, his crew still insisted nine men and women were incapable of considering a guilty verdict.

"I thought I made it abundantly clear," he growled, admiring his watch again, "*seven* hours ago, I'm not asking her to cut *nine*. So, unless some of you are deaf, let's pin it down!"

Mandy, his legal assistant, was quite familiar with McGehee's tantrums. Though only 25, none of the eleven staffers in this room understood him better. And everyone at least suspected why.

"Mr. McGehee," she addressed her boss, a salutation she never used when they were alone, "I think, maybe, the reason we're having a hard time narrowing it down is, well, we're not sure what ..."

"What I want?" he snarled, cutting her off. "What I *want* is to get rid of the ones who not only hate us, but will infect other members of the jury with their poison." He scowled at his associate attorneys, investigators, clerks, Mandy, and the expert psychologist hired for this exercise. Most of them studied their notepads or their feet.

"I was going to say," Mandy replied softly, "we're not sure what sort of argument will mean the most to Judge Bering. You have her figured out better than anyone," she pandered, "so, since we think all of these people are dangerous, maybe you can help us focus on who she'll most likely boot." She tilted her head, raising her eyebrows. "Then we can use peremptories to get rid of the rest," she offered innocently. She referred to peremptory challenges, the final way to reject a potential juror, completely discretionary strikes, no explanation required. Judge Bering gave each side three.

Everyone switched from Mandy to their boss and back again as if watching a tennis match, their collective breath held. McGehee's jaw flexed as he absorbed her suggestion wrapped in a compliment. "Okay," he exhaled, "let's try this." The tension lowered from boil to simmer. She had that effect on him.

When the president appointed Sidney as the government's lead prosecutor in the nation's capital, a friend back in South Bend put forward Mandy, telling him she had aced her paralegal courses in junior college and would have stellar recommendations from her instructors. All of that was true. But when McGehee interviewed the young woman, it was her shapely tanned legs, ample breasts and luscious lips that caught his eyes, not her cream-colored resume. Everyone in the office understood the attraction.

"Judge Bering wants a fair trial. She won't reward anyone trying to *talk* their way off the jury, though. That really pisses her off. So, we have to focus on the ones who are objectionable at their core, because of who or what they are, not simply what they say."

"Number 22," declared Joel Allende, boldly stepping into the breach. McGehee's second chair on the case was a young gun Sidney had come to appreciate. First in his class at Harvard, the ambitious hot shot chose McGehee over a clerkship with a Supreme Court justice, so consuming was his drive to be a top litigator.

"He's the only one of the sixty who contributed to Style's presidential campaign five years ago. He has a favorable view of The Aberdeen Circle, even today, even after everything. He admitted to the judge he thinks President Thorne ..." Joel checked his notes, running the fingers of his left hand through his thick, coal-dark hair, "... and I quote, 'has gone too far' in cracking down on extremists."

"Plus," Mandy said, "he said the death penalty would be hard for him in a case where 'nobody got killed.'" She air-quoted the last three words. McGehee noted Allende flashing his perfect teeth at her, pleased to have her as an ally. He was a good-looking kid, much closer to Mandy's age, but Sidney figured Joel was way too savvy to consider making a move. Still, he felt a tinge of jealousy.

"I know 22 claimed he could put all that aside," Allende jumped back in, "but like you said, sir, his admissions go to the core of who he is. The man will never, ever vote to convict."

McGehee rubbed his dimpled chin between thumb and forefinger. He studied the young lawyer, half considering his argument, half picturing the spirited stud's hands all over Mandy. "How 'bout it, Dr. Pettigrew?" Sidney finally said, addressing the high-paid jury consultant.

"Well," the psychologist temporized from the back of the room, "Our 22 didn't volunteer any of the items Joel and Mandy raise. You had to drag each admission out of him." Shifting to professor mode, he spoke now to the room, not just McGehee. "That tells us he's *not* trying to get off the jury. He wants to serve. With all of these strongly held beliefs, in light of his master's degree and obvious intelligence, he is surely well aware he won't be impartial."

"Meaning?" Sidney asked.

"Meaning he is doubly dangerous. He's what we could term 'a crusader,' someone who has an agenda about which he is passionate."

McGehee nodded. He would never admit it, but Sidney had never considered Pettigrew's argument. "That's true," he offered nonchalantly. "Alright." The prosecutor stood up from a lean against his desk, stretched his five-foot-ten frame to its full length, and shook his arms at his sides like a runner loosening up for a race. "Let's keep going."

McGehee walked to the whiteboard, picked up a dry erase marker, and made three columns, left to right: "Likely," "Maybe," and "No." Under "Likely" he wrote, "22".

"Who's next?"

Until two-thirty the team rehashed the remaining targets' Pro's and Con's, crystalized arguments, finally coming up with their finalists. He then dismissed all but Mandy and Joel, and the trio honed the bullet points to be used in Court at nine, now a frighteningly short time away. They also ranked the rest of the original list for peremptory challenges, depending upon Judge Bering's rulings.

Sidney knew he'd never eliminate all nine about whom he had serious reservations – a huge concern, considering he needed a unanimous verdict. But this was far from the prosecutor's first trial, and he well appreciated that a lawyer never got his dream jury.

At least he'd soon know his "Twelve," and could focus on convincing them to do his bidding. McGehee had never lost a case. He was confident, *very* confident, he would take down Styles.

By this time next fall, President Thorne would be in Fort Wayne, or Bloomington, or Gary, proudly campaigning for the next senator from the Great State of Indiana.

Nine

"It is a simple matter of integrity," Mandela Briggs told the judge solemnly. The last minutes of Saturday morning ticked away. They had been at it since nine, arguing both sides' challenges for cause, the folks who could not possibly be fair and should be stricken by Judge Bering.

"Venireman Number 55," he continued, referring to Emmanuel Arroyo, whose actual name he didn't yet know, "either will not fully respect my client's privilege to take the Fifth, or is by his own admission, dishonest. Either way, that is not a risk this court, or especially the vice president, should be forced to take."

Briggs leaned forward, his hands resting on the large counsel table behind which each lawyer addressed Her Honor. "If he was dishonest about something so fundamental as following your instructions, about my client's basic constitutional rights, then how can we rely upon *anything* he said during *voir dire*?"

As he lowered to his chair, the U.S. attorney began to rise. Carolyn held out her palm, halting his ascension.

"Mr. Briggs, I very much appreciate your concern," she began. Her respectful tone, and having waved off McGehee, telegraphed her decision. "Absent something more compelling, I am inclined to take these people at their word. This is an unfamiliar environment, a strange experience for them, and like Number 55, I don't think many of these veniremen have thought seriously about the legal niceties of our world."

She interlaced her fingers and placed them calmly on top of the sheaf of papers spread before her. Other than the lawyers and their staffs, the courtroom was empty. The media was unhappy about its exclusion, but Carolyn felt it necessary to protect these intimate discussions of the individuals who had spent the last two weeks baring their souls. She spoke now principally for "the record," which her reporter Noah dutifully transcribed.

"This gentleman made clear he was speaking off the cuff, and on further reflection was adamant in his pledge to respect Mr. Styles' decision on whether to testify."

They had been debating about Mr. Arroyo a good ten minutes, and Briggs knew it was over. *Never argue a lost cause*, his mentor drummed into him. *Ready the next battle.*

"I am therefore denying Defendant's Motion for Cause." She lifted the clichéd yellow legal pad from her desk and perused it. "Mr. McGehee, I believe our final challenge belongs to you? Number 58?"

"Yes, Your Honor."

The night before – around three this morning, actually – the prosecutor's team finally settled on five challenges. The last two would be "game time" decisions, used only if things were going their way.

As it turned out, Briggs contested *six* potential jurors, so Sidney felt comfortable the judge wouldn't consider his tally outlandish. The matter was sealed when the Defense surprisingly joined them in objecting to Number 16, which the court had no choice but to grant.

McGehee was two-for-three. This last one would be his most difficult, however.

Number 58 was a sweet, elderly Black woman, 81 according to the lengthy form each member of the panel completed a month ago. Three things worried him.

First, she was nearly deaf, and seemed to have a hard time tracking the proceedings. Her responses were often muddled and mumbled, and the old gal carried a perpetual look of confusion. All this spelled trouble for the prosecution, because the trial would be complicated, the evidence intricate. As the government bore the burden of proof, a juror unable to follow along could be a major disadvantage.

Also, she seemed smitten with "that young man," as she referred to Styles. Someone with her apparent affinity for the defendant was unlikely to convict, and certainly not to agree to the death penalty.

Perhaps most troubling of all, this proud African American woman, whose childhood navigated the tense transition from Jim Crow to Civil Rights, was clearly enthralled by the presence of Mandela Briggs. She glowed every time he spoke. Sadly, McGehee knew, this race-based concern, while perhaps the most legitimate of all, was the one he dared not mention.

"Let me begin by pointing out that this will be a long and arduous trial."

Briggs shot to his feet, "Your Honor!" He was willing to risk the interruption for the chance to cut off the prosecutor at the pass. "Ageism is repugnant to any sense of fairness in creating a jury of one's peers, and a foul stereotype and prejudice that becomes *actual* discrimination if allowed."

Judge Bering suppressed a grin, her face its normal neutral as she intervened. "Counsel, let's allow Mr. McGehee to make his argument before objecting to it."

Briggs bowed respectfully and sat, satisfied his point for her rebuke was a worthy trade.

"Thank you, Your Honor," McGehee resumed, an indignant glare at the defense table. "As I can assure my esteemed colleague, I have the greatest respect for the wisdom that comes with age. My own father, for example, is in his seventies now, and I would *love* to have him on this jury." His team laughed at the feeble joke. Bering smiled wanly. Briggs frowned.

"The issue," he said sternly, "is her ability to adequately take in and assemble the mountain of evidence we expect in this trial. I believe the record reflects how many times she asked for a question or statement to be repeated. And we all observed what I can best describe as a blank stare during several interactions with Your Honor, with me, and," turning with a sarcastic smirk to his opponent, "*even* when Mr. Briggs engaged with her."

"Counselor," Judge Bering interposed, "Number 58 did not try to hide her difficulty hearing. She volunteered that fact on her questionnaire. And as you well remember, I am sure, our original panel was 90 persons, from which I excused several actively serving in the military, unable to adequately read and speak English, and otherwise legally disqualified or exempted from service, *including* those over the age of 70. This nice lady could have gone home, but she chose to stay and serve."

"I understand, ma'am, yet her willingness to be on the jury, which, respectfully, could be its own issue, is not the same as her ability to do so. Once the trial begins, we won't be able to indulge her incapacities."

Briggs stood, smoldering. "Perhaps Mr. McGehee would like to explain what he implies by saying this African American woman's willingness to serve," he held out his arm and leaned in for emphasis, "'could be its own issue.'"

"Mr. Briggs," Carolyn scolded.

"I'm not sure what counsel means," McGehee scoffed, thrilled the defense had taken the bait and highlighted what he could never have raised directly. "But we all know some people want to talk their way off the jury, while others, like Number 58, are determined to be on it. Experience tells us the latter category often has ... an agenda."

"Gentlemen, let's stay on track" the judge snapped. Briggs, once again, returned to his chair, happy to have inserted the subtle accusation of racism.

"Your Honor, if I may continue," McGehee sighed dramatically.

"Please."

"In addition to obvious physical difficulties, which I maintain will impede her ability to follow the evidence, there are her references to the vice president as 'that young man' and how she is 'really disappointed in what they are saying about him.' She smiled every time she looked at him. She admitted to voting for him when he ran for president, and tellingly used emphatic words like 'absolutely' and 'definitely' when the defense asked about her ability to be unbiased."

Carolyn tented her hands and rested her chin on top, giving the prosecutor her full, if skeptical attention.

"By contrast, her disdain for the government's case was equally visible. Her arms were folded and she frowned when I questioned her. She hesitated in committing to objectivity with regard to many issues I raised. My gosh, I had to ask three times whether she would consider the death penalty if the circumstances justified it. 'I suppose' was the best I got. And when asked if the accusations against Mr. Styles had in any way affected her favorable opinion of him, she replied – and I quote – 'Heaven's, No!'"

McGehee laid down his notes and engaged the judge with full intensity.

"The purpose of *voir dire* is to secure a fair trial for both parties, not only the accused, but also the State, which bears the incredible burden of securing the agreement of all twelve jurors." Sidney jabbed an index finger into the opposite palm. "Every ... single ... one!"

Carolyn resisted the urge to roll her eyes. She had a pretty good idea of how criminal verdicts worked. But the guy was entitled to be theatrical, she reminded herself.

"Here, for all the reasons stated, we have someone who, although perhaps well-intended, has neither the desire nor the ability to be an engaged, dispassionate participant."

McGehee raised his arms, as if to summon some kind of divine endorsement. "The law demands more."

He slowly descended.

Carolyn quickly invited a response. "Mr. Briggs?"

"Thank you, Judge Bering." He paused, acting the part of one truly flummoxed. "Given the vagaries of counsel's attacks upon Number 58's integrity, it is difficult to know where to begin."

"Try," she admonished, ready to cut through the chaff.

"Yes, well, I initially note that the mysterious signals the prosecution uses to theorize who she likes and doesn't are, first, imaginary in our view – we saw no such manifestations of fondness and, how did Mr. McGehee put it ... 'disdain.' I'm sorry if he felt a tad unloved, but ..."

"Mr. Briggs, move along," she reprimanded. Sidney glared at his adversary.

"More to the point, nothing of the kind is on the record, so even if the prosecution sensed these purported emotional reactions, there is no objective proof of them."

"Secondly," Mandela scratched the side of his head and winced as if truly mystified by this next one, "the unfounded accusation that Venirewoman 58 is too frail of mind to participate in this case is rather astounding. In America, we strive for a jury of one's peers, not a collection of Yale linguistic experts. We do not discriminate against people for who they are ..." Briggs cast a sideways glance at his foe, underscoring the race card so delicately placed upon the mat. "... certainly not for a minor disability, though she seemed to hear your and my words just fine."

Carolyn again had to keep from giggling. These two really did not like one another.

"And if counsel is concerned the trial may be too complex for her, then I might suggest, 'A,' she may not be the only one unable to understand it – I'm not sure I do, to be honest – and 'B,' perhaps he should have considered a more coherent case before bringing charges against my client."

McGehee made the tiniest move to stand, causing the judge to turn his way. He thought better of it.

"The prosecutor makes clear he is vehemently against ageism and racism, so, all things considered, I can see no reason whatever to grant this baseless challenge."

Judge Bering returned to her notes. Both sides had by now learned she preferred to hear from each side only once, disliking endless back-and-forths. After a brief moment of study, she ruled.

"Motion for Cause denied." She offered no explanation, nor was one expected, so that if the decision were ever made part of an appeal, every possible justification for her conclusion could be raised.

"Alright, gentlemen. Let's take a break until two o'clock. At that time, you can submit your peremptory strikes, and then we will draw names from those remaining so that we can seat our jury first thing Monday morning."

She quickly rose, as did everyone else in a ritual show of deference. Once Carolyn had descended the two short steps to the floor and turned toward her chambers, the lawyers and their teams flew into action: packing, sorting, whispering, and above all, ignoring everyone on the rival side.

They would retreat to their offices, neither more than 10 minutes away. Once there, McGehee and Briggs would guide their respective staffs through final decisions on the last three each side would eliminate.

In less than two hours, the arbiters of fate would be fixed.

Ten

"Congratulations, everyone," Carolyn proclaimed late Saturday afternoon. "We have a jury."

First thing that morning, before the motions for cause, the judge declared a unilateral dismissal of eleven veniremen, all of whom she decided were unfit for one reason or another. Both parties challenged Number 16, so he was dismissed by agreement.

That left nine contested motions for cause. Judge Bering granted four of the defense's, and two of the prosecution's.

With 18 thus gone, Sidney McGehee and Mandela Briggs still faced a disturbingly large pool – 42 candidates – from whom the jury would be constituted. Each side wanted many more gone, but had only three peremptory strikes apiece.

Carolyn collected those very short lists first thing after lunch, and there being no overlap, instructed the clerk to place a folded, numbered paper in a bowl for every one of the thirty-six survivors.

She invited the press pool to return, still grumbling about their exclusion during the striking process. Their discontent faded quickly, however, as she explained what they had missed and, more importantly, what they were now about to witness.

"Mr. McGehee, please select six," she requested, adding playfully, "and no peeking!" Normally, the first twelve remaining on the list of veniremen would be chosen. Judge Bering felt this encouraged the lawyers to focus too intently on people near the front, so long ago devised a drawing to randomize the process.

Briggs followed, then each lawyer picked one more card for the two alternate slots.

Carolyn reminded everyone present that what they were about to witness *must* remain confidential until Monday. "I do not want any of these fine citizens to know they have been selected or excluded until it is disclosed by me, here, in front of everyone. Understood?" Everyone nodded.

"Out loud, please," she commanded sternly. "Does everyone present acknowledge and agree they will not share the results of the final jury selection until Monday, after it has been presented in open court?"

The vice president, the lawyers and their aides, the three lucky members of the media, and even her own court reporter, clerk, administrative assistant and bailiff joined in a loud, jumbled chorus, "I do," "Yes," "I agree," "Promised!" "I swear."

Only then did she carefully unfolded each square, saying the numbers one at a time, the onlookers all leaning forward with anticipation, hands gripped around pens, fingers poised over screens.

When the judge finished, when they had their twelve plus two, she admonished them again about secrecy, and dismissed everyone.

"We will seat the jury promptly at 9 a.m., Monday," she pronounced, "and proceed immediately to opening statements."

Carolyn now scanned her courtroom, as scantly populated as it would be for the next ... for the next however long this tense drama unfolded, she pondered. As of the day after tomorrow, she knew, the now hollow space would be packed: the vice president's guests and his secret service detail, the federal marshals providing courthouse security, the trio of media representatives, slots for observers designated by the president and Congress, and coveted ticket holders. That final group, the majority of spectators, would be chosen by lot each day, thoroughly screened, and sworn to silent scrutiny by Carolyn.

"Are there any other matters until we reconvene?"

The lawyers muttered "No, Your Honor," already packing their satchels and directing their crews.

Neither was satisfied with the collection in whose hands their fate was now placed. They never would have been. They never were.

But those misgivings were quickly forgotten. There was too much work ahead, as now the battle for those twelve souls began.

†††

"As I call your number, please step forward to the jury box," the judge advised. "The bailiff will show you to your chair. Once everyone is seated, I will swear you in, provide preliminary instructions, and then the prosecution will make its opening statement."

All 60 tensed, a few hoping for selection, the vast majority praying to be spared.

Carolyn cleared her throat, and began. "Venireman Number 3."

Aiden Tinsley froze and his eyebrows shot up. Even though the judge had only seconds ago told them what to do if their name was called, adrenaline paralyzed him.

In the span of a split second, multiple emotions raced through his brain and out to his extremities. This mere law student was about to partake in the most consequential trial in the nation's history. He had won the litigation sweepstakes! Young Tinsley considered the weeks of classes he would miss, yet knew he'd be provided every conceivable accommodation. He was as of this very moment, after all, to be a legend in The George Washington University Law School corridors.

Finally sensing all notice upon him, Aiden stood, confidently, and marched his forest green Oxford Skechers from the front pew through the swinging gate at the balustrade's midpoint, and across the checkered front section – the apron of activity where he dreamed of performing his own lawyerly adventures.

A tall, thin, wrinkled woman in a white dress shirt and navy slacks waited at the far opening of what, for all appearances, was a small choir loft: two tiered rows of seven swivel chairs each enclosed by 30-

inch-high paneling, all of the same gouged, inexpensive wood thickly lacquered in a honey-colored coat.

The kindly red-headed bailiff – her silver name tag's black letters read "Bankhead" – motioned him to the last seat on the top, where he stood awkwardly, unsure of what to do next.

"You can sit down," she whispered in a husky, cigarette-ravaged voice, then informed him he would henceforth be known as "Juror Number 1."

Before Aiden had a chance to adjust to his new environment, the spotlight quickly shifted. He heard the echo of Judge Bering's call, "Venireman Number 10," and all eyes shifted to the new star, a middle-aged man in the middle of the front row bench opposite Tinsley's old position, and of whom he had previously taken no notice. A short, portly fellow, he grimaced as he lifted his bulk, hoisted his trousers higher up his belly, and clomped his way toward the box. Now "Juror Number 2," he took his place aside Aiden.

When Carolyn next called the woman on the far-left side of the second row, a silent celebration erupted in pantomime on the front line. The ten still seated there, unchosen, glanced at one another with small smiles and expanding eyes, one woman clutching her chest and a suited man dramatically pretended to wipe his brow. They had escaped, or were reasonably sure they had, and even those who wouldn't have minded being called joined in the discreet festivity.

From her spot back on the fourth band of possibles, Lanta Breckenridge nervously watched the progression's linear march. A second woman joined the emerging jury, followed by three men in a row, the last of whom was only four spots to her right, nerve-rackingly close.

Lanta placed her hands flat on her thighs, studied her bright purple nails, and mutely prayed, *Not me, Lord, not me. I can't miss the children that long. Who will teach them?*

But like a thunderclap, the judge's voice boomed artificially from her microphone. "Venirewoman 45."

Tears welled in her eyes as thoughts of doom crushed down. A young child's hand raised, "Ms. Breckenridge, can you say that again." The chummy laughter entering her classroom in clumps of two and three. Stolen glances at their smart phones as Lanta glared disapprovingly, the Roman Empire having much greater message than whatever text or TikTok dance video was competing for their growing minds.

She gathered herself, as she always did on tough days, and with a deep breath willed herself to her temporary home in the front of the box, newly minted Juror Number 8.

Immediately behind Lanta, Emmanuel studied her reaction, absorbing her emotions. They had never met, but he recalled, several days ago, when she revealed her role as a teacher. That stuck him. A real obligation, something to respect, something to lose if forced to serve here. Arroyo felt worse than ever, more guilty for his selfish effort to extricate himself.

And now she was marked, ensnared. It was at this moment Emmanuel knew what was coming. He *deserved* it. Another man and another woman were chosen. Only two spots left. Yet, there was no doubt in his mind.

"Venireman 55," the judge called out.

Arroyo nodded his head, resigned, resolved. Someone else would have to care for his pair of *Abuela Catalinas*.

Emmanuel now possessed a higher purpose.

†††

Jury Seated in Veep Treason Trial

WASHINGTON – After two arduous weeks of vetting, a jury has been selected for the treason trial of

Vice President Elijah W. Styles. DC Chief Federal Judge Carolyn Bering announced the selections Monday morning, although the names of the jurors are being withheld as a "matter of security."

Seven men and five women were sworn in by the court, as well as two alternates. Fearing influence by a whirlwind of media coverage and a firestorm of nationwide protests, some violent, the judge ordered the newly chosen members sequestered for the duration of the trial, expected to last three to four weeks.

Six African Americans, three Whites, two Hispanics and one Asian comprise the panel, somewhat mirroring the District's actual demographics. Several of those making the final cut had expressed varying degrees of concern about issues ranging from the Thorne administration's policies to the vice president's possible guilt to the death penalty itself.

From an original array of 60 persons, the judge eliminated 11 she considered unsuitable to the case, the parties agreed to a twelfth dismissal, and the court granted six more challenges "for cause", four by the defense and two for the prosecution. Each side then unilaterally struck three more candidates to whom they objected, and the eventual jury was selected by lot from the remaining 36. The somewhat convoluted process is intended to remove those most likely to be unfair, producing the elusive jury of one's peers.

Shortly after swearing in the jurors and instructing them as to their duties, Judge Bering called for opening statements.

U.S. attorney Sidney McGehee, the lead prosecutor, argued the trial will "determine the character of our society," and quoting Dr. Benjamin Franklin, told the jurors they would decide whether the United States remains "the world's longest surviving democracy." He referred to the evidence of treason against Mr. Styles as "overwhelming," claiming it would show he violated his oath of office by making war against his country and giving "aid and comfort to our enemies" by advising and encouraging them "to put him at the pinnacle of power, right into our slain leader's Oval Office chair."

Defense counsel Mandela Briggs countered by mocking the government's allegations. He called the prosecution's claims "misshapen pieces" it is trying "desperately to jam into place." Briggs argued it made no sense for the vice president to plot such an overt act of violence, and concluded, "only Sam Kilbrough knows why he shot President Thorne. He's not talking. And in that silence, we find the most immense and most obvious doubt of all."

The prosecution will start the evidence at 9 a.m. Tuesday morning. Both sides have maintained secrecy about the specific persons they intend to call to the stand. For example, will either side seek to extract testimony from Sam Kilbrough, the former U.S. Secret Service agent who on March 30 attempted to assassinate President Thorne? If so, would he speak if placed in the witness box, or take the Fifth?

It is also unknown if either President Thorne or Vice President Styles will take the stand.

[Read More]

August 3
(One Month plus Three Days before Trial)

"*Sam Kilbrough was not a friend of mine, if that's what you're implying.*"

Hunter Bushida implied exactly *that.*

This was the young FBI agent's third meeting with Blakely Kurtz, and the lies only seemed to multiply with each visit. But this time would be different. Hunter had the goods.

"*Okay,*" *Bushida temporized.* "*Then let's go back to the beginning.*" *Kurtz rolled his eyes, sighing in exasperation.*

Hunter had performed this routine scores of times in his nine years with the Bureau. He knew instinctively they were in the fourth quarter, the clock was ticking down, and although Kurtz didn't realize it, the game was already out of reach. The cinder block walls of their meeting room at the Pekin Federal Correctional Institution in rural Illinois perfectly symbolized Kurtz's future: cold, rough and gray.

"*You say you first met Kilbrough,*" *he scrolled through his pad, even though he knew the dates by heart,* "*November 10, at the TAC office in Brooklyn.*"

"*Right,*" *Kurtz groaned.*

"*Of course, that was only after being confronted with the location data from your phones, putting the two of you there on that date. Up until then, you insisted you and Kilbrough didn't meet until January.*"

Kurtz folded his arms across his chest and frowned. "Fine. So I told you, I'd forgotten." Not likely, Hunter decided. *Kurtz had been TAC's communications director, a fixture on TV and online, a figure who chose words with great care. There was no way someone that fixated on details would actually forget the first time he met a man who, in short order, would attempt to assassinate the president.*

Besides, the November 10 story? Another falsehood.

"Mm-hmm." Bushida tapped his screen and spun it around. "Take a look, Blakely."

The scene was poorly lit, the images grainy. Nonetheless, it took only a few seconds for Kurtz to understand.

Typical bar. Long, lacquered counter littered with stacks of coasters, stray napkins, abandoned drinks, punctuated by a cluster of tap handles bearing insignia of the brands on offer, and a register. On the wall, shelves of liquor bottles in all manner of shapes and colors. A heavy set, seriously tattooed bartender idled slowly from one end of his domain to the other, neither of the two customers in urgent need of his services.

"You recognize this place, right?" Blakely didn't look up, his pupils fixated on the unfolding portrait.

Hunter studied his subject, employing skills honed since embarking on this career straight out of UCLA. Now 32, having received hours of instruction on interrogation by some of the country's best psychologists, years partnering with skilled, veteran agents, and hundreds of his own interviews, Bushida could pinpoint the signs.

Kurtz knew what the video would show, but needed to see it play out anyway. He assumed he was caught dead to rights, yet the consequences of that reality needed time to permeate.

Above all – and Hunter was certain of this – Blakely wanted to tell the truth. Wanted to tell him the truth. The agent had figured this out early on. Blakely's desire to be intimate, though words would be their only intercourse, wasn't an entirely new phenomenon for Bushida.

He wasn't arrogant. Far from it. His Japanese parents were of the best conservative traditions: reserved, respectful, self-effacing; they instilled this reticence in their son. Bushida was an astonishingly handsome man: lush, wavy black hair; square, high cheekbones; pouty, almost feminine lips; a muscular torso crafted by hours in the gym; the long, toned legs of someone who ran 20 miles a week. His ethos and humility forbade him from flaunting these features. Nonetheless, Hunter's Vulcan-like logic whispered that, if using this physical magnetism furthered justice, do it. He could tell Kurtz was under his spell from the first flash of his badge.

Thus, Bushida was confident the infatuated witness would eventually succumb, as had a few other men in the past, and many more women. He played to the attraction, trading the stereotypical, TV edition FBI agent-in-a-suit for a tight-fitting pair of Quantico logoed joggers that showed off his broad thighs, and a long sleeve compression shirt that betrayed every ridge and valley from his abs to his neck.

"Blakely?" he softly inquired, employing his voice to keep the fantasy alive as he drained every ounce of information.

"It's Knock Twice," he murmured.

"What's Knock Twice?" Hunter asked rhetorically.

Kurtz's trance finally broke. He peered into his interrogator's soft brown eyes. "It's a bar."

Bushida nodded.

"In Boston. You obviously know all this." Blakely's face twisted. With anger, Hunter considered? No. Pain. "Why are you asking me things you already ..." His voice trailed off.

Bushida reached across the disfigured metal table and placed his hand gently atop Blakely's, still clinging to the poisonous iPad.

Blakely gasped, frozen, staring at the strong, comforting grip, imagining it for everything he could.

"Watch the video, Blakely," Hunter instructed in a low, barely audible voice. "We have to talk about it ... before we can move on."

Before we can move on, Kurtz repeated silently, and studied the device as told.

He watched himself ramble into the picture and hurriedly, distractedly claim a barstool, on his cell the whole time, scrolling, tapping, looking around impatiently as he waited, nervously checking his wearable every 30 seconds, even though his phone told him the precise time. He ordered a drink, and the unimpressed bartender brusquely *placed a tall, clear substance on a coaster in front of him.*

A full cocktail later, in walked a man whose rigid posture made him seem quite tall, but who in reality was only six-foot. He wore a dark Gore-Tex windbreaker dotted with droplets of rain and a Red Sox ballcap.

"Recognize anyone?" Bushida asked, not with snark, but in the quiet, warm voice to which he had purposefully transitioned. Hunter well knew their session would be played back for hundreds of people in numerous meetings and, ultimately, likely, in more than one courtroom. He needed his tenor to be as far from threatening as possible.

Blakely wanted desperately to move to Bushida's side of the table, to sit next to him, close to him, give him everything he wanted, maybe break down and let the fine man's soothing arm drape around his shoulders, telling him in soft words it would all be okay. Somewhere, however, deep down, he understood this was foolish. He watched the unsmiling FBI agent, nonetheless pleasant.

"The guy sitting down next to me." He looked up, sad. "It's Sam Kilbrough." Bushida was well aware of this, yet Kurtz understood the importance of confirming it.

"Do you see the time stamp up in the corner of the frame?"

Blakely read it aloud. "9:38 p.m., October 31."

Bushida didn't chastise him. He didn't need to point out another lie exposed, that this was 10 days earlier than Kurtz's last admission. He instead bent closer, casually, his expression an easy, seductive invitation ready to draw from what now appeared a free-flowing fountain.

"He said he was glad we had finally met in person," Blakely recalled with a wistfulness that betrayed his hurt. Kurtz recounted how Kilbrough said he'd seen him on TV, admired Blakely's cool, calm rebuttals of daily assaults from the Thorne administration and its allies.

"How did he find you?" Bushida asked.

Kurtz blushed. Even though the agent didn't know, Blakely assumed he did. "RumpUs."

"The dating app?"

Blakely chuckled, not with hilarity, but at the innocence of the beautiful man three feet away. He could teach him so much.

"It's not exactly a dating app," he paused, deciding how scandalous to be. "More, like, a hook-up app. Men Seeking Men."

One of Hunter's thin, dark eyebrows crept up.

"How he figured out it was me, I don't really know. He was pretty vague. Something about a friend of a friend. But, hey, have you seen the guy? Of course I was down to meet him."

"What did you two talk about?"

"Oh, the standard stuff: half-truths, compliments, feigned common interests. He was charming, alright, but looking back on it, something was off. I think on some level," Blakely trailed off, "I was aware of it then, but ..."

"But what?"

Kurtz sulked. "Well, let's say that we didn't even kiss, unless you count a quick goodbye peck on the cheek. I assumed the guy wasn't interested, and that was that."

"You saw him again, though."

"Right." Blakely grinned. "He just showed up at our building. My assistant came in and gave me grief, said 'There's this hot dude in the lobby, says you're friends.' I went out, and there he was."

"Sam Kilbrough?"

"Yep. Well, no. I mean, it was him, but to me he was 'Tom.'"

"Tom?"

"Yeah. Tom Jones. Like the old singer. We joked about that the first night. He was surprised I got the reference."

Bushida smiled.

"Don't worry," Kurtz continued, "I'm not naïve. I knew it was a fake name, which, who cares, right? That's pretty common."

"Did you know what he did?"

"Not that first night. I forget what he said his job was." Blakely turned away, considering whether, at this point, he should be embarrassed at all. "I guess I was distracted. But later, at my office, he said ..." He hesitated.

Bushida had restated his rights a couple of hours ago, before they started. Kurtz had already pled guilty, his sentencing deferred pending his cooperation. He was nonetheless entitled to an attorney, but had no money left, and besides, no one worth a crap would come within a mile of him. His court-appointed counsel was an idiot. And this way, he and Agent Bushida could meet alone.

Still, they were now getting to the serious stuff. Blakely took a deep breath before plunging onward.

"He said, he disclosed I guess, that he worked for the Secret Service. Shocked the shit out of me! Scared me, more than anything. I figured he was about to break out the cuffs, and not in a good way." Kurtz grimaced at his own forced humor.

"What happened next?"

Kurtz hugged himself, physically withdrawing. Hunter needed to keep the story rolling. *"Blakely,"* he called, rising slowly from his seat and placing a firm hand on the frightened man's shoulder.

Kurtz looked up at him, tears welling. *"You have to understand,"* he started, choking back phlegm as he pushed against the urge to break down. *"I hated Thorne. I hated him with every fiber of my being. What he was doing to us. What he* would *do to us if he stole re-election."*

"It's okay, Blakely," Hunter whispered. *"It's okay. But I need you to tell me about Kilbrough."* He grasped Kurtz's other shoulder, and gently pulled him closer. *"What did he say?"*

Kurtz's lower lip trembled. He tried repressing it with his upper teeth. *"He said ... he said he was going to make Styles president."* A tear dripped down Blakely's cheek. *"A gay president. Imagine that!"* The corners of his mouth curled up unconvincingly.

A thousand questions exploded inside Agent Bushida's mind. It was difficult, but he resisted the urge to ask any of them. He fully grasped how useful it would be for the words to flow from the witness' mouth to the jurors' ears without any taint from him.

He pressed Blakely's shoulders with his thumbs, a subtle, personal encouragement, and sat back down, praising his subject with a visage of compassion ... You can trust me.

Kurtz searched his inquisitor. Finding what he needed, he continued.

"Tom. Well, Sam. He said almost everything was in place. That Styles was ready, was going to take care of him – of Sam – of us." Blakely exhaled vigorously. "As you can guess, I was ... bewildered. I asked Sam what he meant, what he was planning to do. He never really said. Very vague. Something like, 'Don't worry, Thorne's only going to get what's coming to him.'"

With a pleading look, Blakely reached across the table for Hunter, but quickly thought better of it. Hunter leaned in, indicating he wasn't put off.

"Agent Bushida," Kurtz begged, "you have to believe me. I didn't know any details. I certainly didn't have a clue Tom, Sam, intended to ..." He flinched at the enormity of the crime.

Hunter dipped his chin encouragingly, though carefully. What exactly did Kurtz think Kilbrough would do? That could wait, however. For now, there was something more important.

"Blakely, that leaves a big question." Kurtz stared, radiating hope and anticipation. "Why did Kilbrough need you?"

He nodded, suddenly confident. "Sure. He said he didn't need anything now, other than, I guess you could say, my emotional support." Blakely reflected. "I was so stupid. Anyway, he said he would get amnesty, or a reprieve or something." Kurtz snapped his fingers, "A pardon he said, that was it, a pardon, and he'd have plenty of money, but he would need," Kurtz formed air quotes, "to *'evaporate' for a while. He knew we helped members of the LGBT community escape Thorne's goons, that we had contacts, our own little Underground Railroad to Canada."*

Bushida bobbed his head, diagraming in his mind the strands he needed to pursue, the corroborations, the follow-ups. But for now, he was satisfied, at least in a way. Whether or not this tree ultimately bore fruit, Kurtz was finally telling the truth. Hunter was certain of it.

But ... was Kilbrough?

The Prosecution

Eleven

Today, it felt real.

For the first time in this process, I saw events in stark relief, not through an opaque cloud of disbelief. Now, all I want to do is sit in a very dark room, close my eyes to make it even darker, and think.

But I can't. I'm "home," with Brady and Anna, who need me as much as I should need them. We've performed upbeat, light-hearted conversation behind forced smiles for the hour since my motorcade dumped me back at Number One Observatory Circle. The truth is, though, "relaxing" with the family only makes matters worse.

For one, we are incarcerated. Yes, a really nice prison – I mean, who should complain about a nine thousand square foot, 33-room mansion? Pretty fabulous, nestled deep within the picturesque, well-manicured grounds of the 80-acre Naval Observatory overlooking D.C. We have way more space and privacy than the occupants of the White House, and between the amenities and obliging staff, well, it's downright luxurious.

Sadly, though, we are not here by choice. House arrest means I only leave the residence for my attorney's office, and now, the courthouse. It's suffocating, and every turn of the calendar only adds to the emotional humidity.

Moreover, there's really nothing for any of us to discuss. All's been said in the 148 consecutive evenings we've already spent together. As a result of my troubles, none of our lives are normal, and none of us want to relive the daily trauma we each endure.

Take Brady. He's as much a prisoner here as I. Being the "Second Gentleman" was a frenzied delight for him in the beginning, his ceremonial, political and social calendars full from dawn until way past dark. He thrived under the media glow, a natural: handsome guy, ex-ballplayer who's always loved crowds, easy talker.

But when the president completely shut me out immediately after the re-elect, Brady became equally *persona non grata*. His circle of supposed friends tightened considerably, and that hurt him. A lot.

After my arrest – April 24, the date none of us can forget – Brady was still free to go wherever he wanted, but what was the point? Journalistic fireflies were replaced by tabloid sharks, his adulation transformed to mockery and contempt. Even a clandestine coffee with a chum metamorphosed into a locus of fist-shaking protest.

And poor Anna. She continued attendance at the Georgetown Scholastic Academy, at least for a while. My exile from the administration wasn't that big a deal among her high school classmates. Freshmen girls have better priorities. Plus, as a political child since age five, Anna was quite skilled at parrying whatever snark came her way. When the indictment came down, however, everything changed.

How do you tell your teenage daughter (a) You are not a criminal, and (b) I am truly sorry for ruining your life. She somehow persisted the balance of the school year. In her intelligent eyes, being a pariah among her classmates, with dwindling support from the staff, was the price of escaping our confinement.

But after a full summer without friends – even the few who might visit her are banned from doing so by their well-connected parents – without the option of an unmolested day out, Anna has become sullen and withdrawn. She's fully aware the President of the United States wants me legally, and literally, dead. I'm fully open to parenting advice on how to deal with that one.

The Solarium is our favorite space in this palace and where, mutely, we presently lounge. The small room is by far the Observatory's homiest spot. As quiet as it is, you can hear the water rippling in the pool outside – thanks Dan Quayle!

None of us have anything legitimately uplifting to share, so we don't talk much beyond banalities we conjure while playacting normality. We grow tired of even those topics pretty quickly, leaving ... silence. The deafening quiet amplifies today's storm of activity.

Anna reads a book. Brady absent-mindedly twirls a glass of Zinfandel, transfixed, waiting until we go upstairs for a "real" conversation, yet one more thing to which I am not remotely looking forward.

All of which leaves me alone with my thoughts, a replay of today's cyclone. Judge Bering announced the jury, and I gotta say, it's scary. That older Hispanic man, the one who owns the restaurants, made it. The guy all but said anyone who takes the Fifth is guilty, and I'm not comforted that Her Honor pushed him to backtrack.

And while I initially scoffed at Izzy's whole "body language" thing, I have to admit I started to see what she meant as jury selection progressed. The guy who wore a suit every single day scowled whenever we made eye contact. The one time I smiled, he pursed his lips and turned away. He's now Juror Number Five. The lady who volunteered her "concerns" about *TAC*? I imagine her neck is sore from all the nodding she did during the prosecutor's not-so-subtle arguments. She's Juror Number Ten.

Oh well, we got some we like, too, including the one Izzy says is in love with me. And, as Mandela reminds me multiple times a day, we only need one vote to avoid conviction.

What preys on my tired mind the most, though, is McGehee's opening statement. I felt helpless, like a human piñata. Emotionally, I'm still bruised and sore. Right from the beginning, he made my fate the price of our democracy.

> *What we do here, together, will determine the character of our society. It will determine the type of government under which we all live. In other*

words, your decisions at the end of this trial will define the very future of our nation.

I thought long and hard about how to begin today, about what my first words to you should be. And with every false start, every sheet of paper I wadded up and threw in the wastebasket, I kept mumbling the same thing. "Not good enough. The stakes are too high." Until, finally, I realized it was right there, right in front of me. I had no choice except to be brutally honest, to tell you, directly, the unvarnished consequences of your responsibility.

Elijah Wilson Styles is not a drug trafficker we need to take off the streets, or a human smuggler, or an embezzling business tycoon, or a contractor ripping off The Pentagon, or even a corrupt politician taking bribes. I have prosecuted every single one of those cases, and obtained convictions, putting bad people behind bars.

No, the hideous crime before us is something drastically worse. The crime aided and abetted by the defendant, unlike all those others I listed, could render meaningless our whole system of law and order, all of our foundations, from free speech to free elections, all of our constitutional principles – in short, everything that makes the United States what it is. The defendant's scheme could have ended two-and-a-half centuries of democratic government, silencing our voices, throwing us into autocracy, subjecting us to rule by a ruthless few instead of an enfranchised public, the powerful instead of the people.

Forget for a moment that Lincoln, Garfield, McKinley and Kennedy were all gunned down by assassins, yet our nation survived. So, McGehee's theory that the life of any one man, even a president, is larger than our national fabric is hogwash.

That may sound harsh, or too coldly academic, considering Magnus was indeed shot. But my point is, this prosecutor isn't interested in the truth, or even accuracy. He wants to inflame passions to get a scalp – my scalp.

Am I the one being melodramatic? Just listen to what he says next.

> *With your courage, the voices of the American people will not be silenced, however, because the assassin failed, the defendant got caught, and you are here to render a judgment to make sure it never, ever happens again.*
>
> *In his diary for September 18, 1787, James McHenry, a Maryland delegate to the Constitutional Convention, took down the events of its last day. He included a question to Dr. Benjamin Franklin as they walked home, from one Mrs. Powell of Philadelphia. McHenry writes, "A lady asked Dr. Franklin, 'Well Doctor, what have we got, a republic or a monarchy?' 'A republic,' Dr. Franklin replied, 'if you can keep it.'"*
>
> *A quarter of a millennium later, it is you citizens, you members of the jury, you twelve who will finally address our founding father's concern. For when it comes to the world's longest surviving republic, it is you who will decide "if we can keep it."*

Seriously? I can only hope at least a few on the jury saw this opening bid as an appeal to blind nationalism instead of blind justice.

You either find the defendant guilty, or you are no patriot. That's insulting.

I do begrudgingly give McGehee points, however, for glazing over the differences between Sam Kilbrough and me ... "the assassin failed, the defendant got caught" ... as if we are one in the same. I am not Sam, and believe me, I know the guy.

It was all fluff and hyperbole, nothing I didn't believe Mandela could handle. Until, that is, our esteemed U.S. attorney spoke factually for the first time, defining the crime at issue, causing my heart to stutter.

> *The indictment against the defendant is straightforward. It is simple. It is direct. It is the only crime specifically laid out in the Constitution of the United States.*
>
> *Treason.*
>
> *Article III, Section 3 of our Constitution says, "Treason against the United States, shall consist only in levying War against them, or in adhering to their Enemies, giving them Aid and Comfort."*
>
> *Congress put that into the Crimes section of the United States Code, where in section 2381 they declared, "Whoever, owing allegiance to the United States, levies war against them or adheres to their enemies, giving them aid and comfort within the United States or elsewhere, is guilty of treason."*
>
> *That's it. Like I promised, nothing complicated. That's the whole law. And at the end of this case, Judge Bering will instruct you to find the defendant guilty if we, the government, prove he committed those acts.*
>
> *We will, I assure you.*

I'm not worried about McGehee proving I plotted to kill Magnus Thorne. He can't. But can his crude rendition of the law mean, if I'm chummy with the wrong people I'm as guilty as they are? Hell, I've known Rachel Maslow for years, and taken *TAC*'s money just as long. Does that mean, if the jury believes they were involved, then I'm involved?

The reality is, I am the one man in this country who could be the peacemaker. I am the best equipped, even as vice president, to build the desperately needed bridges over the yawning divide in America. I am as equally saddened by the excesses of the Thorne administration as the vile groups and nutty lone wolves acting in The Aberdeen Circle's name.

Exactly why Magnus is afraid of me. He didn't worry I'd prevent his theft of an election. No, he was terrified I would calm things down, unite the country, and get all the credit. So, he shunted me off to the side, a steady diet of funerals, or fundraisers with his huge, smiling picture behind me.

Meanwhile, *TAC* failed to follow my advice and speedily, *unequivocally* condemn Tanner's Vengeance, or the fanatics who tried to take Iowa's governor hostage, or all the subsequent violent crazies. The president saw the convenience of an easily definable enemy. His bigotry and homophobia turned into zealotry. He became dangerous. Was I supposed do nothing? Let him crush the helpless to feed his power lust? Yeah, I tried to help, I tried to heal, I tried to stop a tyrant. McGehee, of course, makes it sound sinister.

> *The evidence is overwhelming that Elijah Styles, disregarding the allegiance he owed to the United States, instead betrayed us, making war against us by plotting to kill the president.*
>
> *The evidence will show the defendant was very close to The Aberdeen Circle's leader, Rachel*

> *Maslow, and her gang of TAC terrorists who planned and prepared this plot. He adhered to those enemies of the State like glue.*
>
> *The evidence will also show the defendant knew, extremely well, the actual assassin, Sam Kilbrough.*

The evidence ... the evidence ... the evidence!!

"What evidence?" I wanted to scream. Instead, empty syllables, from a guy who wants to take my gay head back to Indiana on a pike so they'll make him a senator!

Of course I knew Sam. Okay, sure. Knew him "extremely well." He joined my detail the day Thorne introduced me as his running mate five years ago, and I will forever be grateful to Speaker Knall for sending him my way. "You two belong together, I just *feel* it," he'd said. He was right. Sam became more a confidant than a protector.

And not being made of stone – sorry Brady! – I did notice. The man filled his suit like a gymnast does spandex. I rarely saw him out his jacket, that first year anyway, but you could nonetheless tell he was molded without the waste of a single ounce. The first time I touched him, a fraternal side-hug with my arm barely able to reach the full span of his shoulders, I felt the full power of his metallic scaffolding. To be perfectly honest, it consumed a lot of energy not to stare, not to touch, to keep my focus on my work. That never changed, not even after we got to know one another, after we became friends, after we became ... closer than a protectee and his guardian.

McGehee, however, knows none of that. He can speculate, but "evidence?" Of what? Certainly nothing allowing me to force upon Sam any deed against his will.

> *The evidence will show Elijah Styles not only gave aid and comfort to our enemies, but advised and encouraged them to put him at the pinnacle of*

> *power, right into our slain leader's Oval Office chair.*

Did I want to be president? Obviously. In case the prosecutor forgot, I ran for the job at the age of 38, after what all agree was a very successful term as mayor of Dallas. A *gay* chief executive of the ninth largest city in the country: in *deep red Texas*.

Remember, too, my presidential campaign was on fire. Without Governor Thorne's dirty tricks, and the GOP establishment's revulsion to the idea that "someone like him," like *me*, should lead the party, I would have been the nominee! Settling for Veep was my ticket to the top, even if it meant waiting eight years.

That is, until Thorne went nuts.

> *The defendant violated his oath to 'support and defend the Constitution of the United States against all enemies, foreign and domestic.' He did not 'bear true faith and allegiance' to that Constitution, as he swore he would. Instead, he encouraged those enemies to help him gain even more power than he already had.*

Let's be fair. The Constitution was hardly working, was it? The violence perpetrated some on the fringes of The Aberdeen Circle was inexcusable. Thorne's reaction, however, was to thwart due process, civil liberties, human rights, and every principle upon which an equitable society is based. In other words, it was *he* who abandoned his oath with a brutal, lawless, homophobic crackdown. And that was just the tip of his iceberg of illegality, of his plans for domination.

I was trying to save the Republic, for God's sake. Is there anything more patriotic?

> *At the end, we are confident you will see the defendant's guilt as clearly as we do ... as clearly as if he had pulled the trigger himself. Because in the final analysis, what Mr. Styles did was worse.*

I've been in politics for a while now, and I'm used to a good partisan drubbing. Usually, I get to respond in real time, hit back hard. Today, I could only sit there, act skeptical, disbelieving and hurt, all without overdoing it. The jurors' eyes seldom left the prosecutor, but when they did, it was to study me.

What did they see? Hard to say.

But what I hope they see, what I wanted them to see – what I *need* them to see – is a man who loves his country, one who is the hero of this story, not a cold-blooded murderer. A man they can see as president.

Twelve

When Emmanuel opened his second restaurant, in tony Georgetown, the emotional weight far exceeded the original *Abuela Catalina* in his own neighborhood. This was true even though the first venture launched 22 years ago with no history, no financing beyond every penny he had saved and every dollar he could borrow from relatives, and no management experience on Arroyo's part. The risks were enormous and the odds long.

By contrast, the new location was a product of popular demand. Hardly a night passed without a devoted patron of the original begging Emmanuel to give them a place closer to home. Banks lined up to back the expansion, and by then he knew the business inside and out.

Yet, Arroyo suffered terrible anxieties, months of sleepless nights, and a constant expectation of failure. He feared his own ambitions, as if he were daring the fates which had given him comfort, if not wealth, allowing him to put three children through college and fix up their Mount Pleasant abode (he would *never* move). Emmanuel was treated like royalty during annual trips to see extended family in Jalisco.

Por qué, he asked himself constantly, would he jeopardize it all for nothing better than ... *más*?

"*El Nuevo*," as he called Georgetown, was a sensation beyond his wildest imaginations. It didn't matter. As the prosecutor methodically rebuked the vice president's pretensions and lust for power, Arroyo's deep-rooted trepidations came rushing back.

As arrows of accusation whizzed by, Arroyo asked himself whether Elijah Styles had committed any crime other than gambling with his own success, *tal como yo*? Just like me? Was not ambition the heart of both men's sins?

El Nuevo's success had concealed Emmanuel's original misgivings like a pristine layer of snow. Something in the U.S.

attorney's words, however, melted away that fragile cover. A new sensation of guilt engulfed him.

So he watched Mandela Briggs' slow approach to the podium with hope, praying the formidable man would offer redemption not only for his client, but for Arroyo too.

> *Ladies and Gentlemen, the government's lawyer would have you believe your presence here is but a formality. That you are mere clerks, whose sole function is to grip little rubber stamps and smash the word 'Guilty' upon the vice president's forehead. That the painstaking work of the past two weeks, searching for fair-minded, sensible, intelligent seekers of the truth was a farce, a box to be checked.*
>
> *The reality, as obvious to you as to Elijah Styles and me, is that you twelve have an incredible mission: to dissect the government's case, and decide whether the misshapen pieces it is desperately trying to jam into place actually fit together – whether the story it tells, beyond any and all reasonable doubt, is the one that solves the mystery of March 30.*

"The twelve of you," Emmanuel repeated. This is not about my confession, he recognized gingerly, and I am not alone here. All of us are joined to this case as firmly as our creaky swivel chairs are bolted into place. I don't yet know these people, he pondered, but surely they bring their own foibles. And it's not about them, either.

Arroyo looked over to the vice president. *Se trata de él*, he decided, slightly relieved. It's about him.

Briggs tilted his head to one side as his eyebrows lit up his broad forehead. A sense of detached wonder radiated.

> *Does your common sense allow you to believe a sitting vice president could plot to murder his commander-in-chief while thinking, somehow, no one would be the wiser?*

The lawyer let the question hang.

Arroyo twirled it around, weighed it, then glanced at his seatmates. They too contemplated the defense attorney's offer. Was it really that easy, or was this a trap? Was common sense truly the key? If so, is my judgment better or worse than anyone else's?

Briggs maintained his quizzical pose, then spooled out a bit more line.

> *Or that an elected public servant like Elijah Styles, who has earned the president's wrath since their re-election by promoting peace and transparency, would inexplicably turn to violence and secrecy?*
>
> *Or even, as the prosecution preposterously claims, that a rational person would think The Aberdeen Circle, given its sudden notoriety, was the most viable partner for launching a coup d'état?*

The prosecutor had indeed placed some heavy markers in his speech. Arroyo was impressed. But if he was learning anything, it was to avoid impulsive assumptions. Mr. Briggs was already raising good points. Emmanuel actually remembered the vice president on TV, uncomfortably distancing himself from some of Magnus Thorne's bolder actions, calling for calm, while also imploring The Aberdeen Circle to "back off."

> *Mr. McGehee said to you this morning, "at the end of the case, Judge Bering will instruct you to*

find the Defendant guilty if we, the government, have proven that he committed those acts." True enough. She will indeed.

What he failed to tell you is, in determining whether the prosecution has proven anything, Judge Bering will require you be convinced of guilt ... beyond ... a ... reasonable ... doubt.

She will define 'beyond a reasonable doubt' as proof that renders you firmly assured of the government's case. In other words, a reasonable doubt is one based upon both reason and common sense. It arises from a careful and impartial consideration of all the evidence presented ... including gaps in the evidence.

And if, when both sides have concluded, there is any reasonable doubt in your minds, Judge Bering will insist it is your duty to find the defendant not guilty.

As a fair man, Arroyo respected the concept, the two words Briggs drew out, verbally underlined, repeated four times in sixty seconds: *reasonable doubt*. You couldn't just go off on a tangent or bathe yourself in conspiracies, not when a man's life is at stake. Emmanuel was fine with that.

But, didn't common sense allow you to assume certain things too? If one sees black, billowing smoke, isn't it reasonable to suppose a fire, even without seeing flames?

He remembered David, that kid his wife interviewed, and hired, as a waiter at the first *Abuela*. Emmanuel wasn't blaming her. Far from it. He couldn't possibly manage the staff, kitchen, supplies, all of it, without her. The fact remained, though, despite the kid's charm, despite how much the guests loved him, he was a thief. First a bottle of wine, then one of tequila, then another. One or two a week went missing. No one ratted him out. No one saw him pilfer any liquor. But as they zeroed in, quietly cranking up inventory on the preferred brands, their suspicions grew.

When confronted, David denied everything and quit, indignant to the end. For Emmanuel, however, *no había duda*. There was no doubt, reasonable or otherwise. And once David was gone, there was no more missing booze, either.

> *So, as we begin this journey, let us set our direction. Let us take a moment to find our North Star, facing what is factual and honest.*
>
> *The truth is, Vice President Styles was chosen for his high office by Magnus Thorne himself, precisely for his integrity and patriotism. Those were the very words President Thorne used barely five years ago – integrity and patriotism – to describe his excruciatingly vetted new running mate. What Governor Thorne saw in Eli Styles was confirmed by the 84 million voters who selected their ticket. And only last year, President Thorne asked your vice president to serve again. Are we to now believe both Eli Styles' integrity and his patriotism suddenly, mysteriously evaporated, that the man of honor became a man of murder? Is that a conclusion based upon reason and common sense?*

Arroyo was unconvinced. He understood Briggs' argument, but people change. Emmanuel had changed! Had not his own success, if he was being totally honest, bred an entirely new character? In the Georgetown version of his life, he rubbed elbows with the elite. Instead of dressing down in pilgrimage to his less prosperous locale, Arroyo dressed up in homage to his new property – slacks instead of jeans, a nice buttoned, pressed long-sleeve rather than his ratty old sweatshirt. Even a sports coat from time to time.

Maybe Styles had been a patriot. Maybe he did once have integrity. Maybe he still possessed both traits. Emmanuel wasn't buying the suggestion, however, that virtue always survived triumph. The acquisition of power is an unpredictable catalyst.

Briggs pointed a finger toward the Heavens, and continued.

> *The truth is also that President Thorne knew his assailant, Sam Kilbrough, as well as Mr. Styles. He served on both their protective details, first for the vice president, then for the president. It was Mr. Thorne who had the most recent relationship with Kilbrough. Do reason and common sense allow one to conclude Mr. Styles was in some superior position to manipulate Kilbrough into such a wicked deed?*

The saturating news coverage of the attempted assassination and its aftermath left most Americans inescapably familiar with the sordid details. Briggs' here reminded Arroyo of his own skepticism about the Manchurian Candidate conspiracies popular on *FOX News* and *Newsmax*: that Styles groomed Kilbrough for years, placing him near the president so, when signaled, he could shoot him. ¡*Loco!*

> *Mr. McGehee also tries to paint another of the vice president's relationships, with The Aberdeen Circle, as somehow sinister and secretive. The truth is, Eli Styles has never hidden his decade long association with TAC. He has made very public statements lamenting the group's mistakes, while standing by its original purpose of defending human rights. Most coups mobilize public anger or the military. Our distinguished prosecutor says*

> *the vice president used a disgraced civil liberties advocate. Reasonable? Common sense?*

The lawyers are trying to seduce us, Arroyo thought. These stories they shape, these opening statements, weren't much different than cartoons selling cereal to children, or sexy models hawking perfume.

He had to admit, though, they were both good. Like now, turning the defendant's ties to an organization half the country considered terrorists into some virtuous act of loyalty. Yet simultaneously, Emmanuel marveled, Briggs transformed *TAC*'s dark reputation into a shield against the very possibility of his client's guilt. ¡*Magnífico!*

> *And the truth is, Mr. Styles' political fight this past year has been a brave and perilous one for him personally, speaking out against the excesses of an administration of which he is a part. His break with President Thorne was quite open. If his goal was to brutally but quietly topple the most powerful man in the world, do reason and common sense square with his loud, persistent protests?*

Not one ordinarily paying much attention to politics – Arroyo had his own kingdom to run – he nonetheless felt the tremors. A re-election in doubt, with different analysts calculating different outcomes, secretaries of state contradicting county election officials, some votes counted, others disputed, embargoed, or tossed out. It was a mess, and the nervous vibe permeated even Emmanuel's restaurants. Alcohol sales soared.

And so, indeed, he had noticed the vice president's laments, seemingly genuine because they jeopardized his own re-election. "No administration can survive without the legitimacy of its endorsement by the voters," Styles had said.

Thorne's retort was savage. "Perhaps the vice president feels my defeat helps him in four years. Why else would he coddle the dirty vote-riggers trying to steal this election?"

Their break was public and loud and colorful, a conflagration from which no one could avert his gaze. And then the literal fireballs, Arroyo remembered, the explosions at federal buildings in Baton Rouge and Tallahassee, the internet outages, the blackouts, Federal marshals and FBI agents and the DEA and brigades of law enforcement fanning out across the country, culminating in Thorne's national address: "We will not let The Aberdeen Circle hold our nation hostage. We will not negotiate with terrorists. We will not back down."

Yes, Styles' calls for calm, his warnings against a rush to judgment, even if not an overt defense of *TAC* were still, as Briggs says, "brave and perilous" pleas. But were they, as the lawyer suggests, inconsistent with a desire to remove the president? By any means? Or were they, as Emmanuel now countered for the prosecution, mere misdirection, slick sleight of hand?

> *"These few examples but scratch the surface. The uncertainties, ambiguities and inconsistencies in the government's case go on and on. Over the next few weeks, it will be my honor, on behalf of Vice President Styles, to shine a spotlight on the prosecution's allegations. Because the truth is, only Sam Kilbrough knows why he shot President Thorne. He's not talking.*
>
> *"And in that silence, we find the most immense and obvious doubt of all."*

The impressive, sturdy lawyer nodded solemnly, gracefully returning to his table. His expression was neither satisfied nor, as with the prosecutor, gloating. He appeared to Arroyo determined.

Emmanuel buried a heavy head into large hands, massaging the fleshy skin of his face as confusion, and the beginnings of a headache, swirled between his temples.

†††

Knall: No Impeachment Until Jury Decides

WASHINGTON – The House of Representatives will not consider articles of impeachment against Vice President Elijah W. Styles until after resolution of his trial in D.C. federal court, House Speaker Rance Knall (R-Tx) announced Monday. "Too many questions," he said, adding, "I think the people, not the politicians, should be the ones getting at the answers."

The move was surprising, given near unanimous support for such a resolution among members of the vice president's own Republican Party, who hold a super majority in the House. Democrats applauded Knall's move, publicly claiming impeachment premature until all evidence is heard, while privately cheering both the drama within the GOP, and Styles' break with the president.

"I believe the murder trial should have priority," Speaker Knall asserted, referring to the treason charges. "Let the president, and his number two, and anyone else who knows something, lay their cards on the table. After that, hopefully everybody will do the right thing," he said.

"They want him gone," Senate Minority Leader Rusty Deacon (D-Ca) commented, referring to the GOP's 65 seats in the upper chamber, two short of the two-thirds needed for conviction and expulsion from office. "They just don't have the votes here."

"Thorne can't fire him," Senate Majority Leader Hiram Taylor (R-Nb) observed, alluding to impeachment as the Constitution's only legal method for removing a president or vice president. "I'm sure it's driving him nuts."

Vice President Styles has maintained his innocence, and refuses to resign from office. "I have consistently condemned violence as a political tool or tactic," he said in a statement released last month, "and had nothing to do with the horrific assassination attempt."

"Kicking him out of office now doesn't really accomplish anything," Knall asserted in explaining his decision. "Let's instead have the truth ring out from belltowers all across America. Wherever that may lead."

Thirteen

Lying in polka-dot boxers atop a disheveled bed, consuming the catered sterility of a room service breakfast, Aiden Tinsley contemplated an array of jumbled ideas. They were, in no particular order:

- When this was all over, could he, and if so, should he write a book? Scott Turow's *One L* about his first year at Harvard Law launched a storied literary career. Aiden was good with words and entertaining in conversation. Given his budding legal knowledge, why not chronical the trial to end all trials.
- How would he list this experience on his interview profile? Did he really want to be so bold as to include it right up front?

Aiden M. Tinsley, Juris Doctorate Candidate
The George Washington University Law School, Washington, DC
GPA: 3.96 (Expected graduation: June 12)
Juror in United States v Styles

Think of the interviews it would garner, the doors it would open, the conversations it would start!

- How many varieties of cereal did this hotel have? Would he tire of them all before this thing ended?
- Is Fall Recess, and a trip home to glide the gentle Hermosa surf, screwed? As fast as Judge Bering moves things, maybe not. He'd give it a couple of weeks, and then decide.
- Sequestration. Per Merriam-Webster: "to set apart," "segregate," "withdraw" or "seclude." To which, Aiden would add, "boredom."

The fourteen of them, 12 jurors and two alternates, were housed at the modest Hotel Königsstrasse, a 22-room, nondescript structure on

E Street three blocks from the judicial complex and, Aiden noted, also three blocks from Ford's Theatre. He assumed the judge had missed the irony.

Last night had been their first. As soon as opening statements were concluded, the group was escorted down back stairs to the Prettyman Courthouse's underground garage, then ferried the short distance in groups of three or four in a convoy of black Suburbans with heavily tinted windows, accompanied by very serious members of the U.S. Marshal's Service. Their short journey ended under a large security tent at the hotel's rear, through its emptied lobby, and immediately up to their rooms. The only guests were the jurors and their keepers.

Each room had a TV, with all inputs blocked save for Netflix and Max. The Wi-Fi was reconfigured so personal devices could send texts or make calls, but not access the full internet. Books and sports were fine. News sites, Reddit, X and other social media were not. They were told their personal communications would not be monitored, which no one believed.

The idea was to forestall contamination of their objectivity, while allowing them to maintain some level of sanity. Nothing, however, could protect these average folk from the anxious tone of their friends' and families' voices.

Nor could any amount of seclusion cut off the normal human susceptibility to speculation and invention. In fact, their isolation only enhanced wild imaginings about what they were missing, what was being said, and how it should inform them.

And, of course, their secret venue was uncovered within hours of their arrival. By this morning's return trip, the route was lined with RAGErs, TACers and countless other protest and advocacy factions, as well as a horde of simple onlookers, many using their seconds of opportunity to influence Aiden and his colleagues.

From the motorcade, Aiden viewed a hangman's scaffold sporting the vice president's doll-like effigy; a blood-splattered cardboard enlargement of the Constitution; American, Pride, Confederate and BLM flags; a sea of red RAGE ballcaps; a pack of Bikers for Thorne; an old *Styles for President* banner; D.C. Police and National Guardsmen and an occasional drag queen; and lots of signs: square and rectangular, blue, black, green, white, yellow, hand-painted, pre-printed – signs bearing every conceivable message for the world, for the country, and especially for these jurors.

There was one such placard that stuck with Aiden. He didn't know why, or even for sure what it meant. He didn't know if it was deep or farcical. Nevertheless, it remained in the background of his consciousness, biding its time for when his mind drifted during the long hours of testimony.

Styles ♥ Kilbrough

†††

"Please raise your right hand," Judge Bering intoned, as she had done a thousand times before, albeit in lesser circumstances, "and repeat after me."

Moments earlier, precisely at 9 a.m., she summoned the prosecution to bring on its first witness.

"The United States call Ezra Arenberg," McGehee bellowed.

Aiden and his fellows, their interest finally tapped, straightened, focus glued to the familiar man confidently marching to the witness stand, climbing it as a general would scale a tank. His bulky, six-foot-four frame made the wooden swivel seat seem cartoonishly small as he settled in. It protested with loud creaks, causing Tinsley to wonder if it could withstand the occupant's large presence. As the Germanic derivation of his surname indicated, he was indeed a mountain of a man.

"State your name for the record, please," McGehee began with formulistic drama, satisfying everyone's urge to experience what they had seen in the best movies.

"Erza M. Arenberg."

"Your occupation?" as if no one knew.

"Chief of Staff to the President of the United States." He said this with a toothy grin, somehow more warning than pleasantry. In less than 60 seconds, merely by taking his place and introducing himself, Arenberg reinforced his reputation for power. He had run Thorne's White House from Day One, after ruthlessly steering the little-known governor's electoral ship to victory five years ago.

"Mr. Arenberg, how long have you known President Magnus Thorne."

The witness considered this briefly, not searching for the answer, but its most effective wrapping. "Eight years." Arenberg expertly turned his attention from McGehee to the jurors, taking them in one by one as he expounded. "He was Governor of Montana. I was Secretary of Commerce. We worked together to spearhead mass development of lithium production which," he said with an obvious pride, "is now a thriving U.S. industry."

"And did you eventually become involved with President Thorne's first national campaign?"

Aiden noticed the smirk. "Involved?" Most anyone who followed politics knew he was the mastermind of Thorne's rise. Of course, those who opposed the president credited Arenberg with all manner of dirty tricks, voter disenfranchisement, widespread intimidation, even, some alleged, Supreme Court bribery in last year's re-election.

"Yes. I recognized something in the governor, and was pleased to become his campaign manager."

"And after he won?"

"Well, he asked me to stay on and help out. I knew President Thorne had big plans, and thought it my duty to serve my country." Arenberg winked at Tinsley. "Again." A signal, Tinsley guessed, to someone likely to appreciate the witness' fuller biography. Twenty years in the Marines, including well-decorated tours in Afghanistan and Iraq, should certainly qualify as "Again" to a young elite like Aiden.

He wasn't alone, though, among the jurors familiar with that sterling résumé. Or was it legend? Much exaggerated and inaccurately reported, Arenberg left the flattering light uncorrected: *Lieutenant* Colonel, not the full bird assumed by his dominant bearing; mostly administrative rather than combat posts, though only the latter were ever discussed; successful businessman, for sure, but only on a provincial scale; respected member of the Jewish community, with one, or was it two, grandparents surviving the Holocaust (actually, it was one of eight *great*-grands; tragic, yet not quite of searing relevance to his own experience, as he never met the relative in question). Arenberg's roots were indeed deep among the Ashkenazi Jew diaspora trekking into the Holy Roman Empire around the end of the first millennium, but more than forty years prior to Ezra's own birth, his family tree had been firmly transplanted to America.

McGehee wisely skipped the bio and headed straight for the chaos and importance of Arenberg's daily responsibilities, leaving plenty of room for name-dropping, from the King of Sweden to the last Super Bowl MVP. Having ignited the aura, the prosecutor deftly shifted to the matter at hand.

"Am I correct that, given your responsibilities, you had significant interaction with the Vice President?"

"Oh, yes," Arenberg said with embellished exasperation. He turned his large head, topped by its turbulent mass of rich, black curls, and gave Styles a sardonic smile. "I was there at the beginning, when Magnus, er, Governor Thorne, made Eli his running mate."

Master class, Aiden thought, referring to his boss not as "the president," but with the informal "Magnus," showing off their bond. In the same breath, he tossed aside the vice president's importance with the casual use of "Eli."

"Tell us about that, if you would."

"I was against it," Arenberg declared quickly. "I understood the logic. Mayor Styles had run an impressive campaign, had brought a lot of new folks over to the Republican side, had accumulated a lot of delegates and raised impressive amounts of money. All of those were positives." He permitted an abrupt, dramatic pause to serve as preamble to his misgivings.

"But?" McGehee prodded on cue.

"Call it a sixth sense. I know that's not a legal term you guys appreciate," he said, showing the judge a disarming, lopsided grin, "but hear me out."

Arenberg rotated to the jury. "On patrol in Afghanistan, you learn real quick how to listen to the eyes, not the words. It's the same thing in politics.

"I was tasked with vetting the candidates, and I met with Styles twice. He said all the right things, that's for sure. But his attitude was arrogant. His tone was dismissive, like I was wasting his time. His whole presence made it unmistakably clear that, in his view, we needed him more than his career needed us. He wanted guarantees about access, about input, about portfolio. In short, he wanted guarantees of *power*."

"Power," the prosecutor repeated solemnly, underlining his theory of the case, a one-word encapsulation of the defendant's motive.

"Well, I thought we had better options, but it was going to be a tight race, and Governor Thorne felt our best chance was with the mayor."

"So how did you meet Mr. Styles' demands?"

Arenberg chuckled, and with a mocking glance to the defendant said, "Oh, you know. Lots of vague promises about him writing his own ticket, Governor Thorne seeing him as a true partner, blah, blah, blah. It was Magnus – I could still call him that then," he said intimately to the jurors, "who really closed the deal. As everyone knows, he's a persuasive guy. And, he hoped the mayor wanted to do some good."

Aiden watched all joviality leak away. "I'm sure Styles knew it was all BS, but as we later learned, he didn't much care. He had his own agenda."

McGehee decided to highlight the "agenda" comment by ignoring it. "It seems to me President Thorne tried to uphold his end of the bargain?"

"Sure," the Chief of Staff agreed, his tone indifferent, as if the central point were missed. "Styles was a talented talker. He could be useful. *Meet the Press*, *Firefight* on Newsmax, *Sunday Scoop* on XBN. Especially meeting with Democrats. He was the only one on our side they would even think about listening to. At least all of that was true if the vice president was on board with an issue. If he thought it helped *him*. Because for Styles, it was all about taking that next step."

"Next step?"

"Becoming president." Arenberg burst into a deep chortle, simultaneously exuding confidence in his position and disdain for Styles. "Truth is, many days he acted as if he *was* already president."

Tinsley understood the premise: the vice president was ambitious, and in a hurry. Did that make him a potential murderer?

As if reading Aiden's mind, McGehee asked, "Colonel Arenberg, a politician wanting to occupy the Oval Office isn't a crime, is it?"

"Of course not," he answered with a dismissive wave. "Anyone who wants that job needs a lot of drive and passion. And, I might add, a pretty high opinion of himself. What's that old saying, 'Every senator looks in the mirror and sees a president.'"

Arenberg laughed heartily, and Aiden heard several of his fellow jurors join in.

"The thing is," the witness added, turning sharply serious, "there are certain boundaries that mustn't be crossed. There is a difference between earning the job ... and usurping it."

Mandela Briggs stirred, the boom of his voice vibrating through the jury box even before Tinsley noticed his elegant ascent. "Objection, Your Honor." From his table at the far side of the courtroom's well there was urgency, but no panic.

"I believe, Judge, the defense has indulged the prosecution's fantasy of grievance, or vengeance, or whatever it is, quite long enough. This witness is engaging in speculative argument, not actual facts upon which the jury may rely."

Without awaiting permission, McGehee rejoined. "Your Honor, as I'm sure counselor knows, every criminal case involves motive. The Defendant's state of mind is at issue, and this witness has personal knowledge."

"Objection sustained." Judge Bering said immediately.

The cracked whip of her decision awed Tinsley. He had been impressed by her presence from the beginning, and in the first ruling of the trial, sensed she was establishing her authority. Given the judge's Olympian locus atop the bench, the black robe's regal flow, the large, polished gavel ready to strike, he wondered who could doubt her.

"Perhaps, Mr. McGehee," she continued, "we should stick to the defendant's actions."

The prosecutor falsely smiled to mask the rebuke's sting. "Absolutely, Judge." He quickly returned to the witness, who had watched the exchange with bored detachment.

"Mr. Arenberg, did Vice President Styles say or do anything that, as you put it, crossed those boundaries?"

"My gosh, where to begin?" Arenberg paused, as if thinking of his answer, which in fact was well rehearsed. "I'll skip over all of his off-script moments, all of the times he was AWOL when we needed support on an important policy initiative for the American people. The president was often disappointed but always forgiving, but I know that's not why we are here."

Arenberg again consumed the jury box, his face hot, his focus intent. Aiden imagined a volcano's trembling right before an eruption.

"The vice president came to me this past December, the day before the Electoral College was to meet. The day after the Supreme Court ruled in our favor on the Pennsylvania and Texas challenges." That 5-4 decision allowed for alternative slates of Thorne electors, Tinsley recalled. "He was angry." Arenberg paused. "No, that's putting it mildly. He was apoplectic. He said ..."

"Objection!" There was nothing measured about Briggs' protest this time. "Hearsay."

"Mr. McGehee?" the judge asked.

"Offered to show intent, Your Honor."

"Objection overruled." Briggs shook his head mournfully as he retook his seat. Carolyn turned to the jury. "Ladies and Gentlemen, hearsay is a statement made outside of the courtroom, and not under oath." She tarried so as to emphasize what came next. "However, there are many exceptions, including when the statement is offered as possible evidence of motive or intent, irrespective of its truth."

She looked back to McGehee. "That is what I understand the prosecutor is doing here."

"Yes, Judge."

"Okay, then. Members of the jury, as to any out-of-court statement such as this, you are the sole judges of its credibility." She sat back, gesturing to Arenberg, *proceed*.

"Eli said he wouldn't go along with it, that he didn't want to lose his 'legitimacy.'" The chief of staff bracketed the words with his fingers, his tone scornful. "It was all about *him*. And keep in mind, this was a critical juncture for the nation. As I am sure everyone here remembers, people were quite passionate, and here was the vice president threatening to throw gasoline onto the fire."

"Well," McGehee inquired, anticipating the coming cross-examination, "couldn't the defendant simply have been expressing concern over legal process?"

"Absolutely not!" Arenberg growled. "Because the next words out of his mouth were, and I quote, 'Mark my words, Ezra, *your* president won't survive this.' Then, not a week later, Omaha, the CPF offices bombed ..."

"CPF?"

"The Conservative Patriots for Freedom. Major supporters of President Thorne. Seven good people dead, and as the FBI quickly determined, it was *TAC*'s doing."

Aiden looked to the defense lawyer, who wasn't objecting to the sinister implication. Tinsley decided Briggs must fear coming to *TAC*'s defense, thereby strengthening its link to his client.

"Well, Colonel, The Aberdeen Circle's trial is months away. Innocent until proven guilty, right?" McGehee's smirk purposefully punctured his fake generosity.

"I'm not saying he planted the explosives, counselor. What I'm telling you is worse, with all due respect to the fallen."

"And that is?"

"The vice president knew the unrest ravaging our great land. Knew the turmoil. He was at the briefings when our domestic intelligence agencies warned of what was coming, and who was behind it."

Arenberg, jaw clenched, slowly stretched out his arm and pointed, aiming his finger like a spear at Styles. "And he, having sworn an oath to protect and defend this nation, instead protected and defended that vile group of terrorists!"

There it is, Aiden realized. Exactly as Professor Cantwell had instructed in last summer's trial advocacy seminar. All a good prosecution needs, he said more than once, is an easy storyline. No smoking gun required – just a foundation establishing who might not mind seeing the trigger pulled.

"Are you saying, Mr. Arenberg, that the vice president aided The Aberdeen Circle even *after* Omaha?"

"Aided, blocked, tackled ... every conceivable artifice you can imagine to protect them." Arenberg returned to the jurors, his look one of righteous exhaustion. "Look, I get that *TAC* was Eli's oldest alliance, his political powerbase. Politics is a contact sport, and sometimes you need to stand by your friends even when it's tough."

The Colonel balled a fist in front of his chest, knuckles white with intensity. "But this wasn't just politics. This was the security of the United States. We had to get harsh. Everybody remembers how much was on fire. We had to hold the country together.

"And the vice president is out there stabbing us in the back, urging restraint, criticizing our every move, promoting himself as a peacemaker. Even when we learn *TAC* is planning to take down the entire cybergrid, what does he do? He alerts them, making our job that much harder. Every time we took a step, they would find out about it. And who do you think it was that was talking to them?"

Arenberg sighed, laying his hands flat on the arms of the chair, his voice suddenly a whisper. "But none of that compares to Eli sending the assassin, like a damn Trojan horse, right inside the president's tent."

Aiden's jaw dropped, his recovery too slow to hide from the press pool. *Whoa!*

By now, most of America knew the gist of the Sam Kilbrough timeline: well-regarded Secret Service agent becomes part of the vice president's detail, then is promoted to Thorne's, eventually resigning, or fired, a month before the assassination.

This, however, was not part of the endlessly repeated narrative.

"Colonel Arenberg, are you suggesting ..."

"I'm not," he interrupted. "Suggesting, that is. I'm *telling* you what I know. Actual facts upon which the jury can rely." The witness glared at Briggs as he hurled the lawyer's earlier words back at him.

"Go on, sir. Tell us what you know."

Arenberg regarded the panel, the look of a lion about to roar, Tinsley thought.

Fourteen

Everyone assumes I'm rooting for the Black man, Lanta Breckenridge supposed.

In all honesty, yes, Lanta wanted to see Mandela Briggs, a smart, distinguished African American attorney, kick the government's ass. But not for what she branded the racial expectations of those watching.

Rather, it was that slimy, arrogant prosecutor.

The man clearly believed he was lit. The half-smiles and knowing glances and eyebrows arched in artificial astonishment whenever his witness said something he deemed important. If she tried that shit on her 15-year-old pupils, they'd call her out as a total fake. Wouldn't trust her an inch and a half. And here's Mr. U.S. Attorney acting all like we're eatin' out of his hand. *Please!*

Still, she had to admit, this Colonel was the real deal. Breckenridge didn't like him either, but *damn*, he was something. Even though she was no fan of the Thorne administration, it was kinda comforting, in an odd sort of way, to know a dude like this was in charge. Ain't nobody messin' with America if Arenberg's on the front porch.

That wasn't good news for Mr. Briggs, or his client.

They had taken a break mid-morning, and the last thing the judge said, Lanta recalled, was "I will instruct the jury, and this is vital, that you not discuss any of the evidence presented until both sides have completed their case."

Naturally, the first thing the group did when they retired to the jury room was discuss the evidence.

"Did you see the look on his face," the young white girl with the green-tinted hair said two seconds after the bailiff closed the door. Lanta observed the woman crushin' on the vice president during jury selection, surprised she had made it – everything about her screamed radical. But guess ole Mr. McGehee figured he could charm her too.

"I know!" said a bulky Black man Lanta could tell earned his living. Union job, she decided, because he was clearly being paid while here, not at all unhappy about the break from the usual drudgery of his job. "Boss man don't like little Veep, that fo' sure."

Ms. Breckenridge would have swiftly rebuked any of her kids for using such idle dialect. She wanted them to speak intelligently, play the game, improve their odds. Lanta was far beyond scolding her contemporaries, however. They could choose their own path.

"Thas' right," said the tall African American man seated next to Union Guy at the room's long, scuffed up table. "But, damn, he brought the goods, didn't he." Lanta wanted to smack her forehead. This one, dressed in Abercrombie or J. Crew or some such, was clearly an educated man playing to his brother, playing to stereotype. It bugged her.

The two men smiled at one another. She was surprised they didn't fist-bump. No one else reacted, probably, like Lanta, wary of breaching the judge's instructions so quickly. Being honest, though, she agreed with their analysis, tritely put as it was.

By lunch Arenberg had convincingly argued that Elijah Styles was a power-hungry schemer intent on dethroning the president. Worse for the vice president, he stated as absolute fact it was the Defendant himself who inserted the assassin into Thorne's inner ring. Not only that, the confident witness told them it wasn't just a kindly referral of a good employee.

"After the assassination attempt, as you could imagine, we saw to it that every rock was overturned," the Colonel said. "No matter who might be implicated. I'd already learned the vice president maneuvered Kilbrough's reassignment," he said. "Raised suspicions on my part. But I knew it wasn't going to be enough."

"Did you order any further inquiry?" McGehee asked.

"No. This was a Justice Department matter. Not for us to interfere. They reported to me, and I kept the president apprised."

Lanta doubted the angelic hands-off approach. The attorney general, the FBI, all of them worked for the president. If she were Thorne's right hand, she'd be pushing every button to find out who was behind the plot. And Colonel Arenberg was certainly no shrinking violet.

"What did you learn next?" McGehee prodded.

"It was April 21st. I'll never forget that day." This guy, Lanta observed, was normally in full-torque, *move outta my way* mode, but here ... *here* Arenberg really seemed, well, almost human, as if the coming revelation had actually throttled him.

"JoAnn came in, as she had every morning since the event."

"That's JoAnn Degna, Director of the FBI?"

"Right. JoAnn comes in, a real look of horror on her face. This woman is a rock, right? That's why the previous administration appointed her, why we kept her. I can tell, right off, this isn't going to be good. She was, I don't know, hesitant, like she knows she's about to cross the Rubicon."

"What did she tell you?"

"That Elijah Styles had been in constant contact with the assassin, right up until the day before he shot the president."

Initially, Lanta counted herself among the skeptical. She taught her kids all about the Italian Renaissance, Niccolò Machiavelli – even had them read portions of *The Prince*. It was one of her favorite units, and the kids marveled at the diabolical Florentine. But this? I mean, come on, she thought: a sitting vice president trying to knock off his boss so he could take control? Even her little freshmen would have trouble chewing that.

Until now. Until Arenberg recounted, date-by-date, the 43 calls. Probably for dramatic effect, McGehee had him take several minutes to read off each one. Then he revealed "United States Exhibit numbers 7, 8 and 9," the actual printouts of three different service accounts used for the calls.

Forty-three, for Lord's sake!!! Lanta did the math in her head, right before McGehee did it for them: Kilbrough's last day protecting Styles was May 11; by the 18th he was on the president's detail. From then to the shooting, almost one call a week between the Defendant and the would-be killer. What the hell?

"Were you made aware of the substance of these communications?"

"No," Arenberg hissed. "I wanted to call him in," he said, jutting his chin at Styles, "wring his neck and get some answers – maybe not in that order. But ..."

"But?"

"JoAnn said it was part of their ongoing investigation, so I needed to steer clear."

"Were there any transcripts of the calls?" That had been Lanta's first idea.

"She explained to me that all of the calls were made through private carriers, *and* were encrypted." His voice dripped with frustration. "I'd ordered JoAnn to start monitoring his calls after the election, after Eli started going way off the rails."

"She didn't?"

"She said we'd have to get a subpoena, and no judge would issue one against a Vice President of the United States without a ton of probable cause." Arenberg looked at the jurors, moving his head slowly from side to side as if saying, in Lanta's reckoning, *probable cause, huh?*

No surprise then, as they munched their catered sandwiches, soups and salads from a local delicatessen – Judge Carolyn definitely took care of her people – that the conversation focused on a sole topic: *what did Styles and Kilbrough talk about?* The guy Lanta privately named "Banker Dude," a middle-aged white guy who wore a suit every damn day, probably phrased it more in line with everyone's real thinking. "What else *could* they have been talking about."

Now 1:15 in the afternoon, their bellies full, most jurors would confront the urge to nap. Not this group. Not in this case. As Mandela Briggs rose from his seat, purposefully approaching Ezra Arenberg, not even the elderly Mrs. Jackson considered dozing off.

✝✝✝

"Mr. Arenberg," Briggs' low, steady voice began, "you said that, from the very beginning, you opposed Magnus Thorne's consideration of Elijah Styles as his running mate, correct?"

"Correct."

"And you attributed your opposition to, how did you put it, 'a sixth sense.'"

"That's right."

"Now, it was widely reported at the time that the other major contender for the second spot was Senator Pierre Beaufort of Virginia."

"There were many possibilities, Mr. Briggs. Yes, Pierre was one of them."

"Pierre. An old friend of yours who you were quoted as saying, only a few days before the convention, 'would make an excellent choice,' a 'true patriot' and a 'strong fighter for American values.'"

"All true. Senator Beaufort would have made an excellent vice president. Unlike Mayor Styles, he supported almost all of Magnus' policies."

"Pierre Beaufort, your friend, your preferred choice, in an interview with WTVR in Richmond, November 15 last year: 'I'm just not sure what more Black people want from us. My God, the Civil War ended over 150 years ago. At some point, you have to take responsibility and stand on your own two feet.'"

Briggs manner was implacable. "Is that what you mean by a 'true patriot' and a 'strong fighter for American values?'"

"I'm not familiar with that statement."

"Would you like us to play the tape of your old friend saying those words?"

The prosecutor casually rose, his manner denying any real concern. "Your Honor, I object on grounds of relevance. Mr. Beaufort is not on trial here, and while I can understand why Mr. Briggs may want to inject racial animosity into the proceedings," he said, glancing at the jury, "the question is not whether the Senator from Virginia may have spoken intemperately, but whether Mr. Styles conspired to murder the president."

Lanta was offended, though not in the way the defense intended. She found Beaufort's old school racism sickening, of course, and Arenberg's support for the guy was not a plus. But did the Black lawyer really think anyone, especially the six *Black* jurors, was fooled by his naked appeal to race? She hated to admit it, but McGehee was right: that's not why they were here.

"Mr. Briggs?"

"Thank you, Judge. I wholeheartedly agree, Senator Beaufort is not the issue. Mr. Arenberg's credibility is, however. And if you will allow me some leeway, I believe I can demonstrate that his 'sixth sense' may be a bit warped when it comes to my client."

Carolyn Bering pondered the defense lawyer's rather opaque justification. She decided to give him the narrowest of paths forward. "Objection sustained. Mr. Briggs, let's move on from Senator Beaufort."

"Of course, Your Honor." He didn't seem the least surprised or disappointed by her ruling, and Lanta wondered why. Wasn't it pretty much a face plant, an awful way to begin the defense of his client's life?

"In contrast Mr. Arenberg my client, in your opinion, paled in comparison. Arrogant. Dismissive. Not the same kind of 'true patriot' and 'fighter for American values' as your old friend, right?

"It's true, I was not a fan, but I don't recall saying anything about his patriotism." The witness paused, then in a lower, stern register, added, "but knowing what we do now, I sure wish I had."

Lanta cringed. *Ouch.*

"Perhaps, sir, but you did indeed have quite a bit to say about Mr. Styles, very publicly, and very much on the record, didn't you?"

"As Governor Thorne's campaign manager, I obviously had a lot to say about all of his opponents."

"Indeed. For example, in remarks to the Birmingham Chamber of Commerce, you said, 'Mayor Eli, as he likes to be called, took six weeks off after the birth of his surrogate child. I guess to breastfeed.' Are we getting closer to your sixth sense?"

"Oh, come on, Mr. Briggs. It was a joke. Politics is a contact sport. And actually, if you quoted the whole thing, I was objecting to his support for imposing a mandatory leave policy on small businesses. Besides, I'm sure your client has heard much worse."

"Much worse, Mr. Arenberg. Including from you. To *The Denver Post*, 'the problem with the mayor of Dallas is, he's very light on policy, very light on experience – a fellow you could say is very light in his loafers when we need a leader who can wear combat boots.'"

Arenberg chuckled. Briggs smiled at him, contemptuously.

"Fair to say, sir, that your objections to Mr. Styles have more to do with your prejudice than his policies?"

"Not at all, Mr. Briggs. I could care less about his *lifestyle*. What I care about is his loyalty, to the president ... to this country."

Briggs had no delusion Arenberg would admit to being a bigot. Seed planted, he simply moved on.

"Let's talk about Sam Kilbrough. Did you offer any objection to his promotion from protecting the vice president to guarding your boss?"

"A little below my paygrade, counselor," Arenberg snorted. "I wouldn't have even been aware of the change."

"You travel with the president extensively. Didn't you notice this new face?"

"I'm sure I did, but so what. Agents swap in and out. We rely on the director to supervise and handle all of that."

"I see. And the Director of the U.S. Secret Service was who?"

Lanta saw the Colonel's eyebrows nudge up, just a fraction, as if he were suddenly wary. "Daniel Drury." Then she noticed Arenberg tense, a decision made. "You know, your client's chief of police when he was mayor of Dallas."

Briggs leaned over his podium and cocked his ear toward the witness. "And why would you mention that part of his resume, Mr. Arenberg?"

"I think you know."

This was *gooooooood*, Lanta said to herself, a straight up street fight, two bad asses circling one another.

"I'm not sure I do. I am confident, however, the jury would love to hear what you are thinking."

There was that hesitation again, she observed. The Colonel didn't trust Briggs, but badly wanted to share. Lanta had no doubt, though, someone as confident as this man would barrel ahead.

"Drury and Styles knew each other well. *Very* well. It was Eli who got him the appointment. Pestered us like crazy after the election four years ago, during the transition, talking the guy up until Governor Thorne finally told me to make it happen, get Styles off his back."

Glancing to her left and right, Lanta figured they all knew what was coming next.

"And Drury is the one who moved Kilbrough," Arenberg hissed. "Inserted him into the president's team, just like his old boss and benefactor asked."

"Let me see if I've got this straight. You're now saying the Director of the Secret Service was in on this grand conspiracy of yours? That he promoted Sam Kilbrough as part of a plot to murder the president?"

"No, I'm saying he did what Eli told him to do. I'm not saying he knew the plan."

"So, Director Drury was a useful idiot, or at least an unwitting accomplice. Who else are you saying was part of this grand scheme, whether they knew it or not? The agents on duty March 30? The president's scheduler? His secretary? *You*, perhaps?"

Lanta could visualize the steam escaping from the Colonel's ears.

"You're twisting my words, counselor."

"Well, let's look at more of your words," Briggs said contemptuously. "Earlier you told these folks," sweeping his hand toward the jury box, "Vice President Styles was 'out there stabbing us in the back, urging restraint, criticizing our every move, promoting himself as a peacemaker.' Then you insinuated he was giving The Aberdeen Circle inside information to help them – how did you put it? – 'take down the entire cybergrid.'"

Briggs squinted at the witness. To Ms. Breckenridge, it was the same *Are you really sure you want to go there?* look she sometimes directed at a misbehaving student.

"Let's unpack those comments, Mr. Arenberg. First, pleas for restraint, statements against violence, calls for peace ... those are quite admirable goals, aren't they? I mean, you're not advocating riots, brutality and vigilante justice, are you?"

"Oh, come on, Mr. Briggs," the Colonel huffed. "You know damned well that's not what we're talking about." He jabbed his finger at the defense lawyer. "Styles was defending them, undercutting law enforcement, and *that* put a lot of innocent people at risk! Can you imagine planes dropping out of the sky because Air Traffic Control lost radar and comms, or if financial institutions and stock markets were frozen, or worse, electronically raided!"

The more Arenberg surged, the calmer Briggs became. Lanta studied the evolution, the lawyer pleased, relaxed as his adversary spiraled. She looked over to the prosecutor. His normally unworried countenance was, to her, a slight shade darker.

"Colonel, you really want to add crashing aircraft and bank robbery to the vice president's rap sheet?" Briggs chuckled. "How about we stick to the facts. The truth is, the cybergrid attack of which you speak never happened, did it?"

"Only thanks to the hard work of Homeland Security and the FBI."

"And did anyone at either Homeland Security or the FBI ever give you a shred of evidence that the vice president obstructed or interfered with their efforts?"

Arenberg smiled. For the first time in a while, Lanta guessed, he was going to throw a punch. "You mean, other than his multiple phone calls to the Aberdeen terrorists? Other than the mastermind behind the planned attack being, yet again, one of his people?"

Now it was Briggs' turn to act at ease, his face a cool mirror of tranquility. "Ah. I was wondering when you would bring him up. You speak, of course, about Dr. William Van Den Wolk, once chief of technology for then Mayor Styles."

"The very same," Arenberg said with a Cheshire grin. "Your client placed calls to him as well. A *lot* of recent calls!"

"Uh huh." Briggs studied his notes. "Three times between the election and Dr. Van Den Wolk's arrest."

"At least."

"And the nature of these calls, Mr. Arenberg?"

"I wasn't on them, but ..."

"... But the third one was recorded by the FBI, at your insistence, and you've read the transcript." Briggs lifted a thin folder, holding it aloft. "Correct?"

Lanta perceived Arenberg shifting back into neutral. "You obviously know all about it."

"We'll share this with the jury. Defendant's Exhibit 44, Your Honor."

"Without objection," Carolyn looked at McGehee, who said nothing. Most documents had been either agreed to or ruled upon before trial. "Admitted."

"Before I hand it to them, sir, should we read portions aloud together, or would you agree with me that Vice President Styles was trying to learn of Van Den Wolk's intentions, specifically warning him against any illegal actions."

The Colonel burst out laughing, catching himself with an apologetic wave to the judge. "Of *course* he did. He obviously knew the call was being monitored. He was covering his tracks."

"And you know this because you were privy to the first two calls as well?"

The witness frowned. "Those were before Director Degna got permission for a wiretap."

"Thus, as far as you are aware, the first two calls were also aimed at preventing any nefarious actions by Van Den Wolk."

"I doubt it," Arenberg snapped.

"Well, this case is all about 'reasonable doubt,' isn't it? Let's cut to the chase." Briggs folded his hands on the podium and leaned toward the witness. "You cannot provide this jury with a single instance when Mr. Styles aided any plot to attack America's cybergrid, can you, Mr. Arenberg?"

The Colonel glared. Briggs didn't blink. Finally, "Other than common sense, no."

The defense counsel nodded in satisfaction, signaling victory in case the jurors missed it.

"And similarly, the calls to Sam Kilbrough, you've already admitted *no* knowledge as to their subject matter." It was not a question, and Arenberg didn't answer. "Your speculation is simply the number. Forty-three. Right?"

"That and what I said before. It was your client who got Kilbrough access to the president in the first place."

"But in terms of evidence."

"I don't have firsthand knowledge of what they discussed, no. Just the outcome, which was President Thorne being shot."

Briggs tilted his head, giving Arenberg the *I know you can do better than that* expression with which teacher Breckenridge was so familiar.

"Other than sinister conclusions, Mr. Arenberg, did you ever consider alternative reasons for the vice president to keep in touch with Sam Kilbrough?"

"Like what? Like they were best pals or something?" The Colonel snickered at the jury, a couple of whom reciprocated with a chuckle of their own. "I've heard rumors counselor, but we can still be sure of at least one thing they were talking about."

"Did you ever consider that, perhaps, in their three years together, they formed some kind of bond? That Mr. Styles found his service exemplary? That he was just as surprised as you and everyone else about what eventuated?"

"Now who's speculating, Mr. Briggs?"

The lawyer smiled, satisfied the witness was on favorable terrain.

Rampart

"What do you know about Sam Kilbrough's younger brother?" Briggs' tone was sharp, almost scolding.

"Who?" Arenberg's brow furrowed. Clearly off guard, Lanta observed.

"Conor Kilbrough. Age 33. Down Syndrome. Did you somehow miss that in the exhaustive coverage of the attempted assassin's background?"

"That's not something I recall."

"How about Tippy Carver?"

The witness chair creaked as the Colonel shifted uncomfortably.

"You'll have to enlighten me."

"I'm surprised you don't remember the vice president's niece. It seems that during the first campaign, after Mayor Styles joined the ticket, you demanded he participate in a commercial focused on her. Wanted to spend millions putting it on every platform."

"Sorry, Mr. Briggs, that was a long time, and we had hundreds of Ads."

"Tippy also lives with Down." To Lanta's eye, skilled at detecting the mood shifts of her young charges, the Colonel's had just dimmed. "You told my client it would help soften the Republican image if he leaned into that relationship. Ring familiar?"

"No." Arenberg adjusted his suit jacket. Lanta noticed a fresh dew-like glisten on his forehead. "As I said, that campaign is ancient history."

"Okay, then how about last October. Very close election. You certainly remembered Tippy then! Brought the idea up again, *demanding* my client cut an Ad. Do you deny *that*?"

"Objection," McGehee proclaimed loudly. "Irrelevant. Campaign advertisements are neither here nor there. Besides, Colonel Arenberg is not on trial here, Mr. Styles is."

"Exactly, Your Honor." Briggs spun toward her, resolute. "Perhaps I might tie these facts to the witness' concern over the telephone calls."

"Please do," Carolyn advised, leaving no doubt it had better happen quickly.

"Thank you," he said, a slight bow. "Mr. Arenberg, you are familiar with the VPDS?"

The witness puzzled over the acronym for a second, then recognition lit. "Yes, the Vice President's Daily Schedule."

Briggs approached, handing him a bound stack of pages, thick, premium stock it appeared. "Can you identify Defendant's Exhibit 33?"

Arenberg made a show of studying the documents, then, "Yes, it's the VPDS for," he flipped back to the cover, "September of last year."

"If you would be so kind as to turn to September 17, page 32, I believe." The witness glared, pondering a way to refuse the request before reluctantly complying. "Yes?"

"Could you share with the ladies and gentlemen of the jury where Mr. Styles was that evening?"

"A fund raiser. Charity fund raiser." The Colonel tossed the pages in a tangled heap on the small shelf in front of him. This was someone used to *giving* orders.

"For?"

"Center for Down Syndrome Values."

Lanta wondered if she were the only one noting a shift in the dynamic. To her right, she caught the two archetypal Black brothers look at one another, eyes wide. Banker dude pouched his lips in an *Ooooooo* gesture.

"And in U.S. Exhibits 7 to 9, the Vice President's private phone carrier records, did you happen to notice how many of those calls occurred *before* this fundraiser?

"I did not," Arenberg scowled.

Briggs returned to his notes. "A majority, Sir, with 11 just in the week before the event. Do you dispute that?"

"No."

"So, in truth Mr. Arenberg, if one wishes to honestly compile theories on why my client and Mr. Kilbrough remained in contact, it could be they'd developed a bond over their years of professional association. It could be Mr. Styles remains in touch with a lot of associates from his past. It could be he and Mr. Kilbrough were plotting how to murder the president, even though no one knew what turn the election would take."

Okay, sounds ridiculous when you put it that way, Lanta agreed, unless Briggs was playing them as he sighed, stepping from the lectern, hands folded plaintively in front of him. "Or, could it be that they shared a very serious, very worthy common interest?"

Briggs let the question, the *assertion*, hang midair. The Colonel did not bite.

"Nothing more with this witness, Your Honor."

Everyone found the clock. It read 4:48.

"Members of the jury, we will continue tomorrow at 9 a.m. Please remember my instructions not to seek out any information about this case ..." *As if we could*, Lanta mused. "... or to discuss it with anyone, including amongst yourselves."

Bering stood, straightening her robe as the lawyers jumped to their feet. Lanta and her fellows had by now learned the routine as well, standing as Carolyn descended the steps, and disappeared.

Fifteen

Carolyn Bering was satisfied with the trial's first day of evidence, the scrum over Ezra Arenberg. The world outside – the talking heads, influencers, politicos, RAGE red hatters and progressive *Stylites* – those folks could debate the merits of who won what point, armchair legal strategies and the odds of conviction. Her job was more fraught, shackled by real consequence: to safely guide the ship of justice into harbor. Day One serviced this aim quite well, as she set both pace and boundaries, establishing parameters by her measured words, more so with her steely composure.

In many ways, however, today's encore would be as important. With the participants settling into the war's routine, temptations born of familiarity loomed. A juror nodding off. The press pool stretching decorum. The lawyers testing their sense of entitlement. As a judge, she understood these as part of a case's life – the frustrations of the long slog – and her role was to avoid those shoals, which Carolyn would do by exerting consistency, projecting gravitas and demanding excellence.

As an example, the transparency that is democracy's oxygen, as well as the Constitution's Sixth Amendment, require a public trial. So, in addition to the three-member press pool and sketch artist, she allowed 50 members of the public, rotated by lottery, to fill the pews each day – a valued ticket of high entertainment. Rather than leave their behavior to chance, Carolyn instructed her law clerk to draft a one-page agreement, peppered with ALL CAPS and ***bold, italicized font***, admonishing each attendee of the severe consequences of inappropriate behavior, defined in broad strokes as anything beyond silent observation. Debbie made certain they were duly executed after Bailiff Bankhead cross-checked names, addresses and phone numbers.

Thus in control, Bering surveyed her courtroom, perfectly imitating memories of her mother's exacting inspections of Carolyn's childhood abodes. The well's floor was blemished with scuffs and chips from decades of heels and briefcases, its original white shadowed by the dusky grime a weekly mopping and monthly polishing only deferred. The scars and smudges of time also marked the balustrade, walls, and benches. The ornate chandelier offered a yellow haze filtered through slowly baked dust coating its glass bulbs.

This was a cavernous space, but like her childhood apartments, everything had and was in its place. As with Rose, the daughter knew what was necessary, and what was expected. There and then, here and now, order ameliorated chaos.

Yet, Carolyn discovered over time that her domain's physical features only lived as a reflection of the characters seated within its walls. Not so much the anonymous assortment on the benches: here today, gone tomorrow. Nor even the more familiar crew, such as her bailiff, court reporter and trusty administrator. Rather, like any established Broadway venue, the vibe could only be fully appreciated through the current show's company. The intrigue of that red-headed legal assistant's poorly hidden tattoos. The U.S. attorney's leading man swagger. Mandela Briggs' refined grace. The sexual tension on the prosecution side. Yes, Carolyn noticed the cautious glances, the careful avoidance of touching, between McGehee's handsome young associate and his striking teammate.

The large room's current assortment of characters buzzed. All we lack, the judge decided, was Tim Truss, that prolific author of action thrillers he pumped out twice a year – a week or two on *The New York Times* Best Seller list, forgotten as quickly as the cases on Carolyn's docket. She occasionally succumbed to his easily devoured paperbacks, the last one, now that she thought about it, featuring a vice president violently thrust into the seat of power, reluctantly grappling with a country on disaster's brink. *Ruse or Revolution*, was it?

The *Ruse* hero, though, was two-dimensional, a cutout of courage, virtue and, after stumbling onto his path, a decisive, sword-wielding sage. Her defendant? Carolyn had watched Styles closely for two weeks now, still unable to crack his code.

When President Thorne asserted dubious "Emergency Powers" to take over the nation's internet infrastructure, quashing social media and repressing the dissemination of "news" for 24 harrowing hours, it was his vice president who stood in opposition. Brave, said his acolytes, a fighter for free expression, a rampart against tyranny. "Traitor!" cried his detractors, a fool who refused to appreciate the mortal threat *TAC*, or whoever conceived the supposed Great Grid Attack, posed to America's survival.

The Judge didn't see Styles as either. Or anything, at this point, other than an enigma. Did he seek to murder the president and take power for himself, as the prosecution so confidently asserts? Maybe, Carolyn conceded. Somewhere deep down, however, she feared it was the wrong question.

†††

"Mr. McGehee, please call your next witness," the judge instructed at precisely nine o'clock.

"The United States," all fifty of them, the prosecutor's confident tone made clear, "call Mr. Daniel Drury."

A very tall, trim man in a well-tailored navy-blue suit walked from the front benches, through the swinging gate and to the witness box. He remained standing, familiar with the routine. Drury towered over the seated judge, even though her platform was two feet higher than his.

As she swore him in, Carolyn noticed the former Secret Service director had a rather extensive overbite, for which he somehow compensated with a large, confident smile. His bearing was, to her surprise, nothing like the grim, stone-faced stereotype of sunglass-clad, submachine gun toting presidential guardians.

"Mr. Drury, how is it that you came to head the United States Secret Service?" McGehee jumped right in, displaying none of the cordiality allotted Mr. Arenberg.

"Well," the witness began with a bashful grin, "I was appointed by President Thorne, and then confirmed by the Senate."

The prosecutor frowned. "Obviously, sir. The same president who fired you earlier this year, right?" Sidney didn't wait for reply. "What we would like to understand is, *why* were you picked? Why *you*?"

Drury looked a bit puzzled. A good actor, Carolyn thought, as surely the personal attorney he hired left no doubt about the questions to come. "If you mean why did the president choose me, I can say we'd never actually met, but I have to believe he thought I was the most qualified man for the assignment."

McGehee shook his head ever so slightly. "Let's try it this way. What was your job immediately before that one?"

"Chief of Police for the City of Dallas," he beamed. Sidney walked to the jury box, offering them a gentle curl at one corner of his mouth, as in *Now we're getting somewhere*.

"And you were appointed to *that* position by none other than *this* man," McGehee pointed at Styles, "the defendant."

"Yes sir." Drury acknowledged his former boss with unapologetic amiability.

"The two of you had been friends for many years before that, correct?"

Drury pondered the adjective, his forehead furrowed even as his mouth maintained its pleasant pose. "We had known each other, I believe, three years."

"You were Chief of the Las Vegas Police Department when Mr. Styles first approached you."

"Yes sir."

"He was, at that time, with Borgen Railey."

"Yes sir."

"He recruited you."

Drury tilted his head, again offering the politest version of perplexity.

"I'm not sure what you mean, Mr. McGehee. I'm happy, though, to explain why Mr. Styles contacted me."

The prosecutor wasn't about to give the witness that kind of free rein. "Mr. Styles wanted you because of your tech expertise," he asserted, turning to cue Mandy with a thrust of his chin. She rose and delicately retrieved a 3x5-foot foamboard, striding to a waiting easel with the head up, shoulders back grace of a model. There, elegantly, the Vanna White of the courtroom fixed a poster-sized blowup of an old *TechBent* online cover.

ROBOCOP, declared the enormous font behind a much younger Drury, who sported the iconic helmet and breastplate of the old Sci-Fi hero, but whose buckteeth rendered him easily recognizable. Carolyn suppressed a grin.

"Your emphasis on cyber policing, on predictive modeling, catching criminals *before* they commit a crime, that's what caught Mr. Styles' eye, correct?"

"That's true. Actually, more *Minority Report* than this," Drury smiled, indicating the poster. "But Borgen was definitely interested in developing what we were doing, expanding it. They set up an entire unit devoted to what they called 'extrapolative enforcement.'"

"And while this was evolving at BR, Eli Styles left the firm, ran for mayor of Dallas, and once elected, you were one of his first hires, correct?"

"He did call me early on, and it seemed like a natural fit, I thought. The Borgen model, which went way beyond what we did in Vegas, was ready for a test run, and I thought it an exciting opportunity."

McGehee signaled Mandy with his eyes. Ready, she retraced her imaginary catwalk, replacing Drury's fun photo with the gritty mugshot of a disheveled man whose heavy gray stubble, wild hair and sunken eyes colored him shadowy and miserable.

"And who is this?" the prosecutor asked, pointing over his shoulder.

Drury sagged, his happy expression evaporating as he quickly glanced at the image, avoiding it. "That would be Professor Van Den Wolk."

"You don't seem super excited to see him again, Mr. Drury."

The witness opened his mouth as if to speak, but said nothing.

"This was another star of Mayor Styles' team, his new chief of technology, with whom you commenced to work very, very closely, correct?"

"The mayor directed us to work together," Drury snapped, his clear reluctance an attempt to shield against the criminal staring from the tripod.

"On what, exactly?"

"Implementing a pilot of the Enhanced Law Enforcement Program."

"Ah, yes, ELEP." The prosecutor retrieved a document from the corner his table. "Can you identify United States Exhibit 15," he said, handing it to the witness.

"Yes, it's a memorandum from Professor Van Den Wolk to Mayor Styles."

McGehee smiled at an obvious omission. "Is anyone copied on it?"

Drury frowned. "Me."

"And you had a big part in creating it, right?"

"I ... I contributed my knowledge of our efforts in Las Vegas, and my years of policing experience." Drury turned to the jury, almost pleading. "But I'm not a computer scientist, or a programmer."

McGehee raised his eyebrows. "I see," he said flatly. "In any event, as I understand it, ELEP was designed to sniff out crimes before they happened, right?"

The witness hesitated, knowing where this was headed. "Yes."

"It did this by vacuuming up and sifting through communications of every kind, no matter the source, no matter the type, correct?"

"It's not like we were reading people's private e-mails..."

"...Not you, personally, but your supercomputers certainly were."

"Only in a manner of speaking," Drury started, defensively.

"Every e-mail, every text."

"Well..."

"Every post on social media, every phone call. Everything was scooped up and analyzed, wasn't it, Mr. Drury, as long as it was sent, posted or received within the city limits of Dallas."

"Theoretically."

"Uh-huh." The prosecutor considered his prey. The witness seemed to think exposure of these vast privacy intrusions was the objective, to demonize him and vicariously Eli Styles. A nice windfall, but McGehee was after something much more deadly to the defendant.

"And to make this program work, Mr. Drury, isn't it true you needed complete control of the city's internet infrastructure?"

The witness' expression screwed into genuine angst.

"For example," the lawyer prodded, "Let's say ELEP thought it sniffed a drug deal about to go down. In order to facilitate catching the bad guys, it might be helpful to regulate the flow of information, to take over the criminals' devices without them knowing. Maybe stop a warning from getting to a dealer, or send false instructions to a bagman."

"Or to protect innocent victims," he answered, rushing to add, "But never, ever without a court order." Drury still didn't understand where this was heading.

"Sure," the prosecutor appeared to concede. Then he tilted his head, his handsome features adopting an earnestness so piercing, Carolyn thought, it served more as a warning to the witness ... *Be careful how you answer this next one, sir.* The judge noticed the jurors coming to the same conclusion as they tensed and leaned in.

"Technically speaking, though, Mr. Drury, ELEP allowed you to take full control of Dallas' cyber world any time you wanted."

Futility took hold of the former Secret Service chief, his face telegraphing the debate behind it: Quibble and showcase an unnecessary defensiveness, or admit to implied abuses you never considered. "We could have," was Drury's compromise.

"You set up access to every internet service provider allowing you to make, or stop, any transaction or communication coming into or going out of their servers handling the city's digital traffic, correct?"

"Yes."

"And according to Exhibit 15, the Van Den Wolk memo, you could stop a text, reroute a deposit, hijack a phone call, *anything*, instantaneously, before you even notified the carrier of what you had done."

Drury didn't like the sinister spin, but understood the danger of sparring over accusations that, while misleading, were nonetheless true. Frowning, he moved his mouth close to the thin microphone arcing up from the witness box. "Yes," he spat.

"Practically speaking, you could command the entire digital system, if you or Mayor Styles found it necessary."

The witness grimaced, his patience running thin. "That's quite far-fetched, but hypothetically, again, with a court order, maybe."

The prosecutor retrieved the memo from Drury, stepping back across the faux marble floor as he flipped its pages, finding what he needed. "Here," he commanded, thrusting it back at his target, "for the record, on page 19, please read paragraph 14.03."

Carolyn observed McGehee gather the jurors with his eyes while the witness found his place. Every one of them sat erect, waiting for something obviously important.

The former USSS director cleared his throat, hesitant, no longer the forceful presence who originally took the stand. "'14.03,'" he began. "'In the event of an emergency declared by the mayor pursuant to his powers in Chapter 18, Section 106 of the City Code of Dallas, the chief of police shall have authority to requisition and operate, in the interest of public safety, all servers, hubs, routers, junctions or other such devices as may be used by communications carriers, as defined by Code Chapter 24, Section 2, to manage the distribution of information.'"

"Wow," the prosecutor grinned. "That's a mouthful. Would you mind telling the ladies and gentlemen of the jury what that all means?"

Drury stiffened. "It means that during a city-wide emergency, the mayor could facilitate the flow of critical data, to keep our citizens safe."

"Because ELEP gave you the practical ability to control the entire digital grid," McGehee retorted, then snapped his fingers, "just like that."

The witness and the lawyer stared at one another, a silent exchange full of unmasked bitterness.

Finally, the prosecutor broke the standoff. "You said earlier you were neither a computer scientist nor a programmer, correct?"

"Yes."

"And so, the actual creator of this system of absolute control, from a tech perspective, was your memo's co-author, Dr. William Van Den Wolk, yes?"

Drury shifted uncomfortably, not enjoying the reunion. "It was *his* memorandum, Mr. McGehee, to which I contributed my policing expertise. And, as you said, Dr. Van Den Wolk was the one who contributed all of the engineering and programming expertise."

"Brilliant man, right?"

"I know he was well regarded in his field."

"Educated at MIT, Stanford professor, consultant to Microsoft, Google, pretty much all of Silicon Valley."

"I haven't studied his resume, sir," the witness snarled. "As I said, he was well regarded."

"And you two worked closely together for, what, three years?"

"Only on ELEP, which in the scheme of things wasn't much time. As police chief, I was pretty busy with other things."

Carolyn watched McGehee smile at Drury's rhetorical dancing, then scanned her jurors, who also easily diagnosed the witness' attempt to escape guilt by association.

"You are aware that Dr. Van Den Wolk subsequently did work for The Aberdeen Circle, during the year before the attempted murder of President Thorne."

"That was long after we had both left the City of Dallas." There was a glisten of sweat on Drury's forehead, which he unconsciously wiped with the back of his hand. "We haven't spoken in years."

"The defendant," McGehee gestured at Styles, "is the one who put you and the esteemed professor together, right?"

"That's correct." Then, urgently, "We had never met before."

"And do you know who put Dr. William Van Den Wolk and The Aberdeen Circle together?"

"I don't."

McGehee adopted a quizzical expression, turned to Styles, then back to the witness. "As Director of the United States Secret Service, surely you were familiar with the threatening behavior of many *TAC* supporters toward the president. Their constant vitriol. Their hatred toward him."

"We monitored them closely, of course."

"And you knew your former collaborator, the professor, was aligned with *TAC*."

"I may have. I don't recall."

The prosecutor let the feeble response hang, then shrugged. "Let's cover one other thing before we go, Mr. Drury."

Finally, Carolyn thought. The reason she had thought the former director was on the stand in the first place.

"Who shot President Thorne?"

The witness recoiled at the simple question's impact.

"Sam Kilbrough."

"Barely a month before the assassination, Sam Kilbrough had actually been on the president's protective detail, was he not?"

"Yes," Drury responded quietly. This was the drubbing he had anticipated.

"Assigned to the president's detail by ... you."

Carolyn watched the witness twitch. She had seen this before, the calculation, the search for an exit. Would he fence? Would he wilt? Or would he just do the prosecutor's work for him? Despite all Elijah Styles had done for Daniel Drury, Carolyn's analysis of the man gave her a good idea.

"I made the assignment," the witness muttered, then added, a new force in his tone, "Because the vice president instructed me to."

McGehee nodded solemnly, then returned to his table. "No further questions, Judge."

None needed, she thought, and glanced at the defendant. Not surprisingly, the practiced politician was expressionless at the betrayal.

It was, after all, the truth.

Sixteen

Briggs was sick to his stomach, only partially from hunger – he'd choked down a croissant for breakfast and half an energy bar for lunch. Mostly it was anxiety, and the torturous exhaustion of being pummeled. This was the biggest case of his career, with the highest profile client, and he, they, were being destroyed.

As Mandela fantasized running home from the courtroom, home, to hide under a reassuring flannel comforter, he weakly reminded himself that the unfolding disaster was perfectly natural, the assigned order of things: the prosecutor always went first, calling its best witnesses, presenting the government's strongest evidence, molding the jurors' minds toward the sensibility and inevitability of conviction. Only later would he, as defense lawyer, be able to impose his client's agenda, rebutting the prosecution's case like a woodsman hacking at sturdy tree, assumptions splintering, piece by piece, chunk by chunk. Until McGehee rested his case, Briggs knew he had barely a slingshot, taking whatever well aimed potshots he could to ding or scratch the polish of the prosecution's presentation.

So it had been with Drury. "Eli is a great guy," he said during their hours of meetings before trial. "I want to help. These charges are ... *preposterous*!" Yet the ex-director, for whose career Styles had done so much, melted under McGehee's glare. By the time the U.S. attorney passed the witness, Mandela was left mopping up a murky puddle, the vice president rendered a conniving, scheming Dr. Evil. Drury's reluctance to feed the narrative made his admissions sting all the more.

"Let's go back to your initial meeting with Mr. Styles," Briggs had started his cross. There were too many bile-spewing leaks to repair them all, and Mandela knew the jurors would tune out the longer he tried. Start with the worst, long experience told him, and work your way up the list. "This was over a decade ago. He was a projects guy at Borgen Railey, trying to develop a commercial product, right?"

"Yes."

"Not a public official like you – Mr. Styles was years from entering politics. You ran the Las Vegas police department. Why even meet with this nobody, Chief Drury?"

No one had called him "Chief" in quite some time. Drury showed his buck teeth, smiling for the first time in a while. "He was persistent. And, BR had a lot of financial ties to our city ..." the witness chuckled, "... which he made clear to my staff."

"And in this young businessman's hard-won audience, what did you and private citizen Styles discuss?"

"He had seen some of the reporting on our early efforts with what, much later, would become ELEP. He floated the idea of a partnership, said BR was interested in developing it with us. You know, 'if this works, we'll have something valuable to sell.'"

"Knowing how tight city government budgets are, I assume the concept of private funding was attractive to you?"

"Very." Drury underlined his reply with a solemn nod.

"The two of you continued to visit?"

"Many meetings, many. Over the course of a year until we eventually made a deal."

Mandela molded his features, straining to force wrinkles onto his smooth forehead. The next step would require as serious a façade as possible. "And at what point," he had asked, "did Mr. Styles reveal his plot to use your embryonic technology to overthrow the government of the United States?"

It was his best play, Briggs calculated: inflate the prosecutor's claim to absurdity, exaggerating it into such caricature that it burst, more outlandish than awful.

"I mean," he pumped away, "surely that was my whip smart client's intent from the get-go. Develop this sinister software, become mayor, run for president and lose so he could be *vice* president, then groom a Manchurian secret service agent to shoot the president, then use your technical magic to control the entire country while he puts his feet up in the Oval Office."

Drury's mouth was half open, and from the corner of his eye Mandela caught several jurors giggling under their breath.

"Your honor," McGehee stood, affecting boredom, "I'm fairly certain there was no question there, so I'll object to counsel's twisted misrepresentation of the people's case."

"We are in agreement on the 'twisted' part, Judge," Briggs shot back, "but surely my client's intent, as Director Drury understood it, is highly relevant."

Mandela could tell Judge Bering was amused, despite her stone countenance.

"Please rephrase, Mr. Briggs," she allowed.

"Certainly." He returned to the witness. No, Mr. Styles did not express any wicked intentions, just a venture capital guy exploring a good idea. No, as mayor, he never hijacked ELEP for personal gain, or played any role in its use. No, as Secret Service Director, nothing crossed Drury's desk linking the defendant to any plots against the president. And, no, the witness saw nothing nefarious about Styles endorsing Kilbrough for a promotion – only a superior supporting the career of one of his best. And make no mistake, Drury added, "Kilbrough's record was sterling."

It wasn't much. Mandela didn't come close to uncovering all the seeds planted by the prosecution. Nor was such the goal. Stop the hemorrhaging. That was it. Or as much of the bleeding as possible, anyway.

And before Briggs could catch his breath, as Drury was still stepping out of the witness box, the government's next witness, Holt Hancock, entered the well.

As Hancock found his mark with the easy glide of a natural athlete, Mandela decided Hollywood central casting, not the president, cast him for Director of the Cybersecurity and Infrastructure Security Agency. The man pulled Briggs back to high school, where Mandela had been a highly recruited halfback until he tore his Achilles. Yet even at his peak he remained in the shadow of star QB Ricardo Lule. The fact he remembered Lule's name spoke volumes. To Briggs, this was Hancock: the idolized signal caller, the guy everyone wanted to cheer for, the guy everyone wanted to be ... *The Guy.*

Hancock's thick, wavy mop of brownish blonde hair and aqua blue eyes accented apple cheeks boyishly blushed. The witness was indeed young for such a critical post, 36, but considering CISA's mission – protecting the nation's digital infrastructure – it seemed to fit a fresh-faced eagle scout with technical dexterity.

Sadly for the defense, there was nothing juvenile about Hancock's testimony. After 90 minutes of it, Mandela was convinced the jury loved him – he could almost hear the crowd cheering, *Lule! Lule! Lule!* Worse, they *believed* Hancock, swooning over his every word.

He declared Professor William Van Den Wolk a genius, a *legend* to computer scientists like himself, one who disappointedly gravitated to the Dark Side. Van Den Wolk's groundbreaking work in Dallas, ELEP, was beyond visionary. Properly used, it could have had enormous benefits for society, the witness lamented.

And then, after the prosecutor guided him through all the ways VDW and The Aberdeen Circle allegedly plotted to cripple the nation, with the vice president's fingerprints all over the crime scene, came a final, subtle, closing line of questions.

"Five years ago, Director Hancock, did you vote in your home state South Carolina's Republican primary?"

"Of course."

"After Iowa and New Hampshire, it was down to a two-man race, Governor Thorne versus Mayor Styles. Correct?"

"Yes."

"And for whom did you vote?"

Briggs couldn't have jumped faster. He didn't know the answer, but was sure McGehee did. "Objection, your Honor! It's both irrelevant, and a gross breach of the sanctity of the ballot."

Bering turned to the prosecutor, who calmly replied. "It goes to credibility, Judge, the witness' state of mind throughout all the scandalous events he's described for the jury."

She sighed, confident of the correct call and equally certain it wouldn't matter. "Director Hancock, you have a privacy right in the secrecy of your electoral choices. You may answer, but you are not required to do so."

It was Hancock's turn to appear despondent. His eyes downcast, he pondered his answer – or, at least, pretended to, as Mandela had no doubt this was all rehearsed.

Finally, the witness looked up, training his youthful, earnest gaze directly at the vice president. Barely above a whisper, he pronounced in his faint Southern drawl, "Elijah Styles. I voted for Elijah Styles. He was energetic, not all that much older than me, innovative as heck. I thought he was the future. I *believed* in him."

Hancock appeared genuinely distraught, an idealist with a torn heart, not one but two of his heroes betraying their potential, their country, and his own hopes.

"Pass the witness," McGehee declared, spinning on his heels, clearly pleased.

Briggs' stomach grumbled on cue, with *Lule! Lule! Lule!* churning in his head.

"Mr. Hancock," Mandela said as he rose, rounded the defense table, and approached the witness, stopping a respectful five feet away. His stance signaled self-assurance; his expression untroubled. Both were lies.

"If I may summarize, you testified to three main theories on behalf of the prosecution." Briggs needed to recast the damaging evidence in terms more easily undermined, while labeling Hancock as anything but neutral.

He wagged his index finger. "First, The Aberdeen Circle had this master plan to take hostage the entire American internet, demanding the repeal of a list of anti-gay laws. Styles would play the hero and negotiate its release."

The witness leaned forward, his lips parting as he prepared to engage. Mandela didn't give him the chance. "Second," his voice rose as he flashed a "V." Hancock settled back. His bemused, charitable composition signaled the jurors he was totally cool with the defense lawyer performing for his client.

"*TAC*," Mandela continued, "would make the old Russian troll farms that meddled in the 2016 election look like toddlers learning the alphabet. Just before the planned assassination, the Circle would unleash a flood of disinformation on such a massive scale that President Thorne's reputation would be dark as midnight."

Briggs faced the jury box. "Third," he jabbed three joined fingers into the air, "Once in control of communications, there would be nothing but flattering, patriotic news about the new savior, Elijah Wilson Styles."

Mandela directed an incredulous gaze to the witness. "And your story, of course, has the vice president pulling all these strings."

Hancock remained unfazed, combing a long hand through his generous locks, holding the defense lawyer with an unperturbed expression, silently asking, *are you done?* At last he spoke, neutrally, deliberately.

"That's an interesting way to put it, sir. With all due respect, though, my proof to these jurors," he pivoted, nodding at them with his All-Star's smile, "included a lot more detail about specifically how The Aberdeen Circle and Professor Van Den Wolk, with the vice president's help, threatened the national security of the United States."

Briggs initial thrust had failed. The witness was neither intimidated nor ruffled, and didn't bite at Mandela's dramatization. Time for Plan "B."

"Let's examine some of that *proof*, shall we?" Briggs challenged. Hancock nodded, confident, eager. "Putting aside that you guys seemed to know an awful lot about a supposedly ultra-secret plan, you claim *TAC* had enough clandestine agents in place to control ..."

"Actually," the witness interrupted, his palms out in a gentle, apologetic gesture, "what I said was, the FBI gave us evidence showing *TAC* sympathizers had infiltrated the national communications hub for VerizoCom, which routes almost half of all digital transmissions in the U.S., plus several regional centers for smaller carriers. The word I used was 'disruption,' not 'control.' The difference is important, and I chose those terms carefully because I don't want people to be misled."

Mandela was pounding his head against a brick wall. He struggled to appear unmoved. "Be that as it may, Mr. Hancock, the so-called *proof* you cite only hinted at *TAC* supporters being able to cause any trouble, and even if they did, most of the nation's infrastructure would be unaffected. No?"

"I disagree," the director replied evenly. "As I testified, we had significant data showing electronic probes into major banking sites, air traffic control, power transmissions, all of which we monitored and did our best to trace. The FBI's information allowed us to connect the dots, and when we did ..." Hancock exhaled loudly, "we saw just how big this was."

The director shared a pained expression with one juror, and then another, drawing them into his precarious, zero-sum world. "It was like 9/11 all over again, except this time, we could see the planes coming."

"But nothing happened, Mr. Hancock," Briggs argued, trying to sound more factual than insensitive. "Not a single bank account was frozen, nobody lost their electricity, and unlike 9/11, all the planes landed." He spread his arms disarmingly. "The supposed attack was all theory. 'It' never happened, and the level of infiltration you suggest is *not* supported by any evidence."

For the first time, the witness showed a trace of irritation, which Mandela took as a tiny triumph. "Only because an awful lot of good people did their jobs very well," he said. "I believe 37 conspirators have been arrested so far ..."

"... And so far, not a single one has been found guilty of anything."

Hancock tensed, but quickly recovered, refusing to sacrifice his good guy image. "That is correct," he conceded. "So far."

"As for the enormous disinformation campaign against President Thorne you described, unflattering comments about a politician, especially a president, are, well, pretty much the norm in modern America, right? And you hardly need to commandeer the entire internet to do it." Briggs offered a perfunctory smile. "Hillary Clinton running a child pornography ring out of a pizza parlor! Donald Trump covering up extraterrestrial landings because ... well ... he *is* one!"

The jurors tittered at that one, and Hancock allowed himself a grin too.

"The First Amendment goes a long way, Mr. Briggs, but that's your specialty, not mine," he said without any trace of animosity. "Where I, where CISA becomes concerned, is when the volume is turned up so high, and where the content is so false and dangerous, that our very democracy is at risk."

Mandela raised his eyebrows. "That's quite the standard, Mr. Hancock," he mocked. "How would it apply to your own propaganda operation?"

The witness scrunched his handsome features. "My what?"

Briggs swung hard, a new harshness in his tone. "Hadn't the Thorne Administration, of which you were a part, been peddling false and dangerous rhetoric about the gay community for years? Hadn't you been scapegoating The Aberdeen Circle ever since it fought back against that smear campaign? Hadn't the vice president been subject to the most awful, pervasive slanders connecting him to any number of hateful conspiracies? Were those not putting our very democracy at risk?" Mandela glared. "Or are you only concerned with protecting your boss and your power?"

Hancock lifted his chin, leveling his focus directly into his accuser. "CISA doesn't control what people say, Mr. Briggs, and definitely not what they think. But when an organization like *TAC* tries to use cyber warfare to help it overthrow the government ..."

"...Overthrow the government, Mr. Hancock? By being *mean* to Magnus Thorne? By praising Elijah Styles for fighting assaults against vulnerable Americans?"

"By shooting the president of the United States, sir, and using the internet to complete their coup d'état."

Mandela let the words hang, unsure of their impact. He'd finally raised the poised witness' ire, jerking him to the realm of mortals. But had Briggs helped his client? Had he goaded Hancock into going too far? Briggs decided he must charge one more hill, however futile.

He faced his young, no longer glib adversary. "Putting aside this whole *TAC* grand scheme you've championed," Mandela spread his arms wide, mimicking the plot's breathtaking scale, "this jury's sole concern is the defendant. The vice president." Briggs folded his arms across his chest, as if to underline his next words. "With all of CISA's resources, with all your prying and spying and snooping, you have nothing from the lips of Elijah Styles directing, encouraging, or even connecting him to this plot of yours to overthrow, much less murder, the president."

The corners of Hancock's full, ruddy lips ticked up as he steadied himself. "You mean, do we have a recording of your client saying, 'Let's shoot him?'"

"No Director," Mandela shot back briskly, "I mean, quite precisely, do you have one recording, one text, one e-mail, one IM, one *anything* to establish the vice president sought to violently oust President Thorne?"

The witness transformed, becoming solemn, all traces of his buoyant disposition evaporated. "That's not necessarily the sort of thing you advertise, Mr. Briggs. So, no, no smoking gun," Hancock said in a low, chiding tone, "other than the one in Sam Kilbrough's hand." He turned to his real audience, "But that's not how these investigations work. You look for data points, connections, strands of evidence. And in this case, there was no doubt as to Vice President Styles' involvement."

"As you told Mr. McGehee," Mandela said disdainfully, shaking his head. "But all theory, all speculation ..."

"*NO!*" Hancock protested. Several jurors jolted at his uncharacteristic outburst, from which he quickly recovered. "I'm sorry, but no," he continued, visibly controlling his posture, his tone, his breath. "The vice president's plans were not a theory. It's not speculation."

Briggs had calculated he could dilute the CISA director's earlier direct testimony, soften its sharp edges. The decorous, confident witness would politely spar – disagreeing, sure, but without hostility – more concerned with projecting composure, with being liked than scoring points. For hours Hancock concealed his inner beast with an unflinching, protective certitude about his intellect, his team, and their conclusions. But that beast was now unleashed. Mandela pounced.

"Today, in front of this jury, Mr. Hancock, you seem pretty darned certain about what happened, about the Vice President's guilt."

"The evidence I've laid out is compelling. As an analyst, I'd say it is irrefutable."

"As you said, to Mr. McGehee here, less than an hour ago." Briggs rubbed his chin, contemplating - or so he feigned - at length asking in a voice so hushed as to require the jurors to strain and focus intently, "then why didn't you stop it?"

Hancock's deep blue eyes studied his interrogator, his perfectly manicured eyebrows dipping ever so slightly, giving away his sense of a trap. "I'm sorry?"

"If you had all this information, why didn't you stop the assassination attempt, why didn't you prevent the so-called coup? Why didn't you alert every law enforcement agency in the country, the military?" Mandela shook his head in disbelief. "Why weren't you the lead on every national news outlet?"

The witness nodded, not to Briggs, but to the jurors. It was a sensible attack, he understood, and they needed to know it was also an unfair one.

"We had enough material, I admit in retrospect, to connect the dots. But at the time, while it all pointed to something ominous, too much was undefined. The truth was unimaginable. That your client, a sitting Vice President of the United States, was conspiring to overthrow the government and take power for himself ... that was unimaginable."

"And yet, here you are imagining it," Mandela smiled. "Connecting dots, as you put it, only because you happen to hold a pen, and have the freedom to draw any picture you wish."

Hancock didn't flinch. "The evidence is the evidence, sir. And the picture, as *you* put it, is pretty clear."

"Ah. The *ev-i-dence*." Briggs widened his eyes in mock tribute to the word, lilting his voice on each of its syllables. "There were a lot of 'dots' in your testimony weren't there," he chuckled, acting unconcerned about the blows he knew his side had sustained.

And thus, the meat of Briggs' cross: any defense lawyer's strategy when faced with harmful testimony from a solid witness. He knew he couldn't possibly refute Hancock's entire fusillade of facts, so he does the next best thing. Pick a couple of points to belittle, cut at, chop up, tarnish, rough up. Make the jury wonder about those items, just enough so maybe they'll doubt the whole menu. Unlikely, but this is a game of perception, where sometimes going into the weeds obscures the big picture.

"Let's look at a couple of those 'dots,' shall we." Mandela retrieved the remote from the defense table, zapping a document onto the big screen across the well.

"For the record, page 17, U.S. Exhibit 48. You identified this earlier as the transcript of calls your agency intercepted between Blakely Kurtz and Sam Kilbrough, correct?"

"Yes."

"And here we see one example, one you spent a lot of time emphasizing, a discussion on March 10."

Hancock squinted at the screen, eventually pulling out a pair of glasses for his distance vision - or were they for show, to humanize his otherwise intimidating presence?

"That's correct."

"Kurtz is telling Kilbrough he's uncomfortable with the 'special event' they've been discussing, which you insist was the upcoming assassination attempt."

"The context makes that pretty clear."

"So you say, though nowhere in any of their conversations does either of them reference a shooting, or doing physical harm to the president."

Hancock regarded his questioner as one would an errant child, somewhere between a grimace and a smile. "Of course not. No one would say something like that out loud."

"Especially if they thought someone were listening, right?"

"Exactly."

Briggs started his next question as the witness, suddenly panicked, jutted forward, sputtering the beginnings of a protest as he realized his mistake. Mandela forged ahead. "Except, in your direct testimony only a couple of hours ago, you said, and I quote, 'We can rely on them meaning what they are saying because they had no idea anyone was listening. Kurtz was using a burner Kilbrough gave him, and Kilbrough was calling over what he believed was a scrambled line. They thought it was private.'"

Hancock paused, composing himself, then insisted, "That doesn't change anything. Even in a private call, it wouldn't be unusual to use code for something as heinous as a murder. I mean," he turned to the jurors, his tone now airy, "they were talking about killing the president." Two or three in the box nodded, Mandela noticed, still charmed by their guy. Most simply watched the show. Good, he thought, then to the witness, vividly unimpressed, "Uh huh."

His next step, however, was critical. "But the fact remains, the pair may well have known, or at least suspected, someone was eavesdropping."

Briggs noticed taut muscles, from the witness' temples down through his jaw, a tension he hoped the jurors saw too. "They might have," he said reluctantly.

"And if so, well then, so many questions, so many issues arise about this particular conversation. Such as ...," he abruptly stopped, as if his next preplanned taunt had just occurred to him. "Actually, you're the national security expert. Please enlighten us. If Kurtz and Kilbrough, or even just one of them, suspected their call was surveilled, what complications would a good, conscientious analyst have to consider?"

The defense lawyer knew Hancock was sharp, and thus bet on him recognizing quicksand, counting on him not to struggle against it.

"I suppose," Hancock offered magnanimously, "if that's *really* what one thought," as if *no one* would, "we would consider whether misdirection was involved, whether they were trying to mislead whoever was listening."

"Whether what they said was actually what they believed, or even true?"

Hancock folded his arms across his chest, another subtle win for Mandela. "Hypothetically, but again, there is no indication they suspected the call was monitored."

"So you say," Briggs replied impatiently. "Except," he pointed to the sky, or the heavens, or wherever higher reasoning resides, "there was no other reason for them to speak in code, which they in fact did, *and*," he pivoted to the jury, "if Kurtz and Kilbrough *did* fear someone like your CISA or the FBI was snooping, if their words were thus intended to mislead, then your dot becomes the bottom of a question mark," which he drew in the air with his long finger.

"Is there a *question* in there?" Hancock smiled, his charm strained.

"No sir," Mandela said with an unexpected seriousness, "there doesn't seem to be one at all."

With that, Briggs sat, signaling with a gentle wave his passing of the witness. Hancock had spent hours on direct verbally arranging multiple precious dots. The defense smudged but one. Yet, Mandela was confident the jurors' imaginations would spread doubt to the remainder, blurring Hancock's tight weave with memories of a shaky foundation.

Most of all, though, Briggs trusted the advice of his most impactful mentor: "A smart man knows when to walk away." His instincts as a lawyer were of course polished by mock trials, moot courts and the lecture halls of his preeminent Vanderbilt Law instructors. This bedrock lesson, however, came from a higher source. Imogen Briggs. His mother, God rest her soul.

Seventeen

Sidney McGehee fully understood the high bar ahead. He needed a unanimous verdict, not a *single* holdout, to convict the vice president.

Yet, with the dawn of the trial's fourth day, he was confident. In fact, Sidney was relaxed, satisfied the case had progressed according to plan.

Sure, defense counsel threw lots of punches at his witnesses, even landing a few. That was expected, and did not trouble the United States Attorney for the District of Columbia. Each person called to the stand, in his view, had been a net plus. Briggs' somewhat desperate volleys barely scratched them. The prosecutor's case was more than intact. It was strong.

Colonel Arenberg dominated, establishing Styles' blind ambition and shameless disloyalty. Drury was a bit of a wet noodle, but his reluctance to crap on his long-time benefactor enhanced his testimony's credibility. He couldn't deny the vice president's close connection to both the assassin and the dangerous ELEP technology.

Then there was Hancock. The cyber chief got a little ruffled toward the end, but his revelation of Kilbrough and Kurtz's ominous exchange was devastating:

> *Kilbrough: He [VP] says POTUS [the president] "has to go," his words, and they've run out of constitutional options.*
> *Kurtz: What does that even mean?*
> *Kilbrough: There are other options.*
> *Kurtz: Other options?*
> *Kilbrough: You don't want to know, but you guys need to be ready to do your part. It needs to be coordinated.*
> *Kurtz: Shut it all down?*

> *Kilbrough: Shut it all down. There won't be much notice, but you'll know.*
> *Kurtz: And Styles is okay with all this?*
> *Kilbrough: It's the only way. He knows that. He knows what has to be done.*

All faked because they, maybe, suspected Big Brother was listening? *Ummmm ... Okay.* And that was the high point in Briggs' cross of Hancock.

Sidney's mental picture of the scoreboard was thus reassuring, a solid lead in the first quarter, a great start. And he was certain the best was yet to come.

What better explained McGehee's confidence, however, was his take on the jury. Fully vested in his abilities, Sidney was especially cocky about his talent for reading the 12 on his panels. Not because they were vigorously investigated and intently studied before their empanelment, though they had been. Rather, it was his uniquely honed intuition, his knack for interpreting smiles, frowns, posture, squints, yawns, eyebrows. He stitched these threads of reaction into patterns. *This* jury was going to convict. He was sure of it.

Tinsley, the California surfer kid. He wants to be a lawyer in the worst possible way. When I pirouette through an examination, Sidney thought, he's transfixed, taking mental notes, wanting to *be* me. I can see it in his covetous eyes.

Then there was Arroyo, the restaurant owner. This guy was as conservative as they come, a rule-follower, a law-and-order man. Every time Briggs speaks, he balls his right hand into a tight fist, rests his chin on it, and glares in objection.

All of them signaled alliance in some manner of mental Morse code, feeding McGehee's swagger as he stood to call his next witness. They were with him.

"The United States call Michael Fletcher," Sidney announced, using the corner of his eye to glimpse the defense table. He couldn't resist. As expected, to his delight, they were paralyzed with confusion, then scrambled – the associate attacking a thick binder on the floor at the rail behind him, the clownish legal assistant scrolling wildly on her iPad.

A rotund man with unwieldy, wiry brown hair and equally unkempt mutton chops waddled toward the witness stand. With obvious effort, he grumped his thick legs onto the tiny platform and descended toward the chair. The man stopped only when McGehee signaled, waving his palm upward, that the witness should remain standing.

"Mr. Fletcher," Judge Bering intoned, drawing his attention, "please raise your right hand." Hesitantly, as if deciding which arm to move, the witness complied. "Do you swear or affirm to tell the truth, the whole truth, and nothing but the truth?"

"I do," he scowled, offended. In his more comfortable environs, say a pool hall, such an affront to his honesty would have drawn a more contemptuous reaction.

"Your honor," Briggs interjected, studying a screen his tattooed sidekick held, "I'm not sure of this witness' purpose."

"He was one of the people who filmed the president's inauguration," Sidney offered, voice dripping with goodwill. He observed Briggs' wary expression. This was fun.

"We ..." the puzzled defense lawyer began, "Judge, Defendant has already stipulated to the authenticity of all network videos offered by the prosecution."

Judge Bering focused on McGehee, her eyebrows raised.

"I understand that, Your Honor, but I thought it would be helpful for the jury to have some context for the specific segment we want to show them."

She paused, frowning, then, "Make it quick, counselor."

"Certainly," Sidney crooned, and spun to the witness. "Mr. Fletcher, by whom were you employed this past January 20?"

"XBN," he blared into the microphone, his mouth much too close, his voice raspy, his hulky presence clearly out of place.

"And your job?"

"Cameraman. Have been for 28 years, last nine with them."

"And before we show it to the jury, did you review Prosecution Exhibit number 74A for me?"

"Yes," he grumbled, "It's part of what I shot on swearin' in day."

"Specifically, Mr. Fletcher, which part."

"What you showed me? It was backstage stuff. My camera's shoulder mounted so I can move around. The main speeches and stuff, where all the public is, them are all filmed by fixed mounts. You know, the guys on platforms." He said this last phrase with a trace of disdain, as if speaking of a lower class.

Sidney nodded at Mandy, who pressed play. The white screen on the far wall filled with a churn of bodies in a dimly lit space, a cacophony of voices echoing off sandstone walls and marble floors.

"What are we seeing here?"

Fletcher nodded approvingly at his handiwork. "This is the area inside the doors from where Thorne was gonna speak ..."

"The U.S. Capitol interior, behind the doors leading to the East Portico?" McGehee clarified.

"Yeah," the witness groaned, unhappy with the interruption, "that's what I was sayin'." A couple of jurors giggled, amused by the taciturn man's impertinence.

"Go on," Sidney said with a smile, enjoying the slight.

"Anyways, this is where everyone hung before they went outside. Producers thought it would add, I don't know, atmosphere or something." He shrugged his shoulders. "I go where they tell me."

Rampart

To Mandy, McGehee instructed, "21:43, please." She tapped on a tablet, and the video skipped ahead, then froze. Everyone in the courtroom searched the realignment of people. McGehee allowed them, one by one, to find the scene's protagonists.

"Do you recognize anyone in this shot, Mr. Fletcher."

He looked at the U.S. attorney tetchily.

"I recognize a lot of 'em," he huffed. "I do this political stuff all the time. What you want to know is if I see *that* guy," he added, pointing to the defense table, to Styles. "Yeah," Fletcher said nodding at the screen, "that's him at the bottom, in the blue suit with the yellow tie."

"And who is that, walking up to and then conferring with the vice president?" Sidney asked. The timing of his questions was flawless, the screen showing a tall, athletic man approaching Styles, a man everyone recognized instantly.

"That's the killer guy. Kilbrough. I was filming the day he shot the president, too." The camera zoomed in, held for a while, then panned over to the arriving Speaker of the House, Rance Knall, who seemed to study the two men from a distance.

"Let's watch that again," the prosecutor said, nodding at Mandy. She pecked at her iPad, and the video blinked back to Kilbrough's approach. McGehee held up his wrist, pressed his watch, "Go," and they all stared once more at the silent images huddled together, talking intently.

"And ... stop," he ordered as he again squeezed his watch, the video freezing, Kilbrough blurred slightly as he turned to leave. "Forty-eight seconds." Sidney looked at the cameraman. "That's how long I get, timing the exchange between these two as you recorded it."

He walked over to the witness and stood by his chair. "Mr. Fletcher," he began, addressing him with his gaze on the jurors, "did you hear what they were talking about?"

The room was tense with anticipation. So *this* was why such an obscure character had been called to the stand. Sidney smiled as Briggs jumped to his feet, just as the prosecutor planned, drawing even *more* attention to this previously unknown meeting.

"Objection! Hearsay, and, I would add, the prosecution is using this surprise witness without having disclosed to the defense any relevant testimony. He is listed merely as someone able to authenticate certain digital videos."

The Judge looked to the prosecutor, who calmly replied, "Your Honor, I have merely asked *IF* he heard their conversation, not yet its content."

She frowned, not happy that her orderly proceeding was being manipulated. Focusing down to the large man staring peevishly back at her, she said, "You may answer as to whether you heard what they said to one another."

Equally displeased with his interrogator, Fletcher scowled. "No. I was too far away. And that area was super noisy."

"Thank you, Mr. Fletcher," Sidney said pleasantly, and then to the judge, "nothing further." She looked to Briggs, who shook his head, puzzled but wary. "You are excused, sir," she announced, and as he jerkily maneuvered his large frame out of the small chair, Judge Bering addressed the prosecutor curtly. "Next."

"The United States call Patrice Moon."

An elegant African American woman waltzed through the tall wooden doors at the rear and toward the gateway to the well. Poised, chin up, the XBN News chief's entrance set off another mad scramble at the defense table, a picture of disarray McGehee relished.

†††

Mandela now knew exactly what the U.S. attorney was doing, and it pissed him off. Briggs believed in playing hard, but also within the bounds of fairness. As his father said many times in a low, steady voice, *if it's not right you'll feel it, and it won't feel good.*

True, in federal criminal cases, neither side was *required* to reveal witnesses. This was crazy, Mandela thought – the military mandated it in courts-martial proceedings, as did most state criminal codes, and witness lists were universal in civil cases – but despite years of outcry the Supreme Court, which writes the federal court rules, wouldn't budge. Some individual judges, like Carolyn Bering, went as far as they could, encouraging disclosure with pretrial scheduling orders, but enforceability was questionable.

McGehee had placed the cameraman among 427 others on his "List of Anticipated Witnesses," though as an innocuous "Custodian of Records." In actuality, he used Fletcher not only to verify the origins of a video, but to highlight something much more important – an encounter between the defendant and the would-be assassin that Briggs' team not surprisingly overlooked.

The prosecution had dumped millions of records as part of pre-trail "discovery," wherein each party supplies its potential exhibits to the other side. Included were thousands of hours of videos: smartphones, closed circuit surveillance, social media uploads and, like what Fletcher shot, news media "tape" labeled by organization, date, time and location. There were 422 hours of such recordings from XBN alone, another 500-plus from ABC, over 700 hours from FOX, and on, and on, and on.

Under Izzy's supervision, a crew of five paralegals – at tremendous expense to the defense and straining the limited resources of Briggs' small office – cast eyes upon every segment. But most of that had been scanned rather than analyzed, fast-forwarding through much of the mind-numbingly monotonous job. Only the tiniest fraction of a percentage was even remotely relevant. It would have taken a very large squad months to carefully scrutinize every block, and thus, they had missed this chance meeting in a bustling crowd on an innocuous drive labeled "XBN 4423j202033 (unaired)."

Still, Izzy, normally tough as nails, looked as if she were about to cry. This was her team, her job, and she clearly thought she'd let her boss, and their client down. Mandela would love to comfort her, to tell her it was okay, that nobody could find every needle in a field of haystacks. Most vitally, their own client failed to mention this pretty significant get-together. At the moment, however, Briggs had a judge to persuade.

†††

Because Carolyn Bering hated the delay of excusing jurors, the two lawyers huddled beneath her on the far side of the bench. They all spoke in hushed tones.

"Your Honor, Ms. Moon is not on the government's witness list. Your scheduling order requires she not be allowed to testify."

"Mr. McGehee?"

Mandela's mind raced, fireworks of competing thoughts. He had asked for this sidebar, figuring he didn't have much to lose. After all, what could the U.S. attorney say? Calling Moon was clearly an ambush. The Federal Rules may not mandate a heads-up on witnesses, but Judge Bering's scheduling order did. If nothing else, her sense of fairness may lend some help. Judges can have a big impact on a case, the official rules be damned.

On the other hand, Briggs knew the damage was already done. His opponent had revealed a previously unknown exchange between Styles and Kilbrough: one in plain sight, and on the day of Thorne's second inaugural no less. Even if this next witness were somehow disallowed, he knew the jurors' imaginations would be as bad as the truth. That Mandela was fighting to prevent them from learning what the assassin and the vice president said would naturally lead them to imply the worst.

The prosecutor was calm – smarmy, Briggs thought. "Judge, Federal Rule 16 only requires the government allow the defendant to inspect and copy documents or objects that might be relevant to its preparations. Here, we certainly gave them a copy of the video. As to witnesses, we are only required to notify defendants of *experts*, or those who might possess exculpatory or alibi evidence. Ms. Moon fits neither of those categories."

"Fine, but counselor, my pretrial order requires the sharing of anticipated witnesses so that each side may prepare."

"With all due respect, Your Honor, the order goes beyond what the Supreme Court requires." Here, McGehee put on his most deferential mask, still very much like a smirk. "Even so, we complied with its spirit, which asks us to list 'anticipated witnesses,' which we did, scores of them." The prosecutor looked at Mandela, feigning innocence. "We only determined to call Ms. Moon this very morning." Returning a respectful gaze to the top of the bench, he added, "I'm sure her testimony will make clear why."

The Judge was trapped, and they all three knew it. "Very well," she said, "But I expect you will make clear in your questions why notice of this individual wasn't ... *foreseen*." If looks could kill.

Briggs hoped the sly maneuver might result in some helpful judicial retribution later, but for the present, the U.S. attorney was bringing to the stand someone for whom Mandela was completely unprepared. He knew only that whatever Moon was about to say, it wouldn't be good.

†††

"Patrice Donalds Moon, President of XBN's News Division," she introduced herself. She presided over the room, ramrod straight, large navy-colored beads resting immaculately on her dark brown skin inside the collar of a cobalt blue suit.

"Ms. Moon, you contacted me last night, around nine o'clock."

"Correct."

"Please tell the jury for what purpose you reached out."

Moon's head rotated, cyborg-like Mandela thought, and her force enveloped the jurors as she analyzed them before speaking. "Our general counsel advised me of your subpoena for Michael Fletcher, and the dead footage you were going to discuss with him."

"Dead footage?"

"That's the term we use for recordings that are shot, but don't make it on air."

"Okay. Please continue."

"I understood why the video would be of interest, and asked whether we had made any effort to determine what was said between the vice president and Mr. Kilbrough."

"Had you?"

"No. The footage was filmed two months before anyone even knew who Sam Kilbrough was, and as I said, it was never used during any of our broadcasts."

"What did you do next?"

Moon returned her focus to the jury. "I don't like surprises, and not knowing your intentions, I asked our analytics team to look into it. I knew we had occasions in the past where we lacked audio and thought it useful to ... to learn more. Specifically, we have experts who can decipher such things."

"Lipreading?"

Moon offered an indulgent smile. "Basically."

"Why, then, did you call *me*?"

The witness hesitated, taking in a deep breath, not out of indecision, but in a practiced effort to underline the gravity of her response. "I wanted to make certain you appreciated we, XBN, were being fully transparent and completely forthcoming. That we were not trying to hide anything."

McGehee sensed Briggs' coiled energy, ready to spring to his feet with an objection at any second. He guessed, however, his opponent was too smart to fall into that trap. Unfair surprise? Okay, Sidney would tell the judge, but the unexpected late-night call was just as much a surprise to me. Hearsay? No way Bering would sustain that one. While most lay folks had seen enough TV dramas to appreciate hearsay as an unsworn out of court statement, the rule was shot through with exceptions. Here, several applied, but at a minimum, McGehee was offering it to prove "motive, intent, or plan."

Briggs would only make things worse by resisting the conversation's admission, heightening its impact. *If the defense is fighting so hard to keep us in the dark*, the jury would conclude, *this must be really bad*!

McGehee forged ahead. His opponent, tense, waiting for an opening, didn't move.

"What did you discover, Ms. Moon, that you felt was so important?"

The corners of her mouth bent downward and her eyes narrowed. "I never said what I found was important," she said in the scolding voice of a disappointed teacher. Then, to the jury, "That's for others to decide."

The panel was riveted, several leaning forward, all alert.

"Your Honor," Briggs rose, "until both sides have had the opportunity to review this tape," he said, "I do not believe it is proper to allow any ... *interpretations*" – he emphasized the plural – "of what may or may not have been spoken."

Shrewd, McGehee thought. A reasonable sounding stall that didn't reveal the panic the defense must surely feel. The prosecutor didn't bother to respond. He frankly didn't care. A recess would be its own magnificent promo for what Moon was about to reveal, heightening expectancy.

Judge Bering rested her chin on tented fingers, elbows perched on the shelf of her bench as she thought it over, the jurors growing thirstier.

"Mr. Briggs, you may certainly cross-examine the witness as to the reliability of her information. And if you wish to counter it, you will be free to bring an expert during your case in chief." She leaned back into her chair. "For now, let's keep things moving."

"Ms. Moon," McGehee invited her to continue.

The witness gently cleared her throat, her expression a study in control.

"After the subpoena, when we saw this previously unnoticed meeting ..."

"Between Sam Kilbrough and the vice president."

"Correct. As I said, I had someone on staff interpret their exchange. Then we hired an outside expert to independently review that conclusion."

"And?"

"And then they brought it to me. A transcript, along with the clip. Once you know what was said, it's pretty easy to see it for yourself." The witness sighed. "I knew we had something big, so I consulted legal, and they recommended I send our findings to the FBI, which I did. Also, given our acquaintance ..." she gestured to McGehee and back.

"Please tell the jury how we know one another."

"Your wife and I attended Columbia together, and we've kept in touch." *Kept in touch.* She didn't share her and Laura's late-night conversations during Sidney's courtship, or Moon being a maid of honor at their wedding, or the many dinners and parties and events shared over the years, or the potential partners eagerly pushed her way by both McGehees.

"What did you tell me?" he asked neutrally, all business.

"The same thing I told Director Degna. That XBN had information I thought might be relevant to their investigation, and to your prosecution."

McGehee directed Mandy with his eyes, and the Fletcher clip materialized once again on the big screen. This time, a long, rectangular black box flickered at the bottom.

"Your Honor," he said with sudden deference, then pivoted to his opponent, "Mr. Briggs. Before playing it, I ask the witness to first describe what we are viewing here in U.S. Exhibit 74B."

"It is the same Fletcher segment we've been discussing, only this time with closed-captioning, and, as you can see, zoomed in on the two main subjects."

"Does the closed-captioning match the transcript your expert prepared, and thus, what these two men said to one another?"

"It does."

Briggs stood, reluctantly, aware there was nothing he could say to change Judge Bering's course, knowing his continued resistance would further peak the jurors' interest – but he needed to preserve their ability to appeal. "The defense has had no opportunity to review this exhibit Your Honor, nor assess its accuracy or reliability. We renew our objection that no proper predicate has been established, that this is trial by reality TV, interpretive art, and not proper evidence."

"I understand, Mr. Briggs. Ms. Moon will make her expert available to your staff for examination, and you will have ample opportunity during your case to challenge the prosecution's assertions as to what was said."

Briggs shook his head in resignation. The Court gestured for the show to begin.

The jurors were by now well acquainted with the tape, looped at least a dozen times while Fletcher was on the stand. Now spines straightened. There was movement as they positioned for an unobstructed view. The prosecutor waited as long as he could, letting the suspense come to a boil.

Finally, he pointed at Mandy. The familiar dance of the vice president and the assassin rolled forward. This time, only two men filled the screen, no longer a pair of small figures in an undulating crowd. A blinking curser in the captions box spasmodically filled the void with characters, then words, then meaning.

> **Kilbrough: Mr. Vice President**
> **Styles: Sam**

The two looked past one another, as if neither wanted to speak.

> **Styles: So, I guess he's arrived?**
> **Kilbrough: Almost.**
> **Styles: I hoped we wouldn't get to this point.**
> **Kilbrough: But here we are.**

Their eyes locked, the intensity unambiguous.

> **Styles: Are you ready?**

Kilbrough nodded, staring deep into the vice president.

> **Styles: Are you sure? This could end us both.**
> **Kilbrough: More likely me. But I don't think there's much choice.**

Styles looked away, first to one side of the chamber, then the other, then down at his feet.

> **Styles: You know I'll protect you.**
> **Kilbrough: I know, Eli. I trust you.**

The vice president placed a hand on Kilbrough's shoulder.

> **Styles: When everything's in place, I'll ...**
> **Kilbrough: He's here.**

Kilbrough whirled ninety degrees to his right, like a Marine honor guardsman executing a ceremonial turn, and stepped out of the frame.

The image froze, Elijah Wilson Styles standing alone, his face ashen, forlorn. One by one, the members of the jury shifted their attention from his digital image to the corporeal self behind the defense table. They saw, unmistakably, the exact same expression.

Eighteen

The lawyers were back in the Prettyman building on a picturesque Saturday morning in Washington – blue skies, mild temperatures, trees still green and flowers blooming – working with Judge Bering through the motions and technicalities necessitated by the first week's proceedings. The sequestered jurors, however, had the weekend off.

Several heavily monitored activities were on offer for some small reprieve from their isolation: a trip to the nearby National Mall; an exclusive showing of the *Mission Impossible* franchise's newest edition; a private concert by a local jazz ensemble. But before any of that, in the outdoor courtyard of their small hotel, The Twelve were allowed the first of their once weekly "visitations," not unlike the residents of any prison, which, of course, they were in a sense.

Lanta had no husband. That was by choice. Who had time, with a newly retired mother to look after, and roughly 150 young souls to guide through the lessons of the Roman Empire, the Chinese dynasties, and yes, the African kingdoms overlooked by most high school history curricula? Plus, she had a wide circle of colleagues and friends.

So, for her, the job of compassionate caller fell to Beth, her bestie from work. Beth kindly towed a suitcase full of fresh clothes retrieved from Lanta's apartment, through which the U.S. Marshal's Service had creepily pawed for contraband, especially news of the case from the outside world. Included was a loaf of Lanta's mother's homemade gingerbread, perhaps a passive-aggressive protest for Mama's not being invited. Truth be told, the last thing Lanta needed today was her mother's heavy blanket of fretting, conspiracies, and certain tears.

Beth sat across one end of a weathered picnic table, which they shared with the only other Black female juror – Chris? She couldn't remember, they really hadn't spoken much during the week – whose husband or boyfriend joined her. Thus, no privacy, and that indeed was the point, emphasized by the three circulating USMS deputies. Even the slightest mention of the ongoing proceedings was to be strictly avoided.

Beth's conversation meandered from one innocuous topic to the next: Lanta's substitute seemed to be doing a passable job; Sharnelle was indeed, as all suspected, pregnant, and would be gone at semester; yesterday's workshop on adolescent stress was, surprisingly, useful.

Lanta had hoped her mind would feel relief ambling among these mundanities. Instead, it kept returning to the week just spent in a marginally uncomfortable wooden chair, United States v. *Styles* unfolding like an otherworldly, too bizarre to comprehend drama. When it all started, she considered the prosecution's central theme completely wack, a partisan hit job. Plus, she'd always liked Elijah Styles, a truly pleasant man in the nasty whirlwind of today's political climate, and refreshingly intelligent.

Now, however, she wasn't so sure.

The first two days hadn't really moved her. That chief of staff guy was an ass, and the security dude an arrogant poser. On Thursday, though ... that XBN video. My Lord! Did he really say those things? The defense lawyer was clearly shocked. Lanta saw him glance sideways at his client, all *WTF dude*! And Patrice Moon. Now that was a powerful woman who had her shit together. Lanta guessed it took a lot to shake her tree.

Yesterday, however, was worse.

Lanta was big on body language. She could tell more about her kids at Central from the way they carried themselves than what came out of their mouths. When Barbara Vinh entered into the courtroom, her assertive, focused march to the witness stand made it clear she wasn't fooling around. The prosecutor tried to humanize her, bringing up her Vietnamese refugee parents and all the toughness she must have gotten from that, but this woman wasn't having it. She didn't want to be there, and he wasted everyone's time with that jabber. Her answers were shorter than her damn haircut, and just as severe.

In a way, Vinh's stoic, steely bearing made sense. She was a secret service agent, an obviously accomplished one to be assigned to protect the Vice President of the United States. That's not what gripped Lanta, though.

It was Vinh's reluctance. This was a by-the-book operative whose diet was reality and results, no emotion for dessert. The way Lanta saw it, hesitation and doubt were anathema to this woman.

And yet, there it was. The closer McGehee got to what he wanted – to what she told the vice president, to what he said in response – the more her jaw tightened, her breathing regulated, her glare intensified. Lanta could *touch* the tension. She wasn't sure where the prosecutor was heading, but she could tell damn well Agent Vinh didn't want him going there.

Turns out when Thorne was shot, Styles was giving a speech in Dallas where he used to be mayor, to the ACLU, a group still buying what he was selling. Vinh described how, following protocol, they dragged him off the stage – literally *dragged* him – straight back to his armored limo. Vinh personally shoved him inside, throwing herself on top of Styles as the vehicle peeled out even before the door was closed, other agents running alongside, weapons drawn.

"Up to this point, had you told him the reason for your actions?" McGehee asked, piecing the story together. Lanta read Vinh's face. She had used it herself on ninth graders acting ridiculous.

"No sir," she'd said, measuring both words. "We don't have time for conversation during an Evac."

"When did you inform him the president had been shot?"

She paused. Lanta noted the tug of war between Vinh's fidelity to Styles and her obligation to tell the truth. "I didn't."

The prosecutor's eyes widened, as if shocked by her answer. Lanta was genuinely confused. Why would the agent not tell her charge what had happened?

"Did you say *anything* to him?"

"About 30 seconds after we had cleared the scene, I asked the vice president if he was okay. Sometimes a protectee can be injured during an emergency removal."

"And?"

At this point, Lanta had suffered an eerie shudder down her spine. It didn't happen often, but like most folks, she sometimes had a flash, as if remembering a scene instead of experiencing it for the first time. So while Vinh strained, building up enough pressure to force out the words she didn't want to say, Lanta sensed what was coming. And that made it more awful.

"He asked me if the president was dead, and if the shooter was in custody."

†††

About 20 feet from Lanta and Beth, seated in a corner on a pair of rust-speckled white metal chairs, Emmanuel and his wife reviewed the state of his restaurants. Their speech was rushed, constantly switching from Spanish to English depending upon whichever language allowed them to cover the most ground. He had never been away from the business this long and was convinced that, without his constant attention, the entire enterprise would collapse.

On news they had run out of flan Thursday night, he grumbled to Mary, *"Por supuesto que lo hicimos."* Of course we did. "Why didn't you tell me when we spoke last night?" What next? This is what happens when he isn't there to oversee the tiniest details.

His wife quickly wearied of the nitpicking, the fixation on every imperfection caused by his absence. Emmanuel trod toward thin ice.

Mary was doing her best, her burden heavy, and their time today limited. So, reluctantly, he shifted gears.

They covered the children, her garden, his *Mama's* worsening hip, and getting the car to Jorge's for service. These topics didn't begin to hold his interest, however. The more they meandered through the tedium, the more Emmanuel's mind drifted, back to his ventures, and back to his irritation at being trapped in this trial.

It was all a waste of time. *¡Christo, el hombre es culpable!* It was obvious, after just a single week.

Arroyo never trusted the man, and never understood why Thorne chose him as his running mate in the first place. He was gay! And though he understood that was old fashioned thinking – Emmanuel wasn't a bigot, some of his best employees were homosexuals – there was still an element of deception engrained in their kind. Or maybe not even deception, maybe more some need to prove themselves as ... equal, or better than.

The promise during jury selection to be fair and unbiased was sincere, *pero ahora es imposible.* Look at the evidence! Right from the start, that Colonel, now he was *un gran jefe.* Made it quite clear the vice president had one thing in mind: becoming president. And Drury, Mr. Robocop – Emmanuel had to chuckle at that absurdity – a weasel, but nonetheless established *who* wanted to control the internet. And *who* sent the killer to the president's team. *¡Mierda!*

Then yesterday. Everybody probably thought the XBN thing was what mattered. Not Arroyo. *Por seguro, importante.* Nonetheless, he bet the vice president's lawyer would come up with a hundred ways to explain away what Styles and Kilbrough said. Emmanuel could think of several.

That Asian woman's testimony wasn't very remarkable either. Was it really too wild for the vice president to guess he'd been hustled away because of an attempt on Thorne's life?

No, what struck Emmanuel was something more straightforward: the videos the prosecutor played to close out the week. Styles, giving speeches in the last weeks before the shooting. Not exciting or sexy – two on his own row were yawning. But if you paid attention, as Arroyo did, Styles unmistakably showed his desire to get rid of his boss.

> *We cannot survive as a democracy if leadership comes from the tip of a spear rather than the mark of a ballot. If dissenting voices are silenced instead of answered. If power is held by force over consent.*
>
> *That is why I have chosen to use my platform not only to finally, transparently examine the last election, but much more urgently, to rid our nation of its first unabashed, undisguised, unapologetic autocrat. A man whose authority comes from the troops and militias he unconstitutionally deploys to our town squares and city streets in his name, not the nation's. A man who has forfeited any legitimacy he may have doubtfully possessed.*

¡Dios Mio! ¿Como no pueden verlo? How can nobody else see? *This* was the key. This was the vice president saying Thorne had to be eliminated. And still, when the video played, the Korean guy to Emmanuel's right examined his manicure. The girl with the green hair next to him propped her chin in her hand, eyes on the floor. And Mrs. Jackson, bless her heart, was per usual fast asleep.

Is it *me*? Emmanuel wondered. Maybe it was his latent homophobia – *en verdad*, he did not care much for the gay lifestyle, though he knew his kids and his wife thought him a troglodyte on that score. More likely it was Arroyo's belief in loyalty, his offense at the subordinate attacking his number one. Why didn't Styles resign if he felt so strongly? *Because*, then he couldn't be president! It was so obvious.

The last bit the prosecutor played, Styles speaking the very evening before the assassination attempt, was hardly vague.

> *I cannot predict President Thorne's future, but I can say with great confidence his days are numbered. The American people will simply not permit someone who has so tarnished his high office to further defile it. When the president ignores the Constitution, abandons due process, demonizes those who disagree with him and points guns at his fellow citizens, he cannot clothe his dictatorship in the self-serving words, "Emergency Rule," and expect to survive.*
>
> *We are fast approaching a time of action. A time when words are no longer enough. A time when we either restore our democracy, or we bid it farewell.*

His days are numbered? Action, not words? President Thorne cannot expect to survive?

The other jurors were undazzled by the implications, the subtext, the deductive possibilities drawn from the vice president's comments, a small crumb here, an ambiguous line there. For Arroyo, the defendant was all but declaring his intentions. A clear-cut call to arms. *This man is evil, replace him with me!* And less than 24-hours later, Magnus Thorne lay wounded, shot by the vice president's own chosen hand.

†††

Aiden, despite his laid-back vibe, never lacked for moxie. A guided tour of the National Mall, or a movie with the people with whom he'd shared house arrest for an entire week? Supervised visitation with a casual friend, or worse, a classmate, at the same scene of his detention? What the hell would they even talk about?

Nope. For his first day off, Tinsley negotiated directly with Bailiff Bankhead. He was going for a run. A long, long run, and if they tried to deny him that break from the growing insanity of his captivity, he'd act out in a way sure to cause very unwelcomed media attention. He held firm with his threat, convincingly, until from on high, from Judge Bering herself, the word came: *Fine ...*

It was barely 8 a.m. Aiden was stretched, fueled – a smoothie and an apple – his flame and lime Vaporflys laced tight. He exited through a small gate at the rear of the courtyard, which the staff were setting up for the poor souls who would have no such escape. None of his fellow jurors were there to see him, which was by design.

A marshal supervised his departure through a small passageway leading to Seventh Street, at the end of which an unmarked, black BMW i9 waited, engine running, two more USMS guardians inside, ready to trail him and if need be, extricate him from any troubles along the way.

Before reaching the sidewalk, Tinsley retrieved his Oakley Radars from his collar, placing the arms of the lavender tinted shades snugly against his temples, then pulled off a well-worn Rams t-shirt, securing it inside the waistband along the back of his baby blue shorts. Ready, he darted out of the alley, cutting a sharp right and setting a fast pace.

It was a beautiful September day, already 65 degrees, a little warmer than the cool Pacific mornings at home. Definitely not as picturesque as The Strand where he did a regular six miles growing up, waves crashing to his left on the way out, the sun topping the beach-front mansions as he turned to go home. But it would do. He enjoyed the feel of exertion, and this was a part of the city he'd never explored.

Crossing Massachusetts, Aiden faced the intricately adorned Beaux-Arts façade of the old Carnegie Library, now Apple store, and couldn't resist running up its elongated stone steps. At the top he hopped from one foot to the other, arms bent on either side of his head in a Rocky style victory pose, fists clenched so that his sinewy biceps bulged, his best imitation of Stallone's dance. A pair of young women on a bench off to his side leaned in to one another and giggled; not in a mocking way, Tinsley was sure, but with appreciation. They were clearly ogling his tanned, lean body, and he gave them his winning smile and a slight lilt of his chin. Aiden ran shirtless for a reason. He didn't consider himself conceited, just, why hide your gifts?

Down on the street, he picked out the marshals' car, idling near the curb. He could only imagine them shaking their heads, though certainly with at least a tinge of jealousy.

Having been allotted only ninety minutes for this jaunt, he rounded the corner and took off down New York Ave and up Sixth to the Kennedy Playground, where he performed a wide circle around the ballfield, drawing furtive stares from a middle-aged man tossing a football with a friend, and then another guy, this one his own age, doing pullups on an outdoor fitness rig. Tinsley doubted either was gay – I mean, guys look at guys, sizing up the competition, right? – and really didn't care. Not his team, but it didn't bother him either. On that score, he didn't attach any maleficent significance to the vice president's sexuality, though he suspected at least some of his fellow jurors did.

Heading across P toward his next destination, Bundy Field and Dog Park, Aiden wondered how much of this prosecution, in fact, was persecution of the homophobic variety. The president was investing a lot of energy into that kind of hate, and his base was eating it up. The U.S. attorney carefully molded pieces of his case into a queer stratagem to take over the world. Why not? It made for a compelling story. And the plot, if there was a plot, would indeed have resulted in the first gay president.

Still, Tinsley considered himself a pretty analytical dude. Shit, this time next year, he'd be an actual lawyer! That meant he couldn't ignore the facts.

He picked up speed along O Street and onto Dunbar High's football field, where he jogged over to the west end goal line and commenced a series of 20-on, 30-off interval sprints, harking back to his days as a decent high school wideout. As the carved contours of his legs propelled him into a faster and faster tempo, sweat trickled over his eyebrows, down his back, and through the noticeable cleft of his chest, which swelled as he took controlled gulps of air.

He expended his physical reserves and interlaced his hands behind a soggy head, twisting his torso back and forth at the hip. The sun glued salty, wet perspiration to his light brown skin. There was an exhilarating, burning tingle in his muscles. And still, yesterday's evidence intruded. Why were his satisfying physical sensations not enough to disengage these ruminations? This run was supposed to be his escape from the trial. Why was Tinsley so troubled?

Specifically, it was the videoed testimony of Rachel Maslow. It toyed with him, taunted him. The Aberdeen Circle's leader had refused to answer anything. The entire deposition, every question, "On advice of counsel, I invoke my rights under the Fifth Amendment to the U.S. Constitution."

He totally got her strategy. Maslow had her own treason indictment to worry about. Of course her counsel would instruct her to invoke this privilege. Still, as a witness in the vice president's trial, not a defendant, she could have selectively answered at least some of the questions. She could have helped Styles, so important to her organization over the years. Thrown him a bone. Or she could also have thrown him under the bus.

She did neither. She did nothing.

What got to Aiden more than her stonewalling, however, were the prosecutor's questions.

> *"Ms. Maslow, when the defendant called you at 8:47 Pacific Time on the night before the assassination attempt, a call lasting only 29 seconds, he alerted you as to what was going to happen at the North Carolina State Fairgrounds the next day, didn't he?"*

How hard would it have been for her to break silence and say "No," protecting herself and Styles. Or she could have saved us all a lot of trouble and said "Yes," though that would surely sink Maslow as well. Instead, again, the mantra: "On advice of counsel, I invoke my rights under the Fifth Amendment to the U.S. Constitution."

> *"Ma'am, given your very frequent interactions with the defendant, to what degree were you aware of his close, personal relationship with Sam Kilbrough?"*

Whoa! Surely the prosecution wasn't implying *that* kind of relationship. If there was any proof of such an explosive liaison, why only hint at it, and only now, Tinsley considered. Was McGehee just throwing random, tawdry mud? Was Aiden reading too much into a benign question? Maslow could have weighed in, could have simply asked, "What are you talking about?" Nope. "On advice of counsel, I invoke my rights under the Fifth Amendment to the U.S. Constitution."

Tinsley confidently tapped in to his budding legal acumen as he wiped his brow. These queries were intended to send us a message, he decided. They were posed because the government knew Maslow wouldn't answer, a clever way of making its case via a witness who wouldn't fight back.

He checked his watch. Time to go. He cursed Maslow for wasting his outdoor respite. He was ready to pick a side after just a week of trial, and understood that was wrong. A few words from her might have prevented that.

The little surfer dude forced himself to think about something else. Should he put his Rams tee back on?

Nah. He could use some cheering up. He stuck out his bare chest and broke into a slow, purposeful jog.

September 25
(Ten Hours before Trial Week Two)

Izzy's second floor loft was a couple of blocks from Dupont Circle, a vibrant neighborhood convenient to everything. Her space was well-appointed and cozy.

Contrast that with Seb's apartment. Cluttered, cold and seemingly surrounded by nothing but concrete: cracked sidewalks, potholed streets and bland, gray buildings darkened by six p.m. each evening. Nonetheless, he wouldn't give up its walking distance commute to the Post's K Street offices, so when the two spent quiet time together – more now than when they were officially dating – it was at Izzy's.

Atop the thickly stuffed cushion of her lavender love seat, legs curled underneath her, Izzy stared blankly into the generous pour of Malbec she had been nursing.

"Do you not like it?" Seb asked defensively, having brought the vino. She was the connoisseur, her father being one of New York's leading wine importers. Seb couldn't tell the difference between a seven-dollar bottle and one costing 20 times that, but had absorbed what he could from her over the years.

"Huh? No," she answered, returning from wherever she'd drifted. "I mean, yes, or no, I don't not like it. It's fine." Izzy squinted in exaggerated confusion and crooked her head, resting it on his shoulder. "It's good," she sighed.

Seb worked his arm behind her, gently squeezing. "Babe, it's been a monster week. No worries. I'm just here for you, okay?"

Izzy took a swallow. "Babe?" she repeated.

He kissed the top of her fire-colored hair. "I'm fully aware how much you love that little moniker, Sweetie." Izzy gave him a sharp elbow at the invocation of yet another of the sexist nicknames she'd banned. Seb winced, then chuckled as he leaned down and nibbled at the tiny heart on her ear lobe. Mission accomplished. She was back in the room.

Having Seb around was nice. Izzy wasn't sure how to label whatever it was they were doing these days, but in the four years they had known each other, this version was the best. It was, like the Malbec in her hand, fine. Good, even.

They first met at Nuance, the kind of trendy, upscale bar neither preferred. The girlfriend who towed along a reluctant Izzy was work friends with the guy who'd roped in Seb.

He picked her out the minute he and his buddy started thru the crowd, her distinct appearance and animated features drawing Seb like a beacon. Their introduction moments later seemed, to him, superfluous. Her handshake was sturdy, and the hyper-observant young reporter felt it suited her. Several drinks on, Izzy's strength and confidence were even more apparent. Seb was beyond intrigued. He was hooked.

For her part, Izzy regarded the newcomer much more skeptically. He was handsome, for sure – those alluring gold eyes, rich brown skin accented against his eggshell V-neck – but if anything, those attributes put her on guard. To be honest, history taught her men, perhaps fun, were more often trouble. Her initial reticence, however, slowly melted. Seb's quiet intensity pulled at her.

By the evening's end there was no doubt they would see each other again, their attraction undeniable. Too strong, as it eventuated. Yet the fuse was lit: the ferocity with which she adorned the slim, fit curves of her body; Seb's hard yet subtle musculature; Izzy's quick wit and remarkable insight into basic human nature; his ordered, methodical view of the swirl of national life. They were like the pieces of a jigsaw, incomprehensible when scattered as tiny, unexplained fractions, wonderous when fit into place.

For two years they shared sweltering, eager sex and equally zealous reflections on the world. Maybe, if either were willing to submit to a simpler existence, their portrait could have been completed. Instead, Seb's byline was making its mark at the Post, *frequently on page one, and he was an increasingly sought-after guest on studio sets. She was an inventive standout fully devoted to* The Law Offices of Mandela Briggs, *supercharging the firm's success. Neither accepted love as an alternative to ambition.*

Nor was either blind to their compatibility, however, and so here they were. Not together and not apart. Unwilling to lock in or let go.

"I need to ask you something," she said. Seb recognized the change in her tone.

"Yeah?"

"Do you remember that story you ran?" she began, hesitantly, cognizant of blurring the lines between their personal and professional lives. *"The one with the picture you gave me, Kurtz and Kilbrough."*

Seb stiffened. The photo was from a highly placed administrative source who had every intention of bringing Styles down. The assumption was that the rising journalistic star would have it on the front page by the next morning, further poisoning the public against the Defendant and, more importantly, his potential jury pool.

Montes instead smelled a rat. Yes, he verified, the shot was authentic: Kurtz and Kilbrough meeting outside Styles' hotel only moments after the former visited the vice president, and just a few weeks before the latter tried to kill the president.

This meant something else was equally true: the prosecution had withheld this evidence from the defense, planning to spring it on them through the press. Seb figured this out based upon the tiny tidbits Izzy shared as the case progressed. They didn't talk about it much, and only in the vaguest of terms. Izzy knew Seb would never use anything she said in one of his stories and didn't want to torture him with inside info; he thought even the appearance of pumping her for scoops unseemly.

Yet when he received the incriminating photo, something Izzy mentioned a few days earlier crept back. "He wasn't an idiot," she'd said on this very love seat, the two of them drained from a typical long week, mellowed by more than one cocktail. "Other than some phone calls to Maslow, which he didn't try to hide, he cut TAC *off completely. Especially Kurtz, thank God."* News of Kurtz's involvement in the conspiracy was reaching a fever pitch. Montes had reported on it that very morning.

She didn't know.

So, instead of immediately running with the story, Seb chose to warn Izzy. The bombshell could wait a few days.

"I remember it," Seb said. Front page, screaming headline, followed by his appearances on XBN, CNN, MSNBC, FOX. And no hard feelings – Izzy understood that if Seb sat on it, his source would easily find another taker. She appreciated the heads up. "Why?"

"Yesterday, McGehee played the Maslow depo." Izzy paused, wanting Seb's help, his keen analysis, but not to plant the idea for another blockbuster, one Seb would frustratingly be honor bound to bury.

"Pretty uneventful," he said. "It was apparent he forced her to invoke the Fifth over and over to make her reek of criminality. The judge can instruct the jury all day long that it's a constitutional right implying nothing, but only guilty people choose silence over self-incrimination, right? At least that's the strategy."

"I get that," she said, then sat up, unfolding her legs and turning to him, a forging bronze flaring from her gaze. "But out of a seven-hour deposition, the prosecution only played 90 minutes. And our asswipe U.S. attorney was pretty intentional in the clips he used, even though he knew every reply would be the same."

"Right. And?" Seb caressed Izzy's bare knee, brow furrowed. She was stating the obvious. "It's his chance to make uncontested arguments and plant seeds, and you guys are helpless. Hardly surprising."

"One of the questions tripped a wire," Izzy continued, ignoring Seb's remark. Her mind worked that way. He'd learned to step aside when the mental cylinders throttled up. "Near the end, right before we quit. Like, he knew that's where he wanted to leave things. I mean, it wasn't a throw-away. It wasn't random. The bastard was sending us a signal."

Seb shrugged his shoulders, part muddle, part invitation.

She took a contemplative swig, the butterflies on her knuckles fluttering as she fingered the wineglass. "He asked Maslow, you know, you've had all these talks with Styles, so lady, he says ... and listen to how he phrases it ... 'to what degree were you aware of the close, personal relationship between the vice president and Sam Kilbrough?'"

She tilted her head, beckoning him to react. Again, he shrugged. "I guess I considered that more of a reminder than anything. 'Hey, Ladies and Gents, the defendant was really close friends with the hitman!'"

"Could be. For some reason I took it more sinister," she said, troubled. "I thought the jerk was implying Eli and Kilbrough were ... an item."

Seb recoiled, compressing his lips in disagreement. "Mmm, I didn't get that sense at all. Sure, it would make their bond even tighter, but how on Earth would McGehee ever establish *something like that? And if he had proof, why hold it till now?"*

"A grand finale," Izzy whispered.

Seb searched her expression for clues, then carefully touched her chin with his thumb and forefinger, gently aligning her attention to his. "What? Izzy, what is it?"

She sighed. "Probably nothing. I don't know. I'm so tired, and I'm so wrapped up in this case, I'm probably seeing ghosts."

"Izzy," Seb began, controlling his tenor so as not to push her, "I don't know what you're talking about."

"Not sure I do either." She gulped the last bit of her wine and looked up to the ceiling, steeling herself. "Seb, you can't ..."

"...Hey, you know I don't use anything we talk about. Not unless you say it's okay, and even then ..."

"...I know, I know." She put her glass down on the coffee table. "Wait here." Izzy went to the corner of the room, which she also used as an office, and rummaged through some files, returning with a green folder. She flopped back onto the cushions, buried her face into the file, covered her head with her arms, and groaned.

"Okay," Izzy said, feigning calm as she sat up again, "tell me if I'm crazy." She reached inside and retrieved a printout. She handed it to Seb, who saw it was an online profile of Samuel Kilbrough, one of hundreds since the attempted assassination, this one authored by some guy he'd never heard of at a paper in Madison, Wisconsin.

He scanned a pretty generic rendition of the would-be killer's bio, accompanied by a photo of a smiling, much younger Kilbrough. For some reason, Izzy printed it in color. Seb shook his head. They were both exhausted, making good progress on their second bottle, and he wasn't really up to solving mysteries. Izzy could see his impatience.

"This was one of a gazillion pieces I read back when we first took the case, trying to get a bead on what made the guy tick, any clue on why our client put so much faith in him, anything that could help, or screw us."

"I don't see anything here that hasn't been written a thousand times," Seb commented. "Why some online rag in Podunk, Wisconsin?"

"Yeah, not the Post," she said with a smirk, "but Kilbrough went to the university there before the Marines. I was looking for some local flavor. And like you, just now, I didn't get much."

"But? What does this have to do with McGehee's line about Styles and Kilbrough? You said it tripped a wire."

"Exactly! This!" *she exclaimed, grabbing the paper from him and waving it between them. Seb's exasperation was even more evident.* "Okay, so, like I said, I got the distinct impression El Barfo was implying something more than friendship, that he's been suggesting it all along. And to be honest, I've kinda wondered too. Maybe it was McGehee getting inside my head, but I've spent a lot of time with Styles, and we've talked to him about Kilbrough a bunch, and, well – let's just say the whole thing's been nagging me.

"And then yesterday morning, Eli shows up for our usual session, you know, recap the week, talk about the evidence, get his take, blah, blah, blah. And the second he walks in the door, I see it."

"See what?"

"The sweatshirt."

"What sweatshirt?"

Izzy's posture braced, careful as if maneuvering an unexploded bomb, handed the page back to Seb, eyes glued to his.

He took it, watching her watching him, awaiting his reaction. Seb focused on the three-by-two-inch image of Kilbrough. He was indeed wearing a sweatshirt, a gray one emblazoned with the jaunty red-and-white figure of Bucky Badger – Montes possessed a sports nut's encyclopedic knowledge of mascots – marching mischievously toward adventure, one fist clenched while the other held a foaming mug of beer.

"You're saying," Seb deliberated, "you think the Vice President of the United States came into your office yesterday wearing this exact, 20-year-old sweatshirt?"

"Sounds cra-cra, I get that, but I promise he was. He's worn it a lot, which is weird because Styles went to Baylor. No connection to Wisconsin. So it always kinda stood out to me. I figured he'd picked it up during his White House run, you know, before the Wisconsin primary or something. Never really gave it a second thought."

"Until McGehee suggested ..."

"Dipwad succeeded in bringing up a weird feeling, with his 'close, personal relationship' clip. Like, you know, seriously, could there have been

..." Izzy shook her head as if trying to fling the idea away. "The second Eli walked in, that sweatshirt punched my brain. I'd seen it before, somewhere else. I have a good memory for minor shit like that, but I couldn't put my finger on it. Couldn't let it go, either. So, before I came home, I started thumbing through my stuff on Kilbrough."

"And you saw this," Seb said. Izzy frowned. Her little gold septum bar wiggled.

This is scary, Seb thought. One of the things he loved about Izzy was an uncanny ability to see into people. Her instincts were seldom wrong. His journalistic reflexes, however, compelled him to push her. "Alright, well, maybe your initial instinct was the correct one. Maybe it's sentimental from the primary. I mean, he did beat Thorne in Wisconsin. A lot of folks thought he'd win it all after that."

"I was up all night, Seb. Reconstructed his whole campaign schedule. He made two trips to the state, a total of four days, well covered, lots of videos and pictures. He wore a suit, he wore a sweater, and of all places he might have put that thing on, his one speech on the Madison campus, he was sporting a blue dress shirt and a black Patagonia windbreaker. No Bucky Badger."

"Okay, well, he could have gotten it afterward, you know, nostalgic, 'the state that got me close' or whatever."

Izzy looked past him. Ignoring his suggestion, she pressed on. "The hundredth time I looked at this article, I finally noticed it – a tear, not even an inch long at the right edge of the collar. You can barely see it, but it's there."

Seb held the sheet close to face, turning it in the light. She was right. "And so did the one Styles wore," *he whispered,* "a small rip at the collar's right edge." *Izzy slowly nodded.* "Like I said, he's worn it a ton. It's kinda ratty, faded, and yes, that little imperfection."

It had started to drizzle, the ping, plop, tink *of droplets hitting the awnings and drainpipes outside bouncing through the room as the two of them sat in silence. Eventually, Seb, unimpressed by his own words, weakly offered* "they did sort of bond, I mean, Styles' niece and everything. Maybe it was a gift?"

Izzy rolled her eyes. "Guys don't give guys gifts like that, Seb. 'Hey, Mr. Vice President, here's my 20-year-old college sweatshirt I've kept all these years. I want you to have it because we both have loved ones with Down syndrome.' There's only one way Eli acquires that particular piece of clothing."

Seb ran his fingers back and forth behind his right ear, what Izzy recognized as his thinking mode. "So, Sherlock, what do I do with that?" *she asked.*

"Have you told Briggs?"

"Hell no! I don't even know what I'd say."

"How 'bout, 'Our client and the assassin may have been closer than we thought.'"

Maybe, Izzy contemplated. This was perhaps the biggest story Seb would never write. And he was dead on: Izzy had to tell her boss. It could change everything, especially if the U.S. attorney knew more, if he wasn't simply taunting, or bluffing, or speculating, or whatever he was doing. They had to be ready.

Something told Izzy, though, their client may not tell them the truth, the whole truth, and nothing but the truth. When it came to Sam Kilbrough, she wondered if their client even knew what the truth was.

Week Two

Nineteen

Blakely Kurtz. I'd like to rip the little tart's face off – for the lies, for the betrayal, for the naked self-preservation. Not a very dignified assessment, I know, coming from the Vice President of the United States. But it is what it is, and I'm nothing if not honest.

Instead, my game is composure. I mustn't reveal my contempt for the prosecution's "star witness." If the jury sees my loathing, or even senses it, they might give him more credit than he's due. The good news is, I'm quite practiced at controlling every aspect of my physical appearance and emotive signaling. Years in the political arena will do that.

After careful consideration, then, what I instead project is ... pity. Sorrow for the unfortunate thing. The more McGehee drags Kurtz through his eyewitness fable of intrigue, unrequited romance and victimhood, the more compassionate my expression. The hot steam of my anger builds, my malleable face serving as relief value.

> *Prosecutor: "Mr. Kurtz, I want the jury to be abundantly clear about this. When you left Mr. Styles' suite in Cleveland on the morning of February 17, six weeks before the assassination attempt, had the defendant given you any instructions, specifically for Sam Kilbrough?"*
>
> *Witness: "Yes sir."*
>
> *Prosecutor: "What were those directives?"*
>
> *Witness: "The vice president told me to convey to Mr. Kilbrough that, after everything was done, we, meaning The Aberdeen Circle, had secured an inconspicuous location for him through our Canadian friends."*

> *Prosecutor:* "You confirmed those arrangements with the defendant earlier in your meeting that morning."
>
> *Witness:* "Yes sir."
>
> *Prosecutor:* "And from where did you learn about Sam Kilbrough being set up by TAC with a hiding place in Canada?"
>
> *Witness:* "From Rachel Maslow."
>
> *Prosecutor:* "Was this escape plan her idea?"
>
> *Witness:* "No sir. She said to tell Eli it was all arranged, just as he requested."
>
> *Prosecutor:* "Getting Sam Kilbrough out of the country and to a secret location, 'after everything was done,' that was the defendant's wish?'"
>
> *Witness:* "That's what Rachel implied."
>
> *Prosecutor:* "That's what Rachel implied, or what she said?'"
>
> *Witness:* "That's what Rachel said."
>
> *Prosecutor:* "Did the vice president explain the phrase, 'after everything was done?'"
>
> *Witness:* "No sir."

Quite an exchange, all the more for being completely invented. I never said those words. Not to little Blakely Kurtz, and not to anyone else. I'm no fool.

What I *did* instruct Blakely was, tell him everything will be worked out, or will be done, or something like that. And I meant it. Sam had ten days left on the president's detail at that point, had already given his notice. He and I needed to focus on next steps. Sure, I used Blakely to convey Maslow's arrangements for Sam north of the border, but we weren't there yet. I honestly didn't think it would even be necessary, once things settled down, once the country understood the full reach of Magnus Thorne's treachery. Had I known of his crush on Sam, I never would have used Kurtz at all.

> *Prosecutor: "I hate to be indelicate, or intrusive, Mr. Kurtz, but for these ladies and gentlemen to appreciate the credibility of your discussions with Sam Kilbrough, and the seriousness of what was shared, I have to inquire about the nature of your ... association.*

Here we go. "Association?" That's McGehee's PG implication that Kilbrough and Kurtz had scorching, wild sex. *Please.* You have to understand something about Sam. He's a deep guy. Here's what I mean.

Objectively speaking, if one reads what's said online, I'm a decent looking 44-year-old man. Not a stunner, but square jawed, obsessively fit, few wrinkles – surprising given the demands and pressures of my existence – plus, my eyes are, they say, "captivating." Add a thick head of exquisitely (and expensively) styled hair and, well, without bragging, you could definitely do worse.

Kurtz, on the other hand, is seven years my junior, two or three inches taller, still has the sharp-edged build of the gymnast he was in college, and his role as the pretty face of *TAC* online and on air validates his admitted appeal.

Yet, from Sam's perspective, there's no contest. Blakely is superficial, good at repeating preprogrammed platitudes, glib. I feed on minutiae, devour details, evaluate and strategize. For a veteran secret service agent habituated to sussing out the base elements of any situation, where insight is blood and analysis is air, who do you think he'd choose?

Sam in bed with Blakely Kurtz? Not in a million years.

> *Witness: "Sam and I were close."*

> Prosecutor: "Tell us what that means, please."
> Witness: "It means that after we first met – after he sought me out – we started to ... I don't know, matter to one another. We were sharing some pretty intense stuff. That kind of environment, that kind of pressure, it forges a ... connection. You can't help it."
> Prosecutor: "Did you and Mr. Kilbrough become intimate?"
> Witness: "Yes."
> Prosecutor: "Sexually?"
> Witness: "Yes."

Does the Fifth Amendment forbid me from screaming? Would a barbaric yawp constitute self-incrimination or just an honest reflection of Kurtz's absurdity.

Sam needed Blakely the *TAC* communications director, not Blakely the man. The Aberdeen Circle was Thorne's prime target and most aggrieved victim. It was key to toppling the tyrant. Sam desired Kurtz's stature, his status, not his body.

Now, that said, would Sam play upon Kurtz's longings, perhaps indulge his fantasies? Blakely was a guy who hunted gratification on RumpUs. Sam, of course, utilized all available intel to achieve necessary goals. He understood Kurtz's commitment was key, because Rachel Maslow was a coward. Despite the atrocities to her people – to our people, to *my* people – she was way too comfortable as a martyr. She feared Magnus Thorne. But she *listened* to Blakely Kurtz.

So, what would Sam do in furtherance of the mission? The answer is "No" for any scene painted by the prosecutor's lurid, homophobic imagination. But, "Yes" if we stick to the bounds of the necessary, somewhere between Blakely's unrequited longings and Sam's dignity. I guess it all comes down to how one defines "sex."

More importantly, given my literal ass is on the line, what does any of this matter to the jury? Seriously, while they are drunk on the vision of sweating hunks tangled in white sheets, does that help me, or hurt me?

> *Prosecutor: "I assume, as close as you two were, that Sam Kilbrough confided in you?"*
> *Witness: "What do you mean?"*
> *Prosecutor: "Well, you communicated frequently by phone, by text – we've shared much of that with the jury – and you spent time together on several occasions, developing what became, as you've admitted, a sexual relationship. Surely he shared information with you. Personal things. Important things.*
> *Witness: "I suppose."*

Oh, come on, Blakely. Embarrassed? Is it painful admitting Sam never confided in you, at least nothing truly significant? So painful you will lie to pretend he did?

> *Prosecutor: "Did he tell you about the nature and extent of his feelings for the vice president?"*
> *Witness: "His feelings? He respected Elijah Styles, for sure. We all did."*
> *Prosecutor: "Anything beyond respect?"*
> *Witness: "Well, I mean, during the time Sam protected the vice president, they became ... I guess you could say, close?"*
> *Prosecutor: "Close, how?"*

Oh, Mr. McGehee, now what are you trying to imply? Conspirators *and* Lovers? It must all be very titillating for the ladies and gentlemen who will decide whether I live or die. *Sam Kilbrough would do anything, absolutely* anything *for the man he loved ... the man who desperately wanted to be president.*

Your problem is, Blakely can't possibly help you. The young minx may have been deluded into thinking he and Sam were more than they were, but he knows nothing of Sam's attachment to me, or mine to him, a construction of souls transcending anything sordid or tawdry. I've got news for our esteemed U.S. attorney: this salacious secret for which he gropes? Well, I don't have secrets, I haven't in forever. I'm not allowed them.

And for the record, Brady is dear to me. I would never do anything, intentionally, to hurt him. The miracles he and I created – Anna, a storybook political rise, a dynamic public brand – is of a different fabric than what Sam and I shared. With Brady I nurtured a family, an *existence*. With Sam, I tried to free a nation. They were different kinds of love. Those worlds don't intersect; therefore, they cannot collide.

> *Prosecutor:* "Whatever the true nature of their relationship, would you agree Sam Kilbrough believed Elijah Styles should be president?"
> *Witness:* "Definitely."
> *Prosecutor:* "Did he ever say that?"
> *Witness:* "We both did."
> *Prosecutor:* "Can you share exactly what Sam Kilbrough said."
> *Witness:* "Not everything. We talked about it a lot. But I do remember the last time we were ..."
> *Prosecutor:* "Go on."
> *Witness:* "The last time we were together, it was a couple of weeks ... No, less than that. Maybe 10 or 11 days before ... before the ... event."
> *Prosecutor:* "Before he shot the president."
> *Witness:* "Right. Sam said, 'Blakely, you have no idea how dangerous this guy is.' He was

referring to Thorne. I told him I did. That working for TAC, I knew damn well how crazy the president was, how much blood was on his hands, how many lives he had ruined. Sam just shook his head and gave me that look. And remember, he was on the inside for a long time. He knew more than anyone.

"Anyway, he held my chin with his fingers so that I was looking directly into his eyes, as if what he said next was something I really needed to hear. Not only hear, but remember."

Prosecutor: "What did he tell you?"

Witness: "He said, 'If Thorne isn't stopped, what we've seen so far will be nothing compared to what comes.' I asked what he meant. He shook his head, like it was too big to verbalize. But then he smiled, and said, 'Don't worry, it won't happen. We won't let it.'"

Prosecutor: "We?"

Witness: "That could have meant a lot of things. It's what he said next that ... jarred me."

Prosecutor: "What did Sam Kilbrough tell you next, Mr. Kurtz? What did he say after implying the President of the United States would, somehow, be terminated?"

Witness: "He said, 'Eli is going to be a great president, Blakely, and once everyone understands what he's done for us, he will go down in history as America's Savior.'

"It took me a moment to grasp what he was saying. Or what I thought he was saying. I must have stared at Sam forever. When I finally opened my mouth, he put his finger on my lips.

> *'Trust me.'* That was all he said. It was pretty clear Sam didn't want me to force it."

I wanted to stand and applaud. I really did. As a bit of a performer myself, I appreciate Broadway-level theatrics. Blakely was always endearing in his unassuming way, cute perhaps. But, Man! Bravo, *Little One*! This is Tony Award stuff. Makes it sound as though Sam and I had it all figured out: shoot the president, move into 1600 Pennsylvania, and everyone's happy!

The truth is a bit more complicated. Isn't that always the case?

> *Prosecutor:* "Mr. Kurtz, can you tell this jury any specifics about the plot to kill Magnus Thorne?"
>
> *Witness:* "I cannot. In fact, my mind wouldn't go there. I assumed, made myself believe there was ... something else, some other way. Scandal? Impeachment? Something. Anything but murder. Someone as gentle and thoughtful as Sam committing homicide? I mean, this is a guy who was dedicated to protecting the president!"
>
> *Prosecutor:* "What you can tell us, however, is you knew Elijah Styles intended to replace Magnus Thorne as president."
>
> *Witness:* "That is correct."
>
> *Prosecutor:* "We've talked about your familiarity with Sam Kilbrough. What about the defendant? What was your history with him?"
>
> *Witness:* "Ten years. I was Rachel Maslow's executive assistant at TAC when Mr. Styles first approached her. He was running for mayor of Dallas. Three years later, I became comms director, and in that role one of my assignments was to promote 'Everything Eli.' That's what we called it. At first, we thought he'd eventually run

for governor or senator or something. He was ambitious, crazy ambitious, and Rachel made it a priority to do anything we could to support one of us."

Prosecutor: *"One of us?"*

Witness: *"A member of the LGBTQ community. Not just an ally, but a gay man with tons of potential. We all saw it. We were all thrilled. And when he ran for president ..."*

Prosecutor: *"How did that feel?"*

Witness: *"Like Nirvana. You know, recognition, acceptance. Our Obama. I mean, sure, Pete Buttigieg had done it, but he didn't get past Super Tuesday. This time, even as late as the convention, we thought Eli had a chance. It felt like the real deal."*

Prosecutor: *"You were excited, then."*

Witness: *"Beyond excited. Ecstatic. We would do anything for Elijah Styles. In my role with TAC I spent a lot of time with the candidate. Everyone knows the vice president is smooth, eloquent. You see it any time he's on stage. What I learned, though, being around him so much, was the man had a gift. One-on-one, Eli was penetrating. He could look into your soul and ... I'm not sure how to describe this. He's hypnotic."*

Prosecutor: *"What was your reaction, then, when Thorne won and Styles agreed to be his running mate?"*

Witness: *"My reaction? Me, personally?"*

Prosecutor: *"Yes."*

Witness: *"Betrayal."*

Prosecutor: *"How so? What politician would turn down the second highest office in the land?"*

> Witness: "Magnus Thorne is a wannabe autocrat. It's pretty obvious now, to anyone who cares. But even back then, Eli knew that was true. He wouldn't say it this way publicly, but in private, he was super clear: Thorne was a power-hungry crackpot, and a dangerous homophobe too.
>
> "So, when he agreed to team up with the guy, it was heartbreaking for those of us who believed Eli actually stood for something."

And there it is, perhaps the only charge worse than "murderer" – *politician*! Very clever construction by the U.S. attorney. In addition to being gay and all the immorality that entails, Ladies and Gentlemen, this man has no soul! He believes in nothing beyond his own ascension of the political ladder, his accumulation of authority over your lives.

> Prosecutor: "Yet, Mr. Kurtz, you took a leave of absence from TAC and went to work for the Thorne/Styles campaign."
>
> Witness: "Exactly. That's my point about Eli Styles. He can make you believe almost anything. He convinced Rachel, and me, and scores of other people, that he had to take the offer. He must be a part of the administration. That he was the only one who could protect us, from the inside.
>
> "Funny thing is, if Eli had turned Thorne down, I don't think any of this ever would have happened. Thorne would never have been president. Eli gave him the cover to scrape by."
>
> Prosecutor: "If the defendant was as sharp a player as you make him out to be, wouldn't he have foreseen that Thorne would isolate him, just like Kennedy did LBJ?"

Witness: "No, I think Eli had such tremendous confidence in himself, and such high expectations after all he did to get that man elected, he didn't anticipate being cut out. Even if he had, though, his priority was to get the office, to position himself."

Prosecutor: "To position himself a heartbeat away from the presidency, you mean?"

Witness: "Yeah. And, you mentioned Kennedy freezing Johnson, ignoring him. We all know how that turned out."

Prosecutor: "One final topic, Mr. Kurtz. I'll start by asking if you recognize this, marked by the court reporter as United States Exhibit 27."

Witness: "I do."

Prosecutor: "What is it?"

Witness: "It's a note from Vice President Styles to Rachel. Rachel Maslow."

Prosecutor: "How do you know this?"

Witness: "Because I saw him write it, and I delivered it."

Prosecutor: "Please put number 27 up on the screen so the jurors can follow along."

> *R –*
>
> *I can't help anymore. You need to act now, before it's too late.*
>
> *E*

Prosecutor: "Mr. Kurtz, did you know the contents of this card before you delivered it?"

Witness: "Not exactly, but I had a pretty good idea."

Prosecutor: "What did the defendant tell you about it?"

Witness: "We were at his official residence. The Naval Observatory. It became our primary method, you know, in person, of discussing sensitive topics after Thorne started harassing the gay community, and TAC in particular. I'd go because I was much lower profile – Rachel was toxic, thanks to all the attacks. He ..."

Prosecutor: "The vice president?"

Witness: "... the vice president, he had just learned – see, Eli still had good contacts throughout the government, a lot of people who thought Thorne was dangerous, or crazy, or who were just sympathetic about what was happening to us. Anyway, Thorne's people were on to some of our plans, apparently, or so Eli said. Bad things were coming our way very soon, the full force of the president's rage, so it was kinda put up or shut up time, because everything was about to come loose."

Prosecutor: "What plans, Mr. Kurtz? You said, 'Thorne's people were on to some of our plans.'"

Witness: "I wasn't involved in the details, Mr. McGehee. That was part of the role, I guess, of being a liaison: not knowing enough specifics to jeopardize the operation. I don't think anyone was fully aware of all the moving pieces."

Prosecutor: "Except Ms. Maslow, and, of course, the vice president."

Witness: "I couldn't say. I heard things, and in hindsight I can put more stuff together, but back then my knowledge was vague, big picture, cryptic stuff, like the things Sam told me, or that note."

Prosecutor: "Okay. The defendant thought it was urgent to get Maslow to activate TAC's plans – and I think we all have a much better idea now as to what those were. But you said by this point Styles' messages were verbal. Why the sudden need to put something in writing? Wasn't that risky?"

Witness: "I guess he didn't want me to know. Plus, he thought putting the message in his own hand would have more of an impact on Rachel, would make her understand this was for real.

"In any event, she was supposed to destroy it, 'Burn it,' Eli said, as soon as she'd read it."

Prosecutor: "Burn it? Why?"

Witness: "Because, clearly, the idea was to bring down Thorne. I don't mean kill him. I didn't know anything about that, but there was something big planned, something Eli and Rachel and Sam and maybe others, like some of the tech people, had been working on for months. There were lots of rumors, for example, using cyber capabilities to convince the American people to stand up to Thorne, you know, revealing dirt on him that would be more than embarrassing. Resignation level stuff."

Prosecutor: "Like holding banks, the stock market hostage and crashing the economy?"

Witness: "I don't know."

Prosecutor: "Like shutting down air traffic, public transit, creating chaos and panic?"
Witness: "I don't know."
Prosecutor: "Like shooting the president?"
Witness: "No! I mean, that's nothing I ever heard."
Prosecutor: "'Eli is going to be a great president, Blakely,' weren't those Sam Kilbrough's exact words?"
Witness: "Well, yes, but ... Sam, which I said before, he never said anything about physically harming Thorne."
Prosecutor: "Sam Kilbrough may never have used the words gun, bullet, kill or president in the same sentence, Mr. Kurtz, but looking back, isn't all of that pretty clear?"
Witness: "Not to me. Not then. And even now ..."
Prosecutor: "Even now, sir, if murdering the president were not Elijah Wilson Styles' path to the Oval Office, then why burn this piece of paper?"
Witness: "I told you, I wasn't privy to the details, and the vice president didn't tell me everything. Neither did Rachel. That was intentional. But I knew enough to understand this note was, like, the signal. The flare."
Prosecutor: "Final question, Mr. Kurtz. What did Rachel Maslow do when she read the card?"
Witness: "She showed it to me. And then she said, 'Good God, does he want us all to hang?'"

†††

As he descends the stand and escapes the courtroom, all I can do is stare at Blakely. He avoids eye contact. The jury watches him leave, watches me visually castigate him as he slinks off, watches him fixate on the floor with what I hope they perceive as well-deserved shame.

"Mr. McGehee?" The judge calls, and the U.S. attorney stands to announce what my attorney told me to expect: "Your Honor, the United States rests."

Putting yourself in my shoes, as I'm sure you are, you'd think I would feel tremendous relief. The beating is over. Our defense can finally begin. We have a chance to set things right, to inject perspective, rationality and, above all, the golden ingredient for criminal defendants: *Doubt*.

Sure, emotionally there is a fleeting sense of release, a numbed hope not in any fashion celebratory. More as I would imagine leaving a bunker, glad the shelling has stopped and eager for a peek at daylight, however smoke-filled the air. My muted response is driven by the analytical part of my brain, which asks if folks seriously contemplate me selecting murder as the cleanest path to the White House. Have searing innuendo and attacks on my character registered?

Let us be honest. The label "American criminal justice system" is a misnomer, insofar as it includes the word "justice." Before you roll your eyes, I've said this for years. Reforming the process whereby we enforce our communal *Thou Shall Nots* was a major part of my presidential campaign, and before that, my term as mayor. Jury trials are at best approximations, truncated theatrical performances designed to entertain 12 quite random, uniquely unqualified persons displaced from their normal dull lives, for whom the price of escape is a vote at the end. Or perhaps better stated, not a vote, but an *impression* as to which side has better projected guilt or feigned innocence. Like swiping right or left on a dating app, verdicts are little more than subliminal expressions of personal taste and learned fear, sprinkled with a dose of confusion.

I have always been a man of action, planning several steps ahead and then doing, acting, adjusting – in control of my own destiny. That's why this process is so frustrating. That judge on high, the U.S. attorney, my lawyer, those dozen in the box, even the ancient bailiff, all of them are in motion, a symphony, or cacophony, of reactions and decisions all about me, but not *reflecting* me. It's as if I'm being sketched by a blind artist who applies whispered rumors without actual encounter. The resulting caricature, naturally, is wild interpretation, not reality.

I suppose what I am trying to tell you is, for a conviction the government needs a unanimous jury. I need only a single holdout. So, while Arenberg and Blakely and Hancock and "The Note" and the phone logs and the videos indeed paint an unflattering scene, I have no doubt my able counsel will masterfully chip away at this sinister panorama. There will be no conviction, I am certain.

All of which eludes the point. I still intend to be President of the United States. Anything short of a unanimous "Not Guilty" verdict complicates that objective. Thus, once again, it's up to me.

Sidney McGehee may be skilled at legal banalities and scripted persuasion, but he's never riled crowds or debated on national TV, squeezed destitute shoulders or pressed hands pining for acceptance. In essence, a trial is about souls. And I alone grasp what they must see.

Twenty

"Can't we just end this thing?" the president asked, comfortably reclined in his high-back chair, scuffed shoes resting on the memos and papers scattered atop his blotter. "You know, can't we have a witness, someone who heard him say ... I don't know, 'Sam, go kill the president?'"

His pair of advisors dared not turn to one another, exchanging looks of incredulity at the number of crimes proposed in that single utterance. They knew to keep their focus on him, their manner unruffled. This was all part of "the process."

"It's ... the whole thing, it's all a huge waste of time. And bad for the country, too, right, A.R.?"

A.R. Hoffman, White House Counselor and Assistant to the President for Domestic Affairs, sat in his typical Teutonic pose of attention in the wingback at the presidential desk's left corner. "Very bad for the country, sir." Neither he nor the room's other occupant, Colonel Arenberg, had the slightest intention of answering the original question.

"You know, I could have had my generals put this whole thing down." He lifted a heavy crystal tumbler to his lips, taking a healthy slurp of Maker's Mark, lamp light glinting off the presidential seal etched into its side. "Should have, but too many cowards cried 'it's *unconstitutional*.'" Thorne drew out the word disapprovingly as he stared over the rim at the Colonel. Arenberg was one of many providing the unwelcomed advice.

"So," the president continued, clumsily putting down his drink, "where are we?"

"We are in a good position, Mr. President," Hoffman began. The intense man, salt and pepper hair in a menacing crew, suit jacket always on, buttoned, white dress shirt severely starched, had been with the boss from the beginning. From before the beginning. When Thorne inherited his family's middling metals business, he brought in Hoffman, a nerd with a business degree he knew from Montana State, not because of talent but because A.R. was cheap, and loyal. An Ad Man by training, Hoffman's wizardry, along with Thorne's ambition, transformed the small firm into an international behemoth, generating enough cash to eventually buy their home state's governorship.

"McGehee performed as expected, really drew the noose. Styles looked like the ambitious schemer he is, and his ties to Kilbrough, to *TAC*, to the whole mess, are tight as can be. I don't think this jury can wait to convict him."

"Yeah, but that little cocksucker and his uppity lawyer aren't gonna just roll over, are they? No way. They've got something coming, A.R. What are you hearing?"

Hoffman did indeed *hear* a lot. That was his job: be everywhere, know everything. Usually he did. "Well, of course, they don't have to map it out for us, but I dug around, and we have a pretty good idea. They subpoenaed several people. Rhodes, Drury ..."

"Rhodes? My own god damn Treasury secretary! What the hell can that bastard say?"

"Not to worry, sir. We've already had a little sit down with Percival."

"It's the Twenty-Fifth," the Colonel chimed in, never missing an opportunity for insightfulness. "Removal of the president."

"I know what the fucking Twenty-Fifth Amendment is, Ezra. What does Percival have to do with it?"

Hoffman intervened, utilizing the fruits of his finely-tuned radar. "The vice president approached Secretary Rhodes during the whole post-election mess. Tried to get his support for a Cabinet vote declaring you, uh, unable to discharge the powers and duties of office."

"Little Harvard prick. I told you I didn't want him," he said, glaring at Arenberg. "No Ivy Leaguers. You can't trust those smug elitists. Should have gotten a vanilla Jew for Treasury like every other president. Someone loyal who does what he's told."

The Colonel focused on the inflamed vessels zigzagging the whites of Thorne's eyes, blood red bolts the same color as the heavy drapes framing the bulletproof windows along the back. Everything in this Oval Office, from those gory curtains to the Arabian gold carpet to the violent war portraiture lining the walls – Rubens' *Consequences of War*, Copley's *The Death of Major Peirson*, Girodet's *Revolt of Cairo*, Lorenz's *The Last Glow of a Passing Nation*, each an invocation of morbid conquest – was a ghoulish projection of raw, pulsating power. "Macabre," the French leader privately called the décor after his visit. "Insane," the Chinese premier had remarked after his.

Even the president's desk, Arenberg concluded, reeked of insecure bluster. Thorne could have summoned the one made famous by Kennedy and Reagan, the Resolute, built from the oak timbers of the British Arctic exploration ship of that name and gifted to the nation by Queen Victoria. Or the one commissioned by and named for Theodore Roosevelt, later claimed by six of his successors. Instead, he insisted upon his *own* battered and scratched stick of furniture from his days as CEO of Thorne Metals. The First Lady wasn't consulted; this was *his* lair.

"Mr. President," the Colonel finally said, "Rhodes won't be a problem. He called me in a panic when he received the summons. Came over yesterday. We calmed him down, gave him his orders. He'll be fine."

"I'm not so sure," the president mused. "The guy's jumpy as hell. What if that lawyer, what's his name A.R.?"

"Briggs."

"Briggs. What if Briggs rattles him? You know Percival comes from a very pretty world. Not like me. He's never worked a real day in his life. Never been outside a mansion or a limousine. A big, tough Black guy like Briggs staring down at him? He might fold." The president looked into the distance and considered his own remarks, then snapped at his chief counselor, "Did we know about this A.R.? ... this coup?"

Of course Hoffman did. Nothing in this administration escaped his attention. "Well, Mr. President, there were rumblings ..."

"Rumblings? In my own Cabinet? Every one of them begged me for an appointment."

"Not that way, sir. It was Styles. He approached several of them, trying to get a majority, trying to scare them about you calling out the National Guard."

"It went nowhere," Arenberg added. "We heard about it immediately, shut it down, reminded them how much they owe you."

"God damn right!"

"Anyway, you had enough on your plate. No need to bother you with that nonsense."

"Hmmph!" Another swig of the dark liquid, its warmth soothing. "How does any of that, Rhodes, the Secretaries telling him to pound sand ... where does it get Styles? Shows he was trying to screw me, however he could, right?"

"I'm sure that's how McGehee will play it," Hoffman opined, "but our understanding is that Styles wants the jury to believe he would only use legal means to challenge you. That if he planned to, well ..."

"Have someone blow my head off?"

"Right. That he was too by-the-book, too legalistic to consider anything so malicious."

"Bullshit."

"Completely," the Colonel agreed. "Definitely," the counselor concurred.

"I thought Drury already testified?" the president shifted gears.

"Correct," A.R. said, "but Briggs didn't ask him much during the prosecution's case. Sometimes the defense will do that, bring a witness back closer to the end of the case if they think they can leave the jury with a better impression."

The president left his chair and walked past the men to the bar along the far wall. They twisted in their seats to follow his movement, noticing the muted TV in the breakfront below where Thorne refilled his glass. It showed an XBN reporter, "LIVE" on the White House lawn not too far from this very room.

"You know, Drury's another guy I don't trust. Too close to Styles. Weak. Plus, I fired his ass. He'll save his own skin if he gets pushed."

Hoffman nodded, even though the president's back was too him. "Our guess is ..."

"Guess!" Thorne growled. "How do we not know? A.R., your job is to *know*. Drury has to understand his country needs him." He reconsidered, coming to a much more germane conclusion. "His *president* needs him!"

"Drury fully appreciates his position," Arenberg said.

"We could ruin him," Thorne declared, floating a suggestion. "Probably should have by now. Hung him out to dry, you know, the, ah, the ... fool ... incompetent ... failed to protect the president, let his president get shot and all that. Put him in jail for gross ineptitude. Probably gets a nice pension, doesn't he? What kind of horseshit is that?"

It was time to rein the boss in, a not insignificant part of the Colonel's resume, especially when the bourbon took over. "As I'm sure you remember, Mr. President, we decided it would be sounder to leave him something to lose, give him a reason to play ball."

Thorne frowned, but through his fog he was listening.

"Briggs wants Drury to say we canned Kilbrough," Hoffman added, "so he can argue ..."

"Disgruntled secret service agent shoots the president," Thorne allowed. "But we *did* sack his ass, right?"

"Actually," A.R. gently corrected, "we allowed him to resign. Precisely to eliminate the kind of argument you are suggesting."

"Yes," the president said neutrally, searching his memory. "Right, we let him walk. Looked better that way."

"Indeed, sir, and all Drury knows is that Kilbrough wanted out, 'tired' or 'burned out' or some nonsense. That's all Drury can say." Hoffman looked to the Colonel.

Taking the pass, Arenberg said, "I've spoken with him, Mr. President. He understands what to say."

"And what *not* to say," Thorne roared, piercing his chief of staff with doubt.

Arenberg worried the boss had forgotten there were three people in the room. Discreetly, he said, "Drury doesn't know anything about our discussions." His eyes tried to guide the president toward A.R., as in *neither does your White House counselor*. Thorne didn't catch his drift.

"I don't know, Ezra. What if Kilbrough blabbed something to Darby."

He meant Drury, but the Colonel was more worried about what else Thorne might say, and whether Hoffman was getting suspicious.

"Magnus," he said – invoking the familiar in front of someone else was intended as a slap to his creation's face – "you don't need to worry about this. The former director is on board, and he has no knowledge of anything damaging. Briggs may not even call him."

Thorne felt the rebuke, and considered whether to explode. Instead, he took another drink, then, ignoring the insolence, asked another question. "How in the hell did he put on his case in only a week? Do we have the right guy? What's his name again?"

"McGehee," A.R. rejoined the discussion.

"McGehee. Right. I mean, for fuck's sake, does he realize this is the biggest prosecution in history? Ruby blew away Oswald before he could be tried, then Ruby dies of cancer, and those Warren Commission fools chase their dicks around for years and come up with nothing. *Here*, we got the mastermind of the whole thing in front of a jury, and McGehee is already done?"

Hoffman took the lead. "No concern at all, Mr. President. A couple of things are at work. First, there are no cameras in the courtroom, which always speeds things up."

"No spotlight," Arenberg said, "so fewer theatrics by the thespians with law degrees."

Thorne grimaced. "No cameras. That was dumb. Judge could have gotten herself on the cover of *TIME*. Been a real star. You know," he sneered, "she's not bad looking."

"Not her style," A.R. resumed. "Which brings me to my second point. Carolyn Bering runs a tight ship, especially when it comes to trials. They call it 'the Bering Blitzkrieg.'"

"Blitzkrieg," Thorne repeated. "Lightning War."

"That's right!" Hoffman gushed, a bit surprised the president knew his World War II history. "She has the lawyers resolve anything disputed, or technical, well before the case starts so there are no interruptions. The litigants are expected to get to the point fast, or she mows them down. Bering says it's a waste of the jury's time for lawyers to call peripheral witnesses or go in circles or long windups with their questioning. McGehee has appeared before her many times, and Briggs does his research. They both know better."

"Hmmm," Thorne droned, staring into a middle distance. He'd lost interest. The prosecution wasn't the *Circus Maximus* he'd wanted.

The Colonel seized on his mood. "The thing is, McGehee is playing it smart anyway. In a case like this, the defense loves to draw things out, create chaos with irrelevant details, distract the jurors from the central issues. Yammer away at anything they can argue later is 'reasonable doubt.'"

"Reasonable doubt," the president hissed. "What a crock." He lifted his glass, only to discover that it was, once again, empty.

He put his feet on the floor and placed his elbows on the desk, pointing a finger at each of his advisors. "Let me tell you both one thing," he started. "There's no doubt about this, *reasonable* or any other kind. Eli wanted me out, and that little prick didn't care how it happened. So, he's getting what he deserved." Thorne folded his arms across his chest and nodded, agreeing with himself.

It was late, and nothing good ever came from these melancholy meanderings, Arenberg knew. He was about to end it when Hoffman decided a little extra puffery was in order.

"He will get exactly what he deserves, sir," he brown-nosed. "The U.S. attorney really made your case. He joined the vice president and *TAC* at the hip. The jury knows they both wanted you out. He's proven Maslow, Kurtz, Kilbrough were all in league ..."

And then it happened, just as the Colonel had feared. Thorne spoke from his other-worldly place, half aware of his audience, less aware of his words.

"Sam wasn't supposed to fucking *shoot* me!"

A.R.'s features scrunched in confusion.

"I think it's time we call it a night, Mr. President," his chief of staff announced, rising. Hoffman hesitantly followed his senior colleague's lead.

"Expert marksman. Ha!" the president said, again leaning back in his chair. "He was supposed to miss."

Arenberg placed a hand on Hoffman's shoulder, raising his eyebrows at the befuddled White House counselor. *Who knows what the heck he's talking about?*

"I saw it in his eyes, though," Thorne murmured. "It's all because of Styles."

Hoffman's instinct to pump up his chief kicked in. "Rest assured, Mr. President, the jurors have no misgivings. The prosecutor proved the vice president was manipulating the whole thing. They know he's a traitor. Elijah Styles is toast."

"Toast," Thorne repeated, letting the word swirl in his brain. "Toast," he muttered again.

Then he looked to Copley's masterwork, red-clad British soldiers clinging to the limp body of their leader, Major Peirson, uniform stained by his own blood, a large Union Jack aloft above the melee. Thorne mistook the painting as a depiction of "British losers" being routed by the American revolutionaries. It was actually a commemoration of a stunning English victory over the French on the disputed Channel Island of Jersey. No matter to the president, who only saw an enemy rightfully slain. Through his inebriated haze, it was not bleeding Major Peirson, martyr in victory, it was the prone body of his own treacherous vice president.

He whispered in a low, guttural croak, "Dead."

The Defense

Twenty-One

Sitting at counsel table, Briggs took in the judge's unoccupied bench, rubbing his fingers over his throat's smooth skin. Clean-shaven about 4:30 this morning, the same caress would encounter a sandpaperish friction by the end of the court day. Mandela would dampen it with an electric razor before meetings tonight – well into the evening, as usual during a trial – restarting the process early tomorrow with an expensive razor and genuine barbershop-quality shaving cream. Many of his successful Black peers, especially in his opinion those extending their veneer of success beyond reality, chose a rougher look, as in, *I've got better things to do*. For Briggs, it was about professionalism, discipline, detail, traits he projected unambiguously.

Today I finally get the ball, he thought. No more crouching, dodging, weaving. Now *we* direct the flow, to the extent possible in the ether of litigation.

The Secretary of the Treasury was in the house, somewhere in the hallway with his retinue, anticipating a dramatic entrance. Briggs was ready to go, equating his tension to that of a thoroughbred who craves the gate-opening bell, signaling his charge ahead of the competition.

It was 8:32, merely two minutes past the day's scheduled start, still, an unusual delay for the ever-punctual Carolyn Bering, giving Mandela unwanted time to ruminate, second guess, overthink. He resisted such nonsense. He had a plan, and more vitally, confidence in that blueprint. Briggs' strategy was two-pronged: themes and tactics. Quite predictable if the U.S. attorney had done his homework, though Mandela didn't care. It was that tried and true.

Thematically: Deflect, Belittle, Victimize. Make this case about Kilbrough, Thorne, anyone but Styles – *their* motivations and schemes, not the vice president's. Push the prosecution's allegations to a hairbrained, laughable extreme requiring his client to be the most inept, unintelligent criminal ever (obviously not this particular defendant). And all the while, remind the jury exactly who is really under attack: not Magnus Thorne or his gun-wielding RAGE militias, not his lapdog majorities in Congress, but *them*, their democracy, and the man trying to defend the Republic, Elijah Styles.

Tactically: Winnow the case to its bare necessities. Over months, Briggs carefully sifted through voluminous options, conceding the Judge's renowned impatience and, of far more consequence, the danger of wasting a sequestered jury's time. He settled on five or six witnesses to be presented in a rising crescendo of importance and drama. Mandela hoped to yield a superior number – *One* – a single juror unconvinced of the story wielded against his client. Of course, twelve would be better.

It all started with Percival Rhodes.

The United States Secretary of the Treasury was yet another Borgen Railey guy. BR, like Goldman Sachs and BlackRock, were asset management leviathans whose colossal balance sheets seemed to encompass everything, everywhere, at least so far as coin was concerned.

Rhodes, however, was no Whiz Kid like Styles who, in his pre-political life rocketed through Borgen's ranks. Percival, on the other hand, quietly plodded. He eventually became BR's VP for North American operations. The pair never met, Percival's corporate path sober and traditional, Eli's more action hero. Grease vs. glitz. Bond yields vs. flashy acquisitions.

Nonetheless, Rhodes was endowed with the right pedigree: son of long-time Senate Finance Committee chair, the late Prescott Rhodes III; husband to the heiress of a plastics fortune; all the right boarding schools, meeting all the other young beneficiaries of American aristocracy; netted his MBA, *summa cum laude*, from Harvard.

Though Rhodes technically joined BR as a junior associate, his surname, and long list of high-level contacts and well-funded acquaintances, made his steady rise a certainty.

The parallel orbits of these two accomplished men, Styles and Rhodes, finally intersected at the new president's first cabinet meeting four-plus years earlier. Warily they considered one another, neither trustful of the other's station. To Styles, the Treasury post was an undeserved gift bestowed upon a spoiled scion – Percival was Randolph and Mortimer Duke in *Trading Places*, men whose unmerited status was more punchline than honor. For Rhodes, the vice presidency was undignified charity borne of electoral expediency, Eli the lucky hack who helped Thorne check a few boxes.

Now here they were, in the same courthouse, eager to witness the other's discomfort.

"All Rise!!!" the ancient Bailiff Bankhead bellowed, snapping Briggs to his feet, and to his task. The Judge took her perch and looked down at him, his cue.

"The Defense calls Percival ... Bartholomew ... Rhodes," Mandela declared, stretching out each syllable of the sophisticated name, giving its elitism full effect.

A deputy opened one of the oversized rear doors, and in strode a tall man, thinning gray hair gelled rigidly in place, shiny under the overhead lights, his spine a ramrod, his face likewise inflexible. Rhodes traversed the center aisle accustomed to being the object of fascination, his eyes set forward, ignoring the day's lottery-winning spectators. He had been well-briefed on procedures, and with the barest of nods to the judge took his place in the box as if done a thousand times.

Before the witness' right hand lowered, Briggs launched. "Percival Bartholomew Rhodes, United States Secretary of the Treasury, correct?" he began, uttering the title as dryly as if it were a minor postal clerkship.

Rhodes hesitated, nervously fingering the white linen pocket square of his double-breasted Brioni suit. "Yes." Truth be told, Percival's practiced demeanor of regal indifference masked real intimidation. His life rarely involved people of color not in subservient roles. He was unaccustomed to challenge from anyone, least of all an intense Black man.

Mandela guessed as much, keeping stern. Task One: dismantle the pedestal of privilege. "Before Magnus Thorne appointed you to his Cabinet, had you spent so much as a minute in public service of any kind?"

"My family has several charitable organ ...."

"No sir, *public* service, as in government, as in serving the taxpayers, as in setting the policies that will rule people's lives."

"Oh, no, not that. Of course, my father ..."

"I'm not asking about Senator Prescott Rhodes III, or your grandfather, Prescott Rhodes II, founder of the largest mortgage bank in Connecticut, or your uncle, Bartholomew Aster Rhodes, majority owner of New York's largest medical insurance company. I am asking about *you*. Never a smidgeon of public, government service, right?"

Rhodes used his perfectly manicured hand to straighten his perfectly straight necktie. "Correct."

Trifecta, Briggs noted: everyone hated health insurers, mortgages and, of course, politicians. "What you *did* have to recommend yourself to the new president," he continued, "was, well, a whole lot of money. *Billions* in other people's money you managed, and millions which you either personally donated or raised on behalf of candidate Thorne."

During witness prep, the Mexican kid, Joel? ... anyway, the U.S. attorney's associate, instructed Rhodes not to bite at speeches like this.

If there isn't an actual question, wait for one. Resist the temptation to be cute, such as, "is there a question in there, counselor?" The jury will hate you. Let the lawyer be the jerk for badgering you.

Percival was a superb rule follower. He settled his cold gray eyes on Mandela, in silence.

"Twenty-five million dollars, in fact, right Mr. Rhodes?"

"Actually, I only donated two million."

Only. Briggs loved it. "Yes indeed, *only* two million from your pocket," as if Percival had reached into his pants and doled out lunch money, "and another $23 million raised from your family, friends, clients and colleagues."

Rhodes frowned. "Yes."

"And a few weeks after the election, you were named Secretary of the Treasury."

"Yes."

"Straight outta Borgen Railey," Briggs grinned. "Tell us about your time with BR." Briggs didn't care a wit about Percival's experience there, and knew the jury was even less interested. He simply wanted the Secretary talking on a topic where there was literally nothing he could say to endear himself to his audience.

"That could take a while. As you said, I was there a long time." Rhodes gave a slight smile to underline the cleverness of his riposte.

Mandela's face returned the insincerity. "The highlights will be fine."

Rhodes took a deep breath, and with equal measures of boredom, impatience and snobbery, surveyed his journey through the world of high finance. Frowns and yawns dominated The Twelve, and when Briggs judged their opinion of this man could go no lower, he abruptly shifted gears.

"About three years after you arrived at BR from *Haa-vaad*," he mocked, "my client, Mr. Styles, was hired by the firm. Did you meet him?"

"No."

"Never?"

"No." Rhodes worried it was a trick question, so quickly added, "Borgen is a huge organization. I was in finance, and I understand your client was in Mergers and Acquisitions. So, no, to my memory we never crossed paths. Certainly never worked together."

"Did you know Meyer Brook?" The jurors' collective ears perked. Everyone was familiar with the richest man in the world – he adorned the covers of not only financial, but also society, entertainment and sports publications, the epitome of jet-setting success.

"Of course! He is our largest shareholder."

"Did you ever work with him?"

"Quite often. He had a number of business operations outside of Borgen, and in my role as a senior director in the North American Division, and then as its vice president, I coordinated many deals with his external corporations and partnerships."

And now, the humiliation. "As frequent as were your interactions with him, did Mr. Brook ever try to entice you away from BR, offer you the opportunity to work with his global enterprises?"

Percival folded his arms, a defensive crouch he adopted unconsciously. "He did not."

"Not for lack of inquiry on your part, though, right," Briggs smirked.

"I may have made a vague ... sent out feelers, once or twice."

Mandela nodded. He had the goods on all of Rhodes' many efforts, but didn't see the advantage to drawing this out. Instead, "Were you aware that when Mr. Styles left Borgen, he was hired away by Mr. Brook himself?"

Percival steamed, and was terrible at hiding it. The tips of his ears flushed. He cracked his neck. A bead of sweat formed at the edge of his scalp. "I think I knew that."

"Director of Strategic Operations for Meyer Brook's holding company, YieldRose Global, wasn't it? Named after his mother? Anyway, young Eli Styles is at Mr. Brook's right hand. And you, remaining at the old place, still never worked with my client?"

"No."

"Did you ever work for any of the people reporting to my client?" Ouch.

Rhodes gnashed his teeth, then spat, "I suppose so."

Briggs raised his eyebrows, sighing, "so when did you finally meet Mr. Styles, as opposed to one of his subordinates?"

"I believe it was at President Thorne's first Cabinet meeting," he seethed, "maybe a month after his inauguration. We shook hands. That was about it."

"And afterward? Did you and the vice president work together?"

"Never." The word dripped with disdain.

"Socialize?"

Rhodes winced as if Mandela had uttered some kind of vulgarity. "Of course not," then perhaps realizing how his own reply might come across, temporized. "We weren't familiar with one another, didn't overlap officially, or otherwise."

Briggs sensed it was time. Task Two: present the piece of the story best conveyed by someone as reprehensible as Percival Rhodes. *Ripcord*! he screamed inside his head.

"Despite your, shall we say 'distant' relationship, this past December 29, the vice president came to see you, didn't he?"

The Secretary leaned back slightly, betraying a trace of relief. This was what he had been prepped for, what McGehee and his associate had focused upon ever since Rhodes was subpoenaed. "He did."

Percival could not help but add, "At my home," in a tone suggesting such was neither appropriate nor welcomed.

"Why?"

"Why? I suppose because it was a holiday week and no one was in their official office. Plus, I assume, he thought it would draw less attention. There was no motorcade, just a couple of SUVs. When I was summoned to the front door by Manny – that's my butler, who was quite taken aback, as you can imagine – there weren't even lights flashing on the vehicles."

Mandela fixed his elbows on counsel table, resting his chin on interlocked fists, happy to let Rhodes drone on, especially loving the oft-handed mention of Manny, as if everyone had a butler.

"Actually, I'm more interested in why he came to *you*, in particular, Mr. Rhodes?"

"I haven't the foggiest notion. Maybe because I am by law the senior member of the Cabinet, next in the line of succession. After Mr. Styles, of course. But really, I don't know." The Department of State, in fact, preceded Treasury, and before either of them the Speaker of the House and Senate president pro tempore. Briggs skipped the Civics lesson.

"You invited him in?"

"Of course! We went to my study."

"And he told you why he was there?"

"After pleasantries, yes."

"What did my client tell you, Mr. Rhodes?"

The Secretary knew to stick to his script. Mandela counted on it.

"The vice president said he wanted to invoke the Twenty-Fifth Amendment to the Constitution, eliminating the president and putting himself in charge."

"Actually, the Twenty-Fifth would only temporarily make him 'Acting President,' requiring Congressional investigation and action before any permanent consequences. And both the House and Senate are under the control of President Thorne's own party. But I'm sure you were well schooled in all that." Briggs smiled weakly. Rhodes stared back blankly, not sure what land mine he had just exploded.

"In any event, did Mr. Styles tell you why he thought the president should be provisionally removed, and investigated?"

Percival reverted to the carefully fashioned talking points, vetted by the president's inner circle, the Attorney General, McGehee, and who knows how many others. "He said the president's law enforcement activities needed to be stopped. Mr. Styles didn't like the way the president was protecting the American people from the rioters and the terrorists."

"Anything else?"

"Oh, he mentioned the election, doubts about the results and the president's legal efforts against Democrats trying to steal it. But it was mainly the crackdown on violent protestors, cybercriminals and the like."

"What was your reaction to his request?"

Percival straightened his posture with obvious pride, ready to pronounce his enduring patriotism. "I told him I supported President Thorne completely, and that if he didn't, he should resign."

This wasn't to be a debate on the merits of Thorne's police state actions, his nationalizing of Guard troops in multiple states, his banning of demonstrations or mass arrests, or any other of the president's controversial moves. Briggs certainly didn't want to wade into the re-election controversy which, however blatant Thorne's thievery, the Supreme Court had blessed, with Mandela's own client reluctantly presiding over its certification.

No, Percival was here for an entirely different reason.

"In truth, Mr. Secretary, didn't my client actually relate to you reports of citizens 'disappearing' in large numbers, summary detentions, and of particular relevance to you, large amounts of funds electronically confiscated from the president's perceived enemies, all per high-ranking military and national security sources?"

"That's not true," Rhodes snapped. "I've never heard any of that, certainly not that night, not from Eli Styles."

"Which is it, Mr. Secretary? Not true, or just something you claim you've never heard?"

Percival's face became a scowl. He didn't appreciate the insubordination. Or having his words twisted. Or being pushed from his practiced lines. "Your client referenced no Defense or NSA concerns. I would have asked for more information. And as for large unauthorized transfers of financial holdings, as Secretary of the Treasury," here he straightened his tie yet again, lifting his chin in a show of authority, "I would be in the loop on something that significant."

Briggs grinned. "Yes," he nodded, "you certainly would." Percival's eyes narrowed. In his periphery Mandela noticed jurors exchanging glances. "But back to this meeting, to the Vice President of the United States coming to your home a mere eight days before certification of the election. You would agree that was a big step."

"I don't understand your meaning."

"Well, no matter how small his entourage that evening, you would expect the visit would be logged somewhere, right, that people would know? Given your previous lack of interactions, that would stand out."

"I still ..." Rhodes began tentatively, then trailed off with an indecipherable muttering.

"If you were plotting to have the commander-in-chief murdered, Mr. Secretary, would you want to create an official record of your efforts to remove him from office?"

Ah-Hah! Rhodes thought. They told me to expect this. Eagerly, he dove into his canned retort. "Why, yes, I suppose one would, you know, pretend to make a *legal* effort to eradicate the president, so he could later claim his actions were all aboveboard."

"I see. And then, of course," Briggs paused, rubbing his chin pensively, "you would want the president you intended to murder to know, immediately, that you were rallying his Cabinet against him, trying to eject him from the Oval Office. You would want that man, the leader of the world's largest, most powerful military, on alert that you were coming after him." Briggs watched Percival's features melt as he processed the challenge. "Right, Mr. Rhodes?"

"Well, I ... ah, in my mind he probably thought ..."

"Thought what, sir? Thought you would join him in ousting a dangerous man from power? Thought the threats he presented to you might evoke a measure of concern?"

Rhodes gritted his teeth, then hissed through them, "I *was* concerned, of course I was." He closed his eyes for the briefest of moments, intensifying the search of his inner database for an off ramp, anything, trying to remember the "If this, then that" the lawyers had provided him.

While the witness dithered, Briggs leapt into the breach. "So concerned, in fact, that you consulted your wife, Margaret ..." A guess, though a pretty safe one, and who would care if he was wrong. "... then picked up the phone, according to the publicly available White House phone log ..." It wasn't accessible from this administration, but as the lawyer studied a random sheet of paper in his hand, he bet Rhodes would buy it. "... within minutes of the vice president's departure calling Ezra Arenberg, the president's chief of staff, to tattle on my client."

His synapses firing in a million directions, Rhodes couldn't help himself. He just blurted it out. "NO! I didn't call the Colonel. I only spoke that night with A.R."

Bingo! Mandela suppressed a laugh. "My bad," he said, again consulting the meaningless scrap of paper. "That's right. Not Arenberg. A.R. Hoffman, White House Counselor and Assistant to the President for Domestic Affairs. *That's* who you contacted, immediately."

Percival removed a hanky from his inner jacket pocket and mopped the beads of sweat collecting on his forehead. "I did," he said as forcefully as he could. "I thought he should be aware."

"Meaning, thanks to you, my client had just announced his secret mutiny to Magnus Thorne himself." Briggs grinned from ear to ear. "Definitely the smart move if one intends to kill the king, wouldn't you say, Mr. Secretary?"

Rhodes mustered only a slight parting of his lips, and a blank expression.

Twenty-Two

Artificial, contrived, ritualistic almost to the point of charade – Carolyn realized all these elements attached to her lofty lounge, her "bench" as it was called, elevated above the room as much in symbolic gravitas as physical height. This in no way diminished its effect upon her, the rush, as powerful today as when she first ascended the judicial throne those many years ago, appointed by the last Democratic president – the last *ever*, she speculated – a woman Carolyn respected greatly, though they never met.

The panoramic view it afforded, uninterrupted, everyone gazing up at the Judge, infused Carolyn with an energizing surge of command, of purpose, but at the same time obligation, as if her *summus locum*, the privilege to see all, demanded an equal superiority in her actions, her words, even her thoughts.

It was in this weighty, Olympian manner that Judge Bering regarded Ms. Kaylee Nicholson, freshly sworn for the defense. Dark brown hair, parted neatly at the right, hung straight to and past the young woman's shoulders. Her hands, the fingernails of which were clear lacquered – a conscious choice, Carolyn suspected, to avoid commentary any color may have provoked about her seriousness, or judgment, or taste, or maturity, yet another concern with which only women had to grapple – those smooth hands alternated, one resting palm down in her lap, the other flicking her long tresses to her back, exposing the toned span of her shoulders. It was a nervous energy the judge saw frequently, the reaction of people unaccustomed to being on display.

From her chief clerk Debbie's briefing this morning, Carolyn learned enough to suspect this young professional's initial anxiety was likely to fade once the machinery started turning. Her resume and rapid rise within the Thorne administration indicated an abundant intellect.

Assessing her impeccable posture, the judge further predicted an ample well of integrity which, when inevitably challenged, would reveal a steady warrior.

"Kaylee Renee Nicholson," she confirmed, then explained, "Until May 15, I was senior assistant to the White House Chief of Staff, Colonel Ezra Arenberg."

My gosh, the judge concluded, at only 24 years of age this gal was top aide to the leader of the free world's principal advisor. Which begged the question: why would she throw all of that away?

"Give us an idea of your usual duties, Ms. Nicholson, your typical day," Briggs asked. It was an open-ended query, Carolyn noted, a departure from his normal tight grip on witness testimony. He was betting the jury would approve of her, and thus, wanted the next hour or two to flow naturally, shaped by *her* personality, sans guardrails.

"There really was no 'typical day,'" Kaylee said with stern confidence, the earlier unease abandoned. "My responsibilities tracked whatever the Colonel was focused on. His schedule often changed by the minute, and mine just followed his. Basically, whatever rose to the president's attention at a given moment." She said this almost casually, the judge thought, as if the worries of the world were no more than a shopping list.

"But what did you *do* for the chief of staff," Briggs directed. He wanted the jurors to understand this was no mere errand girl or filing clerk.

"I started as an intern, during the campaign, putting together briefing files for Mr. Arenberg, literally manilla folders with five or six pages containing information about whatever event, you know, speech, fundraiser, TV appearance, what have you, was next. Then, after the election, he gave me a full-time position as one of his assistants, doing kind of the same thing, but more policy and issues and such."

"And two years ago, he put you in charge of all the assistants?"

"Right, though it didn't change much. I had been shadowing the Colonel pretty much from the beginning, but now he wanted me to rely on the others more for the research aspects and focus on, I guess I would call it 'continuity,' making sure we stayed on track, being consistent."

Carolyn noticed Kaylee gesturing more, relaxing as she traversed familiar terrain, even looking away from the attorney for quick snapshots of the jurors to gauge their approval.

"And that meant notes," she said. "A lot of notes. At the end of the day, I would prepare summaries, minutes, action memoranda, basically documentation of everything we did on a given day, or what it might mean for the next."

Briggs drew the panel's attention to an important buoy in the witness' narrative. "I assume, then, you were with Mr. Arenberg a good portion of the time."

"Almost every minute."

"And that included his discussions with others."

"Definitely. He was very serious about having a record of who said what, you know, the commitments people made, the opinions or information he received, the directions he gave. The chief of staff counted on me to keep up with all that. I mean, there were some national security issues. I had a clearance, but not for some things. Ninety-nine percent of the time, I'd say, I was there."

The judge assessed her panel, every single one of them fully engaged, indeed tantalized, because like Carolyn they realized the young assistant, very much an insider, could only be here to reveal something no one was supposed to ever hear.

"Why did you leave, Ms. Nicholson. You were 26 when you resigned, correct?"

"Yes."

"A 26-year-old who, fresh out of college, went to work for the president's closest confidant, became his senior assistant, interacted daily with the nation's highest political officials, dealt with the most important issues on the planet, and then ..." The judge admired Briggs' seamless melding of words and movements, spreading his arms wide to encompass all the world and its possibilities. "... and then, you sacrifice all of it."

In her days as a courtroom combatant, Bering would have at this juncture slowly, deliberately, dramatically walked to the jury box, searching their faces as she approached, only then posing the next burning word. Briggs simply lowered his head, and in a voice so intentionally low one had to strain to hear, muttered, "Why?"

This was the gateway question, the premise for everything of greater consequence to follow. When Kaylee initially met Izzy, "why" was the key the exotic legal assistant needed. Same with Briggs when they gathered at his office a few days later. To understand her testimony, to *trust* her testimony, "why" was first necessary. And yet, having recited her response a dozen times for her parents, for her fiancé, for her best friend, for Briggs, she still hesitated the way a cliff diver pauses at the rocky edge, anticipating the long fall to the cold waters below.

Judge Bering observed her internal agony. The jurors, like nosey neighbors, also latched onto Kaylee's struggle. Briggs coaxed with his eyes, *You're here, no turning back,* JUMP!!

"I couldn't participate in what was happening anymore," she finally declared to Briggs, then, looking up at Carolyn, her protector, "I knew what was happening wasn't right, and there was nothing I could do to stop it." But *you* can, right? Carolyn felt the witness beseech her. Bering couldn't turn away, couldn't pretend to shuffle papers, couldn't even clear her throat, until Kaylee turned, and with renewed confidence announced to the jurors, "It was a decision of conscience."

"Was there anything in particular, Ms. Nicholson, that provoked your departure, a straw that broke the camel's back, so to speak?"

McGehee leapt to his feet with an urgency he abhorred, an act he knew would garnish this turncoat's testimony with more meaning than it deserved. But he saw no choice. She needed to see his fortitude, the ferocity with which he would attack her. "Your Honor, I renew the United States' objection to this testimony, to the disclosure of any privileged discussions this employee may have heard," he paused, "or upon which she may have eavesdropped."

Carolyn steeled herself against a protective instinct, any kind of emotional attachment, anything other than pure detached fairness. This young woman could take care of herself, she intuited. At the same time ... "Mr. McGehee, I am fully aware of the Court's ruling on your motion, as is Mr. Briggs, and I am sure the witness has been thoroughly advised on what is and is not permissible." Briggs nodded. Kaylee nodded.

"Then the government would request *Mizzzzz* Nicholson," he drew out the prefix, emphasizing her youth, her immaturity, her inconsequence, "be instructed to tread very carefully, in light of the serious laws in place for the protection," now to the jury, "of *our* national security."

The judge presented Kaylee with the most pleasant, reassuring smile she could muster, almost a wink. "So instructed," she said casually.

"With that out of the way," Briggs said dismissively, "you were about to tell us your reason for leaving. Please continue, ma'am." Touché, Carolyn thought. The gravitas and respect of "Ma'am" eclipsing the disparagement of "Ms."

"It was more of a snowball effect. Too many occasions where I became uncomfortable with what we were doing." She squinted. "Or maybe why we did it."

"What is the first such occasion you can recall."

"I remember a meeting the Colonel had with the FBI director, JoAnn Degna." She looked at the U.S. attorney. "Without revealing anything of a classified nature," she said preemptively, forcing Bering to smile, "Mr. Arenberg was following up on a request he'd made about the teachers' unions. He said something to the effect of, 'JoAnn, we need them fired.' He was referring to gay and lesbian educators. 'The president wants them out of the classrooms and away from our kids.'"

"Why did President Thorne, according to his chief of staff, your boss, want to fire thousands of LGBTQ teachers?"

"It was all part of the same thing that went way back. The conservatives in Congress, The Freedom Caucus, the Truth Battalion, Speaker Knall, they all wanted to limit gay rights, especially with the public backlash against The Aberdeen Circle."

The witness pushed her cascading hair off her shoulders, something Carolyn no longer perceived as a nervous tick, but a flexing of sorts, a subliminal accompaniment to her growing confidence.

"Anyway, when *TAC* came out strong against the president's re-election, he saw them as a threat."

"Objection, Your Honor. Speculation. *Mizzzzz* Nicholson can't possibly know the president's mind."

The judge suspected the witness could return the volley. "Without a better predicate, Mr. Briggs, I'll have to sustain."

"Ms. Nicholson, how do you *know* President Thorne considered *TAC* a threat to his re-election?"

"Mr. Arenberg told me that many times, in the context of policies we were asked to work on, you know, looking into things the president wanted to pursue. I recall at least one time, on an Air Force One trip to raise money in Los Angeles, when the president himself asked him, or told him, something to the effect of 'Ezra, *TAC* is coming for me, and we've got to fight back. What can we do to obliterate these queers.' I remember the word 'obliterate' specifically."

"And queers?" Bering was inescapably drawn to the defendant, to his reaction, as was half the courtroom, everyone stealthy in their glances. His face was stone.

"Well, or fags, or something derogatory like that. It was the way he referred to them, especially after *TAC* came out against him the way they did. He took it very personally."

"Were there other suggested actions against the gay community?"

The prosecutor sighed theatrically, again to his feet, an exaggerated exasperation. "Judge, the United States objects to this irrelevant smearing of a president who, I should remind counsel, is the victim of an assassination attempt orchestrated by his client. His alleged reactions to The Aberdeen Circle's threats do not disprove any of the defendant's ties to that terrorist group, to the assassin, or to the plot to kill President Thorne."

Nice speech, Carolyn thought, and trained her attention on Mr. Briggs.

"I believe the president's schemes," he replied, "to destroy the LGBTQ community are *highly* relevant, Your Honor, not only validating many of the vice president's purely legal actions, but also giving credibility to the testimony of Ms. Nicholson."

The judge tugged at her ear, considering her desire to prevent a political sideshow while taking the defense's point. "Objection overruled. But Mr. Briggs, let's not get bogged down here." He nodded, message received: Move it along.

"Ms. Nicholson, did other presidential designs on gay Americans weigh on you?"

"Really cracking down on marches and protests and such. The Colonel told me, 'The president needs us to find more ways around the First Amendment,' or similar words. There was also discussion about declaring known homosexuals as a national security threat, and using that to revoke licenses, government contracts, pretty much anything that required a federal permit. I remember the Colonel saying something to the effect of 'the god damn president thinks it's the 1950s,' you know, back when they had laws barring gay people from certain employment.

"And in particular, he mentioned pressure on the IRS to go after high-profile LGBT people, entertainers and such, specifically, I remember Mr. Arenberg mentioning Linda Luther, you know, that Netflix comedian, and also the governor of Maine."

"And this all bothered you?"

"Yes. But more when the Colonel told Director Degna, 'You need to find something.'"

"This was during that same meeting in his office?" She nodded.

"You need to answer for the record, Ms. Nicholson," Carolyn prompted.

"Yes, it was during that same meeting. And she said, 'Find what, exactly.'"

"But you didn't quit," Briggs asked.

"Not then. I thought the Director made it pretty clear she wasn't going to manufacture any evidence, and Mr. Arenberg didn't press it. I wasn't comfortable, but I didn't think it would go anywhere." She flung her hair back again, then, with a lift of the chin, "I didn't think any of it would go anywhere."

"So, what changed?"

Bering grew impatient. There would be no parade of political grievances in her courtroom. She noticed McGehee ready to pounce, and would use him to shut it down. Still, Carolyn was curious where, exactly, Briggs was going.

"The assassination. The attempt."

Briggs drew his expression into a question mark, as though not privy to what was coming. "How did that change things," he asked, feigning a light tread.

Kaylee looked down. From her vantage, the judge could see the witness molding each palm flat to its corresponding knee, bracing herself. "When I first heard about it, I was in the West Wing. I had a small, like, cubby 20 feet or so from the Colonel's office. But I was in Mr. Arenberg's, arranging some materials for his return – he traveled with the president to North Carolina that day – and the TV was on. It was always on. That's when I saw."

Nicholson's naturally light skin, a girl Carolyn concluded didn't spend much time outdoors, became a deathlike pallor.

"I was obviously worried about President Thorne. They weren't sure if he'd been hit. I mean, you could see, when the Secret Service was pulling him off the stage, he was moving his legs, he was on his feet, his eyes were open. It was all so crazy, the chaos, the camaras bouncing. It was hard to tell what was really going on.

"But then, after, I don't know, a minute or 90 seconds or ... it seemed longer, I'm not sure ... I was watching a replay and ... he was there ... it was ... *him* ... my heart came up into my throat. I couldn't believe what I was seeing. It was Agent Kilbrough. I couldn't breathe. There were three or four people in the room by then, but I was so focused on the screen, I honestly can't tell you who was there. I recognized him before anyone on TV identified him. I thought I was going to throw up."

You look like you might now, Carolyn observed. There was no doubting the shooting shocked her, as it had the whole nation. The trauma Kaylee now relived, however, was palpable, even six months after the event. And Kilbrough? Her terror was off the charts. Why? As much as Nicholson was in the presence of President Thorne, the Colonel always at his side and she at the Colonel's, Kaylee surely would have seen him on duty. Did that familiarity deepen the agent's betrayal to the level of nightmares?

And what was Briggs up to, the judge wondered. Trying to buck up the witness' credibility by showing how deeply attached she was to this president? Make her concerns about Thorne's worst impulses seem more reluctant, and therefore, more reasonable?

"Did you know agent Kilbrough, Ms. Nicholson?" Briggs prodded.

"*No*," she said, a beat too fast. "I'd seen him on the president's detail, many times, but there would never have been a reason for us to talk."

"Was it the reality of a former member of the president's own protective detail committing this heinous crime, someone you had seen many times, is that what upset you?"

She shook her head, and her mouth opened, but no words came out. Finally, Kaylee straightened her pose, and forged ahead. "I had recently seen Sam Kilbrough in the West Wing, meeting alone with Mr. Arenberg."

Briggs arched his eyebrows, highlighting his next question. "Was that unusual?"

"Yes. And it wasn't on the books. All of the Colonel's appointments are logged. By law, they have to be. But Mr. Arenberg didn't even tell *me*. Also, it was rare for the Colonel to meet with even the *head* of the president's detail. Maybe for a big foreign trip or something, but usually that kind of coordination was handled levels below the chief of staff."

"Okay, well, couldn't the senior agent have delegated to Kilbrough that day?"

Kaylee frowned. "That wouldn't make sense. He had a deputy. And if it were so important that it required the Colonel's personal attention, I can't see him sending an underling." Carolyn noted Nicholson again repositioning her hair, ready to charge. "Plus, the meeting was on March 23, exactly one week before the assassination. And Kilbrough had already left the service anyway."

Bering watched a recognition slowly seep across the panel. Briggs took his time, letting the jurors anticipate his next question, one by one, before he even asked it. Then, quietly, "I believe the jury has already heard testimony, and seen documentation, that Agent Sam Kilbrough resigned from the United States Secret Service on February 27."

Carolyn could feel the implications simmering as Briggs waited, eventually asking, "Why, then, Ms. Nicholson, was your boss, President Magnus Thorne's chief of staff, meeting with the shooter seven days before the assassination?"

Her throat trembled, and the judge, even though sitting a mere four feet away, strained to hear the reply.

"I don't know."

Twenty-Three

District of Columbia Chief Judge Carolyn Bering had seen the full range of lawyerly emotion: the crush of defeat; the elation, or perhaps simple relief, of victory; shock, anger, exasperation, disbelief. The attorneys she most respected avoided the highs and lows, inate equilibrium allowing them to flow with the tide of evidence, improvising, tacking, always focused on the next rather than the past.

Sidney McGehee was such a player. He'd strutted about her courtroom many times since his appointment as U.S. attorney, ever prepared, resilient, confident to the point of arrogance – though not without some justification, she conceded.

To dispatch with Kaylee Nicholson, a witness capable of bruising or even derailing his carefully crafted case, he would need all those traits. Carolyn could nearly hear the whirl of the brash prosecutor's brain, hand to holster, safety off, ready to draw.

Using her time as a litigator, the judge traced the contours of the coming assault in her own head, point-by-point, each vulnerability targeted, as she was certain Mr. Briggs had forewarned the now exposed witness. But Briggs couldn't answer for her, or stand between her and the government's table, or shield her with anything more than whatever she possessed from their prep sessions. Those sittings covered each volley, every thrust, all the angles of McGehee's likely approach. Now, Carolyn sensed the defense lawyer in vigilant prayer, hoping Kaylee remembered enough to survive.

"You 'don't know' what Ezra Arenberg and Sam Kilbrough discussed in this supposed meeting," *suuuhhhh...pose...idddd*, the word chopped up and drawn out to fog the air with incredulity. "That's a fact, Ms. Nicholson."

He didn't need an answer, but she gave him one anyway. "Yes."

"Could have been anything, could have been the Colonel's concern for a former employee. Kilbrough resigned February 27, so Mr. Arenberg could have been checking in on the guy. Could have been pumping him for information, something the agent had learned in his time with the Service. Maybe, even, something about the vice president, whose protection Kilbrough headed before Mr. Styles arranged his suspicious transfer to the president's detail. Could have been the Colonel investigating the administration's growing concerns over your friend the defendant's dangerous activities!"

Bering winced as the witness took the bait. "The Vice President isn't my friend," she protested, almost like she had been slapped.

"No? What time this morning did the subpoena *compelling* your testimony tell you to be here?"

Nicholson flinched. "I wasn't."

"You weren't what?"

"I wasn't subpoenaed."

"That's right, because if you had been, I would have received a copy and would have known you were coming. Instead, you *volunteered* to sit there, for the defense, for the vice president, right?"

"I suppose so."

"Well, did someone pressure you? Threaten you? Blackmail you?"

"No. I wanted to do the right thing."

McGehee nodded as he paced, a pantomime of processing her virtuous intentions. "Hmmm. The right thing," he repeated. "The *right thing* would have been to cooperate with the investigation launched in the weeks after the shooting. Yet, when the FBI, Agent Hunter Bushida, I believe it was, met with you ... not a word about some sinister conclave between Ezra Arenberg and the soon-to-be-assassin, correct?"

"He didn't ask me about it." The judge noticed the skin tighten over Briggs' knuckles as he squeezed his hands together.

"He ... didn't *ask*? You tell the jury this conspiratorial story today, but back when the authorities were trying to piece things together, it didn't seem worth mentioning?"

"The White House Counsel, Mr. Ginsberg, told me to be very careful, to only answer the specific questions asked." Kaylee looked to the jurors, pleadingly Bering thought. "I was still working for Mr. Arenberg, and ..."

"And you're saying that Mr. Robert Ginsberg, White House Counsel, the top lawyer for the president's executive staff, told you to withhold information from the FBI?"

"Not like that, no, but ..."

"Did you tell Mr. Ginsberg about this gosh awful visit Mr. Kilbrough paid to your boss?"

"It didn't come up, not directly anyway. And I assumed he knew."

"What does that mean?"

"Well, in my first meeting with Mr. Ginsberg, he wasn't really asking me specifics, just telling me how the interview process worked, what the agent would ask, how I should respond. That sort of thing. Later, I mean, when the date was coming up, this was really weighing on my mind, so I asked Mr. Arenberg directly."

"You asked Ezra Arenberg about his alleged conference with Mr. Kilbrough?" McGehee was basically crooning, in the judge's estimation, a big smile, as if they were all about to hear the most fabulous tale.

"I did."

"And pray tell, what did he say?" McGehee chuckled.

"He said something to the effect of, 'Me? Kilbrough? Here? You're mistaken, Kaylee. A few words in passing back when he was on duty, but a sit down? Never!'"

"I said, 'Colonel, I saw him, sitting in this chair.' I could tell he was angry. I know what that looks like. Pressing his lips together, his neck gets red. But he didn't answer me. He just said, 'Is there anything else.' So, I left."

"Uh huh. Never occurred to you that maybe you hadn't seen what you thought you did? I mean, you never went into the room during this alleged meeting, did you?"

"No, but I was in the doorway. I'd seen Agent Kilbrough a hundred times. I know what he looks like. It was him."

"And you've already admitted there was nothing on Mr. Arenberg's log."

"Which, like I said, was strange. Every meeting gets noted."

"Who keeps his log?"

"His secretary."

"Sarah Zinsky."

"Yes."

"Is she reliable? Trustworthy?"

Carolyn stiffened, a pang of sympathy for poor Kaylee. Glancing at Briggs, she noticed he, too, understood the trap, and also that it was fair game.

"She had been with the Colonel for years, even before all his political work. I always thought she was competent."

McGehee wasn't letting go. "Reliable? Trustworthy?"

The witness gave herself up. "I would think so."

"Would it surprise you if she were to testify that no such encounter ever occurred, that she would have written it down?"

"I don't understand how she could say that," Nicholson fought back. "He *was* there."

"The White House Visitors' Registry lists everyone who enters the compound, with a badge issued, appointment window noted, entry and exit times recorded. Right?"

"Yes."

"After Mr. Arenberg corrected your assumption, did you ever check the Registry?"

"He wasn't on it."

"So, the Colonel's lying, Ms. Zinsky is covering up for him, and the security personnel at the gates all failed to do their job."

A glistening sheen emerged through Kaylee's modest cosmetics. Hair slipped over her shoulders, which she didn't push back. "I can't answer for them," she began, "but I know what I saw."

"I have another question, Ms. Nicholson. Weeks after the shooting, you were still working for the Colonel, even after you realized, in your mind anyway, that your boss had met with the assassin, and, as you believe, lied to your face about it. Add all your grave concerns about President Thorne's intentions. Why did you stay *until May 15?*"

An obvious assault, Bering recognized. She guessed at how Briggs might have mapped out Kaylee's answer.

The witness straightened, recovering a bit, her flex confirming the judge's assumption. "I thought I was doing good work. Performing a valuable service for my country by trying to stop what I could, you know, giving honest advice to the Colonel."

Ah, there it is ... Carolyn spied the long hair finally being put back into place again. *She's ready to fight.*

"That all ended during my last meeting with Mr. Ginsberg."

"Okay, well," the prosecutor stumbled. He knew better than to open this can, but Nicholson barreled ahead as he tried to talk over her. The judge showed McGehee her hand. *You asked for this, Mr. U.S. Attorney.* She nodded at the witness, *Proceed.*

"The day before my interview with the FBI, which was right after I confronted the Colonel, Mr. Ginsberg showed up unscheduled. I had just spent several hours doing prep with one of his associates the day before, so it was kinda weird. And his whole attitude had changed. It was ... he was *furious*. He really laid into me about not speculating or saying anything I didn't know for certain. He never came out and said it, but it was obvious what he was talking about. It was pretty clear he had been put on alert."

Kaylee stared through her adversary as he stood from his chair in a rhythmic, unworried motion, not springing into action, but gliding. "I wasn't comfortable lying," she added, like throwing a rock at a lion, Bering imagined, "and I felt as though that's what he was telling me to do."

McGehee slowly paced around the prosecution table, behind his assistant Mandy and his associate Joel, one corner, then the next, until he stood in the well, never taking his eyes off his prey, no concern written into his manner, only concentration.

"That's when I left," Nicholson said. It sounded like a valediction.

What the cocky prosecutor did next, a lopsided sneer, showing only enough teeth to make it more of a snarl, reminded Carolyn of The Grinch, that cartoon character who so disturbed her as a small child. She understood exactly why. The same malevolence, the same assuredness, the same thought-bubble: *Now you listen to me, young lady! Even if we're horribly mangled, there'll be no sad faces on Christmas.*

"'Poof.' You're out! Without a word to the press. No dramatic letter of resignation. No nothing. You just vanish. And these grave dangers to the union which you claim drove you to a monumental decision of conscience? Well, those, you keep all to yourself. You don't tell, you don't warn, *anyone*."

As fast as Kaylee thought she had escaped, riding a wave of righteousness, McGehee wrenched her back. "I told Mr. Arenberg," she stammered. "I told him why I couldn't stay."

"Your Honor, United States Exhibit number 42." He wiggled a finger at Mandy, and a couple of clicks later, an embossed page of notepaper covered with bright blue chicken scratch dominated the big screen.

"Can you identify this handwriting?"

"It's Mr. Arenberg's," Nicholson admitted, her eyes moving right, left, right, left as she interpreted it, her spine stooping a fraction with each line.

"It's my understanding he would scribble out something for just about every conversation, and Mrs. Zinsky would keep them organized for future reference."

"That's correct."

"No such note regarding any meeting with Sam Kilbrough, by the way." McGehee smiled faintly. "Does that surprise you?" Kaylee's mouth opened, but she paused, not sure how to avoid sounding fanciful. The prosecutor quickly filled the breach. "Never mind. Instead, I'm sure the jurors and others here are having as hard a time reading the Colonel's scrawl as I did. Surely, you can decipher it." He held out his palm. *Please do*!

Painfully, she recited the words. "*Nic out. Asked why. No specifics. Burn out? She thanked for opp. Will stay week, transition/brief Emil.*'"

"'Nic' refers to you, I presume, and Emil was the deputy assistant who would be taking over your desk, right?"

"Yes."

"According to the Chief of Staff to the President of the United States of America, you provided no specifics whatsoever about your voluntary resignation, leaving him to speculate that it was 'burn out.'"

"That's what he wrote," Kaylee said in a tone dripping with disapproval. The judge couldn't tell if she had given up, or simply trusted the jurors to doubt the Colonel.

"Indeed, you did stay the week, trained your replacement, and left on May 15th."

"Yes."

"And crucially, Ms. Nicholson, you kept your appointment with the FBI, sat down for a two-hour interview with Agent Bushida, and never once mentioned Sam Kilbrough's alleged meeting with Ezra Arenberg, am I right?"

"Mr. Ginsberg was there, as my lawyer, and I guess I felt ..."

"Ms. Nicholson, if you could please answer the question, which was not about your feelings, but whether you informed Mr. Bushida of your *theory* about Sam Kilbrough."

"He didn't ask that specific question, and I followed Mr. Ginsberg's instructions."

Carolyn surveyed the jury box: lots of downcast eyes, folded arms, and melted lips.

The U.S. attorney, feeling full stride, wheeled away from the witness, to whom he had been inching closer and closer during his assault upon her. With his back turned, he retrieved a thick sheaf of papers, bound by three gold clips at their long edge, thumbed the pages dramatically, and then studied the top page. Finally, without facing her, he called out as if to no one in particular, "Ever heard of Carver House Publishers?"

Terror seized Kaylee. Briggs instinctively rose to her defense – an attention drawing mistake, in Carolyn's humble opinion.

"Objection, Your Honor. If Mr. McGehee intends to cross-examine the witness with a document, it must be identified, and her counsel given an opportunity to review it."

"Overruled, counselor. Premature. The government has not yet made any reference to a specific document."

McGehee turned to the judge, bobbing his head in thanks, or agreement, or gloat. Then, angling toward Nicholson, holding the heavy volume as if a holy relic. "Have you? Heard of Carver House Publishers?"

Kaylee, girding herself, answered. "They are helping me with ... my agent felt Carver House would be the best to ... advise ..." The gears of her ramble stuck.

"Your book," the prosecutor proclaimed, the subject word more condemnation than noun. "It's been barely four months since you quit working for President Thorne, and you've written an incendiary tell-all." He bounced the bound manuscript on his open palms to accentuate its heft. "Four Hundred and Eighty-Six pages of *your* words."

Bering tried to work out whether it was actually Nicholson's manuscript in the U.S. attorney's hands, or if this was an elaborate con. No such book was on the list of pre-admitted exhibits, nor had it been mentioned before now. The ploy, or the book, whichever it was, gave Kaylee the appearance of having her clothing ripped off. Violated. Her counsel, Carolyn discerned, was equally stunned.

"Surely you knew," McGehee mocked as if speaking to a child, "publishers must submit books by people with security clearances to the NSA, Justice, and other agencies."

Of course that's how he'd acquired the draft, it dawned on the judge, humbled by her tardy comprehension. But until he tried to introduce the thick document into evidence, or read from it, there was nothing Briggs, or she, could do.

Nicholson didn't speak, her composure disintegrating.

The prosecutor was too smart to trouble himself with any of those mechanics. Instead, he unsheathed his sharp sword, deciding to end the engagement in one swing.

"Tell us, Ms. Nicholson, and please speak clearly so Noah, here, can get it down precisely ..." He paused, pivoted to take in the jurors, giving *them* his full attention, extending the witness' masterpiece toward them. "... how much did Carver House pay you for this?"

Every eye was on Kaylee. Her tense lips. Her shallow breathing. The long brown hair now over her chest as she slumped. Her hesitation only focused the glare.

"Seven Hundred and Fifty Thousand."

For entirely different reasons, Kaylee and the prosecutor both looked to the floor.

Twenty-Four

Surprise Military Witness Will Cap Week for Styles Defense

By Sebastian Montes

WASHINGTON – As the vice president's treason trial races to the end of a dramatic second week, sources confirm one of the nation's highest-ranking military leaders has been subpoenaed for Friday. The identity of this surprise witness was not revealed.

Since the beginning of Elijah Styles' defense on Tuesday, lead counsel Mandela Briggs has cast his client as a patriotic guardian of democracy, seeking to undermine the prosecution's case for motive. First up was Treasury Secretary Percival Rhodes, who admitted the defendant's attempted use of nonviolent means, the Constitution's Twenty-Fifth Amendment, to remove the president from office. Next was Kaylee Nicholson, former senior assistant to Thorne's chief of staff. She alleged an ominous administrative campaign against LGBT Americans, before stunning the courtroom by claiming her boss, Colonel Ezra Arenberg, met in his West Wing office with Sam Kilbrough exactly one week before the latter's assassination attempt, an allegation the chief of staff immediately denied in a fiery statement.

Thursday saw a pair of lesser-known witnesses. Denise Carver spoke of frequent interactions between her daughter, Tippy, and her brother, Styles, tearfully highlighting his extensive advocacy on behalf of Down Syndrome awareness. Tippy and Kilbrough's younger brother, Conor, share that diagnosis. The defendant's team stresses that his many contacts with his former bodyguard focused upon charitable goals, not plotting a sympathetic dimension to the vice president.

The day concluded with Dr. Thomas Patel, the North Carolina trauma surgeon who treated President Thorne's injuries after the March 30 shooting. Dr. Patel agreed the wound to the president's upper arm was never life threatening. Briggs' questioning portrayed the bullet's entry site as an illogical location for someone intending to cause death. In questions laden with implication, the attorney murder. Mrs. Carver's warm retellings also depicted a more suggested a skilled marksman such as Kilbrough, at close range, would have selected the head, neck, or a vital organ, if murder were his goal.

Overshadowing those witnesses, though, was the leak after adjournment regarding the defense team's aim to use a respected armed forces figure to show President Thorne had more provocative and threatening plans in store for the nation.

[Read More]

†††

Lead with your hardest punch. That was the advice of Sidney McGehee's trial advocacy professor at The University of Chicago. Don't waste time with preamble. Don't dress your point in layers. Don't be restrained. Be forceful, on message, and above all, unapologetically clear.

The dauntless United States Attorney for the District of Columbia lived by these words, always on the attack, persistent in his drive toward unconditional surrender. His problem at the moment, however, was that the stunning, equally confident redhead with four stars on each of her shoulders was not yet his witness.

"And for those of us perhaps unfamiliar with military parlance, what is CASCOM? What does it do?" McGehee's opponent asked General Jacqueline Harken. Briggs was nearing the end of a methodical, Sidney thought plodding review of the witness' storied military career. Taking his time, year by year, the defense counsel played out the narrative: West Point; Apache helicopter pilot decorated for her service in the Middle East against ISIS and against Al-Shabaab in East Africa; Purple Heart for wounds suffered in the fierce battle of Raqqa in Northern Syria; her promotions to Brigadier and head of the legendary light infantry division, the 101st Airborne. Ten years ago, she earned her third star, tapped for leadership of the U.S. Combined Arms Support Command "CASCOM," the current topic of education. Briggs had not learned the "hardest punch" rule, McGehee mused.

In fairness, his adversary understood that a pair of African American jurors, both men, were ex-Army and would eat this up. *That* was the reason for the extended inspection of her resume.

"Primarily, CASCOM is responsible for education in and training for LSCO ..."

"LSCO?"

"Large Scale Combat Operations, and multi-domain operations, including IMT ... ah," she pried herself from the acronyms with a lift of her brow, "Initial Military Training, including war fighting competencies in a decisive action training environment. Basically, providing soldiers who can immediately contribute to their first unit of assignment."

This trip down memory lane gave the prosecutor time to study her, to probe for vulnerabilities. On the surface, General Harken was formidable, what with her erect bearing, the full-dress midnight blue uniform perfectly tailored and pressed, with rows of multi-colored ribbons on the left breast and medals on the right. Surely Briggs wouldn't go through each one – how tiresome.

"Then, six years ago, the Army awarded your fourth star, and President Vance appointed you to your first term as Vice Chair of the Joint Chiefs of Staff."

"Yes sir." Her voice was crisp. The cadence steady.

"President Thorne re-appointed you two years ago, and announced just before this last election that you would succeed General Joshua Nelson as Chair of the Joint Chiefs."

"Yes sir."

"Tomorrow, in fact, you are scheduled to be sworn in to that highest of all positions in our uniformed services, the first woman ever to hold that rank."

There was difficulty, McGehee noticed, in the general's acknowledgement of this latest achievement. Her steely gray eyes remained fixed on the defense lawyer like micro-radars searching for an edge. It dawned on Sidney these two had not rehearsed. They had not even met, he concluded, or else Briggs would have avoided this discomfort, whatever it was.

"Yes sir," she finally answered, holding back the rest. The prosecutor jotted a note.

"General Harken, who are the Joint Chiefs of Staff, and what is their role in relation to the defense and national security of the United States?"

"We are the senior officers for each service branch – Army, Air Force, Navy, Marines, National Guard and Space Force, as well as Chairman Nelson and myself – with the responsibility of advising the President, Secretary of Defense and National Security Council on all military matters. The Chair is the president's principal advisor, by law, and we are the Chair's counselors, so to speak, although any of us can be called upon by POTUS or SECDEF. Additionally, we have a joint role to ensure the readiness of our men and women in uniform, whether that be policy, planning or training."

Last night, once Sidney learned Harken would take the stand, he devoured materials hastily collected by Mandy and Joel. Biographies, news reports, anecdotes, interviews. The Colonel and A.R. Hoffman reached out as well. And McGehee called around, and around. The most useful tidbit, however, came from the Chief of Naval Operations, one of Harken's fellow Joint Staff members. Yes, the man passed over for Chairman: not because he wasn't the most talented and deserving, but for the simple reason that "Jackie" was a woman, a promotion well-timed for the president's re-election.

"Ma'am, if I could turn your attention to last October, the weeks just before the election," Briggs said. She nodded, unflinching but, the prosecutor perceived, braced for something rough. "You had just been named as the next Joint Chiefs Chair."

"The president had made the announcement, yes, to take effect in one year, assuming I were to be confirmed by the Senate."

"Had you previously met with the president about this quite significant promotion?"

Her calculus was quick, but Sidney could detect it. Not a word would be wasted. Her breathing was controlled. Her movements minimal. Her jaw slightly lifted, as if to give her the tiniest better vantage. Nothing was too small to manage.

"Yes. I often sat in for the Chair, and on one such instance, just after Labor Day, President Thorne informed me of his intent to discuss my name with the majority leader, and assuming that went well, to make an announcement."

I often sat in for the Chair. Quite the understatement, according to Hoffman's read last night. Washington was terrible at keeping secrets, but in this case had defied expectations. Turns out, General Nelson, age 79, was ... how did A.R. put it? ... "a tomato short of a BLT." The old man was too revered and respected to shove aside, and, Hoffman added, would have pitched a major fit if anyone tried to replace him.

The solution was his personal protégé, Harken, who Nelson thought of – literally on his more confused days – as the daughter he never had. So, yes, more often than not the president received his briefings and advice from her.

"Help me out here, General Harken. The law, 10 United States Code 154(a)(4)(A) to be exact, says the Vice Chair shall not be eligible for promotion to Chair?"

The witness demonstrated unease. Only the flicker of an unwanted emotion, but it was there. McGehee didn't know what was coming, but she clearly did.

"I so informed the president, who pointed out the next part of the regulation, which allows for exception."

"I believe you, he, are referring to Section (4)(B). Here," Briggs said as Izzy handed him a solo printed sheet of tiny black text, "let me read it. It says, 'The President may waive subparagraph (A),' that's the part saying the Vice Chair can't be promoted, 'if the President determines such action is necessary in the national interest.'"

Ah, McGehee thought, absorbing the point. Harken didn't respond. She didn't need to. Her service was beyond valuable, the president's faith in her boundless and complete. Go ahead, Briggs telegraphed the prosecutor, just try impeaching this witness: President Thorne himself says she's not only *necessary*, she's in the freaking *national interest*.

"So, before he made it official, and announced it to the world, did Magnus Thorne discuss anything with you about, oh, I don't know, his philosophy, or yours, or his needs, or expectations?"

Harken calculated. Sidney deciphered the faintest squint as she recalled the conversation. To study her was really all the prosecutor could do right now. Take notes, assess, scour for chinks in the general's armor, *any* way in, so that when it was his turn he could undo the damage surely coming.

"The president said he needed loyalty." She paused, her countenance banishing any hint of complicity with this line of inquiry, imparting that she was *not* okay revealing conversations with her commander in chief. "I assured him my loyalty to the nation, and to the Constitution, was unwavering."

"Was he satisfied?"

"He asked about my loyalty ... to *him*. I replied that I could think of no greater loyalty than to guarantee him my best, most objective advice on all matters."

McGehee didn't doubt Harken said those exact words. But where had Briggs gotten these details? How was he even aware of the conversation?

"And did he discuss with you anything about the imminent election?"

"He said he expected ... trouble. Said there were certain groups who intended to interfere with, 'rig the election' were his words. He asked if I agreed with General Nelson that we should use the military to keep any of that from happening."

"How did you reply?"

She wasn't about to trash her mentor or reveal his infirmity. That much was obvious to Sidney. Yet, he easily recognized a tension in her already stiff posture, a dilemma she had seconds to resolve. Probably a waste, but McGehee decided to throw her a lifeline, to be her friend.

"Objection, Your Honor. This has gone far enough. The advice given by a member of the Joint Chiefs to her commander-in-chief is a private, privileged discussion, and forcing disclosure in open court will have a chilling effect on the integrity of future discussions. Moreover," he threw in for good measure, "none of this is relevant to whether Mr. Styles plotted to kill the president."

Without waiting for the defense's reply, Judge Bering spoke. "I think I understand where this is going. Your objection is overruled. But Mr. Briggs, let's get to the point." Then to the witness, "General, you may answer. However, you are not required to disclose anything that would impede national security, or which is classified."

Nice move, the prosecutor conceded. The Court's given her an out. We're about to discover, he decided, how much skin she has in this game.

Harken acknowledged Bering's ruling with a small dip of her head, then turned to the jurors for the first time. As she shifted, the overhead illumination struck her from a different angle, accentuating a burnt orange tint to her hair Sidney hadn't previously made out. It was medium in length, not as long as the high school yearbook pictures he'd reviewed, when it flowed with adolescent abandon, nor as short as her well-documented combat days, but a compromise, practical, the way he guessed Harken organized everything. He hoped her pending answer would also strike a balance.

"I told President Thorne I didn't know specifically what he and General Nelson discussed, but that in my view, *Posse Comitatus* prevented the United States military from operating on American soil against American citizens."

"You are referring to an 1878 act of Congress which prevents federal troops from civilian law enforcement?"

"Yes sir."

"How did he respond?"

"He said he was sure I would have a different opinion if these people — he didn't specify who — were trying to overthrow the government. Then he moved on to another topic. We never talked about it again."

"But General Harken, I'm sure you are aware that, on multiple occasions, starting at polling places right before the election, again during the period of disputed results, after the Supreme Court's ruling, and as recently as s few weeks ago, President Thorne has deployed U.S. troops, on American soil, against American citizens. Dozens have been killed, many more injured or detained."

Briggs avoided a specific question, thus avoiding an objection from the prosecutor. Instead, his expression pleaded for a reply, trusting her. From his angle, McGehee couldn't see their unspoken exchange, waiting a beat too long to intervene.

"I am aware, sir."

Briggs waited. So did General Harken. "And?" he finally prodded.

"And ... the matter can be complicated, Mr. Briggs." She refocused on the panel, deciding to direct this discussion to them. "First, for none of these occasions was I consulted, nor was I provided any advance notice. Had I been, I would have expressed my concerns, as I did after the fact. Second, I am not in the chain of command, so to speak. Contrary to popular belief, how the movies and TV shows portray it, members of the Joint Chiefs do not exercise military command over combat forces, not even the chairman. We provide advice and counsel, when asked. Finally, not to defend any specific incident, but most of these occurrences involved national guard units directed by state governors."

"But it's pretty common knowledge President Thorne called those governors, all Republicans like himself, and told them what he wanted."

"I understand, but as long as the troops are not federalized, as long as they remain under state control, *Posse Comitatus* doesn't apply." She frowned. "Like I said, it's complicated."

"It wasn't only National Guard troops, though, was it General Harken?" The defense lawyer wasn't so much confronting the witness as guiding her, Sidney realized. Again, where in the *hell* had he gotten his information?

"In Ann Arbor ..." she began.

"...Michigan, where the governor is a Democrat ..."

"Yes sir. Troops from Fort Campbell, the 101st Airborne, were dispatched to put down ... disturbances."

"Your old unit?"

"Yes sir."

"And by 'disturbances,' you mean protests. Large, loud, but peaceful, mostly students upset over the election controversy, the disqualification of ballots and flipping of the state's electoral votes to President Thorne?"

Her demeanor became the watchfulness of one tiptoeing through an uncleared minefield. "I believe the president was concerned about potential violence."

"How did you learn of this deployment?"

"Our DJS," she immediately corrected course, remembering the aversion to acronyms, "director of the Joint Staff, transmitted an action report as they were mustering, including the orders."

"Orders from whom?"

"Ultimately, of course, from the president. It issued from the Secretary of Defense, which is SOP." She apparently decided that one was well enough understood.

"How did you respond?"

"I called the commanding officer to inquire."

"Did you advise to 'stand down.'"

"No. Only the president can countermand orders."

"Was this a legal order?"

McGehee stood. He didn't like the trajectory. "Judge, unless counsel is going to claim the 101st had something to do with the vice president's plan to take out the president, this is all irrelevant to the jury's consideration, and a waste of their time."

"Mr. Briggs," Bering asked, "where *are* we going with this?"

Plaintively, he replied, "We are laying the foundation for Mr. Styles' completely legal efforts to challenge the president's illegal actions, Your Honor."

She pursed her lips. "This trial is about the assassination attempt on March 30, Mr. Briggs, and whether your client had anything to do with it. Let's move on."

Sidney won the objection, but wasn't sure he liked the court's framing.

"The prosecutor mentioned the vice president, General Harken. Did you have any communications with him about these domestic military actions?"

"I did. He called me after the news broke of the engagement in Ann Arbor."

"You mean before the media blackout? Before the arrest of journalists covering the massacre? Before internet cell coverage was blocked in and around that area?"

McGehee fumed, but grasped the unfriendly terrain, the literal accuracy of Briggs' statements. This was territory – were 13 deaths a massacre? – where he best not quibble.

"I am not sure of the exact timing," she said calmly, also not willing to fan the flames. "He wanted to understand how it was possible, and if it could be stopped."

"What did you tell him?"

"I explained that the commanding officer had followed an order received through legitimate channels."

"Can an officer refuse to follow an order, if," Briggs glanced at the prosecutor indulgently, "*hypothetically*, it is illegal?"

"Yes, and in fact, that is what the vice president asked. However, as I told him, that officer can then be relieved, and someone more ... someone willing to execute found."

Judge Bering adjusted, straightening to her full seated height. The defense lawyer sensed imminent intervention and took the hint. *Move On!*

"It is, as you said General, rather complex." He scratched the back of his head, contemplative. Then, as if he had just stumbled onto something, the very darkness of his pupils seemed to widened, his brow creasing. "Let's talk briefly about something much simpler."

Twenty-Five

Yes, he'd been left with a mess. Sidney prided himself on being well-informed. Investigation. Preparation. Always two steps ahead.

Yet, he had never heard of Bonsal, North Carolina. Not until ten minutes ago, when incoming Chair of the Joint Chiefs, four-star General Jacqueline Harken, designated it the situs of a secret American disgrace.

Oddly, as his brain twisted and clutched at the outlines of a counterattack, the prosecutor's initial notion was, "Why did she go there?" Whether what happened was right or wrong – there had been rumors of these clandestine detention camps from many sources – she must realize this would end her exalted new role before she even took it; unless, shrewdly, Harken calculated the political cost as too great for President Thorne. And what about violating national security, the unauthorized disclosure of classified information? *Will I be indicting and prosecuting her next*, he pondered.

But McGehee's focus quickly returned to its usual mode, even as the disclosure pulsated throughout the room. Crafty, Briggs was, dropping this bombshell. Nevertheless, as the prosecutor stood to begin his cross-examination, the self-assured U.S. attorney knew *exactly* what he was going to do.

"You said you learned of Bonsal from," he checked his notes to underscore a fidelity to facts, "the Office of the Provost Marshal General, who heads up the military police."

"The OPMG leads the *Army* Military Police Corps, yes sir, and I heard directly from Marshal General Orea."

"You knew him?"

"Her." She corrected Sidney neutrally, but with obvious purpose. "We were classmates at West Point."

"As I understand your testimony, General Orea was," checking his pad again, "concerned?"

"Yes sir. Very."

"However, you were in the dark."

"That is correct, sir. I told her I would check into it."

"And, according to you, this top-secret operation involved the FBI, the Departments of Justice and Homeland Security, North Carolina's governor and its State Highway Patrol, FEMA, and, of course, the U.S. Army's Military Police Corp. Maybe others. Yet, despite the wide array of officials involved, this American Auschwitz was still, *somehow*, so cloak-and-dagger that nothing leaked, not even the second highest ranking member of the president's own Joint Chiefs knew of it?"

"It was, as near as I was able to discern, a compartmentalized action, which means it was purposefully designed so that none of the participants would have access to the full reach of the plan, or even understand the impact of their role in it. That is a basic security protocol for special ops."

"Twenty or so specialized trailer homes set up, almost overnight, in an area where plenty of folks live, surrounded by several squads of U.S. Army police, plus highway patrol checkpoints popping up all around the nearby Old Highway 1, with strange government vehicles racing around, helicopters and drones overhead. I mean, General, it all sounds a bit Tom Clancy, don't you agree?"

She wasn't rattled. This was a warrior, after all, a woman who had literally killed people, taken a bullet in combat, and survived the broken bones and bloody wounds of a crash landing while saving her crew. Definitely not someone he was going to intimidate.

"I don't read Clancy, Mr. McGehee," she said dryly. "I find reality hard enough."

He smiled in unison with the jurors mostly doing the same. "Fair enough," he said as unflappably as possible. "Still, wouldn't you think, if indeed there had been a mass detention of American citizens as you speculate, practically in the middle of people's backyards, at least one individual would have spoken up? That our hyper-alert journalists and vibrant social media would have kicked up some dust?"

"I can say with confidence, sir, this operation was executed by highly skilled professionals, most of whom would have been, as I said, unaware of the ultimate objective. These were seasoned operatives quite skilled at ..." she sorted through her options, "discretion." Then she added, "Hiding in plain sight is also not a new concept."

In addition to being a successful lawyer, McGehee considered himself more than an amateur onomatologist. To him, the meaning of one's surname included an almost spiritual connection to the centuries of ancestors bearing the same calling card. It was as if a piece of each Baker's or Zhang's or Silva's roots passed along with their genes. In the general's case, Harken, of Irish origin, meant "dark red." Sidney attributed the derivation less to her fiery locks and more to the color's symbolic power to stimulate, activate, dominate. He could see all of this in the woman 12 feet away.

"Let's agree then, General, that after your inquiries, you discovered not a single file, document, or photograph describing or even mentioning this supposed operation," McGehee charged, "and that's despite your highest of security clearances!"

"That is true, and also not surprising. They are called 'Black Ops' for a reason."

"So, the lack of proof ... *is* your proof? I would love to have that luxury in the courtroom, General," he chuckled. "It would make my job a whole lot easier." Sidney was taking a chance. Harken was accustomed to salutes, not snark. If he could get her to lash out, just once, it might help.

"True, Mr. McGehee, it is much like your charges against the vice president – from what I gather, courtesy of our hyper-alert journalists and vibrant social media." She said this flatly, but in the calmness of her voice, the prosecutor heard the click of a disengaging safety. "That is to say, no actual 'proof' of any illegality."

Then, giving her full attention to the jurors, she ... Sidney couldn't call it a smile, yet her expression softened, inviting the panel in, to reason with her. "Unlike your case, however, mine, neither 'speculation' nor 'supposed' as you've incorrectly labeled it, is built upon direct evidence from sources I trust. Like General Orea, who I've known over 30 years. Like Director Degna, whose surveillance teams suddenly lost sight of prominent *TAC* activists in the same 48-hour window after Bonsal opened. Or a high school friend of mine – I'm sure you remember I am from Raleigh." He didn't, actually, and her accent was no longer evident.

"You see, she lives in Holly Springs, just a few miles from the site we've been discussing. Locals do, as you say, notice things, and they do talk. Everything she told me was consistent with the operation I have described today, and with the desire to keep its specifics quiet."

Harken was coolly briefing the jurors, not lecturing them. McGehee watched as a curtain of concern descended over them.

"And one other item, about which Mr. Briggs did not inquire, concerning President Thorne's intentions on the day he was shot." Her head pivoted, and she stared deep into the prosecutor, challenging him. More like an invitation to duel. "May I?"

He tried his best not to show the anger he felt: at the impertinence of the General's disloyalty to her president, and therefore, her country. At his own missteps into the quicksand of her duplicity. If he shut Harken down, Briggs would simply bring it up again on re-direct. "Of course," he said pleasantly, not a care in the world, glancing at his watch as if this whole thing were a terrible waste of time. *Never let the jurors think you are hiding evidence.* Another wise lesson from his professor.

"The Fairgrounds, where the assassination attempt occurred, is exactly 21.3 miles from the Bonsal position," she began, again intimate with her audience. "The rally was less than a week after I first heard from General Orea. Every stone I turned over revealed more ominous clues. While we were in the SitRoom after the shooting, one odd fact struck me. Call it intuition, because it really shouldn't have mattered. Marine One, that's the Sikorsky VH-3D Sea King used by the president, had been flown down for the event."

Harken was pensive. She let her words soak in a moment. Sidney was as much on edge as the twelve in the box. "That's ... unusual," she began again. "The trip from Raleigh-Durham International to the Fairgrounds is less than ten miles, hardly enough to justify the logistics. Presidents rarely use the helicopters domestically, other than to or from Camp David or Andrews, unless they plan to tour a disaster site or have some similar need. So, I called the C.O. for HMX-1," she paused, a coy upturn at the right corner of her lips, "that's Marine Helicopter Squadron One. Colonel Rawling. I asked him one question. The flight plan. What was President Thorne's intended route."

She turned back to the prosecutor, and waited, patiently. Clever woman, McGehee thought to himself. She's pointed the gun at my head, and now she wants me to pull the trigger. "Yes?" he asked, as boredly as he could. "What did *she*, or he, tell you?"

"He," Harken said neutrally, ignoring the attempt at self-deprecation. "Colonel Rawley was as perplexed as I was, though I didn't inform him of my discoveries. He said that the president wasn't using the helicopter from RDU *to* the Fairgrounds, only for the return. 'Weird route back,' he told me. 'I guess he wants to impress the country folk with the bird, 'cause he's sure flying over a lot of near empty space.'"

Sidney saw her neck muscles tense. "Marine One was to fly southwest before doubling back to the airport ... right over Bonsal."

"Let me get this straight, General," Sidney barked, snapping the jurors away from their fixation with the witness. "You're saying that, on the day he was shot, the president intended to fly one of the most recognizable aircraft in the world over the exact location of his sinister, highly classified, super-secret plot against American citizens, a concentration camp in the middle of suburban Raleigh-Durham, North Carolina. And this was to accomplish, what, exactly?"

She remained cool, not about to test the frail limb onto which he invited her. "I can't imagine, sir, what he intended." Then, for good measure, "I would have advised against it."

"This was March 30, ma'am, six months ago. Where to begin ... though I'll be quick, Your Honor," he said lightly to the judge, "as I fail to see how any of this bears on the defendant's plot." Then, his face brandishing the appearance of a spontaneous idea, "Unless, perhaps, General Harken, are you suggesting the president's deviousness justified the defendant's actions?"

"I will leave it to the jury, sir, to decide what the vice president may or may not have done. But if you are asking me whether there is anything that would justify President Thorne's shooting, the answer is, obviously, 'No.'"

"Okay, well, good to know," he said. "But surely, if the president were removing American citizens to secret detention sites, without due process, that would also be something you wouldn't condone. Am I correct?"

"If it were clear that's what was happening, I agree."

McGehee feigned puzzlement. "Isn't that what you are telling us happened?"

"I am saying there were certainly matters of concern, and I was doing my best to explore and address them."

"Did you alert the media?"

"That would be inappropriate. We have a chain of command."

"Did you address this with the entire Joint Chiefs?"

"No. Because General Nelson asked me not to do so."

"So, you raised the matter with your immediate superior?"

"Yes sir."

"And he said?"

"He said he would handle it."

"And did he?"

"I know he spoke to President Thorne, because I was summoned to the Oval Office."

"You discussed the situation with your commander in chief?"

"Yes sir."

Sidney contemplated his next move, choosing what he hoped was the safest route. "Can you disclose any portion of your conversation, General, without violating national security, or compromising classified information?" Yes, he mused satisfactorily. Let this whole diversion end indecisively, with no answers, snug under a *Top Secret* blanket.

"I can, because nothing specific was discussed," she said.

For a moment, McGehee thought he should leave it there. But the witness seemed to think so too, and that was too tempting. "Okay. What, then, was said?"

A dramatic pause? Sidney wondered. Or was she aiming?

"President Thorne said, 'I understand you are taking a look at Bonsal.' I confirmed that I was. He said ... 'Don't.'"

She left it there. McGehee pressed. "Was that an order?"

"I interpreted it as such."

"Did you follow it? I mean, you obviously didn't go public with your *grave* concerns. You didn't resign, not with the biggest possible promotion of your military career so tantalizingly close."

Harken's head tilted ever so slightly to the right. Sidney sensed she was sizing him up, but with a definite tinge of curiosity. About what he wasn't sure. Finally, she spoke, in the manner one would imagine for a commander sending precious troops into battle. "My duty, sir, is to the Constitution of the United States. If any offense is committed against it, or its people, my responsibility is clear."

Her hands reached out to the railing of the witness box. She wasn't seeking stability, but to expand her presence, to assert control. "I serve at the pleasure of the president. Whether I stay or go is up to him. Either way, my obligation remains the same."

"And the vice president?"

Her forehead creased. "Sir?"

"Was his duty, responsibility and obligation to that same Constitution?"

"Yes sir."

"Would you defend your country against a violent overthrow of its government?"

"Of course."

"If the vice president plotted exactly that, as we have shown this jury, then as citizens, they have that same duty to preserve, protect and defend, don't they General?"

Harken's look was steel. "There is none higher."

September 30

(Friday Evening, End of Trial Week Two)

Long, long ago, partisanship rendered the American public a wildfire-torched landscape, scalded skeletons and fiery embers in its wake. After his election, President Magnus Thorne quickly abandoned outreach to "moderates" and "independents" and "voters in the middle." Styles may have helped at the margins, Thorne concluded, but his victory was sealed by red meat appeals to his scorched base. And by God, that's how he would govern.

Accordingly, when it came to putting together his Cabinet, Thorne didn't try to placate demographic sensibilities, a Black nominee here, a woman or Hispanic there. Hell, he already had a gay vice president, didn't he? With a near super majority in the Senate ready to confirm his picks, the new president's choices were based solely on two factors: repayment, and loyalty.

For the Justice Department, David E. Smith conveniently checked both boxes. He was a skilled, cutthroat corporate attorney for the nation's financial heavyweights. More impressively, he'd led the legal storm troopers in every significant right-wing cause of the past 20 years. And Smith cajoled his clients into coughing up tens of millions for the president's campaign. Above all, however, as Thorne for America's general counsel, he proved there was no hill he feared charging.

"Don't worry yourself, Meyer," Smith said now casually to his very agitated guest. Meyer Brook was the richest man in the world, founder of wildly successful biotech, aerospace and cybercommerce ventures, and largest shareholder of the behemoth trading house, Borgen Railey. "It's all under control."

Fresh from his dubious maneuvers to secure Thorne's second term, the attorney general reigned as most powerful member of the president's Cabinet. Which meant, of course, he was the only person who could keep someone like Meyer Brook out of POTUS' hair.

"I'm not going to be left hanging out there, David" Brook said, nervously twirling the ice in his vodka tonic.

Smith regarded his former and, once this nasty government service stint ended, future client with as respectful a countenance as he could project. The ample attorney general's double chin and fleshy neck rolls bulged above the white collar of his pale blue shirt. His corpulent hands rested, interlaced, on the large mound of his belly.

"Meyer," he placated, "you can trust me." Today's job, in Smith's palatial sanctum at the Robert F. Kennedy Building, was to steady the markets – which meant steadying Meyer Brook.

"But what if this Kilbrough fellow starts blabbing? What if he decides to cooperate?"

Smith emitted a grumbling, staccato burst of air reminiscent of Jabba the Hutt, a moniker given him by his many detractors. "First of all, Meyer, who exactly would he talk to? I am the one holding Kilbrough's fate. The U.S. attorney works for me.

And we are offering him a life sentence, and that's only because he missed." Smith shoulders jogged up and down as he happily grunted at his joke.

"Besides, who cares if Kilbrough talks? What's he going to say?" Smith waved his hand dismissively.

"But what about ..." Brook stopped short, unsure if he could say it out loud.

Sensing this, Smith prodded, grinning, "Go ahead. This office hasn't been bugged since J. Edgar met his maker."

"What about the rumors?" Brook hedged.

The attorney general became more serious. "You mean, that the president hired Kilbrough to shoot at him? No one's going to believe that."

Brook anxiously drained his cocktail, then headed to the liquor cart to fix himself another – this one stronger. Smith waited until his guest had returned and taken a generous sip.

"Meyer, you've known Magnus, what, six years?" Brook nodded. "Well, I've known him way longer. The whole idea is crazy."

Brook grew bolder. "So there isn't going to be any secret pardon?"

"Secret pardon?" Smith emitted another guttural gurgle. "There are no secrets in this town. At least," he added, turning serious again, "not from me."

The two men stared at one another, until finally Smith muttered, "Meyer, what's really bugging you? I know you didn't fly all the way down from Manhattan to gossip about conspiracy theories."

Brook shifted uncomfortably in his massive, throne-like chair, identical to the one in which Smith sat next to him. "Styles," he said.

Smith raised his eyebrows. "Styles? What about our soon-to-be ex-vice president?"

"You're right, David. I don't believe the nonsense, that Thorne got himself shot so he could promote himself to dictator and roll out the tanks." His jaw tensed. "That's not to say I don't have grave concerns about the president's response to March 30, and what it's doing to the economy, especially my little companies." He paused. "But what you all are doing to Eli Styles terrifies me more."

Brook took a healthy swig, and leaned across the gap between them. "Mr. Attorney General, everyone knows Styles was my boy."

Smith tried to suss out Brook's meaning. The old man's body lacked even a fibre of sentimentality, so he couldn't possibly be interested in rescuing his former protégé. And as well connected as Brook was, he must recognize he'd easily survive any taint as Styles' political patron.

What did that leave? What could spook a man as indestructible as Meyer Brook?

"You see," Brook started, looking more pale, unsteady, his assured façade failing, "I'm actually more worried about what Eli might have to say."

Puzzled, Smith rearranged his bulk. "I don't understand, Meyer. Eli? He's the one who went to TAC, encouraged them. He's the one who involved Kilbrough. Kilbrough, don't forget, was on Styles' personal detail for years. Those two were close."

The attorney general lingered, examining Brook for the effect of his words, deciding how much to reveal.

What Smith didn't appreciate was that the octogenarian with the thinning pate of wispy gray strands, the sunken sockets, and the splotched, bulbous nose, was likewise studying him. Brook, too, was deciding how much to share.

"Look," the attorney general eventually said, "no matter what the vice president does, none of this has any provable connection to you. Yeah, you were the man's benefactor for years, but you've since been a great friend to President Thorne."

Brook's expression remained uneasy. Smith sensed something askew, but continued anyway. "Never fear, Meyer, he'd be a fool to give up his Fifth Amendment rights. No good lawyer would let him, and Briggs is great. If Styles does testify, by the time Sidney McGehee is done with him, no one will believe anything he says. He'll be finished. And the country will be ..." He skipped a beat, choosing his words carefully, "glad to be rid of him."

Meyer Brook nodded somberly. Surely the attorney general was aware he and Eli met that very morning. The vice president was under house arrest, for Christ's sake, multiple agencies following his every move. They could not have missed Brook coming and going from Mandela Briggs' office. So why, then, wasn't David fishing for information?

For now, Brook would leave well enough alone. He would hold back what Eli confided. The trial was over soon, and he frankly didn't know who or what to believe. In fact, Brook was completely sure of only one thing: he wanted to be on the winning side.

"Perhaps you're right, David." The titan of the pecuniary realm placed his next bet. "Anyway, Rance Knall suggested I give you a little something to make my old apprentice a tad less interested in talking about ... inconvenient topics."

Smith chuckled as Brook handed him a plain folder, which the attorney general didn't open. He didn't need to – it was undoubtedly worth its weight in gold. "Good advice from our dear Speaker," he purred. "McGehee, I'm sure, will make very good use of this."

Brook nodded, solemnly. "Tell me, then," he said, asking the attorney general the same question he had posed to Eli Styles six hours ago. "What really happened? And no bullshitting, David. Only what is one hundred percent certain."

He eased back and waited. The truth would be useful.

The lies, however, would be invaluable.

Twenty-Six

Mandela went out of his way to show his judges respect. He was always on time, with extra copies of whatever the Court may need and whose overwhelmed clerk may have forgotten. He never argued past a magistrate's signal that his or her mind was made, or threaten appeal if things were going badly. He didn't crowd the bench or lavish insultingly disingenuous flattery. Above all, not once in his career had he lied to a robed lord.

It was thus an unusual circumstance for him to be summoned to chambers, late on a Saturday morning no less, and find himself seated before a seething Carolyn Bering. Her fingers pinched the edges of a thin, blue folder as her narrowed eyes perused its contents. Given this particular jurist's reputation as the most reserved, measured member within the D.C. circuit, her bare furor was all the more troublesome.

Yet, Briggs fully understood why he was there. He had invited this. Moreover, it was a choice he would repeat if offered the opportunity.

To his left sat the United States attorney, pensive in the glow of the Court's silent heat, probably trying to figure out what *he* had done wrong. Briggs was surprised his foe was so obviously out of the loop. He'd expected McGehee to arrive fully armed.

"Gentlemen," she said in a forced, husky tone to bleed off a soaring pressure, releasing the word before there was an explosion. Briggs got it. This was the biggest case in her storied career, and he was about to make it bigger. "Where to begin?" The corners of her mouth were indeed turned upward, but the half-hearted movement was closer to a grimace.

Briggs calculated he could weather the storm. She wouldn't yell, and retribution was hardly in character for Carolyn Bering. Still, he hated the very idea of having disappointed her, or worse, of her believing he had been disrespectful.

She inhaled, then released the air in a heavy gush of resignation. "First, for logistical reasons, court will convene an hour later than normal on Monday, at 10:00 a.m." The stare she directed at Mandela was as hard as concrete. This judge's schedule was sacrosanct. It clearly pained her to alter it.

The ostensibly minor modification confused him, though. What did she mean, "court will convene?" What was happening at ten? She had buried the lede. Briggs didn't dare utter a syllable, however. He also did not look at the prosecutor. *Dude has no idea!*

"You and your staffs will need to be here at eight, however, as the Secret Service needs everyone in place by then, and will not allow any of you to leave the courtroom unescorted from that time forward."

As sharp as Mandela was – he accepted his acumen not in a braggadocious way, but in the confident manner a premier sprinter would realize his speed – this made no sense. The Secret Service? Were they already priming the E. Barrett Prettyman Courthouse for the grand arrival in case imminent objections were overruled? When, then, was the hearing? Is that what 10 a.m. was all about? The Big Man's representatives couldn't get here any earlier? What time would they serve their brief, so he'd have a chance to prepare a response, or at least formulate his oral argument?

"Your Honor, I hope I'm not interrupting," McGehee tread carefully, "but may I ask what we are talking about?"

For a brief moment, Bering and Briggs were in unison, each taking in the U.S. attorney, the judge with surprise, the defense lawyer with a fleck of sympathy.

Bering looked at Mandela, her mouth opening slightly as if to speak, her features overriding the effort, contorted with renewed frustration. *You didn't tell him either?* was the easy telepathy.

Bering cleared her throat. "It seems, Mr. McGehee, that your adversary has subpoenaed the President of the United States, for live testimony on Monday morning."

U.S. attorneys were a pretty cocky bunch in general, this one at the head of the class. Which made his muteness all the more remarkable. Frozen. Waiting. Waiting for the judge to explain, to add the "And ..." There was none. Only a question.

"Did he not serve you with a copy of the subpoena, Mr. McGehee?"

"We did, your honor, at 8:13 this morning, twelve minutes before it was served on the White House." Briggs took quite the risk, jumping in while she addressed his counterpart. But it was obvious McGehee's office had somehow botched the receipt. Mandela wasn't trying to help the guy. He actually detested the preening egomaniac. Still, Briggs guessed he would catch the blame regardless, and so decided to circumvent the scuffle altogether.

The Court tented her fingers under her chin, glaring at him. "You get no points for obeying the strict letter of the law, counselor. It's your lack of adherence to the spirit of the requirements that has me concerned." Her words were chosen so carefully, so Bering-like. Mandela absorbed the blow, letting her vent.

Federal Rule of Criminal Procedure 17. Subpoenas. The clerk issues them blank, signed and quite official looking. The requesting party then fills in the empty spaces and serves them. No ironclad requirement to notify the other side, or even the Court, on any particular schedule, but common practice is to advise both in a timely way. When you don't, well, Briggs appreciated the consequences. Which is why he sent them copies, but not in time for either to do anything about his plans.

McGehee filled the void. "Your Honor, the United States obviously takes tremendous issue with this bullsh..." Regarding him for the first time that morning, Mandela saw the prosecutor trembling with fury, catching himself at the knife's edge of decorum. "Baloney," he corrected. "This baloney." He shot holes through his adversary, who let him. "There are a number of problems – executive privilege, national security, relevance – not to mention the logistical issues, the delay this will cause."

McGehee, flushed with anger and refusing to even look at Briggs, kept his sight on Bering. "I think the defense realizes its back is against the wall and is trying to force a mistrial so they can regroup, now that they know our case."

The Court gave him free reign. She even leaned back in her chair, perhaps enjoying the pummeling? Mandela patiently waited it out. It was the least he could do.

"We can have a motion to quash ready by this afternoon," he barreled on, "and perhaps the Court could hear us by the end of the day?" McGehee's confidence was growing. "I assure you we are willing to take our chances on appeal, and I am positive," he seemed about to stand and supercharge his argument by pacing the floor, "the Supreme Court will uphold a guilty verdict without forcing the president's attendance."

Not an unreasonable request, Briggs conceded. His own reply brief was already written. His senior associate had been working on it for weeks. All Ryan had left was to tie his sections to whatever the prosecutor filed.

Mandela anticipated Bering would move with lightning speed. He bet she would do anything to avoid blowing up the trial, thus wasting all these jurors' time. The only real issue was, would she allow him to call a clearly pertinent witness, and if she did, how long could the might of the Executive Branch string this out?

"Furthermore," the U.S. attorney raged, the Court allowing him to spend his indignation, most of which flew past Mandela without notice. Briggs was busy reviewing his mind map for the coming fight to justify his high-stakes maneuver. This presidential subpoena wasn't ego, he repeated to himself. Nor was it a Hail Mary. It was necessary, he believed, to demystify the man upon whom he wanted to focus this trial.

Eventually, the prosecutor sat back, fatigued, having exhausted his repertoire of righteous punches. For now.

Bering shuffled at the papers in her folder, a final procrastination before turning over her first few cards. "Mr. McGehee," she said, a soft voice not matching her strained eyes, "I certainly appreciate your position, and ordinarily I would be quite receptive to some of the measures you are suggesting."

That wasn't the opening Briggs expected. Nor the prosecutor, over whom a curtain of bewilderment fell. "Your Honor," he started, nearly breathless, his earlier energy dispersed. The Judge held up her hand gently, not in admonishment but in condolence.

"I have been informed by Mr. Ginsberg," she said, referring to the White House Counsel, "that the president is not going to oppose the subpoena."

The room drowned in silence. The crisp fall day outside triggered neither the air conditioning nor the heat, hushing the normally ubiquitous rumble of the ancient HVAC system. Only faint sounds of traffic and someone's distant, high-pitched laugh wafted through the cozy room. Briggs was briefly stunned, then overcome with the tingle of anticipation. Not in a million years did he dream that ...

"Well, Judge, the People certainly have objections of their own," McGehee burst out, defiant. "It is, with all deference to the White House, *my* case!"

Bering nodded sagaciously. "I agree, counselor. And you are welcome to file whatever briefing you wish." Her eyebrows arched, and she placed her hands, palms up, on the surface of her neat desk. "If I may offer my advice, however, I wouldn't do that."

McGehee was crestfallen. Her face regarded him warmly, a rare gesture from someone for whom public emotion was nearly nonexistent. "I share your skepticism," she said, "but with the witness' consent, and the wide latitude given criminal defendants in the exercise of their rights to a fair trial, there is no way I am going to bar President Thorne from the courtroom."

Abruptly, she zeroed in on Mandela, a violent tide breaking, all pleasantness gone. Behind the judge's gaze, he imagined her retrieving the prosecutor's sword as if for a fallen comrade, brandishing it forebodingly. "Mr. Briggs, make no mistake of my intentions." One of her small hands was balled into a fist, rotating inside the other's palm. "You will get your witness. But your lane of inquiry is going to be vanishingly small, and your margin for error hypothetical at best. This case is about the vice president's alleged complicity in the attempted murder of his superior, nothing more. I trust the United States attorney will point out any deviations from that subject matter."

She paused, daring Briggs to the fill the gap. Wisely, he didn't. "Do I make myself clear?"

"Yes ma'am."

The scolding was worth the pain. As she said, he would get his witness.

†††

At one corner of the president's desk, Colonel Arenberg sat with his head buried in his hands. At the opposite angle A.R. Hoffman appeared ready to spring, his rear barely grazing his seat. Behind them, to the near side of facing sofas, Robert Ginsberg paced, fixated on the golden carpet, remembering what his wife had called it on her solo visit to the historic place: Saturday morning puke.

For the moment, they were the only three in the room. There were traces of the temporarily absent yet most important occupant, though. A suit jacket tossed onto the cushion of one of those blue and crème striped couches. A drained tumbler with three melting ice cubes sitting atop the bar cabinet against the far wall. Still, none of them spoke, his presence palpable, his latest tirade lingering.

The door from the interior corridor leading to POTUS' private study – a smaller office, dining room and lavatory just off the Oval – swung open as forcefully as it had been slammed moments ago. A renewed man entered. "Ahhhhh," Magnus Thorne exhaled. "So much better."

His three guests stiffened. Was this merely the eye of the storm?

"Now," he said, knuckles on hips Douglas MacArthur style. "Anything else?"

Who would enter No Man's Land, where a hail of bullets was the typical toll? A.R. and Ginsberg cast their hopes on the Colonel, the closest to the president, the one who, albeit in private and infrequently, could use his first name. Arenberg received their silent plea, rolled his eyes, and plunged in. What the hell.

"Boss, we don't want to belabor this, but hear me out."

Thorne trilled his lips, shook his head, and walked over to the Waterford decanters, grabbing his favorite solution and releasing the liquid into his glass.

"We get you're insistent on doing this. Matter of pride. Totally understandable. But preparation is the key. You simply can't take the stand in," he checked his wrist, "36 hours. It's a trap, and Briggs is ready." The president's back remained to them as he stirred his drink with an index finger which, tilting back his head, he then licked. "With all due respect, sir," the Colonel continued, "if we're going to beat him, we need to be ready." Hoffman and Ginsberg nodded, vigorously. The cowards, Arenberg thought.

Thorne pivoted, took a generous sip, and mutely addressed each of his advisors, one by one. His shirtsleeves were rolled up. He was the rough and tumble Montana businessman again, primed to brawl.

"God damn it, boys, we're not discussing this anymore. That sonofabitch took a chunk out of my ass yesterday, with one of my own generals, and I'm gonna set things straight." He dared them with his eyes.

"I spoke with the U.S. attorney," Hoffman offered gingerly.

"Shhiiittttt," the president groaned. "That bastard hasn't exactly been defending me, has he A.R.?"

"He's trying, Mr. President. He is confident he can buy us as long as we need to organize. I know Robert, here, would kill to have the extra time with you." Ginsberg looked horrified at having been dragged into the crossfire.

Thorne turned chillingly calm, twirling the tiny blocks in his booze, and flashed his trademark crooked teeth. "Let's talk about my tie. For Monday." He took another sip. "Red, or blue?"

Twenty-Seven

It's not so much nerves I feel, though I have plenty reason for preoccupation.

There's Brady, for one. More morose with each passing day, to the point he's even bringing me down a bit. Were it possible, I'd send him away. Much better than his brooding on the front row, sending off signals of negativity and defeatism that are then attributed to "the Styles camp," when I feel no such pessimism. At home, Brady doesn't want to talk about it, other than subtle digs announcing his – what exactly? Concerns. Jealousy. Suspicions. All about Sam Kilbrough, of course. It's all so tiresome, an unwelcome departure from his previous sunny encouragement.

Then we have those twelve mini-judges in the box, like a dozen easter eggs with their own subtle shapes and colors. I found the game of trying to "read" them pointless when this whole thing started. But now, I actually think I have a knack for it. My worry isn't that we don't have several on our side, it's the herd mentality thing: the stronger, more hateful, more dominant members of the jury pushing the weaker, more sympathetic ones into an unfortunate decision. Weeks of forced isolation swelling the urge to capitulate, no matter my cruel fate.

Perhaps the greatest trigger of, again, *not* nerves, *not* fear, but a tingling, charged rush vibrating throughout my body, is the imminence of a verdict and its accompanying loss of control. Sure, there are appeals, but that esoteric exercise won't involve me. Trial is the only game, and I need a triumph, a resounding and unanimous victory, not the whimpering fizzle of a hung jury or the finesse of a higher court's lofty opinion which no normal person will read. Put me in, Coach. I got this! I can't win if I don't play.

In other words, I desperately need to testify.

These are the anxieties I'm *trying* to explain to Mandela in my millionth or so visit to his austere, purposeful offices. Don't get me wrong, I comprehend his admonitions. The arguments against a criminal defendant testifying are legion. Sure. *But ...*

"I hear you, I really do," is what I say to Izzy and Ryan. He listens to them. "What I'm not sure you fully appreciate, though, is my sense of where we are. The battlefield." I need to redefine Mandela's cookie-cutter vision of this case, because it's not like anything he's managed before. And of *me*. I am not the typical client.

"You said yourself, these jurors need to see the case through *my* eyes, the threats to *their* liberty *I* was fighting for on their behalf. Well, I think we've offered them a lot to consider, but the way I see the landscape, they aren't *feeling* it."

I'm standing. I do better when I expand my presence, physicalizing my words. "I was there, on the front row, witnessing Thorne's unscrupulous maneuvers from a perspective no one else can bring to life!"

Izzy is frowning. At least that one never hides her emotions. No worries. I'm not done. "And you were the ones who upped the ante by inviting the president to our little party," I say to Ryan, giving him my most serious expression. "Genius, by the way, I'm not criticizing," just in case they think I'm not on board. I am.

That's because Magnus is an ass, and unlike me, his self-control is crap. Everyone else was shocked when he didn't object to the subpoena, when it was announced he'd be there tomorrow morning. Not me. I know the man. He's delusional and loves the sound of his own voice. Convincing when not challenged, true, but Mr. Briggs will skillfully knock him off his pedestal. It won't be enough, though, because cross-examination can only get you so far with a pathological liar.

"The president's appearance makes it absolutely essential for me to take the stand. Not only does it paint a vivid contrast," I guide my hands across an imaginary canvass, "the raging bull versus the watchful owl, but I can also counter whatever nonsense he spouts. Someone has to mop up, provide context."

Ultimately, I get to decide. I am the defendant. It's my case, and my life on the line. Still, I want the team on board. I want them to acknowledge my persuasive abilities. I've been influencing people almost as long as Briggs, and with much bigger audiences.

I can tell Ryan gets it. Izzy remains discernibly opposed. Mandela listens patiently, trying to decide how to talk me out of it. He gives me his most tolerant face, scanning his notes – he showed the courtesy of scribbling feveringly as I spoke – pretending he's considered my arguments earnestly. Then he clears his throat.

"I will grant, Mr. Vice President, that you are a skilled orator, and more admirably in my view, an exceptional conversationalist. You have shown the ability to connect with all manner of people from diverse backgrounds. Including, maybe especially, people who disagree with you."

The flattery is as thick and delicious as were Mom's peanut butter and jelly sandwiches. Plenty of feel-good carbs.

"The witness box, however, is not a podium. Nor is it the guest seat on *Meet the Press* or *Fox News Sunday* or *XBN Duel*. It is more akin to," Mandela sports a cautionary look, "a dart board. Or an archery target. Pick your metaphor." Young Mr. Townsend is now nodding along with his boss.

"The U.S. attorney is, frankly, praying you will step onto the stand and raise your right hand. Not because he's smarter than you, though he doubtless believes that, but because he appreciates the odds are stacked overwhelmingly in his favor."

Sidney McGehee. Sanctimonious, disingenuous hack. My lawyer is correct, he wants to square off *mano-a-mano*. He sees a little queer boy in need of a good bruising. Probably beat up kids like me in the immaculate bathrooms of his so-called "public" high school, with its über-tax-base, privileged two-parent homes, and a football stadium that cost more than all of my campuses combined. What better way to launch his political career than to demolish the traitorous vice president. Secure the death penalty for Styles, and on to the United States Senate. Magnus Thorne will be first in line with an endorsement.

"He knows the rules of this peculiar game we play, and with all due respect, Mr. Vice President, you don't. There will be no flowery speeches from your chair, no matter how much you and I try and tell your side of the story. Hell, you'll be lucky to finish a complete sentence. The guy will be on his feet with objections every 10 seconds, and I'm sure you've seen enough of this judge to know she holds a very short leash."

"But," I say, because here I own the experience of countless high-profile debates, "he'll look like a bully, or an obstructionist, or just plain rude. The jurors will want to hear from me, and they won't appreciate his interruptions, like he's trying to hide something."

My counsel puckers his lips, an affectation merely feigning thoughtful respect, which he quickly refutes. "Could be." He nods, again in staged contemplation. "Could be. However, by this point the jurors have accepted him, and me, as impolite and brutish." He grins. "After all, we're lawyers." Ha. Ha. Ha.

"The larger point is," he proceeds, "you won't get an unimpeded path to the jury, or to the truth. Your discourse will be chopped up into unrecognizable fragments, and it will actually be *you* who comes off as either disorganized or incoherent."

He's ignoring my rhetorical boxing chops, so I remain unconvinced.

"Mr. Vice President, everything I'm telling you applies with equal measure to Magnus Thorne. I guarantee his advisors, and especially his lawyer, are deeply disappointed in his decision to appear tomorrow. Far from ingratiating himself with the panel, I expect his appearance to be a mess. Best to leave that as the final impression."

Conceivably, he's right. But to risk my survival on Thorne's implosion leaves me fragile, vulnerable, and impudent. The president's diabolical master plan was to become an all-powerful dictator. "I needed to stop him," I say, not initially realizing I'd spoken the words out loud. From around the long, scratched table, Mandela, Izzy and Ryan stare as if I have uttered something revealing, begging me with their eyes to say more. So, I do.

"In my view, there are critical stories to tell. President Thorne was a clear and present danger to American democracy. Despite great peril to myself, I fought him. I defended our system. I defended our people, even, paradoxically, the rights of those who love him and hate me. The fact that Sam Kilbrough took matters to the extreme ... well."

The rest should be obvious, such that it doesn't matter how I finished that train of logic. The reality is, Sam idolized me. Sam desired I become president. He thought he was a patriot, and in all honesty he was. Who else can make that clear, portraying the assassination as *his* motivation. His *infatuation*?

I am not a religious guy. God knows I tried; pun intended. I remember bussing tables in Russell Hall's cafeteria, the girls' dorm at Baylor, student employment which paid my tuition. Humiliating job, all those rich, piously Christian young ladies looking down their reconstructed noses at me. Somehow, I thought if I prayed a little harder and believed a little deeper and banished my confused sexual urges, maybe I'd gain their acceptance, which I crazily thought I needed. Instead, ironically, I got faith. Faith in the possibilities of hard work and perseverance. Faith in myself instead of approval from an amorphous, ubiquitous deity who may or may not be sitting on some cloud, passively laughing his ass off at his followers. Faith in the ends justifying the means.

And that brings me full circle to why I cannot yield the stage to Magnus Thorne. Why I have to speak to this assemblage of my nominal peers.

"This prosecutor will tear you apart," Izzy interjects in her endearingly unvarnished way. Are they seriously playing good cop/bad cop? "The nicer and calmer you are, the easier it is for him to punch you; the more combative, the less likable you become. It's lose/lose times a thousand," she says.

"Best to keep alive the mystique of the valiant, selfless warrior for democracy," Ryan adds.

They throw everything at me, the full tour of the mistake I'll be making, blindfolded into a minefield, all the insinuations and discrepancies that will blow up in my face.

"And think of Brady, and especially Anna," Briggs piles on in his best imitation of compassion. "There could be the hints of a relationship with Kilbrough that, they will say, went beyond the professional, or the charitable."

The day dims and the conference room's artificial lighting becomes more noticeable. So does my assuredness. Instinct has taken me to some strange places, but never, ultimately, let me down.

I can still be president, but only if I fight for it.

Week Three

Twenty-Eight

This president was adept at the multitudinous uses of force: brute, demonstrative, overpowering, and perhaps most effective, the subtle or merely threatened. Thus, the Secret Service agents about the courtroom were concurrently ornamentation and intimidation. Trademark dark suits snug upon fit physiques, well-trimmed scalps, spit-shiny shoes, earpieces, strong manicured hands within easy distance of serious weaponry's obvious protuberances, and, of course, their eyes: searching, watchful orbs from whose pupils radiated cool calculation. These guys and gals were not playing.

This King's Guard, an outward manifestation of might presaging right, swelled Emmanuel Arroyo's favor toward Magnus Thorne, for whom he'd voted twice – voting even though in D.C. it didn't matter, because the Democrats always won. He wasn't alone in his awe. As Emmanuel and the others emerged through their side door and mounted the single step to the dual rows of wooden seats, he read it on his fellows' faces. Arroyo hadn't said much in the past few weeks, but he had listened, studying them, learning their tells for boredom, dissatisfaction, surprise or confusion. Now, as they took their usual places, each expression confirmed this was no ordinary day, and would be no ordinary witness.

Absent were the normal murmurings in the audience pews, the frenetic moving of boxes and files and pads about counsel tables, the intense whispering of the journalists near the back, the light banter from increasingly chummy Bailiff Bankhead, the easy meandering of the marshals. All was replaced by a hushed, nervous anticipation.

While Emmanuel absorbed this tableau, his interest settled on the witness chair, specifically, the cracked burgundy cushion tied with thin yellow ribbons to the spindles at its back. Far from special, it was worn, flattened. No presidential eagle, talons clutching arrows. It was the same cushion, he mused, upon which the asses of many less significant mortals had rested, yet in a few moments the most powerful man in the world would occupy it. Right here, not 20 feet from Arroyo himself! Oh, how he wished Mary could be here to see.

Only the judge and guest of honor were missing. It was 9:58, two minutes before the day was scheduled to start. Judge Bering was never late, something Arroyo admired. He quickly pondered whether that might change today, whether the logistics of such a significant personage would alter even her tightly run operation. And he tried to imagine the choreography, the protocol, when the big man entered. Do we rise? Even the judge? We should respect him, or at least his office, Emmanuel decided, but then his view shifted to the defendant, and his sense of justice caused him to wonder if standing unfairly exalted the witness at the expense of the accused. No one had given them instructions.

The entryway from the judge's chambers was on the opposite side of her bench, so that only the top few inches were visible. Arroyo trained his sight on that narrow band of dark wood and waited, occasionally glancing at his watch as its minute hand ticked toward the tiny XII at the top, then one past the hour. Ten-o-two, -three, -four, and the tension all around tightened. Who was making whom wait? Heads swiveled left and right, from the back of the courtroom to the front, from agent to agent, seeking any sign of imminent approach. Nothing.

Finally, at 10:07 – Arroyo verified it – he saw the top of the judge's familiar hairdo emerge as she darted up the steps in a delayed hurry to her post. A normally businesslike manner had hardened, her eyes cast down as she arranged her pen and papers and gavel as if in practice for the more serious control she would soon need to exert.

Then, with an almost imperceptible sigh, she greeted Emmanuel and his brethren, "Good morning, ladies and gentlemen," as she did each day, though her smile was forced. "I apologize that we are running a little behind." All nodded forgiveness and understanding.

Just as quickly, she addressed the defense lawyer, who to Arroyo was completely unaffected by the changed environment. "Mr. Briggs, please call your next witness," Bering called out as naturally as she could.

The defense lawyer said nothing. Instead, in what appeared a prearranged signal, he inclined his head to an agent standing against the wall off to his left, who then whispered into his sleeve. Like magic, both hallway doors swung open. Emmanuel ran the fingers of his left hand over the stubbly hairs covering his scalp. They came back damp with perspiration. He wiped them on his corduroys as a presence consumed the open entryway. President Magnus Thorne, in person.

The man stood tall and commanding, staring forward, arms at his side as if newly arrived in some esteemed foreign capital, preparing to walk the red carpet. Arroyo trembled, charged by a current radiating from the majesty of the president's office.

"You may come forward, sir," the judge called sternly, startling Emmanuel. *Rude* was his first reaction, until he looked at her. Impatience? Annoyance? No. His careful observations over the last weeks led him to conclude Carolyn Bering was beyond that sort of petty thinking. *¡Astuto!* Cunning. Clever. She'd seen an opportunity to give the exalted witness an order with which she knew he must comply, and had deftly taken it.

Thorne tugged at each of his monographed cuffs, flashed his famously crooked teeth, and started down the center aisle, unhurried, glancing from side to side and graciously nodding his acknowledgment to the day's lucky attendees. Somehow, the collective decision was to remain seated in frozen reverence, a response the jaunty president didn't seem to mind in the least.

As he pushed through the gate leading into the well, Thorne reached out his hand to the prosecutor, who stood and took it, smiling warmly at the man who'd nominated him. As this anointment occurred, Arroyo couldn't help but notice the other side of the gesture's coin: the president's back was fully turned on his traitorous number two. He continued ignoring Styles as he approached the bench and, still beaming, reached up to the judge, holding his arm at a distance requiring her to either refuse his courtesy, or stand. Emmanuel smiled at the gamesmanship as Bering leaned forward reluctantly, and they shook.

At long last, Thorne took over the appointed chair, immediately swiveling toward the jurors, charming them with his attention. Arroyo would later swear to Mary that the president, of *all* the United States of America, had locked eyes with none other than her very own husband. He told her with complete certainty, "*Nunca nos hemos conocido, pero él me entiende.*" We have never met, but he *gets* me.

††††

... to tell the truth, the whole truth, and nothing but the truth. So help me Almighty *God.*

The dude was larger in real life than Aiden expected, which was surprising because he thought TV was supposed to make people look bigger. Kind of a massive head, proportionally, and his mouth was huge, like those mismatched teeth could reach out and devour you. If the man had any anxieties about being here, about dissing his own vice president, it sure didn't show.

"Mr. Thorne," Briggs started, and here Tinsley noticed two things. First, the defense lawyer's gait, his manner. Confident without being cocky, immediately dispelling any nerves or intimidation about the task at hand. Also, the surnamed salutation. No "Mr. President." *You're just a witness, like any other.*

"Let us begin with the summer of your first nomination, the convention in Nashville. I'm sure you remember it well."

"Like it was yesterday," Thorne beamed.

"Great! So, surely you recall Tuesday, the second day of the convention, when you went before the cameras and announced to the nation, 'After thorough and serious deliberation, I have chosen Elijah Wilson Styles to be the next Vice President of the United States,' calling him, in *your* words, 'far and away the most qualified person in America to assume the presidency, should the need arise.'"

"Of course," the president nonchalantly conceded. Then Aiden perceived a switch flip, Thorne's face transforming into the sour, fighting scowl he'd seen whenever a reporter's question agitated the president. "Which is why his eventual betrayal hurt so badly."

Briggs was undeterred. "Integrity, and patriotism, were the qualities you highlighted when revealing your personal choice for the second highest office in the land. Integrity, and patriotism. Please, Mr. Thorne, would you share with the jury the basis for that high praise? In other words, tell us how your exhaustive consideration of Mr. Styles led you to reach those conclusions."

The president kept his focus on the lawyer, refusing to acknowledge the presence of the man who tried to have him killed. His anger melted away as quickly as it had arrived. Thorne regarded the defense attorney sheepishly, then fixed upon the jurors. "It's no secret, Mr. Briggs, that in politics ... well, let's just say sometimes we who practice that fine art are a little given to hyperbole." He winked. Tinsley heard a couple of his comrades chuckle, most at least smiling at their inclusion into this inside joke. It was a trite, bullshit escape from the question, the young man concluded, immediately rooting for Briggs to whack him.

"Ah, I see, yes. Hyperbole. Exaggeration. Embroidery. But I assume it is not your regular practice to outright *lie* to the American people, to folks like those sitting before you in that box." They all spun from Briggs to the president, eager for his reply, for his confirmation that, no, while he may embellish – naturally, every elected official does – he'd never lie. Or as Aiden viewed it, no politician would ever *admit* he lied.

"Therefore, sir, with all due respect, my question remains. How did you, whose job requires a keen insight into those he encounters, conclude that Elijah Styles was a man of integrity, *and* patriotism?" The attorney's deportment was severe. His challenge reminded Tinsley of the glove slap used to demand a duel.

"It wasn't a lie. It was more aspirational. *Me* giving *him* the benefit of the doubt. But as long as we're all being truthful here, Mr. Briggs, I'll share this one. That assessment, about integrity, patriotism, and so on, it was all a huge mistake. We bought into the mayor's carefully crafted public image, and I'll admit he's a good salesman. The truth is, I should have gone with someone I knew better instead of a guy I interviewed, literally, for an hour over coffee in the middle of a convention.

"I wanted unity. I wanted competence, and he appeared to be pretty damn smart. I also wanted to break ground for this country, and I did, putting the first gay man in history on a national ticket. I'm proud of that, and only wish he had done a better job of representing his kind ... um, you know, his people."

Whoa, Aiden gasped. *His kind*? Maybe it was growing up in sunny SoCal, land of Live and Let Live. Or coming of age when gay everything was so far beyond mere acceptance, into the category of "whatever." The president was forty years his senior, of a different era, and obviously from a different planet when it came to the LGBT community. Tinsley, his attorney cap snugly on his head, wondered if Briggs should pound away. If it was me, he decided, I'd let it go, let the comment speak louder by speaking for itself.

"Let's talk about your actions, Mr. Thorne, in the days and weeks after March 30."

Aiden smiled.

"Before you had even left the hospital ... By the way, what exactly was your injury?"

For the first time, Tinsley concluded, the president appeared the slightest bit uncertain. "I was shot in the arm from close range," he said gravely.

"Uh huh." The lawyer consulted a thin, stapled report. "According to Dr. Patel, in your discharge summary – for the record that's Prosecution Exhibit number 87," he made the aside to Noah, the reporter, "the bullet 'abraded the brachium,' that's the upper arm, 'requiring debridement, application of antibiotic, and loose dressing to prevent irritation during the healing process.'"

Thorne glowered, but didn't respond.

"So, a flesh wound, treated with ointment and an oversized bandage, correct?"

"Dr. Patel informed me I was quite lucky, if that's your point, Mr. Briggs." He recovered his cheerful façade and asked, "Have you ever been shot?"

"Only shot at, Mr. Thorne, during my final deployment with the Army. In Iraq. But like you, I was quite lucky." He stole Thorne's grin. "As I was saying before that detour, while being treated, you barked out a few orders from your bed, I believe."

"Of course I did. When there is an attempted assassination of the president, one must assume our nation is under attack." The president faced the jurors with his chest puffed out, assuming the aura of superhero, his custom-tailored dress shirt ready to rip open and reveal a large red "S". "When it comes to protecting American citizens," his scrutiny leapt from Mrs. Jackson to Banker Dude to Aiden, "I don't fool around."

"Executive Order 17484, which I've marked here as Defense Exhibit 111," Briggs held the single sheet at arm's length, like it was toxic, "do you recall it, the first one you signed?"

"Most definitely. It federalized the National Guard in all 50 states, and ordered them to secure each state capital and all urban areas with a population of, I believe it was 100,000."

"Yes, I see that," the attorney said, reading the document, still at a safe distance. "It also includes rules of engagement, such as 'Shoot to Kill,' though no mention of 'Who' to shoot, or under what circumstances."

"Our troops needed flexibility. After all, we had no idea what we were dealing with."

Tinsley remembered that day, as he was sure did everyone else on the panel. It was terrifying. Tanks, armored vehicles and lethally geared soldiers seemed to be on every corner. No one went anywhere, which he figured was probably the point.

"The thing is, Mr. Thorne, you were by then very well protected, under heavy guard at Raleigh Regional Medical Center. The gunman, who you actually *knew* – we'll get to that in a moment – was under arrest." Briggs' expression twisted in confusion. "I guess I'm scratching my head here," and he literally did, "What was the threat? Why did you feel the need to, essentially, put the country under martial law. Ronald Reagan didn't take any such steps when he was shot in 1981, nor did Gerald Ford in 1975 when there were two attempts on his life. Even after President Kennedy was actually murdered, Lyndon Johnson tried to project calm, the opposite of your actions."

Thorne didn't hesitate, showing not an ounce of misgiving or remorse. "Different times, my friend." The president firmly placed one hand on the witness stand's shelf to his front, and the other atop the wood rail to his left, closest to the jurors. It was an open stance, Aiden noticed, a posture of power from which he could swivel his imposing torso as he alternatively lectured the defense counsel and The Twelve.

"You see, back then, we basically had one enemy. Mother Russia. None of my predecessors you listed had to worry about cyberwar, or the power of liberal social media agitators, or domestic terrorists, like The Aberdeen Circle." Thorne had coiled into disgusted irritation. Tinsley wondered if it was his memory of the dangers, the impertinence of being doubted, or both. "Unlike Johnson and Reagan, I wasn't taking any chances." Then, directly to the panel. "Not with your safety and freedom, I wasn't."

The strategic circling by Thorne and Briggs, Briggs and Thorne, was fascinating. Their verbal swordplay reminded Aiden of Frankie and Aleo, two of his boys back in Hermosa, both effortlessly nasty with the boards. They were like oceanic gladiators, performing skills they didn't even know they had, didn't think about, just conjured on the fly. Those two were only impressed by unrideable waves, and when Aleo conquered a bomb screaming ragdoll, Frankie would find one even more threatening. One up, one up, one up, exactly like the present battle, except words, not water, suits instead of shorts.

"That's an interesting perspective, Mr. Thorne, though I'm still not sure I understand exactly what it is we good citizens," he took in the entire courtroom, "were being protected *from*. Regardless," he theatrically waved away those misgivings with the back of his hand, "there are four things concerning this Executive Order you signed about which we are quite certain."

The attorney took three menacing steps in the direction of the witness, the president, which garnered the attention of his protectors. In Tinsley's mind, however, the movement had a clear purpose. A message. *I'm not afraid of you.*

"First," he pointed his index finger skyward, "there were no riots." Briggs paused, shrugging his shoulders, palms displayed disarmingly.

"None whatsoever. Anywhere. Which is strange, because from your disputed re-election until that day, there had been protests and marches and rallies on a daily basis. It seems your ... unfortunate event, well, it didn't incite anyone to do anything. And whatever grand takeover scheme you concocted for The Aberdeen Circle ended up a fantasy."

The president was not amused, his mercurial aggressiveness frothing. "I'd say that was exactly the point," he spat. "All that firepower made them think twice."

He had more to say, but in a lesson for the budding young law student, Briggs wedged into the nanosecond of Thorne's breath, jamming the intended tirade. "'All that firepower,' you say. Glad you brought it up, because, despite the lack of any calamitous uprising, there were, indeed, people killed. Dozens, in fact, all across the country, shot by troops sent into the streets," he held E.O. 17484 like bloody dagger, "on orders from you!"

The president expanded his upper body and made to reply, but Briggs simply raised his voice, and rumbled on. "A mother in Butte, a pair of college students in Knoxville, and perhaps most telling, three patrons of a popular bar right here in D.C."

"All violating the curfew. None of them, *none*, would have come to any trouble if they'd stayed home," and indicating the jurors, "like I'm sure these good people did."

It was clear to Aiden that pure adrenaline was propelling Briggs, who ignored the president's callousness and proceeded with his checklist. "Third," punctuated by what Tinsley remembered as the Boy Scout salute, "massive arrests, thousands, mostly of people minding your illegal curfew in the privacy of their own homes. DEA, FBI, ICE, local police, all scouring the landscape for your enemies!"

"Not *my* enemies, Mr. Briggs," Thorne jumped in, "enemies of America!"

"And mostly LGBTQ citizens."

"You're damned right. Deny it all you want, but we'd been watching *TAC* for a long time. This was a nest of terrorists, and believe me, they fully intended to take me down, to overthrow the government," his cheeks flushed, veins bulging, "and to put *THAT* traitor in *MY* chair!" he snarled, thrusting a finger at his vice president without looking, still refusing to recognize him.

Fascinating to Tinsley was how the witness' sudden fury only served to infuse his interrogator with added calm, another example he would gladly adopt. Briggs studied Exhibit 111, letting the president's heavy panting dominate the courtroom. He very slowly looked up at Thorne, *are you done*, then walked to the jurors, letting his next words bounce off of them and back to the man he now demonstrably shunned.

"Perhaps most interesting of all is the time stamp on this Executive Order, 12:37 p.m., barely 90 minutes after the events at the State Fair. Awful darn quick, wasn't it? Almost as though this document was prepared in advance, Mr. Thorne, like you *expected* this whole thing? That ointment and bandage flesh wound appears to have been quite the convenient justification for grabbing total control, wouldn't you agree?"

The president ground his teeth, his jaw so tight Aiden swore he could hear a crackling noise in the dead air. All at once, another metamorphosis overtook the leader of the free world. Thorne contemplated his adversary benignly, showing not a trace of animosity, waiting patiently for Briggs to see his reflection in Tinsley and the others.

When the defense lawyer finally wheeled round, Thorne spoke, slowly, his voice measured and lathered with an accent of reason. "I know it's hard for people like you, on the outside, to fathom all the serious intel that crosses my desk. Some of it would make your stomach catch and your toes curl. But I'm not afraid," he said, thrusting his thumb into his chest so violently Tinsley recoiled, as did the jurors on either side of him. "That's my job, Mr. Briggs, not to be terrified or shudder or shut my eyes, but to *deal* with it. Like I said, the Aberdeen people were very, very dangerous. They had recruited thousands of mindless followers. And my unfaithful vice president was fully in bed with them."

The president folded his arms across his chest, as defiant as he could make himself, conjuring a glare that shot through Briggs' cranium. "So yes, we reacted fast, before Styles and his culty band of traitors could destroy our nation." He looked to the floor and nodded his head, suddenly withdrawn, until the contemplation ended and he assimilated the entire panel, leaning toward them. "My friends, you have no idea how close they came," then, his tone even more ominous, "You have no idea what I did for you."

Aiden carefully scrutinized Briggs, inches away, lightly resting against the wooden rail. The law student's respect for the man had been growing by the day. His calm, his precision, his daring. As he pushed off and unhurriedly paced toward his table at the far end of the well, Briggs did not appear the least rattled, or even concerned. Was he done? Had he no rejoinder for the president's bravado?

Reaching his chair, however, in what was barely more than a whisper, the confident defense attorney gave his answer. Without rancor, consumed by sincerity, he simply uttered, "In other words, Mr. Thorne, you're telling us, 'Pay no attention to that man behind the curtain. The Great Oz has spoken. Just trust me.'"

✝✝✝

What was it George Jefferson used to say? Lanta reminisced. *Good God*, she thought, can't believe I'm reaching that far back, Mama's show, which I tolerated only 'cause she loved it, but *Man*, appealing mainly to the nicer, softer racists, it was patronizing as hell. Anyway, she remembered now. "Honkies." That's what George used to say struttin' about his *deee-luxe apartment in the sky*.

And that's exactly what these two were, the president and the prosecutor. Honkies. A couple of privileged white men explaining away all life's inconveniences. Lanta wasn't sure who they thought they were fooling.

Over two hours in, and they'd covered a lot. The dangers of *TAC*, how it'd mobilized tens of thousands. How much Thorne really loved the LGBT and the Qs. After all, he'd appointed a gay man to the second highest office in the whole land, hadn't he?

All those pictures the defense lawyer'd brought up before, the president and Kilbrough, back when the future assassin was his protector, the two smilin' and laughin' and pattin' each other on the back like they was best of friends? Oh, that's only Magnus Thorne being his considerate self. Certainly never hatched any plans with the guy.

Rehabilitation. During the break that's what the little law school boy called it. Hmmm. Bringing back from the dead sounded more accurate to her. Aiden was his name? Nice enough kid. Rich. Entitled. A little arrogant, but what did it matter to her. Their paths would never cross again. Never would have in the first place, if hadn't been for the random collision of this case. She had to admit, though, the boy understood this trial more than she did.

Right now, Thorne and McGehee were trying to repair the damage Briggs had done them over the internet fiasco on the day of the "flesh wound" – Lanta had to laugh at this magical imagery from the defense. For real, because till then she'd bought into the idea his injuries were way more serious. Anyway, yeah, she remembered how, starting right after the assassination, getting any real news was virtually impossible, especially for someone as untechy as her. All gazillion stations, from the old school networks like ABC to Bravo to even the Food Channel, they'd been co-opted by something called the Emergency Alert System. What you saw was some really, really old dude at a plain desk with a big EAS logo on the wall behind him, and all he did was read, over and over, the same bullshit that didn't tell you nothin', except the bad guys were coming to get you, stay home or go home, be calm, listen for further instructions.

Scarier, even than the tanks Lanta saw on her way back from school – urgent early release protocol – more than the helicopters and F-16s or whatever the hell they were screeching across D.C., was the internet. Nothing worked. Nothing loaded, not the news sites, not Insta or TikTok, just spinning wheels or "You are not Connected to the Internet." No messages would send, e-mail servers were "down," phone service was super spotty, mostly busy signals or that annoying three-tone followed by, "I'm sorry, the number you have dialed is no longer in service ...." This went on forever, least till the next afternoon if her memory served. Seemed longer. And now these two are saying it was no big deal?

"I presume, Mr. President, this was a risky step for you, politically."

"Absolutely. There is nothing more precious to most Americans, after God and family, than their internet, their ability to communicate. But once Mr. Hancock, my CISA director, explained the imminent danger *TAC* posed, their plans to take down whole industries – banking, commercial, air travel, you name it – I had no choice." This he said dripping authenticity, Lanta feeling the embrace of his pleading eyes.

"The defendant's lawyer made a big deal about how fast this happened after the attempt, as if that somehow implicated you."

"You bet it was fast." He stuck his chest out once again, proud of his decisiveness. "We'd discussed this, Mr. Hancock and I, my whole national security team, many times. We had a good handle on their plans, and frankly weren't far from going after them. I personally believe that's why they moved up the date for coming after *me*."

"But, and no offense intended here, sir, was it really necessary to shut *everything* down, to completely deprive people of access to information?"

Thorne grew instantly somber, a mask Lanta puzzled out was one of many he strapped on as the occasion called. She folded her arms – didn't care if signaling resistance offended him.

"It was the only choice, the only way to stop *TAC* in its tracks and safeguard our essential systems. I know, I know," he repeated, the earnest dad comforting his children, "it was a huge inconvenience. I wish there had been another way. But better not to be able to check your Facebook page than to see your checking account drained to zero, or a couple of airliners collide in midair."

Maybe, Lanta conceded. Although, Facebook? When's the last time he'd been online. She for sure didn't understand all this cyber stuff, but what did any of it have to do with the man on trial? What proof did this mighty figure have that his understudy was trying to replace him, and that tanking the internet was part of the coup?

Her eyes widened, however, when the fancy prosecutor read her mind.

"During this trial, Mr. President, we have shared abundant evidence with the jurors of the defendant's connections both to The Aberdeen Circle, and to Sam Kilbrough. Specifically regarding the cyber-threat, can you add anything to the picture?"

Now Thorne was pensive, Lanta saw, and she almost laughed. He mutates from one form to another more than those Animal Planet lizards. Chameleons, she corrected herself. Regardless, this is why she hadn't voted for Thorne. Either time! She never could land on exactly who he was. The vice president may be guilty as hell – she hadn't decided that one yet – but damn, his boss here was too slick by half.

"I'm not hesitating because I doubt his guilt, Mr. McGehee. I'm just making sure I don't divulge anything classified." He thought about it a moment longer, then transmuted into a *What the Hell* posture, like he was going to treat them to the inside scoop. "I'll offer this, and what I'm about to say is coming from our best national security analysts," he whispered conspiratorially, drawing the panel into his confidence. "Professor Van Den Wolk was Eli's guy, all the way. They developed that ELEP program together in Dallas. It should scare the pants off you, violating every word and letter of the First Amendment, destroying basic liberties in the name of some crazy algorithm that supposedly predicts a crime might be committed. My point is, we know the two were in touch directly before I was shot. We know the professor had his tentacles into a number of systems across the country. And, while I can't be too detailed here – sources and methods, you understand," he winked, "we are certain Eli, my own number two, gave Van Den Wolk the green light, just like he did Maslow with his handwritten note, that it was 'Go Time.'"

Thorne leaned back, satisfied. Lanta surveyed her companions with the corners of her eyes, and saw many of them were as impressed with the president as he was with himself. Man hadn't said a damn thing, and yet they were prepared to shout "Hallelujah!"

She was ready for him to go. This staged back-and-forth did nothing for her, and Lanta could predict what was coming next. They'd talk some more about Styles being disloyal, treacherous, ruthless. About Bonsal being a harmless holding pen for super bad traitors, and how brave Thorne was to go face them down in person, least till he got winged.

Instead, the U.S. attorney surprised her, for once.

"Mr. President, the defendant's lawyer brought up the issue of a pardon for Sam Kilbrough. Mr. Briggs never actually asked you about it, though. So, I will. Would you, under *any* circumstances, issue one to the man who attempted to take your life?"

Now that's worth sittin' here for, Lanta figured. First interesting question all afternoon. But she wasn't stupid – Ms. Breckenridge spent her days with wily teenagers. When it comes to intrigue and scheming, they had the game down pat. This was no gambit. She was certain of it. McGehee, Thorne, they scripted this.

The president covered his lips with hands joined in prayer, elbows resting on the shelf in front of him, as thoughtful as he could be. "Yes," he said. "I would."

Lanta narrowed her gaze, ignoring the collective inhalation, a shriek, all of the excited murmuring, guessing at Thorne's purpose as the judge's gavel demanded silence.

"Now, I'm not crazy," he began with a self-deprecating smirk. "There would be conditions, of course, such as, 'stay the hell away from me,'" he laughed, most of the courtroom joining him. "There would need to be serious mental health treatment, ironclad monitoring." He bobbed his head, happy with himself. "But there's one more condition, the most important of all, before I'd consider it."

Later that night, alone in her hotel room, Lanta actually felt proud of herself. She'd guessed it. She'd figured out what Thorne was going to say. And to her mind, it was brilliant.

He'd melded, again, this time every inch the rough and tumble Montana minerals magnet, his posture steel, an equally stout set to his face. Thorne held up a fist, using it to punctuate his final condition. "Sam Kilbrough has to come in here, and tell the truth about Elijah Styles." And for the first time, he looked at his vice president.

Twenty-Nine

Carolyn imagined the angst in Mandela Briggs' office last night. His uncharacteristic harried features told all. He'd lost a very important argument, and unlike the surprise subpoenaing of the president, this time he gave her a heads-up, sending a message through Bailiff Bankhead about 20 minutes ago: his client was testifying.

After the exhausting drama of Magnus Thorne, Judge Bering had calculated they may finally be done. Each side had thrown its best punches. The prosecution was confident it had shown the defendant as an ambitious schemer who would stop at nothing to gain the ultimate prize. That the president stuck the landing, assuaging the sinister stench the defense raised, dispelling the notion he was some kind of megalomaniac. Briggs, too, had reason for optimism, painting the vice president's concerns as legitimate, his motives pure, and the U.S. attorney's evidence circumstantial at best.

So why would the defense chance blowing it all up by delivering Styles into McGehee's clutches? Did the defendant fear the jurors – *all* of them – were considering guilt? Conceivable, sure, but in Carolyn's experienced estimation an undivided "not guilty" was equally possible. Most likely, in her view, was a hung jury where the twelve were irretrievably split. Not satisfying to either side, yet she was certain Briggs would rather have a hung jury than a hung client, even if it meant doing this all over again.

Then, an epiphany as she reached for the door from her chambers. Yesterday, when the judge banged her gavel to close the day, she noticed Styles intently tracking Thorne's triumphal departure. The image's meaning was unclear at the time, but now Carolyn understood. The president's strutting exit was a gauntlet thrown, one the vice president was incapable of resisting. Styles would ignore sage advice and rise to the occasion: conquer the monster, restore his reputation, burnish his honor, for America, for the world!

Bering, however, suspected more than those impulses. She had studied the man closely the past month. There was a ceaseless calculation behind his eyes. Unlike in her previous death penalty cases, *this* defendant didn't display the wounded carriage of a caged animal. There was no brooding desperation. Styles maintained a watchfulness, like an eagle surveying his environs for opportunity. The vice president's impressive mastery of composure failed to conceal, from this judge's practiced intuition, the coiled energy of a man eager to strike. In her gut, Carolyn believed Styles held grander plans, ambitions only he failed to fathom as impossible. *He still intended to be president*, she realized, and this jury was a necessary rung to that holy grail.

"Mr. Briggs," she sighed, bracing herself for another eventful session. "Do you have any further witnesses?" as if maybe, by some miracle, his client had come to his senses.

"Yes, Your Honor. The defense calls Vice President Elijah Styles."

If yesterday's proceedings were saturated with anticipation and excitement, today's commenced with utter shock rippling through the audience. The jurors exchanged equal measures of amusement, curiosity and thrill, while Seb Montes and his fellow journalists mutely showed bewilderment before furiously attacking their tablets, dreaming of banner headlines: "***Stunning***," "***Risky***," and depending on how he fared, maybe "***Daring***."

No one's reaction was of more interest to Bering than McGehee's. The determined prosecutor registered none of the disbelief permeating the rest of courtroom. Of course he didn't, she decided, because there was a tab in his brain for every alternative, a branch on his strategic flowchart for every eventuality. He was cocky, incapable of being overwhelmed by any situation. Instead, the judge saw *hunger*. Sidney

McGehee didn't produce a knife, fork and napkin or smack his lips, but his mien was close to that cartoonish picture. It was as if his parents had wheeled out a shiny new bicycle on Christmas morning, and he knew just what he was going to do with it.

Styles now looked up at her, waiting for her to commit him to the truth. She administered the oath. He sat. Briggs approached, and their rehearsed choreography began.

"Mr. Vice President, before we move into substantive matters, let's make one thing very clear for the jurors. You do not have to testify. The Fifth Amendment to the United States Constitution explicitly states that none of us, as American citizens, can be forced to bear witness against ourselves."

"I understand."

"And yet, here you are. In the box, facing the triers of fact, willingly exposing yourself to cross-examination by a professional prosecutor who, literally, wants you executed."

Carolyn noticed the slightest twitch in McGehee's torso as he considered rising. "That's a very mean way to phrase it," however, isn't an objection, so he restrained himself. The death penalty was, indeed, his endgame – why show weakness by wincing at its mention?

"I realize, Mr. Briggs, that my safest move would be to stay over there," he pointed at the vacant chair he'd occupied until now, "and let you two give final arguments. Other than innuendo, speculation and presumption, there is absolutely no evidence I've done anything other than try to save our Republic." He tried to temper his grandiose comment with a disarming smile. "I should be content to let these good people reach their verdict. I'm sure they're ready."

Indeed they were, Bering was certain. But she could also see The Twelve's fascination with the defendant, the idea of whom lawyers and witnesses had painted in strident, conflicting strokes. Now here he was, flesh and bone.

"Those same insinuations, however, if unanswered, are as dangerous to our democracy as President Thorne's autocratic abuses. If I let those delusional conspiracy theories go unanswered, who would ever speak truth to power again?" He shrugged, palms up, plaintive. "Who will stand up for our principles the next time a would-be tyrant threatens us from within?"

The judge marveled at the ease of his performance, impressed by the resolute set of his features. "This isn't about clearing my name. I believe the evidence does that for me. This is about standing up for what's right, making sure our institutions hold," he bathed in a sheen of sincerity, "making sure the democratic values we cherish are preserved." To the side, she noticed McGehee's subtle smirk, his subliminal warning to the jurors, *blah, blah, bullshit.*

"Let's go back to the convention five years ago," Briggs jumped in, "to your nomination as vice president. The ladies and gentlemen on the panel heard Magnus Thorne's take, his rather amended view of whether your patriotism or integrity had anything to do with the selection. I think it would be helpful to get your recollections."

Styles started to answer, caught himself. Carolyn marked his silent reckoning, retrieving the image of an old college beau as they skid across the choppy waters of Lake Freeman, his tongue tucked into a corner of his lips as he turned the small boat's head into and through the wind, assuming a more advantageous course.

"I have frequently been asked why," he said. "Why he picked me. Only the president knows for sure. I could tell you what he said when we met in his suite the night before the announcement. The lavish praise. The promises. The opportunities."

Styles focused on Mr. Arroyo, Bering presumed because the defendant had concluded, as had she, that he was one of the most likely to convict. "You've heard all that before, though, from other witnesses. If I may, there's a better question. Why did I say 'Yes?'

Why did I agree to join a ticket with a man about whom I had misgivings, even then?"

"Objection, irrelevant," the prosecutor snapped. "President Thorne is not on trial, Judge. And the defendant's political calculations have nothing to do with the plot for which he has been indicted."

Briggs waited a beat to see if Bering wanted a response. She didn't.

"I believe the witness' frame of mind and motivations are in issue, Mr. McGehee." She indicated for Styles to proceed. He returned to his audience.

"If, as the prosecutor frames it, 'political calculations' were my concern, I can assure you I would have politely declined the offer. His polls were grim, and I frankly didn't think he had much of a chance. My campaign manager, my husband, pretty much everyone whose opinion I valued begged me to say 'No.'"

Briggs coaxed his client onward. "Then why did you agree?"

"Because I believe in this country. I knew Magnus Thorne and I were cut from different cloth, that he'd never have considered me if I hadn't amassed enough delegates to jeopardize his nomination. But I started my campaign to make a difference, to push policies improving average Americans' lives, expanding opportunity and securing liberty."

Cue the soaring music, Carolyn thought.

"As we sit here today," Styles continued, "despite the peril to my family, my career, my very life, I would do it again. I never imagined the president would defy norms on a scale that would have made Richard Nixon and Donald Trump blush. I never dreamed, not in my worst nightmares, that his agenda would be about power and control rather than the well-being and freedoms of our citizens."

The vice president adopted a defiant pose, chin up, brow furrowed. "There are no regrets on my end, Mr. Briggs. In fact, given what I've learned about Magnus Thorne and his designs, it is vital for me to have assumed this role. I honored my oath to protect and defend the Constitution, and," waving his hand across the jurors, "all of you!"

Bering developed a sinking feeling as Styles drew deeper from his well of lofty platitudes. He was so used to campaign rhetoric, to dazzling audiences with the fervor of his voice, he was blinded to reality. The jurors were recoiling from the conceit of his self-congratulation. She'd seen those expressions before.

Briggs sought safer ground. "Mr. Vice President, a central tenet of the government's case is your history with The Aberdeen Circle, and particularly its leader, Rachel Maslow, and Blakely Kurtz, from whom we heard last week. Let's talk about that."

"Gladly." He melted into a lighthearted ease.

"As I understand it, your first interaction with *TAC* was right before you announced your candidacy for mayor of Dallas."

"Yes, January, ten years ago. About two weeks before I declared, I met with Ms. Maslow at her offices in Portland."

"Why? Why did you want their support?"

"You have to recall that, a decade ago, The Aberdeen Circle had a sterling reputation. It was forged in response to the brutal Tanner Centurion murder, and in just three short years had grown into America's foremost protector of civil rights. Whether race, gender or identity, *TAC* gave voice to millions wanting nothing more than equality. I was proud to receive its support."

"And more recently? You have to acknowledge the organization has had its share of controversy."

"Absolutely, as is the case with many well-intended groups that experience meteoric growth. There were instances where they messed up, and I've said so. Like failing to quickly and forcefully condemn bad actors only loosely affiliated with *TAC* who sullied its name. Violence is always wrong, no matter the cause." When Styles said this, the judge thought back to her childhood, of Nancy Reagan's "Just Say

No" campaign. One member of the panel frowned. Another crossed his arms. The whitewashing of Aberdeen's troubled recent history was not going over well.

She could tell Briggs felt the vibe too. He shifted focus. "You communicated with *TAC* often during the time from election day until March 30, true?"

"Yes. There was a lot of anguish on their end. President Thorne had used The Aberdeen Circle as a whipping post during the election, focusing on its problems and ignoring the organization's many good deeds. I did what I could to try and lower the temperature, on both sides. Unsuccessfully, as it turns out."

"Were you aware of any plots by *TAC* to do the president harm, or to overthrow the government?"

Styles laughed, a bit too eagerly in Carolyn's opinion.

"I'm sorry, but I find that theory ridiculous, Mr. Briggs. To think that an association devoted to justice and equality, under intense public scrutiny, as we've just discussed, would hatch a scheme so over the top is, well, absurd. Moreover, to think this group of ordinary folks, last time I checked with no tanks or F-16s, could organize such a coup ..." He trailed off, shaking his head.

"Then your many interactions with Ms. Maslow and Mr. Kurtz weren't to plot Magnus Thorne's demise?" Briggs was trying to get back on track, giving the government's allegations a farcical coat.

Seeing his prompt, the vice president turned serious. "Far from it. I was trying to direct their energies in a productive direction. Protests, marches, sure. But some in their ranks felt the pull of desperation and wanted to act out accordingly. My efforts were to keep anyone from damaging *TAC*'s standing any further, to avoid giving the Thorne administration, and their RAGE followers, any excuses for more retribution."

"You heard Blakley Kurtz, though, sitting right where you are now. He said, among other things, that you were involved in Sam Kilbrough's activities, knew about a supposed safe house for him in Canada, that Kilbrough anticipated you becoming president, and that you, indeed, intended to replace Magnus Thorne."

Carolyn watched the defendant contort with pain, stabbed by the very idea of Kurtz's accusations. To her it was his first honest reaction, though of uncertain provenance. Was he wounded by audacious fabrication, or scorching truth?

"That was difficult to hear," Styles began, mournfully. "I suppose I shouldn't have been surprised, regardless of his story, considering what the government has done to him."

McGehee rocketed to his feet. "Objection. False conjecture, and an insulting implication, Judge, certainly beneath the dignity of this man's office."

"Sustained. Mr. Vice President, please testify only to the facts as you know them."

Styles focused intently on the prosecutor as he replied, "I understand, Your Honor. I only meant to say that Blakely and I had an excellent professional relationship. Were he not under federal indictment, I would have been stunned by his ... inventions."

Briggs retook the reins. "Specifically, did you have anything to do with, or any knowledge of, a Canadian escape plan for Mr. Kilbrough."

"No."

"Did you tell Mr. Kurtz you intended to replace Magnus Thorne as president."

Bering made out the witness' ordering of his next verse, a tiny tremor in his facial muscles. "In a sense, yes." That raised a few eyebrows in the jury box, she saw.

"Explain, please," Briggs said.

"I don't recall anything specific, but considering how grave things were, I'm sure I shared with Blakely my plans to pursue the Twenty-Fifth Amendment, and if that failed, the court of public opinion. I am confident," he halted, caught himself, "*was* confident, that the truth would lead to his resignation, or his removal from office. And so, sure, in that way, I thought it might fall to me to assume his duties."

"Did anything in particular derail your efforts?"

"Sam Kilbrough shot the president," Styles said, his visage a billboard of vindication. Nicely done, Carolyn allowed. She was not surprised the defense attorney spurned a follow-up question. The jurors would get the irony.

Briggs casually made his way toward his table at the far end of the well. She speculated he may not be finished, though it would be a great ending. Then he wheeled back toward his client, feigning one final, insignificant notion. "Oh," he said matter of factly, "one last detail." The judge suppressed her awe at his pretend indifference.

"The government has made quite the fuss over a note you sent to Rachel Maslow."

"The one I supposedly told her to burn." Styles eyes twinkled.

"Exactly. It said, 'I can't help anymore. You need to act now, before it's too late.' Sounds sinister."

Styles played along. "Yes, quite cloak and dagger."

"Did you write it?"

"Yes."

"And to what effect?"

"President Thorne was planning to have her arrested. I had that on good information from someone at Justice who was horrified at the manufactured charges." He glared at the prosecutor, as if McGehee were in on it. "I'd tried to run interference, but this was high priority, coming, I was told, straight from the top. When I realized I couldn't stop it, I sent her the note. She'd resisted hiring a lawyer or going public, for fear of appearing paranoid. Rachel needed to know she was out of time."

Briggs contemplated the answer, calmly guiding the jurors to do the same. The judge identified several bobbing their heads. Satisfied, Styles' counsel gave the judge a slight bow. "No further questions."

Thirty

On a lark during sophomore year at Purdue, Carolyn took a workshop in marine biology. Something to do with a cute guy she'd been admiring – Mark? Matt? Doesn't matter, nothing ever developed beyond a single awful date. But the course was fascinating, chock full of the peculiar realities of a world she'd never before considered.

One factoid from the class popped into her consciousness as Sidney McGehee stood for his cross-examination: the concentration of an odor in seawater is measured in parts per million, one odor molecule for every million molecules of ocean. Sharks can smell blood from hundreds of meters away, in concentrations as low as one part *per billion*.

McGehee rounded the last corner of his table slowly, to Carolyn's mind circling, eyes fixed into some middle distance, head tilted back as if sensing what he was programmed to devour. This would be the prosecutor's signature moment, Bering recognized, defining his path to the top. The blood he sniffed, she suspected, was the soft arrogance of Styles highly polished persona.

"Mr. Styles," he started in a carefree, almost gleeful tone, "thank you for agreeing to take the stand." The prosecutor placed a hand on his heart in mocking gratitude. "Before we knight you as grand defender of our democracy, however, there are a *few* nagging questions we should get around to."

The judge observed several jurors inch to the edge of their uncomfortable wooden swivels. She pondered whether they savored the deliciousness of a slaughter, or were electrified by the prospect of a titanic joust.

McGehee casually reached back, Mandy placing a heavy book in his hand, which he studied for a moment, then held up for both the panel and witness to see. The cover was a black-and-white portrait of the vice president from the shoulders up, engaging the camera in a meditative pose, the title in large white script at the top. "*Rampart*. Interesting choice. I'm curious. How'd you come up with that name?"

"I didn't," the defendant replied, voice neutral, wary. "It's my secret service call signal."

"Right. You obviously like it. I mean it's plastered on the front of your autobiography. 'The defensive wall of a castle or city, a protective barrier,' I think is the definition. Sort of fits with how you envision yourself, your whole theme here today."

"My publisher liked it," Styles said.

"Thought it would sell, did they?"

"I suppose so."

"Hmph," McGehee grunted dismissively, then fingered a marker, opening the hefty tome. "Anyway, let's take a peek at something you wrote, something I find amusing in light of your presentation today." He scrutinized the text. "Page 147, in the chapter called 'Making Capitalism Work,' you say ...

When Meyer Brook named me director of strategic opportunities, I was given carte blanche, with only one mandate. "Make Success!" I used that freedom to implement the core principles of business which remain my North Star for a booming American economy: invest in workers first, listen to them, let them be accountable for the fruits of their labor, and the consumer will follow.

"Then blah, blah, blah, and you go on to cite a couple examples of companies you claim to have 'turned around.' Umm, Regency Tool & Die is one. Remember that?"

"Yes."

The judge was a bit puzzled by the line of inquiry. In the witness, though, she sensed a measure of discomfort.

"Putting aside that you oversaw the layoff of half the workforce, 700 good union folks ..."

"Objection, Judge Bering." Briggs was on his feet, equally baffled. "While no doubt the vice president would be happy to debate his past business accomplishments, I'm sure the jurors would prefer we discuss matters actually relevant to this trial."

Carolyn looked to the prosecutor with curiosity. He smiled.

"Mr. Briggs is absolutely correct, Your Honor. Let me get straight to the point." He faced the witness, asking pleasantly, "How much did you make off the sale of Regency, Mr. Styles?"

The witness seemed puzzled. "Well, nothing directly. I'm sure that came into consideration at year's end."

"Really. Okay, well, let's digress for a quick second here." McGehee returned to the thick autobiography, thumbing it. "Page 78 of your book, there's a very moving description of your first date with Brady." The prosecutor gave an approving look. "I'm sure you recall the location?"

The defendant failed to reciprocate McGehee's fake warmth. "Of course. White Rock Lake."

"You describe it as one of your favorite hangouts, something you wanted to share with your soon-to-be-husband. In fact, the two of you were married on its shores."

Carolyn couldn't fathom where this was going. Nor, she could tell, did the witness or his lawyer, though warming Styles' image was certainly not the destination.

"It was a special place."

The prosecutor leered, then motioned Mandy, who summoned to the screen a chart with names, tables and numbers. Dollars, actually. Lots of them.

McGehee leaned on his table in a casual, conversational pose, clearly enjoying himself. "Can you identify this document, Mr. Styles?"

The vice president studied it, and as he did so, Bering detected a faint dampness on his scalp, spreading slowly to his temples.

"It is a balance sheet."

"For Regency Tool & Die. Correct?"

"Yes."

"Assets, Liabilities, and then the final section. Equity. That's the value of the shareholders' ownership, right?"

Styles choked out his reply. "Yes."

"Next page, please." Mandy cycled up a new sheet with more lines and figures. "If we look at the third largest owner of stock, that would be who?"

The witness stared at the document blankly, swallowed, then answered. "White Rock Cap."

McGehee positively beamed. "White Rock Cap! What a creative name. It's a holding company registered in the Cayman Islands whose principal owner is ..."

"Your Honor," Briggs shouted, "this line of questioning has gone beyond irrelevancy into bad theater. The financial details of a company my client dealt with a dozen years ago, while he was in the private sector, is of no consequence to the issues in this trial."

"Mr. McGehee?" the judge asked. On the one hand, she wanted to see where this landed, certain her jury did as well. On the other, what *did* this have to do with anything?

"My esteemed colleague makes the defendant's integrity and patriotism key pillars of his case. Therefore, his character is very much an issue. If the Court will allow me just another minute, I will make the connection clear."

She looked at the witness, whose pale cast told her this was for real. Cutting the U.S. attorney off now would be a mistake. She reluctantly indicated he could proceed.

"Mr. Styles, would you like to tell the jurors the name of White Rock Cap's principal shareholder, or shall I?"

Something suddenly shifted inside the defendant. His back straightened, and the color returned to his face. "I am. Or, at least, Brady and I are. The stock is held in our names jointly. Sort of a college fund for our daughter." He radiated the affectionate glow of a loving father. Carolyn's old oceanic studies flooded back again, the vice president as her favorite sea creature: the octopus, a master manipulator with the magical power of assuming the exact hues and silhouette of its immediate environment, vulnerabilities hidden behind a gush of ink. Only here, the prosecutor was fixed on the scent.

"Uh huh," McGehee said loudly, accentuating his skepticism. "Quite a lucrative fund, too. Years later, when Borgen Railey finished its turnaround – I *love* that term," he winked at the jury, "of Regency Tool & Die, White Rock Cap's share of the gain was $11 million. Sound about right?"

"I don't know the particulars."

"Part of the amazing transformation of Regency were several military contracts which you, using your office as vice president, steered its way. If need be, the company's former CEO is willing to come flesh out the details for us."

"I did what I could for a lot of small domestic companies. We were trying to restore the American economy."

McGehee chuckled. "In very exclusive ways, it seems. But putting aside the potential conflict of interest or ethical concerns, I want to nail down two quick facts, Mr. Styles, and then we'll move on."

Carolyn kept tabs on Briggs, waiting, her patience running thin. He had to shut this down, she knew. But it was a devil's choice: Allow the vice president to flounder in clarifications and evasions that, from the look of him, would come off quite disingenuous; or, accept a patina of guilt by invoking Styles' Fifth Amendment right against self-incrimination. Carolyn considered warning Styles herself, but that would just make it worse. For what, exactly, was his lawyer waiting?

"First," his associate Joel handed him a two-inch bound stack of 8½-by-14-inch sheets, "these are your federally mandated financial disclosures for your time as vice president." He handed it to the witness, who reluctantly took possession like it was a poisonous snake. "Prosecution Exhibit number 129," he said to the court reporter.

"Can you show us where you reported the $11 million windfall from your very astute investment in Regency?"

Styles tossed the document onto the small shelf in front of him. It landed with a dramatic thud he immediately regretted. "I wouldn't know, Mr. McGehee. Those documents are obviously prepared by accountants. I wouldn't know where to begin."

"You could begin, I suppose, by telling those accountants about the sale, right? Their names and contact info are listed on the last page. But we don't need to bother them, because you know you never told them."

"I don't recall."

"And you never listed your little profit on your income taxes, either, did you?"

Finally, Briggs stood. "Your Honor, we can have a second trial, right here, this week, on these new claims, never before raised by the government, and I am confident we can put all of this into context. However, I renew my objection on grounds of relevance. None of this has anything to do with the charge of treason."

"No need, Judge. I'm sure these good people have heard enough about the defendant's significant hidden interest in multiple companies he, shall we say, helped along. My friend at the Manhattan U.S.

attorney's office tells me she's days away from an indictment, so I'm content to let *her* handle it."

"Your Honor!" Briggs was angry, for the first time losing his careful composure. She waived him off, not too happy herself. The prosecutor had abused her leeway.

"Mr. McGehee, I do find your line of questioning irrelevant, and so sustain the objection." Then she turned to The Twelve. "Ladies and Gentlemen, whether or not the vice president's financial affairs were handled in accordance with legal requirements is a matter that would be, as indicated, a trial within itself. It should have no impact on your deliberations in this case, which is about an entirely different matter. I therefore instruct you to disregard that entire exchange."

She had done her best, though regrettably, knew it was too little, too late. The prosecution's dagger had come from nowhere. This affair had nothing to do with the actual merits of the case. Yet, it struck at the carotid of the defendant's authenticity. That, she could not undo.

Bering appraised the U.S. attorney, infuriatingly flashing the smug sureness he wore like a ritzy overcoat. She gathered herself, refusing to let him fracture her respectability. "Mr. McGehee, anything else?"

He half ignored her, heaving his energies back at his quarry. "Mr. Styles, despite your many wild claims and aspersions against our president, you never resigned."

"I did not. Running away would do nothing to defend our nation, though it definitely would have made my life easier."

"In fact, on January 6, you certified the vote that you now claim was tainted and illegitimate! A tad inconsistent, wouldn't you agree, unless the point was to certify your own additional four years in office."

"It is well established that the vice president's role with regard to the Electoral College is purely ceremonial. You can ask Mike Pence about that. Congress can object and vote on any state's ballots. My only power is to acknowledge the certified results."

"Even if the president you are certifying is a despot, a dictator, a direct threat to democracy, all of which you claim Magnus Thorne to be? You're saying the Constitution requires you to stand there, meek and obedient, and just sign off?"

"I respect the Constitution, Mr. McGehee, which you seem to believe is a matter of convenience. Moreover, I feared what Magnus Thorne would do if he didn't get what he wanted. Things could have gotten a lot worse, a lot faster. I'm sure you recall the presence of federal troops in the House chamber during the counting of the votes. Despite what the president says, they weren't there to ..."

Carolyn's mind drifted, catching only snippets of the action.

"... the truth is, Mr. Styles, you are as much responsible for the Enhanced Law Enforcement Program as Professor Van Den Wolk. He may have written lines of code, but Elijah Styles was its greatest champion. And the two of you were, as these logs show, increasingly in contact as the day of the assassination came closer."

"I was merely ... I was trying to chase down rumors, most of which were started by Thorne's people, by the way. Outlandish things such as you've floated in this trial, like massive takeovers of banks and communications. I wanted to verify that his work for The Aberdeen Circle involved no such nefarious plans, and that those types of subversions weren't possible anyway."

"The foremost expert in cybersecurity, Mr. Hancock, was quite confident those threats were not only real, but on the cusp of being realized. We all heard him. Where's your expert, Mr. Styles? Why isn't the professor here to back up your story?"

Briggs rose, mouth agape, letting his facial contortions herald his words. "Judge Bering, the U.S. attorney is well aware Dr. Van Den Wolk cannot be forced to testify. We wish he would, but Mr. McGehee is prosecuting him too. We are confident the professor will explain the absurdity of the government's fantastical notions in his own trial."

The prosecutor lunged, and the witness parried. The usual precision of the judge's focus, however, was impossible. She'd lost control, however briefly, by allowing the matter of offshore accounts and hidden profits into the case. It was a lapse which might have enormous consequences for the accused.

"Ah, yes, the great doctor is under indictment, refusing to explain his actions," McGehee reported whimsically, then quickly added, with mock sincerity, "which is, absolutely, his right. I take the right against self-incrimination quite seriously."

The taunting exchanges finally snapped Carolyn back. "Gentlemen, that's enough. If you have objections, please address them to me, and avoid the sidebar remarks."

Being honest, she considered herself a darn good judge. Pleasant without being friendly. Punctual. Knowledgeable. Even-handed. All the D.C. bar polls gave her high ratings. The judicial blindfold of equity, Bering knew, required resistance to empathy at all costs, no matter how harsh that may sound. Impartiality demanded it. Yet the judge felt that tender emotion now while witnessing Styles, who she'd inadvertently disarmed, endure the death of a thousand cuts. She had no way to muffle the vile bell she'd allowed the prosecutor to sound. But Carolyn could get back into the game.

"Mr. McGehee, let's wrap this up."

He countered her rebuke with an exaggerated innocence, before focusing again on the witness. "Your professor aside, Mr. Styles, surely even you can see how this all appears. Your increasingly hostile assaults against the president before he takes a bullet, your admitted friendship with the assassin, your long collaboration with the high-tech genius possessing the expertise to bring the nation's internet to its knees, your affiliation with The Aberdeen Circle and its legions of dangerously inflamed followers. Are these the ingredients for a peaceable debate?"

To the judge's trained eye, the vice president had gradually deflated, this hyperconfident man's life force leaking from his punctured virtue. He ignored the jurors, from whom he had been laboring so hard for admiration. Instead, breathily, he spoke only to his nemesis, the man now the hub of his existence.

"I'm not a violent man, Mr. McGehee. You can ask anyone who has known me for years. That's why I spoke out so publicly, why I begged the Cabinet for help, tried to get *TAC* to see reality. Since you keep bringing it up, that was the whole point of ELEP as well, to stop crime *before* anyone gets hurt."

Styles was near tears. Real ones or an affect, Carolyn could not assess. But also, she believed, a reflection of his desperation. "Why would I want the president dead?"

Bering absentmindedly rubbed her cheeks, her mind fading as the witness spiraled. McGehee was only getting started.

Thirty-One

The federal penitentiary nestled into the Maryland countryside only 45 minutes from the Prettyman Courthouse in central D.C., meaning the prisoner could be summoned on very short notice. This was by design. A pair of designs, actually, but only Sam Kilbrough was aware of the dueling, though quite similar plans.

As it turned out, neither Thorne's team, nor the vice president's, had requested his presence at the trial of the century. That was always a possibility, depending on how the evidence developed. Kilbrough was the *Break Glass in Case of Emergency* option. No one wanted to risk his testimony unless it was absolutely necessary.

The U.S. attorney's office, despite the president's bold challenge for Kilbrough to "tell the truth," decided Styles did enough damage to himself to ensure conviction. The defense obviously believed they could at least prevent a unanimous jury, thus garnering a mistrial and second chance at redemption, maybe even an actual "not guilty" verdict.

Sam didn't like either outcome. A hung jury meant a retrial: too much delay, and him still behind bars. A conviction would strengthen the president's already too powerful status. An acquittal wouldn't be accurately translated as *insufficient evidence to convict*, but instead the media and vice president would herald proclamations of *complete exoneration*. And then what could Kilbrough do?

So, the evening after Styles slinked off the stand, right after Inmate No. Z48-C1023 finished off his bland meatloaf, mashed potatoes and green beans, he called his lawyer. Thirteen hours later, he was in a Bureau of Prisons van, wearing a well-tailored navy-blue suit. At 80 miles-per-hour, under escort by both state troopers and the U.S. Marshal's Service, Sam was on his way to the courtroom of Carolyn Bering.

†††

In an unusual move for this judge, she of the rocket docket, of not wasting a precious second of a jury's time, a recess was declared at 3:48 on Tuesday afternoon as the defendant left the stand. There wasn't time to get far with another witness, assuming defense counsel even called one, which Bering doubted he would. Regardless, in fairness – she swore it was not remorse over her role in Styles' troubles – the judge granted Briggs the evening to regroup, conference with his client, and sort through their options.

"Nine sharp counselors," she instructed. Had it been her client, she'd tell the defendant that calling more witnesses was unlikely to help. Who would they call? After already poking serious holes in the government's case with their best choices, who was left to move the needle in his direction? Additional testimony was unlikely to bury the vice president's own words. Plus, any one of their marginal candidates could say something unfortunate under McGehee's hectoring, leaving the defense in even worse shape.

The prudent course was to go straight to final arguments. Let Briggs spin the immateriality of Styles' *alleged* financial shenanigans, remind the panel there was no direct evidence of guilt, and highlight the dirt under the president's fingernails.

This is the advice Bering expected from someone as smart as Briggs, and after the defendant's whooping, she was sure he would take it. McGehee, likely feeling pretty good, undoubtedly had his final argument prepared. The jury could be deliberating by the afternoon.

Such was the plan, anyway. Until the call. It reached her office early Tuesday evening as she worked on "the charge," the instructions and definitions she would give the jury to guide them to a verdict, along with the ultimate questions they would answer.

Carolyn accepted the unknown gentleman's polite and profuse apologies "for disturbing you so late, ma'am." Yet, even after he repeated himself, she was still unclear whether she had really understood him.

In fact, she did. Which was why, 90 minutes later, the two opposing lawyers joined Judge Bering in chambers, along with her chief clerk and her court reporter in chambers, all anxiously awaiting their most intriguing guest. This would be on the record, and in the unfamiliar man's own words.

†††

Although Zee's knock was a gentle tap, it nonetheless startled everyone in the room. "Mr. Martin is here, Your Honor," the judge's administrator announced. This was the first McGehee and Briggs heard the name. Until now, Bering had revealed nothing, offering no explanation for their unusual after-hours conclave.

"Thank you, Zee. Send him in, please." A tall, lanky man of uncertain ethnicity strutted through the door toward the judge, long arm extended. She leaned over her desk and took it without standing, her features manifesting formality.

"D'Artagnan Xavier Martin," he announced, "but please call me Dee." A member of the Texas bar – Bering's clerk had been busy researching the lawyer ever since his unanticipated call – Martin seldom appeared in federal court, never before the ones in D.C. He had been chief counsel for the House Judiciary Committee back when Rance Knall was its chairman. The other two attorneys didn't even know that much. Searching their mental databases, they came up empty. "Thank you for agreeing to see me."

"We appreciate you coming in," the judge replied formally.

"Absolutely," he said with odd cheer, as if their gathering was the most ordinary thing in the world. "I truly wish I could have given everyone more notice, but as I explained to the court, the decision only came this evening." He smiled broadly, to the judge's thinking a stark contrast to his coming message.

"I'm sorry," McGehee said, most definitely not apologetic, "what decision?"

Still standing at the edge of Bering's desk, Martin pivoted to the prosecutor, radiating upbeat energy. "We haven't met, sir. Dee Martin," he said for the second time. They shook hands, McGehee only half rising, then Martin and Briggs completed the process. "May I?" He asked, pointing to the only unoccupied chair. Bering inclined her head in assent.

He sat, positioned to the judge's right. Briggs was in the center, McGehee to the left. They repositioned their chairs to directly face, and size up, the mystery visitor.

Martin had a short, blunt nose with large, oddly circular nostrils, hard enough to ignore without the unkempt hairs screaming to escape. His cheeks were flat, dotted with pockmarks, the skin a light caramel. The stranger's ever-present grin exhibited uneven teeth stained by either cigarettes or coffee, or both. He projected an unbothered air. "As I was telling the court earlier this evening ..."

"If I could interrupt," the judge broke in, "before we start, I want to advise everyone that I have asked Noah to record these ..." She fished for the right word. "Proceedings." They all turned their heads and politely acknowledged the reporter. Carolyn nodded at him, his fingers arrayed over the keyboard, ready to begin. Bering recited the time and date, listed all attendees, then commenced her short preamble.

"I received a call from Mr. Martin approximately two hours ago, wherein he informed me of his representation of Mr. Sam Kilbrough, currently incarcerated at the federal maximum-security prison at Muldrow. I was told his client had made a request to testify in our ongoing trial. Realizing this situation is, to say the least, unusual, I instructed Mr. Martin to come to my chambers as soon as possible. When he indicated he could do so immediately, I gave the same directive to counsel for the United States and for Defendant Styles. Now that we are all present, with the transcription of our conference being taken, I ask Mr. Martin to bring everyone up to date so we can decide how to proceed."

She surveyed the stunned faces of her two combatants. "Are we ready?"

"Wait." It was McGehee again, uncharacteristically off balance. "What happened to Kilbrough's defense lawyer in North Carolina, where his criminal trial is pending. I met with him and the U.S. attorney down in Charlotte a couple months ago, to see if we could come to any kind of arrangement." He eyed Martin with skepticism. "Did he fire that guy, because I sure don't remember you being there?"

Martin ran a hand across wooly coils of short golden fuzz covering his skull, a gesture appearing to indicate gravity. "No, no, you are absolutely correct. I wasn't there. He is still most definitely in Mr. Calloway's capable hands. As far as any trial down *there* is concerned, that is." The odd ebullience returned. "I am more of a, how should I put this, a trusted advisor, carrying out Mr. Kilbrough's wishes."

McGehee stared blankly, no more informed than before Martin's answer.

Judge Bering quickly steered things back on course. "Gentlemen, as I said, this is an unusual circumstance. I would prefer we let Mr. Martin brief you, so you know what I do. Then we'll have plenty of time for questions. Okay?" The prosecutor and his counterpart viewed this interloper with equal suspicion. Neither replied. "Sir, you have the floor."

"Thank you, Your Honor. Anyway, as I was telling the court, my client has been following this trial very closely, as one would expect, given his interests." Martin chuckled at his own understatement. No one else did, causing the odd lawyer to adopt an abruptly severe manner.

"The thing is," he continued, "after watching both the president and the defendant testify, Mr. Kilbrough is quite ... *disappointed*." The happy-go-lucky charmer had vanished. "He feels the jury is being, how should we say this, being misled. And with his unique perspective on events, he feels he owes it to his country, to which he is quite loyal, by the way – you know, ex-Marine, lifetime of public service and all that – he feels he needs to set the record straight."

Judge Bering watched her lawyers, whose reaction was much the same as hers had been. Dumbfounded. She knew it was about to get even weirder.

Briggs spoke up, his first words of the bizarre encounter. His voice was steady, concealing roused nerves. "As I understand you, Mr. Martin, your client is prepared to waive his Fifth Amendment rights against self-incrimination?" McGehee nodded along, he and his counterpart briefly on the same page.

"Mr. Kilbrough has no intention of incriminating *himself.*" Another chortle, as if this were humorous. "To answer your question directly, yes, he understands his right not to testify, and believes it important to forego that privilege."

"Will he sit for a deposition, so that we can be better prepared," McGehee jumped in. His question was posed not to the lawyer, but to the judge. Martin answered anyway.

"No," he said sharply. "The jury will be the first to hear what he has to say."

Now Briggs tagged in. "What, exactly, is the anticipated nature of this last-minute testimony?"

"I am afraid I am not at liberty to say. You will have to hear that from Mr. Kilbrough himself."

McGehee's mouth was agape, a stance Bering had never before seen from the U.S. attorney. He addressed her angrily. "Judge, this is ridiculous, and against every protocol in our procedures. A witness can't demand to testify at the time and place of their choosing, with no advance warning or opportunity for the parties to make ready. It's outlandish, and I think you should bar his participation."

There was an uncomfortable pause as, rather than responding to McGehee, she looked to Martin. The man's smile returned, this time more creepy than ingratiating.

"Judge Bering anticipated one of you might make that argument. The problem is, as I explained to her, my client has zero intention of being silenced. He has – what do people younger than me call it – receipts. Audio. Docs. All backing up his first-hand account of what really happened. Yeah, she has the power to keep Mr. Kilbrough out of her courtroom. But I suspect Her Honor wants these jurors to make a decision based on the truth, the whole truth, and nothing but the truth."

Martin sat back, satisfied, before raising his eyebrows while he studied his fingernails. "I should also mention, if he is blocked from appearing here, my client will release a video statement outlining what he *would* have said. Pretty awkward!"

McGehee's face reddened. Briggs glared. Judge Bering frowned.

"On the bright side," Martin said, "at least doing this our way, both sides get to ask him questions! If you don't like what he has to say, you can do your best to impeach him."

To relieve the building tension, the court called a break. Fifteen minutes later, she gave the lawyers her recommendation. They were free to dissent, she said, and she would not force the witness upon them if both objected. But her observations were cogent, and her guidance reasonable.

Key to the outcome, however, was the lawyers' confidence in their own skills as litigators, and their mutual prayer the assassin would hurt the other side more. Styles had told Briggs many times Kilbrough wanted to "destroy Thorne." Speaking for the president, Arenberg had advised the U.S. attorney, "Sam will bury that little shit once and for all."

Kilbrough would be present at 10 a.m.

Thirty-Two

The handcuffs were removed, but not the watchful scrutiny of the witness' former colleagues in the Secret Service, seven of whom were strategically positioned around the courtroom. The shackles had been one of Kilbrough's demands. Because both sides wanted his favor, with the reluctant approval of the security forces, off they came.

In another break with protocol, the witness was not called to the stand with the jury seated. All of the men and women with guns – the USSS, the Bureau of Prisons transport guards, the U.S. marshals – insisted Kilbrough be placed in the stand *before* the audience and then jury were seated. Those services, in fact, wanted to eliminate public attendance for the day, arguing fewer bodies meant greater control over a dangerous man. Judge Bering nixed that idea. Her courtroom would not be governed by fear.

In consequence, the day's lucky public guests, and this session's privileged journalists, entered with Kilbrough already on display like the marquis animal at a zoo. The assassin everyone had read, heard and seen so much about was ensconced upon the same rickety wooden swivel occupied 48 short hours earlier by the man he shot. With fear and awe, the audience maintained an overwhelmed gawk.

It was the jurors, as Bailiff Bankhead did her daily duty escorting them to their pen – perhaps because they were in close proximity to him, or maybe because they were more invested – who showed the greatest shock. They had greeted most witnesses, except maybe President Thorne, with the neutral palate becoming their role as dispassionate arbiters of the truth. For Sam Kilbrough, there was no such sanguinity. Arroyo, Breckenridge, Tinsley, Mrs. Jackson, Banker Dude, Union Guy, and all their colleagues were unanimous in a dazed, spellbound recognition.

"Mr. Kilbrough, thank you for your appearance today," Briggs started, seeking to gain rapport without being friendly – the man had fired a bullet into the president. His tone, therefore, was polite, but distanced. "You are in a unique position, as I'm sure you're aware, to clear up certain ambiguities for these jurors."

"Yes sir," Kilbrough said respectfully. He did not have the manner of a killer. He was, if anything, urbane. A handsome, fit man who radiated soft rectitude. His bearing denoted the easy confidence of someone at peace with life's provocations.

"Let's dive in, then. By way of background, you resigned from the United States Secret Service February 27, approximately one month before the events of March 30 in North Carolina." *The events*. Quite the bland phrasing for an attempted assassination, but the defense lawyer wanted to keep the temperature low.

"That is correct."

"What was your last assignment?"

"I was a member of the president's personal protection detail."

"Before that, you served in the same role for my client, the vice president."

"Yes sir."

"You made the switch from Styles to Thorne last year on May 18, right at the beginning of the general election season, about nine months before you left the Service."

"Yes sir."

"From May 18 until February 27, then, you had regular proximity to the president. I mean, we're talking feet or inches, armed to the teeth with lethal weaponry, right?"

"Yes sir."

"And to be blunt, Mr. Kilbrough, if your transfer had been a plot by Elijah Styles for the purpose of murdering the president and securing his own promotion, you could have made that happen on May 18, or February 27, or any day in between, couldn't you?"

"I could have." Kilbrough shifted his focus away from the lawyer for the first time. To the rapt panel he added matter-of-factly, "Were the government's case true, it would have made my actions a lot simpler." Amazingly, his words came off rational, not cold. "But the move to the president's detail was not, as you phrased it, 'a plot' by the vice president to murder Magnus Thorne."

Briggs did a poor job of hiding his glee. Styles assured him Kilbrough would destroy the prosecution, which worried the experienced litigator. How could his client be *that* certain unless he knew something more, a prospect troubling in itself. Nonetheless, this first remark was quite beneficial. Tiptoe, *carefully,* a little deeper into the cave, Briggs told himself. If Styles could be trusted, the next question would pay off.

"Last week, Kaylee Nicholson told these ladies and gentlemen she witnessed you meeting with the president's chief of staff, Ezra Arenberg, in his office, only days before the shooting. The government's lawyer here," he waved in the direction of McGehee, "suggested she was very much mistaken. He pointed out there was nothing on the Colonel's calendar, in his notes or the White House visitors' log, and no one to corroborate her testimony." Kilbrough looked amused. Almost holding his breath, Briggs asked, "Did you meet with him?"

"I did. March 23. At the Colonel's invitation." A noisy clamor reverberated until Judge Bering slammed her gavel in a single, sharp crack.

"Then why no record of it?"

"Because that's the way he wanted it. There are times when the president or his team want to do things off the books. Usually offsite, but I have personally escorted people into 1600 under those circumstances, and believe me, they aren't taken through the main entrances, they don't sign in, and any trace of their visit is wiped."

A lawyer's general adage is, *never ask a question to which you do not know the answer*. This, obviously, was uncharted territory. Given the witness' last response, however, and the vice president's certitude about Kilbrough, Briggs forged ahead.

"Tell us, please, what that meeting was about."

Kilbrough gracefully swung on his chair so that he gave the jurors his full attention. Their eyes, he saw, were wide with expectation. "It was our last meeting ..."

"Objection," the prosecutor shouted with an urgency he hadn't previously displayed, jarring many in the courtroom. "Hearsay! Out of court statement, and from an interested, and dare I say, uniquely unreliable declarant."

The defense lawyer countered McGehee's uproar with a bewildered tranquility. "Your Honor, Rule 801(d)(2) is pretty clear, statements made by an opposing party are not hearsay. In this trial, the government, which the president's chief of staff represents at the highest level, is most assuredly the opposing party."

McGehee's lips parted as he raised his hand, but Briggs spoke over him. "Moreover, this meeting *should* have been recorded, taking place as it did in a public office. As Mr. Arenberg has chosen not to disclose its contents, this is the defense's only avenue to that critical evidence. Finally," he added, regarding his foe unsympathetically, "if the U.S. attorney has any concerns about the witness' credibility on this point, he will have his chance to cross-examine him. Not to mention, he is free to recall the Colonel, should they wish to dispute anything Mr. Kilbrough is about to say."

"I understand the government's concern," the judge cut in, forestalling any further argument, "as well as the rules regarding hearsay. I agree with the defense's analysis. I also find, under Rule

807, there being no other evidence the defendant can obtain through reasonable efforts, considering the absence of any records whatsoever about the meeting, the jury should be entitled to consider his recollections." Turning to them she added, "You are the sole judges of the witness' credibility."

In other words, there was no way she was keeping this from them. "Objection overruled. Mr. McGehee, you are free to bring Mr. Arenberg back, of course."

"Mr. Kilbrough," Briggs said seductively, the panel's appetite whetted. "You were going to tell us about your meeting?"

"Well," he opened, composed, as if his words were merely an extension of his service to his country, "first of all, I told the Colonel it was a bad idea for us to meet, in the White House of all places, so close to the action date."

In the tiny press area three benches behind the balustrade separating combatants from spectators, Seb Montes' jaw dropped. It was a remarkable reaction for a journalist who had seen and reported upon the truly unimaginable, whose unflappability was as necessary to his trade as paper and pen. He wanted to run from the room, be the first to report what he had just heard! But who would dare miss whatever came next?

Briggs stammered, "The ... action date?"

"Yes sir. This was my final meeting with Mr. Arenberg, but not my first. We decided back in January that I would shoot the president. Actually, the plan was for me to shoot *at* the president. Nicking him was my idea."

Not a soul in the courtroom stirred. Only a few had even resumed breathing.

On the jury, where one would expect exchanges of shocked and confused expression, there was no movement at all. The Twelve maintained an unyielding focus on the witness, waiting for clarification, or at a minimum, some confirmation they had indeed heard him correctly.

Among the flummoxed was Mandela Briggs, who unfortunately had the floor and thus the obligation to continue his line of inquisition. Whatever tentative track he intended, however, had been thoroughly washed away. *The plan was for me to shoot* at *the president.*

"You are saying, Mr. Kilbrough, that the chief of staff to the President of the United States was aware, in advance, you were going to shoot his boss?" There was no assertiveness in Briggs' voice, as if he too was sure there had been a misunderstanding.

"Aware? Most definitely. He was very enthusiastic about the idea."

Sometimes things were too good to be true, and that was what worried the defense lawyer at the moment. He feared a trap, that the greater his descent into this lunacy, the more impossible any escape. Yet, what choice did he have but to step delicately onward?

"Why would Ezra Arenberg want you to shoot at the president?"

"I should probably make it clear, the Colonel would never have given the green light without the president's blessing. But to answer you directly, the objective was two-fold: sympathy, and getting Elijah Styles out of the way."

"Wait, what?" Briggs muttered, the fog in his thinking becoming denser. "The president? Are you also claiming Magnus Thorne knew you were going to shoot at him?"

"No sir," he began. Perhaps, finally, a retreat? But Kilbrough immediately continued in a solemn, deep voice, "the president himself told me he was, to use his exact words, 'All in.'"

The room spun, or so it seemed as one attendee, then another, snapped out of their disorientation, concluding Sam Kilbrough must either be desperate, or crazy. A wave of disappointment washed over Briggs, his fleetingly star witness careening into implausibility. The defendant's counsel prepared to step back, to align himself with the sudden pervading disbelief, to let Kilbrough sink by himself.

That is, until he caught a glimpse of his client. Unlike everyone else in the room, the vice president remained riveted, taking in the witness' bizarre assertion with complete approval, encouragingly bobbing his head up and down. Eli Styles was no fool, and right now he was signaling his attorney to press on.

"Magnus Thorne told you to shoot him." Briggs stated it neutrally, not as a question but as an assertion.

"Shoot *at him*. Yes sir, he did."

Briggs saw his off-ramp. "The same president who testified here Monday, under penalty of perjury – a federal crime, by the way – and said nothing about staging his own assassination?" There was heat building in his words as he flung them at Kilbrough. "I'm sure you can imagine he would call your present accusation ... preposterous!"

The witness was not shaken in the least, his air of serenity unbroken, eyes cool. "First, Mr. Briggs, I also swore to tell the truth, as I assure you I am. Second, and with all due respect to you and the United States attorney, no one ever asked the president if he had advanced knowledge of the shooting of March 30. He most certainly did."

Kilbrough returned to his primary audience, drawing them in one at a time as he spoke, his language slow and steady. "Third, Magnus Thorne may be willing to deny a lot of things, to exaggerate, to lie. But even he isn't crass enough to deny his own words, in his own voice."

With that he looked across the bar, to the first bench, to his own counsel, D'Artagnan Xavier Martin. Everyone followed Kilbrough's line of sight. When all attention was fixed hard upon him, the funny looking man withdrew a tiny cassette from the inside pocket of his off-the-rack suit, the kind of cartridge obsolete for 20 years and thus possessing an antiquitous charm of authenticity. He held it aloft for everyone to see.

†††

After hearing the playback in Judge Bering's chambers – Dee Martin conveniently provided the rare machine capable of doing so – Sidney McGehee argued ferociously against admittance of the tape. "It amounts to an illegal wiretap, Judge!" he rambled, all color drained from his normally telegenic face. "The president most certainly did not consent to being surreptitiously intercepted. If that's even him on this ... thing!"

Briggs suspected the prosecutor was wrong. Fortunately, his associate had written an entire article about it for his law review. "Judge," young Ryan Townsend practically whispered, intimidated by his unexpected participation, "18 U.S. Code 2511 governs the recording of communications." She motioned for him to proceed. Ryan gulped, then added with a tad more confidence, "as Mr. McGehee may have overlooked, section 2(d) exempts parties to the communication, which Mr. Kilbrough most definitely was."

Judge Bering quickly dispensed with hearsay, reliability, overly prejudicial and other such legal spaghetti, leaving the U.S. attorney thankful all of this occurred outside the jury's presence. "And, of course Mr. McGehee, you may call an expert to dispute authenticity, if there's any doubt." He knew there wasn't.

As they returned to the courtroom, Sam Kilbrough remained in his seat, assiduously avoiding any show of emotion. He clearly remembered his conversation with Thorne. Yes, he recorded it, confident the audio would be useful. But he recalled every single word without it. People tended to remember chats in Aspen Lodge, the president's private residence at Camp David. Plus, Sam was the one who insisted on the meeting.

With everyone in place, Carolyn signaled Zee, who pushed play. Noah took down everything.

Unidentified Voice No. 1: Right this way, Mr. Kilbrough.

Sam Kilbrough: Thank you.

UV1: The president is finishing up a call and will be along in a moment, sir.

[Pause, approximately two minutes]

President Thorne: Sam, what the fuck are we doing here? Ezra says you're getting cold feet.

SK: Thank you for seeing me, Mr. President. And, no sir, no cold feet. I only told the Colonel it was important for us, for you and me, to be on the same page.

PT: Well, Jesus, man, why the hell couldn't we do that through him. Do you know what an ass-whipping it is getting someone in and out of here without being seen? You trying to blow this thing up?

SK: Of course not, sir.

PT: I'm the one getting shot at, you know. What the hell, son? From now on, Ezra's your only point of contact. Understand?

SK: Yes sir.

PT: Alright, Sam, I'm in the middle of a million God damn things here, so get on with it. What do you need? Colonel says he already gave you the pardon ...

SK: Right ...

PT: ... but I don't want you using that thing until I tell you. Got it? Not one shit stinking second before I tell you.

SK: Yes sir.

PT: Understand?

SK: Completely.

PT: What else? Got everything you need?

SK: I do. Mr. President, I know you understand the gravity of what we are going to do. An assassination attempt is, to say the least, a major step. Once I pull that trigger, there is no turning back ...

PT: ... Good God, Sam. That's why you're wasting my time? No one's ever going to know. Boom! It's done. Media off my ass. I'll have every reason in the world to crack down even harder, snuff out those woke pussies once and for all. And the beauty of it is, that little bitch friend of yours, our beloved vice president of nothing, will take the fall. Can't wait to fully disgrace that worthless pansy.

SK: I don't know, Mr. President.

PT: You've got them all wrapped up in this, right, Sam? TAC. Styles. When the shit hits the fan, they're all behind it, that's the way it's got to look, or this whole thing is a waste of time. I'll throw those gay lunatics into Bonsal with the rest of the trash. Maslow, all the left-wing nuts, GONE!

[Pause, approximately 20 seconds]

PT: Are we done?

SK: Yes sir. And thank you for seeing me. I needed to hear your commitment, Mr. President, that you are fully behind this plan.

PT: God damn right I am. I couldn't be more all in if I pulled the trigger myself. Now you just do your part, Sam, and we'll all have what we want.

SK: What is that, sir?

PT: Total control ... We'll finally make this country great again!

SK: Yes, Mr. President.

PT: And Kilbrough?

SK: Yes sir.

PT: Don't forget to miss!

[Pause, approximately 40 seconds]

UV1: This way, please.

[End of Tape]

†††

One of a litigator's most vexing dilemmas is, when to quit. When is "good" enough? When does one declare victory, take it to the house?

In the hushed wonder of the E. Barrett Prettyman United States Courthouse on this bright blue Wednesday morning, such was Mandela Briggs' predicament.

He had mere seconds to make a decision, as Judge Carolyn Bering was among the first to regain her composure, and was already summoning his reply with a studious regard.

There were so many questions he wanted to ask. So many "Why's." The crushing temptation to wrap up Kilbrough's gift in a neat red bow was tempered only by the fear that, in his greed, he might strangle his own client. *Leave well enough alone,* he told himself.

Nevertheless, unceasing calculations spin in the head of any good trial lawyer, forecasting risk and reward, totaling up the score. Those assessments whirled in Briggs' mind too, with the result of a single loose end he could not ignore.

"Mr. Kilbrough," he said, confident in this final gamble, "you are a skilled marksman who fired from point-blank range." Briggs paused, not from uncertainty, but for emphasis. "And yet, you didn't miss."

The witness studied his inquisitor, then set his expression so as to underscore his message, which he delivered in a measured cadence. "If I had missed, as the president expected, it would have been a one-day story. *Deranged ex-Secret Service Agent Shoots, Misses*. It would have given President Thorne every excuse to seize total control exactly as he planned, without inviting the kind of scrutiny his intentions deserved. This trial, and its spotlight, would never have happened. I knew if he were actually hit, he'd be forced to go after the vice president with a vengeance."

Briggs caught Kilbrough's eyes. The man was ready to continue, but was encouraging Mandela for one final prompt. Kilbrough's look all but scripted the words.

"Why did that matter to you, Mr. Kilbrough, so much so that you were willing to shoot the President of the United States?"

"Because Magnus Thorne is a dangerous man." For the first time, he wavered, juggling the composure of his emotion and the precision of his words. The former gave way to the slimmest welling of his eyes, a sheen noticeable to the jurors on the front row. There was a catch in his voice as he continued. "I love my country. I've devoted my life to it, as a Marine, as a member of the NYPD, and in the Service, all with the same goal of protecting our democracy and our freedoms.

"The president does not respect any of those ideals. And while the people can elect whoever they want – that's the way our system works – I was around Magnus Thorne night and day during and after the election. He lost. He understood that, and his people did too. I heard their plots and schemes to subvert the process, to bury votes, to intimidate election workers and officials. I heard it all, first hand."

Kilbrough swallowed hard. "When the American people rose up, and they knew only a tenth of what I did, I had a front row seat to Magnus Thorne the would-be dictator. I couldn't stand by and watch that happen. So, when things started looking really grim for the administration, when I heard their plans to pound the country into submission in ways you cannot begin to imagine, I approached Arenberg with the idea for staging a shooting, pitching it as a way to avoid a lot more bloodshed in the streets, a lot more arrests.

"Thank God, he bought into the notion it would create enough shock and sympathy, letting them seize control with less resistance. You know, the perfect justification. And when the president came on board enthusiastically, I was confident the one little piece of the plan I *wasn't* sharing would be enough cause an investigation so intense, everything would be revealed. That it would bring down their entire house of cards."

Kilbrough turned from the jurors, momentarily raising his focus to the ceiling, then said, in a near whisper to the judge, "I hope I was right."

Thirty-Three

"You, a veteran of the Secret Service sworn to protect the president, literally *shoot* him. Then you swagger into this courtroom with an alleged recording made on 40-year-old technology – not verified or authenticated, by the way – and expect us to believe, "A," Magnus Thorne was in on the plot, and, "B," putting a bullet into the leader of the free world makes you some great American patriot. Do I have it about right?"

Sidney McGehee's renowned composure was a luxury he could no longer afford. Plus, he was angry. *Very* angry. He and everyone else knew that was Magnus Thorne's voice.

The high-flying U.S. attorney's most illustrious prosecution was on life support. He had been lied to by the Attorney General and by the president's chief of staff. Both assured him Sam Kilbrough, if needed, would be helpful.

As Briggs maneuvered the assassin like a wrecking ball, though, McGehee recalled one slight hesitation from his boss. "Of course," David Smith, the rotund AG had offered, "I wouldn't recommend using him unless you have to, Sid. You know, who wants to link arms with the guy who committed the nasty deed?" followed by the guttural laugh that scraped McGehee's spine. Foregoing Kilbrough sounded like cautious, reasonable advice, and Sidney agreed as a matter of strategy. But he had to wonder, what had Smith known?

"My patriotism, Mr. McGehee, is for these people to judge, however they define it. All I can do is explain the threat I perceived, and my efforts to stop it."

"By shooting the president?"

"By trying to expose him."

Kilbrough's unyielding dark brown eyes yanked at the prosecutor's furor, absorbing him, convincing him with their tranquility that no amount of hammering would dent his certitude.

"Part of the government's case against Mr. Styles is the involvement of one of his main backers, The Aberdeen Circle, in this plot against the president. You do not deny, do you, meeting on multiple occasions with Blakely Kurtz, *TAC*'s communications director?"

"I did."

They were on CCTV together, twice, once making google eyes in a bar, once outside Styles' hotel. So, this concession was not a big win. But it could be a beginning. McGehee had to find some path to self-preservation. He reminded himself it was the vice president on trial, and no matter Magnus Thorne's bizarre involvement, if Styles was connected to the scheme, it didn't matter if the president was too.

"Was the purpose of your meetings, as Mr. Kurtz testified, to secure a safehouse in Canada?"

"One of the purposes, yes."

"I'm baffled as to how you planned to escape *anywhere*, but putting that aside – why did you need a hideout at all, if you had a signed pardon from the president?"

"I didn't need a hideout."

The prosecutor looked at Kilbrough with the frustration of a driver who's navigated onto a dead-end street. As he searched for a way out, the witness spoke up.

"May I explain?" The last three words you want to hear during your cross-examination.

"Let me guess," McGehee cut him off, aware Briggs would come back to this later if he didn't address it now. Might as well frame it in cynicism. "You're going to say the president needed you to involve *TAC* any way you could. Another slice of his devious master plan."

"That was part of it. He and the Colonel definitely wanted *TAC*, and therefore the vice president, implicated. This was an easy way to do it. *TAC* and Kurtz were unaware of the details or even the date. As far as they knew, I *would* need a refuge."

Made sense, McGehee thought. Only an idiot would meet with Kurtz so brazenly, and this proficient ninja was far from an idiot. He knew they would be seen. He *wanted* to be seen. It was a set-up to draw in the Aberdeen crowd, showcasing the president's diabolical side, thus further destroying McGehee's lawsuit.

From the ash heap of defeat, however, the guileful prosecutor smelled something *off*. Some hidden opportunity. It began during Briggs' examination, as Kilbrough pilloried the president. Twice McGehee glanced at Styles, finding a complexion of relief, joy, gloating. But when he returned his focus to the witness, there was no reciprocation, no obvious rapport between Kilbrough and the vice president. Only a single furtive, disapproving look from the man saving the defendant's ass.

Moreover, Kilbrough *asked* Sidney if he could explain himself. Clever witnesses like him answer questions with as few words as possible. They are coached to *never* volunteer. Yet he was offering to share. Come to think of it, Kilbrough demanded the opportunity to testify in the first place! Was it solely to screw the president, or did this methodical operative have a larger mission?

Finally, there was that most recent answer, served up uninvited. "That was *part of it*," he'd said when McGehee asked if the Kurtz meetings were a ruse. Seconds later, a tantalizing utterance the prosecutor couldn't shake: *TAC and Kurtz* were unaware of the assassination plot details. Was the omission of Styles on purpose? McGehee thought Kilbrough too shrewd for such an oversight. Nothing matters more to a lawyer than words: their use, their emphasis, and most definitely their absence. Something told him to go for it. Hell, he could hardly make matters worse.

"Why else did you meet with Blakely Kurtz, besides the safehouse request?"

Kilbrough exhibited a hint of relief that the prosecutor followed the bread crumbs. He took a deep breath, as though steadying himself for a plunge.

"Because the vice president's plan *did* require that I disappear, at least for a while."

✝✝✝

McGehee felt a bit like Alice in Wonderland, a fable he'd never enjoyed, finding the protagonist silly and indecisive. Presently, though, he was gaining sympathy for the poor girl, thrust into an upside-down world where little made sense, rules were fluid, and logic did not exist.

"The *vice president's* plan?"

"To remove Magnus Thorne from office."

As he controlled his own expression, McGehee suddenly imagined Briggs' reaction, though he dared not look. "Blakely Kurtz told us the defendant was confident he would soon be president. I assume that was related to this plan?"

"Yes, and to be honest, I was optimistic as well. In the beginning."

"Optimistic about helping Elijah Styles become president?"

"Definitely."

"By murdering Magnus Thorne?"

"Never," he snapped, an unprecedented glimmer of resentment from the graceful witness. "And that was the problem."

McGehee hated ceding control. It was contrary to his training as a lawyer, his comfort as a leader, and his Type-A personality. But he was a competitor, with the courage to take risks if they increased his chances for victory.

This, he concluded, was such an occasion. He was going to pass the ball to Sam Kilbrough. "You deny any intent to kill the president?"

"I do. As noted, I had every opportunity to murder him, were that my purpose."

"Then please explain what you mean, when you say you were optimistic about the defendant here becoming president. That is, until the 'problem' of murder arose."

Kilbrough again offered himself to the panel, his relentless ability to command their attention yet again on display.

"To make any of it understandable, I suppose I need to begin at the beginning."

"Go ahead." Kilbrough sighed, whether from regret or resignation was hard to tell.

"Elijah Styles is the most impressive man I have ever met," he started simply. "I have to admit, I was a little disappointed when Director Drury assigned me to his campaign during the primaries. Call it a hunch, but I didn't see the Republican Party nominating a gay man, which meant after the election, I was unlikely to make a presidential detail. That had been my ambition ever since I joined the Service. My vision was to do an eight-year POTUS run, then ride off into the sunset. Whole new career. Something that didn't involve threats and high-value targets.

"But from the moment I met Rampart," Kilbrough softened into fond recollection, "that was his signal, which I came up with as leader of his first security team. It's how he struck me: strong, protective, a fortification against all that is malevolent. Anyway, I knew right away he was the person to lead this nation. Not just his ideas, most of which I liked, a few of which I thought were too progressive, but also his idealism. He was positive, uplifting, the kind of person who saw the value, or at least the potential, in humanity."

What have I wrought, the already dejected U.S. attorney mused. This ode to the vice president jeopardized a narrative of depravity McGehee painstakingly spent days attaching to the defendant. Trying to stop the witness now, however, would only alienate the jurors, enraptured as they were with him.

"Over the next four years, as the vice president came to trust and rely on me, confiding in me more and more, I learned how dangerous Magnus Thorne was. We were only aware of half the story, as much as the vice president was frozen out, but that was a hundred times more than the public knew, more than enough to conclude POTUS had one objective. He wanted to be the next Putin, if you remember that guy, how he suffocated Russia's democracy and became supreme leader. Or, for a more modern example, try Annalise Lindner in Germany, who took the Alternative für Deutschland from a fringe party of über-right fanatics to complete domination of Germany.

"All the things this jury's heard about Thorne are true. Using the military, the security services, manipulating control of the internet, illegal detentions. He was even integrating dozens of RAGE militias with their local law enforcement to become his private army. I often wondered why Eli didn't resign, go public, try to prevent Thorne's re-election, which we both feared might be our nation's last unless he were stopped."

McGehee knew he'd unleashed this, and regretted the miscalculation. But at this point, with that damned audio, Magnus Thorne was ruined anyway. Let Kilbrough run wild with his Styles worship. Sidney would paint him as a lunatic fanboy who, by the way, shot the president. Kilbrough couldn't change that inconvenient tidbit.

Still, McGehee must channel this, extract some useful nugget. "Mr. Kilbrough," he interjected, "it is beyond question the defendant was behind your re-assignment to the presidential detail. Even he admits that, but says it was motivated by a desire to advance your career, and that your charitable connections brought the pair of you too close."

The prosecutor assumed his most contemplative pose. "However, here's what puzzles me. Why would you want to leave the side of a leader you so admired, and go to work for someone you obviously loathed? Why would you want to pledge your life to protect a man you considered the next Adolf Hitler?"

McGehee fixed on Styles while asking this last question, and the sight cuffed him like an arctic blast. The defendant's face fell with each syllable, eyes signaling the witness not to answer, or at least not tell the truth.

Kilbrough caught the plea as well, and his response was in a quiet voice. "The move had nothing to do with my advancement," he began cautiously. "It's true we'd grown fond of one another, but my transfer was for one purpose. We needed eyes and ears inside Thorne's world. Nothing could accomplish that better than me being on his personal security team."

"So, Colonel Arenberg was correct. The defendant used his influence with Director Drury to move you inside the president's camp!"

"Yes, but make no mistake, sir. I was more than willing to do this. For my country."

"You were willing to be a Trojan Horse for Elijah Styles' sake, too, weren't you?"

Even softer, "Yes."

"Your mission, then, was to collect intel, anything the vice president could use to take down Magnus Thorne."

"At that point it was to prevent his re-election. Which I respected, because it meant the vice president would be out of office too. He was willing to make that sacrifice to save the nation."

"How noble of him. Of course, it would also make Styles the *I Told You So* front runner in the next cycle, wouldn't it?"

"If that's what he thought, he never told me."

"Uh huh. Okay, then, Styles never abandons the president, the election passes, Thorne wins ..."

"He didn't," Kilbrough cut in with a flash of anger. "Valid votes were thrown out, electors threatened, and Congress intimidated on January 6. I was with the president that day, and let me tell you, he was delighted at the pictures of bayonetted guardsmen in the U.S. Capitol, supposedly there to protect the Members. Of course, the only threat to them were his own RAGE militias storming the building."

Kilbrough's emotions roiled. He soon made plain why. "I remember Thorne jumping up at one point, when Eli was on the screen, pained at having to preside over that travesty. The president said, 'Lil' faggot's not quite sure what to do with that gavel, is he boys?' and doubled over laughing."

The witness' memory of Thorne's vulgarity provoked an unmistakable passion. More intriguingly, Kilbrough had again called the defendant "Eli," the prosecutor noted, filing it away.

Quickly trying to smooth the edge to his outburst, Kilbrough added, in a slower cadence, "That's when things changed."

"Changed how," McGehee asked, no longer dreading where this could go.

"We realized that stopping Magnus Thorne had gone from difficult to almost impossible. Eli told me none of the Cabinet members were willing to openly oppose the president, so the Twenty-Fifth was out. The Republican majorities in both houses of Congress, more interested in their own power than in Thorne's blatant illegality, meant impeachment was off the table too. The few media outlets willing to tell the truth were drowned out by much louder conservative voices. And Thorne strong-armed the social media companies so their algorithms buried stories about his crimes. Only pro-Thorne messages had any reach."

"Why, then, did the Colonel, or the president, believe a fake assassination would be useful? Sounds like they had it all under control."

"They didn't. And you have to understand Magnus Thorne. His actions provoked massive protests, and those really dug at him. He needed to be adored, and now he could hardly go anywhere without chaos. He was infuriated, almost desperate. Plus, boycotts were really starting to hurt the economy, and that was a risk for all Republicans. So, he clamped down even harder. It was a very, very destructive cycle."

"And that's why you suggested it? Show him a way to justify his tyranny?"

Kilbrough looked over at Styles. "I felt there was a good chance Thorne would go for it." A somber veil descended over the witness. "But that's not where the idea came from."

McGehee turned to defendant. The vice president's features were sheer terror. "The idea to shoot President Thorne came from Elijah Styles, didn't it."

Kilbrough didn't move at first. Then, almost imperceptibly, his head bobbed, once up, once down.

McGehee was paralyzed by his case's sudden whirl. *His* good fortune. Afraid to push for more, but convinced he must, he gently chided, "For the record, Mr. Kilbrough."

"Yes," he whispered.

"Yes, what?"

Kilbrough scowled at McGehee, wanting to leap from his chair and strangle the prosecutor rather than articulate the words. "Eli believed there was no other way," he said under his breath.

"I'm still confused, Mr. Kilbrough. You said you were supposed to miss, that hitting the president was your idea. How did the defendant think shooting and missing would possibly help *him*? Wouldn't that play right into the president's hands, just like you pitched the idea to Colonel Arenberg?"

He emitted a mournful croak. "Eli's idea wasn't for me to fire and miss."

McGehee stared, hoping to coax words best spoken without prompt.

Briggs was suddenly on his feet, to what effect he was unsure. Perhaps a few spare seconds may give Kilbrough pause? Hadn't his client assured him they were tight? "Your Honor, may we take a short break? I think it would be prudent for the witness to confer with his counsel, given his own pending criminal trial."

"*NOOO!!!*" the witness shouted, face flushed, before Judge Bering could respond. The unflappable man of steel was gone.

"No," he repeated more evenly, eyes glistening. Sam stared directly into the vice president's pleading features, the pair joined, neither yielding across the 20 feet separating them. A tear traversed Kilbrough's cheek.

"Eli wanted me to kill him."

†††

What happened next depended solely upon one's vantage point, though logically the events occurred as they did.

Judge Bering banged her gavel, repeatedly, attempting to extinguish the gasps and cries of astonishment. She never fully regained control.

McGehee shouted follow-ups, Briggs objections. Neither had any impact.

The witness carefully wiped his face, maintaining an intense visual embrace of Styles. A few heard Kilbrough say, or thought they heard, *I loved you*, or *I love you*, as if the difference mattered.

The vice president's practiced façade of brainy curiosity and deep empathy had liquified into black extinction, a bubbling stew of hatred and betrayal. Were his angry glare across the courtroom physical, his hands would be encircling Sam Kilbrough's neck.

Bailiff Bankhead frantically herded the jurors toward their meeting room, more on instinct than of any real purpose. Arroyo, Breckenridge, Tinsley and the others stumbled along in general confusion. Some felt relief. All were uncertain as to their charge, now that everything had blown to hell.

Seb Montes strained to hear above the din – the unhappy witness, the devasted defendant, the determined judge, the flummoxed lawyers, the stunned jurors, the enraptured audience – he caught enough to report the story, over and over, on CNN, XBN, countless streaming services, podcasts and, of course, in his own *Post*, online that evening, front page on doorsteps the next morning.

As obvious as it may seem, however, *Eli wanted me to kill him* did not officially end the trial. Kilbrough somehow reached the finish line, stumbling through the mayhem, painfully revealing the vice president's insistence that murder was the only option. Sam would be a hero, a *pardoned* hero, and as president Styles would rejuvenate the nation with Kilbrough at his side. Then Sam recreated his dreadful realization that Eli was every bit as insane as the president he wanted to murder. Equally wrenching, he admitted his foolhardy investment in the life Eli promised for them, one without Brady. Just another lie.

The trial of the century would require various formal maneuvers before the final fall of Judge Bering's polished wooden mallet.

Motions, deals, pleas, and her signature on this order and that judgment would eventually signify its abrupt and chaotic end.

That is because the wheels of justice move slowly.

The daggers of politics, however, unsheathe with lightning speed.

Epilogue

Knall To Be President At Noon

Thorne Resigns Hours After Styles

By Sebastian Montes

WASHINGTON — President Magnus Thorne resigned Thursday night, effective at Noon today, telling the nation "America needs a full-time president and a full-time Congress" freed from the pressures of impeachment. In a televised, often defiant address from the East Room of the White House, Mr. Thorne told an assemblage of loyal staff and supporters that leaving the office to which he was only recently re-elected in a highly disputed vote "is contrary to every fiber in my body" and "a stain upon the integrity of our country's democracy." However, he acknowledged the "forces arrayed against us have their own agendas" and "will never allow us to achieve the great things we had planned for our people."

Thorne's sudden announcement came barely 24 hours after the stunning testimony of former Secret Service agent Samuel Kilbrough at the treason trial of Vice President Elijah W. Styles, who resigned late Wednesday. Both leaders found themselves in political peril, under thick clouds of controversy and intrigue.

With each of the nation's two highest offices vacated, the Constitution elevates Republican Speaker of the House of Representatives, Rance Travis Knall, to the presidency.

Shortly after Thorne's departure, the eight-term congressman from Sugar Land, Texas, will take the oath of office.

Just six months ago, on March 30, Kilbrough shot and wounded President Thorne during an appearance at the North Carolina State Fairgrounds. In a quick, and what many now describe as highly politicized investigation, Vice President Styles was indicted for treason. He was labeled the mastermind behind the attempted assassination, with the goal of propelling himself into the White House.

At trial, weeks of evidence against Mr. Styles, and the defendant's own claims targeting Mr. Thorne, were eventually trumped by the surprise appearance of the assailant, whose devastating testimony not only confirmed the defendant instigated a plot to kill the president, but Thorne's own bizarre plan to evoke sympathy, and justification for unprecedented crackdowns on dissent, by having Kilbrough fake just such a shooting.

Within hours, the vice president agreed to resign, plead guilty to the lesser offense of conspiracy to murder, a ban from ever again holding public office, and a recommended prison sentence of nine years.

Mr. Thorne was approached in the Oval Office yesterday by Speaker Knall and Senate Majority Leader Hiram Taylor (R-Nb), members of his own party. They later confirmed in a statement from the White House driveway their advice to the president that he could not survive impeachment proceedings in either chamber. "Not a single member of our conference," Taylor said, "has indicated support for Magnus Thorne remaining in office."

[Read More]

†††

Light filtered through the large bay windows of the Oval Office, striking the very new president on the back of his squarish head, illuminating like a fractured corona the spindly, unkempt strands of hair dotting his mostly barren scalp. "When the majority leader and I first arrived, he said he was gonna fight it," Rance Knall cackled. It was a placeholder of a laugh, a punctuation, not in an overdone way but genuine and intimate precisely because it was *you* in the room. The man oozed country charm.

"I had to explain to him, 'Well,' I says, 'you still have some support in the chamber, mainly the RAGE wackos and such, but most are running for the hills. Plus,' I told him, 'it don't hurt none that I have twice as many friends in the House as you ever did, and unlike you, they really like me.'" On this note he slapped the desk, *his* small desk he had ordered moved over from the Speaker's office because it had accompanied him his entire political career, from state representative for the 28th District, Fort Bend County on Houston's southwest side, through his term and a half in the state senate, and finally his election to the U.S. Congress 15 years ago.

"Now, you gotta understand ole Magnus. I knew from the moment we first met, back'n he was guv'nuh, the guy was tough on the outside, but t'warnt nothin' on the inside. Kinda man who'll puff out his chest and shout and pound his fist and give orders, but at the first sign of trouble craps his pants." Knall looked down, contemplative.

"I wanted to feel just a little sorry for him, but hell, it's hard to feel bad for someone who's messed up six ways from Sunday. All started with pickin' Styles. Told him it was a bad move. A real Icarus, that one. Wasn't hard to see he'd stab Thorne in the back first chance he got. And with Magnus freezing him out and humiliating him? Well, damn, it just became inevitable."

Knall's face abruptly softened as he fixed on the room's other occupant, a strapping man seated in a burgundy wingback directly across from the desk. "I'm sorry, boy," he said compassionately. "I know you were fond of ole Eli. But trust me – you're good to be rid of him."

Knall leaned back in a massive red-leather chair that swallowed his small, slouched frame. He steepled his fingers and bounced their tips rhythmically against his chin. His eyes narrowed. His guest, who had known the new president as far back as he could remember, recognized the hum of deep-down thought. He knew to sit there and wait. Uncle Rance – not his real uncle, but his late father's best friend – had his own pace.

"I don't feel guilty, though. Not one damned bit, son. When ya boil it all down, those two bastards deserved each other, and they sure as shit deserved what they got." He looked across the desk, life twinkling in his light blue eyes, those kindly, grandfatherly eyes that had suckered more than one fool. The guest's father, who endured the most hellish days of Iraq with Rance Knall, said he was the bravest, smartest man in the world. And the meanest son-of-bitch when crossed.

Magnus Thorne had shrugged off Knall, dismissing him as a bumpkin, a minion there to comply. Eli Styles treated Uncle Rance with pseudo-respect to his face, but called him the village rube behind his back.

"Most I can say," Knall laughed, "I'm glad I helped it along a little."

He shook his head firmly from side to side. "That ain't fair, now, is it? Wadn't me a'tal." Then he grinned at the tall, handsome, sandy-blond pillar of a man absorbing his story as he had since he was knee-high. "Was *us*, Sam. *It was us. We* helped things along. Didn't we ever."

Printed in the USA
CPSIA information can be obtained
at www.ICGtesting.com
LVHW091306151124
796649LV00041B/458